MAESTRO

THE LEGEND OF DRIZZT

Follow Drizzt and his companions on all of their adventures
(in chronological order)

FORGOTTEN REALMS®

HOMECOMING
BOOK II

MAESTRO

R.A. SALVATORE

MAESTRO
Homecoming, Book II
©2016 Wizards of the Coast LLC.

This book is protected under the copyright laws of the United States of America. Any reproduction or unauthorized use of the material or artwork contained herein is prohibited without the express written permission of Wizards of the Coast LLC.

Published by Wizards of the Coast LLC. Manufactured by: Hasbro SA, Rue Emile-Boéchat 31, 2800 Delémont, CH. Represented by Hasbro Europe, 2 Roundwood Ave, Stockley Park, Uxbridge, Middlesex, UB11 1AZ, UK.

FORGOTTEN REALMS, WIZARDS OF THE COAST, D&D, their respective logos, the dragon ampersand, Neverwinter, and The Legend of Drizzt are trademarks of Wizards of the Coast LLC, in the U.S.A. and other countries.

All characters in this book are fictitious. Any resemblance to actual persons, living or dead, is purely coincidental. All Wizards of the Coast characters, character names, and the distinctive likenesses thereof are property of Wizards of the Coast LLC.

Printed in the U.S.A.

Cover art by: Aleksi Briclot
First Printing: April 2016

9 8 7 6 5 4 3 2 1

ISBN: 978-0-7869-6591-5
ISBN: 978-0-7869-6602-8 (ebook)
620B6518000001 EN

Cataloging-in-Publication data is on file with the Library of Congress

Contact Us at Wizards.com/CustomerService
Wizards of the Coast LLC, PO Box 707, Renton, WA 98057-0707, USA
USA & Canada: (800) 324-6496 or (425) 204-8069
Europe: +32(0) 70 233 277

Visit our web site at **www.DungeonsandDragons.com**

Prelude

BY LOLTH'S FURRY LEGS!" BRAELIN JANQUAY EXCLAIMED, SHAKING his head in disbelief at the sheer slaughter unfolding in front of him.

Hundreds of demons, thousands of demons, had swarmed into a circular cavern in the Masterways, the complex of large passageways that were the main entrance of Menzoberranzan. They were just outside the city.

Dark elf wizards and priestesses lined the cavern walls. The bombardment of magic raining down upon the Abyssal forces was beyond anything Braelin had ever imagined, let alone witnessed. A hundred lightning bolts slashed an equal torrent of fireballs. Magical storms pelted the intruding demons—zombie-like manes and simian balgura—pounding them down, tripping them on the icy floor where they were finished off in a haze of steam as fireballs exploded atop them.

The drow trap had sprung to devastating effect, but the demons kept coming.

"Can they kill them all?" the astounded Braelin said.

"Be ready," Tiago snapped at him. "Some will get through, and if you fail me on the flank, know that I will not be merciful."

Braelin stared at the upstart Baenre noble for a few moments, doing well to hide his utter contempt. Jarlaxle and Beniago had warned him of Tiago's volatile temperament and haughty attitude. Jarlaxle knew the inner workings of the Baenre nobles better than anyone outside the immediate family, and Beniago was Tiago's cousin. Still, Braelin had spent the last decades serving in Bregan D'aerthe. He had lived more than half his ninety-five years with Jarlaxle's band, and most of those years had been outside the city. Now, back in the fold of Menzoberranzan, Tiago's arrogance, the venom dripping from his every word—and those of many of the other drow, particularly those nobles in House Do'Urden, where Braelin now served—appalled him.

Nothing had changed other than Braelin's escape from, and perception of, the stilted reality that was Menzoberranzan. He had been so accustomed to it in his earlier days, so numb to it, but now every word jarred him, and it took all of his self-control to hide his true disgust at the nefarious ways of his own people.

The cavern walls continued shaking from the magical barrage being poured upon the attacking demon hordes in the larger chamber to the west. One brilliant flash set Tiago and Braelin back on their heels.

"Ravel and his lightning web," Tiago remarked, managing a nod despite the sour look upon his face. Ravel, the former Xorlarrin House wizard now of House Do'Urden, was making quite a name for himself with that ritual addition to the common lightning bolt. Having witnessed it first-hand on several occasions, the two drow standing at the front of the corridor defense could only imagine the scores of demons now melting under its devastating effects.

No sooner had Tiago finished the remark than there came a cacophony of stunning proportions, ground-shaking and with explosions echoing along the corridor walls likely all the way back to Menzoberranzan. Even out here, some hundred strides from the battle, Braelin could feel the heat of the magical conflagration. He loosened his grip on his swords just a bit, having a hard time imagining that any demons would come out this end of that slaughterhouse.

"The magical confrontation nears its end, then," Tiago added when the shaking at last abated. Like the wizardry displays in times of celebration, spellcasters always liked to end with a grand display.

Braelin nodded. Ravel had told them all that the lightning web would strike as the cavern slaughter was winding down, and the ensuing crescendo only confirmed that. Almost certainly, then, the demonic reinforcements had slowed to a trickle, and so the wizards and priestesses had pulled out their last great display.

"The slaughter in the cavern nears its end!" Tiago shouted.

His call carried back to all tendrils of the regiment with the weight of an undeniable command. As the weapons master assigned to this day's primary war party, Tiago stood in full command of the warrior forces around him, including nearly a hundred foot soldiers and ten times that number of orc, goblin, bugbear, and kobold slaves.

Braelin listened carefully as Tiago barked orders, setting groups in place, organizing teams to go forward and cover the retreat of any wizards or priestesses who could not magically escape the cavern. Certainly there were dimensional doors set up to get many back into the city, but those were to be used only by the extra spellcasters who had come out for the ambush. Many of the others, including those of House Do'Urden, had been assigned to the war party, and so would soon be returning to find their place among Tiago's command.

What struck Braelin most about Tiago's stream of orders was the tone of the weapons master's voice, one that showed him to be less than pleased by these events. Braelin had noted that combination of imperiousness and frustration from the beginning. His associate, Valas Hune, perhaps the greatest of Bregan D'aerthe's scouts, had come to them hours earlier with word of the vast demonic force approaching. Such information had elevated today's events above Tiago, had demanded magical communication with the city's rulers. Sorcere had emptied herself of wizards, Arach-Tinilith had sent forth all her priestesses-in-training, and many of the major Houses, including Baenre and Barrison Del'Armgo, had sent forth a cadre of their greatest spellcasters.

And that left Tiago sitting back in the peaceful corridor, clutching his unbloodied sword as a great victory was won in the ambush cavern in front of him. Braelin found himself truly amazed at how desperately this weapons master craved battle. And with demons, no less!

His anger was unrelenting, and Braelin knew it all stemmed from Tiago's failure to secure the head of Drizzt Do'Urden.

Movement in the corridor ahead signaled the return of the spellcasters. The priestesses came first, showing little urgency, which confirmed that the slaughter in the cavern had been near-complete—and which only deepened the scowl on Tiago's face. They, including Saribel Do'Urden, Tiago's wife, moved past Tiago and Braelin and the other melee commanders to take up their positions in the third rank—near enough to offer healing to any who might be wounded.

Then came the wizards, moving more swiftly, and with those in the rear of the procession glancing back somewhat nervously. Ravel led the way, along with Jaemas Xorlarrin, who was rumored to be the newest member of the Do'Urden House Court. Both stopped when they got to Tiago, Jaemas waving the others into position among the second rank of warriors.

"I have never seen such a horde," Ravel said to Tiago. "We obliterated them by the hundreds, but they simply kept coming."

"Kept coming without regard!" Jaemas exclaimed, seeming equally at a loss. "They marched without hesitation over the bodies of scores and hundreds of their Abyssal kin, and so they too were obliterated. The entire cavern is deep in the piled, empty husks of demons sent home."

Ravel started to add to that, but could only shake his head.

"But there are more remaining?" Tiago asked, and it was obvious to Braelin and everyone else who heard him that he was hoping the answer would be yes.

"Balgura were spotted in the Masterways beyond the chamber," Ravel confirmed, "rushing to join their comrades in oblivion."

Braelin sighed, but tried to disguise it as a cough—unsuccessfully, he knew—when Tiago turned a glare over him. He had battled demons before, of course, as was true of every drow who had grown up in Menzoberranzan, but he counted balgura among his least favorite foes. They looked like some joke of the gods, resembling great apes with orange hair and massive limbs. Every balgura Braelin had ever seen stood as tall as the tip of his finger if he held his arm straight up over his head, and four times his weight. Yet, despite that imposing size and the sheer strength that accompanied it, balgura were surprisingly agile and quick, and while one alone could prove to be a dangerous adversary, these howling and scrambling beasts were pack hunters, fighting in frenzied coordination.

Frenzied—Braelin thought that a fitting word for this particular type of demon.

The drow was brought from his thoughts by screeching sounds echoing down the tunnel walls.

"They've seen the carnage in the cavern," Ravel remarked. "It's amazing that they find no deterrence in climbing over piles of dead comrades."

"Perfect soldiers," Tiago replied. "A pity we do not possess more of their ferocity in our own ranks."

"You had no more tricks to play on this group?" Braelin dared to ask. "Balgura are better dispatched with magic than the blade."

Tiago glared at him again.

"Everything is better dispatched with magic," Ravel replied flippantly, and he gave a dramatic sigh and walked away.

Tiago turned to watch him go, letting his glare follow the wizard. "You are only next to me because of Jarlaxle's assurances," Tiago said to

Braelin. "Are those assurances worthless, then? Would it serve us both better for me to assign you to stand second to some other warrior?"

Braelin stared at the noble son of House Baenre for a long while. A big part of him wanted to take Tiago up on that offer, though he knew it wasn't a sincere question and indeed, more of a threat. Still, to be away from Tiago would bring relief on so many levels . . .

But the Bregan D'aerthe warrior could not ignore the truth. There was no finer warrior to be found at House Do'Urden—none even close—and indeed, few in all of Menzoberranzan could match Tiago's prowess in battle. Malagdorl, perhaps, and Jarlaxle when he was in the city, which was not often. Beyond that, were there any warriors, weapons masters even, who would serve better in battle than this young upstart noble beside him?

"Of course not," he answered, and bowed politely. "I will show you my worth when the blood stains the stones."

He meant it, and he knew that he had to mean it. Tiago wasn't keeping him close out of any favors to Jarlaxle—as far as Braelin could tell, Tiago didn't think much of Jarlaxle at all. Tiago had accepted Braelin as his second because Jarlaxle had told him that he'd not find a more worthy battle companion. Now it was incumbent upon Braelin to live up to that billing.

Or perhaps, Braelin reminded himself, Tiago wanted him as second because Tiago wanted to keep Jarlaxle's eyes and ears in House Do'Urden very, very close.

With that unsettling possibility in mind, Braelin pointedly reminded himself that if he did not acquit himself well in battle, Tiago would find a way to get him killed in battle. Perhaps Tiago would even do the deed himself if a balgura could not.

Braelin knew that beyond doubt once he looked again at Tiago's expression.

The shrieks of the approaching beasts increased, and Braelin tossed that unsettling thought away. He had no room for such doubts now that battle was upon them, and his life was dependent upon the coordination between he and Tiago.

"Wife!" Tiago called, turning back and motioning Saribel forward. He swung back around just in time to duck behind his shield and catch a leaping balgura with it. The weight of the blow sent him skidding backward, the demon sliding, too, past Braelin's right flank.

Braelin stabbed with his right-hand sword, his left blade going forward to fend off the rush of another wild, orange-furred demon.

The balgura to his right hissed and spat in protest, and the sword sank in deeply indeed. That seemingly mortal strike didn't fell the creature, though, and it apparently did not even notice as it swung around at Braelin.

But then came Tiago, out from behind that strange and beautiful shield, with his magnificent sword sweeping down from on high to split the wounded demon's head in half.

Braelin somehow managed to fend off the clawed hands of the demon in front of him and extract his sword from the falling balgura's ribs. With both weapons in hand, the skilled drow warrior fast turned the flow of battle back against the ferocious beast.

Tiago came by him, yelling, "Forward!"

Braelin was about to argue—he didn't really have anywhere to go—but Tiago's deadly sword flashed out from under his shield, stabbing Braelin's foe in the side. So fine was that blade, Vidrinath by name, that a mere sweep of Tiago's arm had it slicing through the thick demon's torso, nearly cutting the thing in half.

Braelin tried unsuccessfully not to gasp, then to keep up as Tiago leaped at the incoming swarm of demons, even as they leaped at him.

He kicked aside the dying beast's last clawing strikes and went down to one knee, his swords in a double-thrust to stab up at a balgura that had leaped at him. The demon landed and stumbled, skidding on torn feet, easy prey for the drow warriors in the next rank.

Feeling quite pleased with his clever maneuver, Braelin started ahead once more. And then he wasn't so pleased with himself, and nearly forgot that battle was upon him as he noted the movements of Tiago Baenre Do'Urden. The drow noble more than matched the ferocity of his wild opponents. He leaped every which way, batting at clawing hands and biting maws with his fabulous shield, taking the life from one demon after another with that magnificent sword.

Engaged once more with a demon, Braelin lost track of Tiago's battles. After his balgura was finally dead, it took Braelin some time to locate and watch the leaping, scrambling blur that was Tiago. He shook his head in disbelief as he realized that for every attack Tiago blocked, one or more was getting through.

A gash opened on Tiago's arm—he nearly lost his grip on Vidrinath—but the wound closed almost as it appeared.

Braelin glanced back at Tiago's wife, High Priestess Saribel, to see her in a constant stream of spellcasting. With Tiago as her singular focus, waves of Lolth-given healing magic flowed at the noble son of House Baenre.

And Tiago trusted her, obviously. He had left his companion behind and recklessly rushed into the midst of their fierce enemies. If Sanibel let him die, Matron Mother Quenthel Baenre would not be merciful.

That realization, and the understanding that Tiago had planned this long before, brought an unsettling thought to Braelin. Though Tiago did not need him as a flanking protector, could he say the same? He did not have a high priestess standing behind him imparting unlimited healing.

And though he was of House Do'Urden now, was he really? Braelin Janquay was Bregan D'aerthe, minion to Jarlaxle, loyal to Jarlaxle.

Tiago had to know that.

Tiago wouldn't care if he died in this corridor outside of Menzoberranzan.

Tiago might even welcome that. Might, indeed, have made his attack in the hope of killing off Braelin.

All thoughts of catching up to the Baenre faded, and Braelin braced himself defensively, letting the monsters come to him.

◆ ◆ ◆

TIAGO ROLLED SIDELONG up over one hunched, simian demon and felt the explosion of pain as the balgura bit him hard on the hip. His fine adamantine armor kept the teeth from tearing too deeply, but oh, he felt the pain.

The exquisite pain followed by the ecstasy of healing warmth, the embrace of the goddess.

He rolled over the balgura's head, turning as he landed so that as the ape-demon turned to pursue, Tiago's readied sword cut it from belly to throat. A high sweep of Vidrinath took the head from the next demon in line.

He found himself laughing now as a trio of the beasts leaped at him to bury him under their bulk, in his turn he had noted Braelin Janquay.

Braelin understood now that Tiago considered him expendable, and that was a message the eager young weapons master wanted Jarlaxle to hear.

"Bregan D'aerthe," he spat from under the pile of clawing and biting ape demons, his shield, magically expanded to its fullest diameter now, keeping the bulk of the attacks away, his sword arm finding its openings to stab ahead and violate demon flesh.

And the pain continued, clawed hands and toothy maws finding their hold, and the pleasure of Saribel's healing washed over him, and the young drow knew true ecstasy.

◆ ◆ ◆

SARIBEL COULD ONLY hope that her tireless, frantic efforts would be enough to keep Tiago from great harm, or even death. If he perished here, the priestess would take her own life rather than face the wrath of the matron mother.

Tiago was doing this to her purposely, forcing her into servitude. There would be no gratitude for her efforts here, no words of praise, no tender appreciation later on. She would only know his contempt, forever his contempt.

"Until I am Matron Mother of House Do'Urden," she resolutely managed to tell herself between spells, and she growled out her next as she nodded with determination. With patience and fortitude, she would gain the upper hand.

Or maybe she should just let him die out there, she thought briefly. How easily she could interrupt the healing spells and let the demons rend him to bits.

It was a fleeting thought, of course, and not just because of the threat to her life should he die. Her marriage to Tiago made her a Baenre as well as a Do'Urden, and that was something she would never jeopardize.

The thought was buried a moment later, as word filtered down that the matron mother herself had come onto the scene.

Saribel redoubled her efforts, throwing every breath into a spell, filling Tiago with the blessings of Lolth.

"What is that fool doing?" she heard behind her, and recognized the voice of the terrible Quenthel Baenre.

Globes of fire appeared in the air. Glorious flames, hotter than hellfire, rushed down in killing lines, incinerating demons all around the battling young weapons master.

A sweep of Vidrinath felled another, the last one near to Tiago. He leaped around, his face a mask of insulted rage. But that expression changed when he took note of Matron Mother Quenthel.

Indeed.

Quenthel motioned to Braelin, ordering him forward.

"He is reckless," the matron mother whispered to Saribel as she turned to leave. "And ambitious." She paused and caught Saribel's gaze.

"He is brilliant," Quenthel told her. "And you will bring him to me later, uninjured."

Saribel wisely didn't pause in her casting to even acknowledge the matron mother.

◆ ◆ ◆

QUENTHEL BAENRE DID not magically flee the scene, as would have been expected of so important and powerful a figure. She walked openly down the corridors of the Masterways and back into Menzoberranzan, the Clawrift on her left and the huge side chamber that held Tier Breche along the wall to her right. Word had spread of the glorious victory in the tunnels, of course, and so she wanted her people to see her returning from the field of glory, humble and magnificent all at once.

Her sister, High Priestess Sos'Umptu Baenre, was waiting for her back in the main cavern, as ordered, along with a powerful contingent of the House Baenre garrison—enough to deter any murderous hopes some plotting matron mother might entertain.

The Baenres were cheered all the way back to their compound. Matron Mother Quenthel soaked in that glory, and understood that it was a necessary and not superfluous parade, both for the reputation of her House and her as matron mother. All along that path she was reminded of the damage that had come to her beloved city.

Destruction due to the idiocy of her missing brother.

Quenthel knew Gromph had summoned the Prince of Demons into Menzoberranzan, quite unannounced.

The monstrous behemoth had left now, but had cut a swath of absolute destruction in his wake. Demogorgon's slashing tail had dug trenches in the walls of Sorcere, nearly toppling major parts of the structure. The beast had torn down the gates and walls of several houses, including two of the ranking Houses with matron mothers sitting on the Ruling Council.

And Demogorgon had dug a trench, for no apparent reason other than he could, halfway across the city and back—to this very exit into the wilds of the Underdark.

Many drow had been slain on the beast's journey, Demogorgon's massive tentacles whipping out to grasp unfortunate dark elves, wrenching them in to be devoured or hurling them halfway across the city to splatter into a stalagmite or stalactite. Many others had clawed their own eyes out, driven mad by the gaze of the godlike demon.

All because of Gromph.

Quenthel could barely contain her growl.

"There were greater demons than the manes and balgura out in the caverns," Sos'Umptu informed her, something Quenthel had already suspected.

"Your priestesses spied them?"

"Lurking beyond the circular cavern, yes."

"Named beasts?"

Sos'Umptu nodded. "Beasts recognized, yes."

"And?"

"The spells of banishment failed," Sos'Umptu admitted.

Quenthel stopped her march and stared hard at the priestess. Sos'Umptu could only shrug.

"You should have been out there among the priestesses," Quenthel said, her voice betraying great concern.

"There were many high priestesses positioned in that cavern," Sos'Umptu replied with her typical lack of discernable emotion. "Their spells are as potent as my own. Though they knew the demonic names, they could not banish the beasts."

"They erred in identifying—"

"No," Sos'Umptu dared to interrupt. "It is as we feared, Matron Mother. The barrier of the Faerzress itself has been harmed. The demons cannot be banished."

Quenthel turned away, staring instead at the looming compound of House Baenre, her face showing that she was trying to process this startling and dangerous news.

"But we can kill them," Sos'Umptu offered. "When we return to your chambers, I will bring forth a magical divination of the circular cavern where the battle was primarily waged. You will see, Matron Mother. The beasts are piled many deep—empty, destroyed husks."

Quenthel looked at her incredulously.

"We won!" Sos'Umptu said, and she did a fair job of acting as though she cared. "A glorious victory! Few of our children of Menzoberranzan were wounded, fewer still killed, and the demon horde is piled high in death."

Quenthel's expression became very slightly more incredulous.

"A thousand Abyssal creatures dead, do you think?" Quenthel asked.

"Perhaps twice that," Sos'Umptu replied.

"My dear Sos'Umptu, they are demons. Do you think the Abyss will run out?"

◆ ◆ ◆

AN EXHAUSTED MINOLIN Fey walked into the nursery in her private quarters at House Baenre. She faltered immediately and nearly fell over, seeing a young woman standing over Yvonnel's small bed

"Who . . . ?" she started to ask, but stopped, her eyes going wide, as the woman—likely not yet twenty years of age—turned and flashed her a perfectly smug and wicked smile.

"You do not approve, Mother?" the girl, who was indeed Yvonnel, asked.

"How?"

"It is a simple spell, though an old one," Yvonnel explained. "A version of a haste dweomer employed by wizards in the days before the Spellplague, before the Time of Troubles, even. A wonderful spell, speeding the movements and attacks of the recipient, but one that came with the unfortunate—or in this case, fortunate—side effect of aging the recipient as if a year had passed."

Minolin Fey was only half-listening to the explanation. She was caught by the sheer beauty of this creature in front of her. Sheer beauty, she knew, beyond anything she could have imagined. Painful beauty; to look upon Yvonnel was to despair because one could not be so beautiful as she. Her skin glowed with smoothness, like satin and steel woven as one, delicate yet impossibly strong. Her soft touch could ignite every nerve in one she seduced, teasing with softness even as her fingers closed around the moaning victim's throat.

"Haste," Yvonnel said suddenly, and more emphatically, breaking Minolin Fey out of her near stupor.

"You . . . You know the arcane arts?" Minolin Fey stammered.

The young woman laughed at her. "I am one with the Spider Queen, who sought to make the Weave her own. Or have you forgotten?"

"N-no," Minolin Fey stuttered, rather inanely, and trying to decipher the statement. Yvonnel claimed to be one with the Spider Queen? How high were her ambitions after all?

"You are often overwhelmed," Yvonnel said with a nasty little laugh. "No matter, your most important duties are behind you now."

She felt her expression turn curious.

"I am born, and clearly weaned," Yvonnel explained. "I have no need to suckle at your breast, nor any such desire. Not for nourishment, at least."

The way she finished that thought had the high priestess's knees trembling. Despite the awfulness of the thought she knew that she could not begin to deny Yvonnel of anything she wanted. It took all of Minolin Fey's willpower not to throw herself prostrate on the floor at that moment, begging Yvonnel to take her, or kill her, or do whatever she so desired.

In that moment of terror, not just of Yvonnel but of her own weakness in the face of this mighty being, Minolin Fey truly appreciated the girl's claim that she was one with the Spider Queen.

She was—that was clear now. This was not a child standing in front of her, not even one infused with the memories of Yvonnel the Eternal. No, this was something much more.

With a deceptively childlike laugh, Yvonnel went through a series of movements and chanted softly. A slight glow came over her, and her hair, already thick and halfway down her back, grew a bit longer and curled at the bottom.

"I am two full decades of age now," she said. "Do you think any young warriors would find me attractive?"

Minolin Fey wanted to answer that any living creature would fall before her, that any drow in Menzoberranzan—in all the world—would not resist her for more than a heartbeat.

"Twenty-five, I think," Yvonnel remarked, and Minolin Fey looked at her with puzzlement.

"Twenty-five years," the girl clarified. "I seek an age that will afford me the respect I need, but also an age of perfect beauty and sensuality."

"Is there any age where you would not be such, either way?" Minolin Fey heard herself saying.

Yvonnel's grin let the high priestess know in no uncertain terms that she was caught within the web of this one's charms.

"You will do well when I am matron mother," Yvonnel said.

"I am . . ." Minolin Fey felt as if she had just been granted a great reprieve. "I am your mother," she stammered, nodding eagerly. "My pride . . ."

The girl waved her hand, and though she was across the room, the magical slap hit Minolin Fey so hard it sent her stumbling to the side.

"No more," Yvonnel said. "That duty is behind you and forgotten. You will survive and thrive, or you will fail, on your loyalty and service moving forward. I would think nothing of destroying you."

Minolin Fey cast her gaze down, staring at the floor as she tried to find some way out of this.

And then she felt a soft touch on her chin—and such a touch! A thousand fires of pleasure erupting within her as Yvonnel so easily lifted up her face to stare her in the eye. Minolin Fey feared that she would go blind, being so near such beauty.

"But you have an advantage, Priestess," the girl said. "I know that I can trust you. Show me that I can respect your service, too, and you will find a wonderful life in House Baenre. One of pleasure and luxury."

Minolin Fey braced herself, expecting another slap, another brutal reminder of how quickly that could be taken away.

It didn't come. Instead, Yvonnel gently brushed the tips of her fingers down the side of Minolin Fey's face, and that touch, so impossibly soft, so wondrously calling out to every nerve to bring them forth and lighting them with sensations of pure pleasure, left in its wake a line of pure ecstasy.

"Come," Yvonnel said. "I believe it is time for Quenthel to learn the truth of her niece."

"You wish an audience with the matron mother?"

"You will get me that meeting immediately," the girl answered. "I give you this one task. Do not fail me."

Minolin Fey held her breath then, feeling very trapped. The way Yvonnel had said that made it quite clear to her that it was one task for now, but there would be an endless stream of subsequent tasks later. And her personalization of the last remark, bidding Minolin Fey not to fail *her* instead of simply not to fail, showed the high priestess that this dangerous child would simply not accept failure.

This strange little daughter to whom she had given birth was the promise of great reward and the promise of perfect pain, tantalizing and terrifying all at once.

It was bad enough for Minolin Fey that in Gromph's absence she survived only at the sufferance of Matron Mother Quenthel. But even worse was the thought that her only chance at flourishing might well be this dangerous child, whether reincarnation of Yvonnel the Eternal or avatar of Lady Lolth herself—or some weird mixture of the two.

Dangerous. So very dangerous.

◆ ◆ ◆

"WHO IS THIS that you bring to my private quarters?" Quenthel asked when Minolin Fey entered her chambers in House Baenre unannounced.

"Look closely," the young drow woman said, holding her hand up to silence the high priestess, and surely that, even more than her sheer beauty, tipped Quenthel off to the truth, as was revealed deliciously to Yvonnel by the expression on the matron mother's face.

"How . . . How is this possible?" Quenthel stammered.

"You were killed in battle by a rogue drow who still lives, and yet you, too, still live," the young woman answered. "And you would ask me how a few compressed years of aging is possible? Do you think it impossible, Aunt?"

Quenthel's eyes flared with anger at that impertinence, being referred to as someone's aunt. She was the Matron Mother of Menzoberranzan!

"Are you so meager in your understanding of magic, both divine and arcane, that such a minor feat seems impossible to you?" Yvonnel prodded, and she couldn't suppress her sly grin as Minolin Fey gasped at the insult.

"Leave us," Yvonnel told the high priestess.

"Stay!" Matron Mother Quenthel roared, for no better reason than to counter the demands of the upstart young woman.

Yvonnel looked over to see Minolin Fey trembling with uncertainty and palpable fear.

"Go," she said softly. "I will win in here, and I assure you, if you remain, I will remember your hesitation."

"You will remain here," Quenthel said firmly, "or you will feel the scourge of the matron mother!"

Minolin Fey wept and shook at the conflicting demands, appearing as if she would just crumble on the spot.

"Ah yes, the five-headed scourge of Quenthel Baenre," Yvonnel said. "A fine weapon for a high priestess, but a meager baton for a matron mother. I am sure I will do better."

Quenthel's eyes and nostrils flared as she reached for the scourge and brought it forth; the five snake heads of the whip, each imbued with the life essence of an imp, swayed eagerly and hungrily.

Yvonnel laughed at her and told Minolin Fey to go.

Still some dozen strides away, Quenthel grabbed her other weapon from her belt—a magical hammer—and with a growl, she brought it swinging about.

An image of that hammer appeared in the air behind Minolin Fey as she turned; it cracked her on the shoulder, sending her sprawling. From her hands and knees, she couldn't help looking back at Quenthel, as did Yvonnel.

"I did not give you permission to smite her," the girl said evenly.

With a growl, Quenthel swung again, more forcefully. Yvonnel crossed her arms in front of her and waved them out wide. Again the hammer appeared, this time aiming for Yvonnel's face. But as the spectral image descended, it hit a shimmering field the girl had enacted. As it plunged through, it came out instead in front of Quenthel, and she yelped as her own hard strike smacked her in the face and sent her stumbling backward to the ground.

Not even bothering to stand back up, Minolin Fey scrambled away, making curious mewling noises all the way to the door. She slammed that door behind her as she exited.

"You dare!" Quenthel cried, unsteadily trying to stand, blood streaming from one nostril and from the side of her face.

"I 'dare'? You think that a simple trick?"

"Some dimensional warp of space," Quenthel spat, blood coming with every word.

"Against the likes of a spectral hammer?" said the girl incredulously. "Do you not understand who I am?"

Quenthel found solid footing then and hoisted her snake-headed scourge, replacing the hammer on her belt. She advanced, growling with every step.

Yvonnel put her hands on her hips, as petulantly as she could manage, and shook her head and sighed.

"Really, must it come to this?"

"You are an abomination!" Quenthel retorted.

"You have so quickly forgotten the Festival of the Founding in the House of Byrtyn Fey?"

That stopped the advance of the matron mother, and she stood there, suddenly unsure, her eyes darting about.

"Expecting a yochlol?" Yvonnel teased.

They both knew the truth now.

"Did you not tell your brother to marry Minolin Fey so that I would be born in and of House Baenre?" Yvonnel asked. "You even named me, did you not? Oh yes, except that you were instructed as such. Yvonnel the Eternal, born once more to be your successor, yes?"

Now Quenthel was herself looking for an escape.

"And here I am."

"You are a child!"

"I am, in body."

"No!" Quenthel demanded. "Not now, not yet! You are not old enough—even with your magical physical advancement, you are but half the age to begin your training in Arach-Tinilith."

"My *training*?" Yvonnel asked with an incredulous laugh. "Dear Quenthel, who in this city will train me?"

"Hubris!" Quenthel said, but there was not much conviction in the roar.

"Yngoth is the wisest of the snakes on your scourge," said Yvonnel. "Go ahead, High Priestess, ask her."

"High Priestess?" Quenthel yelled in protest. She came forward, closing the ground, lifting the scourge for a strike.

"High Priestess Quenthel," came the response, but not from Yvonnel. It came from one of the heads on her scourge, from Yngoth.

Quenthel looked at the snake in shock.

"She believes herself matron mother," Yvonnel said to the snake. "Tell her the truth."

Yngoth bit Quenthel in the face.

She staggered back, trying to sort it out, but not quickly enough understanding the terrible danger to her. Yngoth bit her again, and by that time, the other four scourge heads had also sunk their fangs into

Quenthel's tender flesh. Fires of poison burned through her. She should have thrown the scourge aside, of course, but she couldn't think quickly enough in that terrible moment.

The snakes struck again, and again after that, each bite filling her with enough venom to kill a score of drow.

She stumbled, but still she held the scourge, and still the snakes bit at her.

She fell backward, the weapon falling beside her, and as she writhed in fiery agony, the snakes bit her again.

And again.

She had never known such pain. She cried out for death to take her.

And there was the child, Yvonnel, she saw through bleary, bloody eyes, standing over her, looking down at her, smiling down at her.

Darkness closed in from the corners of her vision. She did see Yvonnel reaching down; she did feel Yvonnel grasping the gathering of her gown. She felt light as darkness engulfed her. She was light, she believed, because Yvonnel lifted her up with just that one hand, so easily hoisted her from the floor.

A pinprick of light broke the darkness—perhaps the tunnel to the Demonweb Pits and eternity.

But that pinprick widened, and Quenthel felt as if cool waters poured over the burning venom coursing in her veins. It was impossible! No spell could defeat that amount of deadly poison so quickly.

But the light widened and Quenthel realized that she was in her chair again, in her throne, the throne of the matron mother. And there was the young woman, Yvonnel, staring at her, smiling at her.

"Do you understand now?" Yvonnel asked.

Quenthel's mind wheeled—she was terrified that Yvonnel was reading her every thought. She should be dead. The poison of any of her snakes would kill a dark elf. The repeated bites of all five would kill a dark elf in mere moments.

"You live," Yvonnel answered the obvious question. "Yet no priestess could have administered enough healing, divine or alchemical, to pull you back from the death brought by your snakes' venom."

Quenthel's eyes widened as her gaze drifted lower, as her eyes focused on the scourge, her scourge, that Yvonnel carried. The five snakes wrapped lovingly around Yvonnel's beautiful black arms.

"Fear not, I will fashion my own scourge," Yvonnel explained. "Indeed, I look forward to it."

"Who are you?"

"You know."

Quenthel shook her head helplessly.

"You wonder why you are alive," said Yvonnel. "Of course you do! Why would you not? Wouldn't I be better served to let you die? Oh, I see," she said with a perfectly evil grin. "You fear that I saved you from the snake poison so that I might make your death even *more* painful!"

Despite herself, Quenthel began to tremble and to gasp for air.

"Perhaps it will come to that, but it need not," said Yvonnel. "You are fortunate, in that I do not wish to yet reveal myself to the Ruling Council and the city, and thus, I desire your services. You see, for all who look upon House Baenre, you will remain the matron mother. Only you and I will know better."

She paused there and cast a grin at Quenthel. "You do know better," she said.

Quenthel swallowed hard.

"Who am I?" Yvonnel asked, and those five snake heads of Quenthel's scourge unwrapped from the girl's arm and came up hissing and swaying ominously, reaching Quenthel's way.

"The dau—" Quenthel started to reply, but stopped when she noted Qorra, the third and most potent viper, moving to strike.

"Think carefully," Yvonnel said. "Prove to me that you are not too stupid to properly serve my needs."

Quenthel forced herself to close her eyes, to reach into the memories and wisdom of Yvonnel the Eternal.

"Take your time, my aunt, my sibling, my daughter. Who am I?"

Quenthel opened her eyes. "You are the Matron Mother of Menzoberranzan."

The girl's smile sent a thousand waves of warmth cascading through Quenthel, and the snakes slithered back into the loving embrace of Yvonnel's arm.

"Only you and I will know that," Yvonnel explained. "Prove your worth to me. I will be in need of powerful high priestesses, of course, and perhaps a new headmistress of Arach-Tinilith. Are you worthy of such a position?"

Quenthel wanted to reply, indignantly, that she was already the matron mother. How could she not be worthy?

But she said no such thing. She nodded meekly, and accepted the scourge when this young woman, this mere girl, handed it back to her.

"Other Houses hold you in contempt," Yvonnel explained, walking aside as Quenthel composed herself and straightened in her throne. "They hold the name Baenre in contempt. That cannot hold, of course. They will conspire, and if those conspiracies come to fruition, you will be their target, for now at least." She spun gracefully on her heel, her smile wide. "Perhaps they will kill you," she said happily. "But perhaps not. And in that event, and if you have served me well in the tendays coming, then you will survive this. You will serve in my House Baenre, and in my Academy, and you will know honor and glory and great power.

"You see, I do not fear you, because you know now, do you not?"

Quenthel nodded.

"You will never turn against me, because nothing any of them can do to you will be as awful as what I would happily do to you."

Yvonnel bounced over and kissed Quenthel on the cheek, and as she pulled back, the five snakes of Quenthel's scourge came up beside her other cheek, their flicking tongues tickling her.

"Go back to your matron mothering," Yvonnel said, skipping away. "I will inform you when I need you and what I need from you."

And with that, she was gone.

PART 1

The
Puppetmaster

THERE COMES A POINT IN A LIFE WELL-LIVED WHERE THE GAZE GOES beyond the next horizon, to that inevitable time when this mortal coil feeds the worms. Life is a journey, a beauteous walk surrounded by such vastness of time and space that we cannot even truly comprehend, and so we make sense of what we can. We order our corner of the world and build security if we are fortunate, and perhaps, too, a family as part of a larger community.

The immediate needs consume so much of our time, the day-to-day trials that must be overcome. There is a measure of satisfaction in every small victory, in every meal earned, in the warmth of shelter on a cold winter's night.

This is the climb of life, but for those who are lucky enough, there comes a place where the mountain is topped and the needs are satisfied, and so the view grows grander. It is a subtle shift in the omnipresent question of a rational being, from "What can I build?" to "What will I leave behind?"

What will be the legacy of Drizzt Do'Urden? For those who remember my name when I am no more, what will they think? How much better might be the lives of those who follow me—my progeny, perhaps, if Catti-brie and I fruitfully go that route—because of my works here? I watched Bruenor bring forth the sarcophagi of King Connerad and King Emerus, the lava-encased bodies flanking the throne of Gauntlgrym. No less will they be remembered in Mithral Hall and Citadel Felbarr—all the Silver Marches for that matter—for many centuries to come.

Am I destined to become such a statue?

On a practical level, I doubt it, since I expect that much of my remaining life will be spent outside of Bruenor's domain. I will never forget him, nor he me, I am sure, but I sense that my days beside him are nearing their end. For all the love and respect I hold for King Bruenor,

I would not plan to raise my children in a dwarven mine. Nor would Catti-brie, I am sure.

The road is wide open in front of us—to Longsaddle, of course, but only for now. One thing I have come to know in my two centuries of life is that the span of a few years is not a long time, and yet it is often an eventful time, with unanticipated twists and turns. Wherever that meandering road might take me, though, beside me goes an understanding now that my journey is less and less often what I need to do, and much more about what I want to do.

So many options, unbound by the shackles so many must wear. I am a fortunate man—that, I do not deny! I have sufficient wealth now and I am at peace. I have love all around me and am responsible to myself alone—and responsible to my wife only because I choose to be.

And so what will I do? What road shall I choose? What legacy shall I foment?

These are good questions, full of the promise of sublime reward, and I only wish that every man and woman of all the goodly races could find a moment such as this, a time of opportunities and of options. That I am here in this place of luxury is nothing short of remarkable. I do not know the odds of such an outcome for a homeless drow, a hunted rogue in the wilds of the Underdark, but I would bet them long indeed. So many fortunate twists and turns have I found on my journey, encounters with grand friends and marvelous mentors: Zaknafein, my father, and Montolio deBrouchee! And Catti-brie, who helped me to find my heart and a courage of a different sort—the courage to stubbornly exist in a place where my people are not welcome.

And Bruenor, yes Bruenor—perhaps Bruenor above all others. It is incomprehensible that I was befriended by a dwarf king and taken in as a brother. Yes, it has been a reciprocal friendship. I helped Bruenor regain his throne, and walked beside him on his wider journey to bring his people together under the great homeland of Gauntlgrym. Between us, it seems, sits the very definition of friendship.

With all of this, here I am. So many battles I have fought, so many obstacles overcome, yet I cannot deny that good fortune has played a tremendous role in leading me to this place and this time. Every man, every woman, will find battles, will find enemies to overcome, be they goblins or disease, an ill child, a wound that will not heal, a dearth of food, the chill of winter, unrequited love, the absence of a friend. Life is a journey from trial to test, from love to hate, from friendship to grief. We each deal with unsettling uncertainty and we each march on, ever on, following the road that will ultimately lead to our grave.

What grand things might we do along that road? What side avenues will we build, which might start our children on their own walk, perhaps?

So I have found this turn of perspective. I have scaled the peak and look now upon a grand, grand view. I can thank a woman whose warm embrace brings me peace. I can thank the greatest friends any man might ever know. I can thank a dwarf king who found a rogue on the side of a lonely mountain in a forsaken land and called him friend, and took him in.

But I am an elf, and lo, there looms another mountain, I fear. I think often of Innovindil, who told me to live my life in shorter spans, in the expected days of those shorter-lived races about me. Should Catti-brie and I have children, I will likely outlive them, as I will almost surely outlive Catti-brie.

It is a confusing thought, a paradox entwining the greatest joy with the most excruciating agony.

And so here, on this mountaintop, surveying the grand view, I remain aware that I might witness the dawn of another few centuries. By the counting of elves, I have lived but a fraction of my life, yet at this still-early moment, it feels so full!

I am a fortunate man.

Should I see those distant dawns, there are surely dark valleys ahead, and after such certain moments of profound loss will I find the strength to climb the next mountain, and the one after that, and the one after that?

I will, I know, because in my grief the first time, when I thought these friends lost, my love lost, my life lost, I came to understand the truth: that the road will roll beneath your feet whether you step lightly with hope and swiftly with determination, or whether you plod in misery, scraping the dirt with heavy boots.

Because the perspective of that journey is a choice, and I choose happiness, and I choose to climb the next mountain.

—Drizzt Do'Urden

CHAPTER 1 ◈

Tidying

THE WAGON BOUNCED ALONG THE WEST ROAD, THE COFFIN, TIED down as it was, still managing to grumble and bang—so much like the battlerager it carried. They had collected Thibbledorf Pwent for his final journey.

Penelope Harpell and Catti-brie drove the wagon, with Drizzt astride his magical unicorn, Andahar, close beside them. They were bound for Gauntlgrym, after four tendays spent in Longsaddle, where they had dropped old Kipper and the other Harpells who had helped King Bruenor retake and secure the dwarven homeland.

They could have used some sort of a teleport to bring the battlerager's body home to Gauntlgrym, but the winter of the Year of the Rune Lords Triumphant, or 1487 by Dalereckoning, had broken early and so they had decided to take an easy ride instead. Besides, big changes were afoot in the North, so it was said, with upheavals in Waterdeep and grumblings that Lord Neverember had angered more than King Bruenor with his blustery ways.

"I miss him," Catti-brie said to Penelope on the second morning out from Longsaddle. Drizzt had urged his unicorn ahead to scout, leaving the two women alone. The auburn-haired woman glanced back over her shoulder and cast a wistful grin. "I did not know him much in the latter days of his life. I saw him not at all, alive at least, in these years of my rebirth. And still, I cannot but feel a sense of loss with him back there in that box."

"Never a more loyal friend than Thibbledorf Pwent, so claims King Bruenor," Penelope replied, and she put a comforting hand on Catti-brie's forearm.

"So he truthfully claims," said Catti-brie. "Pwent would have caught a ballista spear flying for any of us. His life was to serve."

"A good life, then, if after all these years you still feel the pang of loss at his passing."

"I do." She gave a helpless little chuckle. "It is a strange thing of this second life I know. Many of those dearest to me are here again. My beloved husband, the Companions of the Hall, but still there are times when I feel out of place, as if the world I knew has been left behind and this new world is meant not for me, but for those who have yet to write their tales."

"You are half my age," Penelope reminded her. "There is a large book in front of you, dear Catti-brie, and one with half the pages yet blank."

Catti-brie laughed again and nodded. "It just feels strange sometimes, out of place."

"I understand."

"What does?" Drizzt asked, riding back to join them.

"The world," said Penelope.

"Particularly you," Catti-brie teased.

"It would seem as if I have missed a profound discussion," Drizzt said, falling into line beside the wagon. "One worthy of repeating?"

"Not really," Catti-brie said. "Just the lament of a silly young woman."

"Bah, but you're not so young," Drizzt teased, and Catti-brie shot him a phony glare.

"We were discussing the books we write of our lives," Penelope explained. "It would seem that Catti-brie has a few chapters to add."

Drizzt nodded. "I understand," he said, and he did indeed. "We have just climbed a great mountain in reclaiming Gauntlgrym. The scope of that achievement remains hard to fathom. Perhaps now is the time to let out our breath and to wonder what the next great adventure might be."

Catti-brie and Penelope exchanged a glance then, tipping the drow off.

"So you are plotting your course," Drizzt said.

"We know what we must do," Penelope said seriously.

"The Hosttower?"

"It must be rebuilt, or Gauntlgrym will prove a short-lived victory," said Catti-brie. "There is no doubt that without the power of the ancient magic delivering the water elementals to the prison, the fiery primordial will soon enough break free. The resulting eruption will ruin Bruenor's kingdom . . . and what else? Will Neverwinter again be buried under a mountain of ash? Waterdeep, perhaps?"

"You know this?"

"I know this." Catti-brie held up her hand to display the Ring of Elemental Command that Drizzt had taken from the body of the drow wizard, Brack'thal Xorlarrin, and given to her.

"How long do we have?"

"A decade?" She didn't seem very certain.

"And how long to rebuild the Hosttower of the Arcane?" Drizzt asked. "Can you even hope to accomplish such a task? Is the magic still understood? Do the spells remain to access? It was built many ages ago, by all that I have heard, and we have since passed the Time of Troubles, the Spellplague, the return of Abeir . . ."

"I do not know," Catti-brie bluntly admitted.

"We cannot know until we begin," Penelope added. "But all of the Ivy Mansion will join in as we can. We will open our library and cast our spells as needed."

"We cannot know the course until the first stones are reassembled," Catti-brie agreed.

"You cannot know that you will know the course even then," said Drizzt, and the women had no rebuke for that logic. They were in wholly unexplored territory here, dealing with magic that the world had not seen in millennia.

"We will find assistance from many quarters," Penelope replied. "Your friend Jarlaxle controls the city, and he understands the urgent need for this. He believes, too, that rebuilding the Hosttower will serve his own needs."

"The Harpells will ally with Bregan D'aerthe?"

"Jarlaxle allied with Bruenor," Catti-brie reminded him.

Drizzt started to reply, but bit it back and just heaved a confused sigh instead. What else might be said of Jarlaxle other than a confused sigh, after all? Once again, Jarlaxle had saved Drizzt's life when Doum'wielle, wielding Khazid'hea, had mortally wounded him. Surely the level of Jarlaxle's involvement in securing the Forge and the lower levels of Gauntlgrym went well beyond what the friends had witnessed, and could not be understated. Jarlaxle had convinced House Xorlarrin that to wage war against Bruenor's legions would not serve them well, and had he not done so, how many dwarves would have gone to their graves under the barrage of Xorlarrin magic?

"I expect that Jarlaxle will provide great insight," Drizzt had to admit. "He has contacts across Faerûn and beyond. He consorts with dragons! Likely, he will prove to be your greatest resource in this journey."

Again the two women exchanged a look, and Drizzt stared at them curiously.

"He will be valuable, but more so will be the Archmage Gromph Baenre, I expect," said Catti-brie.

Drizzt felt as if he would simply slide off Andahar's side and crumble to the ground. "Gromph Baenre?" he mouthed in reply.

"He has lived more than eight centuries and has ready access to, and intimate knowledge of, spells that were long forgotten before the Time of Troubles even. Is there anyone in the Realms, save perhaps Elminster himself, wherever he might be, more prepared for such a task as this?"

"He is Baenre," Drizzt said evenly, as if that should be enough—and normally, it most certainly would be.

"He is indebted to Jarlaxle, and cannot return to Menzoberranzan. Or so said Jarlaxle, though I know not why."

Drizzt had heard as much. He tried to focus on those truths and set aside his deeper fears—fears of House Baenre that every dark elf who was not Baenre had judiciously whipped into him from his earliest days.

"You really intend to pursue this?" he asked at length.

"I have no choice."

"You have every choice!" Drizzt insisted. "This is a Baenre, and a wizard beyond the power of all but a very few. Elminster himself would deal carefully with the likes of Archmage Gromph Baenre! He is drow through and through, and he is Baenre through and through, and so not to be trusted."

"He needs Jarlaxle."

"For now. But that may change, and if it does, what will it concern Gromph to destroy you, all of you, and take the tower for his own?"

"He can have the tower as his own!" Catti-brie retorted. "As long as the magic is flowing to Gauntlgrym to keep the beast in its pit."

"And what blackmail might Gromph demand of King Bruenor when such power as that is in his control?" Drizzt asked.

The responding expressions, winces of discomfort from both, showed that the two were well aware of that possibility.

"Jarlaxle will prevent that," Catti-brie said.

"Jarlaxle has little power over the Archmage of Menzoberranzan!"

"What choice do we have?" Catti-brie yelled back at Drizzt. "What choice, my love? Are we to abandon this quest and so abandon Gauntlgrym, and so let the primordial roar forth once more to lay devastation about the Sword Coast?"

Drizzt didn't really have an answer to that.

"Jarlaxle has assured us that Gromph's position is compromised right now," Penelope added. "This will be to Gromph's benefit as well, and he is pragmatic above all else. And Luskan is fully under Jarlaxle's control—even Gromph does not dispute that. Would the archmage deem it worthwhile to do battle with the whole of Jarlaxle's band?"

Drizzt was hardly listening by that point, his stare locked by Catti-brie, the woman silently pleading with him to trust her with these decisions. And Drizzt knew that he should. Catti-brie's understanding of what needed to be done was much greater than anything he might discern.

But he feared that she did not as well understand the webs of the drow, how easily she might be caught in those ultimately sticky filaments, and how difficult it would be to ever escape.

◆ ◆ ◆

"ANY GUILT YOU might feel is surely misplaced. If it hadn't been you, it would have been someone else," Jarlaxle remarked to Gromph when he caught up to the archmage in a suite of rooms Gromph had taken as his own in Illusk, the ancient Undercity buried beneath the common graveyard of Luskan.

Gromph arched an eyebrow at the mercenary, his expression uncertain, but certainly not appreciative.

"We have word of other demon lords walking the ways of the Underdark," Jarlaxle explained. "Zuggtmoy, the Lady of Fungi, is rumored to be holding court among a large gathering of myconids. Orcus is said to be about, as is Graz'zt. The Underdark is less inviting than before, it would seem, and that is no small feat."

"Rumors," Gromph muttered, denying the premise.

That made sense to Jarlaxle and confirmed many of his suspicions. Gromph knew what he had done. The archmage understood that his mighty spell had wrenched Demogorgon from the Abyss and in doing so, had likely broken the protective planar barrier formed within the magic of the Faerzress.

"It would seem that your summoning was part of a larger invasion by the Abyssal lords," Jarlaxle said.

"Rumors!" Gromph emphatically roared. "Have you considered that perhaps Demogorgon brought them forth?"

"He would not," Jarlaxle replied, shaking his head resolutely. "No, there is something bigger afoot."

"Concern yourself with the matters of Luskan, Jarlaxle," Gromph warned, his voice ominous and threatening. "Leave the greater truths to those of greater understanding."

Jarlaxle bowed at that, as much to hide his knowing grin as to mollify his volatile brother.

"Where is that creature you claim as a peer?" Gromph demanded.

The one you consider your tutor? Jarlaxle thought, but very wisely did not say. "Seeking answers, I would hope."

"In the Abyss?"

Jarlaxle nearly laughed out loud. "Where Kimmuriel always seeks his answers," he replied. "At the hive-mind, of course. The illithids know everything in the multiverse, if one is to believe Kimmuriel."

"Bring him to me."

Jarlaxle's expression grew doubtful.

"I wish to speak with him," Gromph added. "Bring him here, as soon as you can."

"Of course," Jarlaxle replied, though of course he had no intention of doing any such thing. Kimmuriel had gone to the hive-mind of the illithids to search for answers, and that was no place Jarlaxle ever intended to visit. But the psionicist had also gone there, posthaste, to get away from Gromph. Jarlaxle hadn't pieced it all together yet, but he was quite suspicious that Kimmuriel had played more than a little role in the disaster Gromph had brought about by inadvertently summoning Demogorgon to Menzoberranzan.

It might prove beneficial to keep Kimmuriel at the hive-mind for the time being in any case, and not just for Kimmuriel's own sake. If any race in the multiverse could aid in rediscovering the magic that had created the Hosttower of the Arcane, it would be the illithids. Time itself, the passing of millennia even, seemed no barrier to those strange creatures and their vast repository of knowledge.

"Perhaps Kimmuriel will garner some information as to how we might be rid of the demon lords," Jarlaxle offered, and that, too, was an honest hope.

"Demon lord," Gromph corrected. "We know of one, Demogorgon. The rest is speculation."

"Even if it is just one . . ." Jarlaxle conceded with a shrug

And that one alone was catastrophe on a monumental scale. Who was going to remove Demogorgon, the Prince of Demons, from the Underdark? Not Gromph, who had fled the scene screaming and tearing at his own eyes. Not Jarlaxle, who had no intention of doing battle with any demon lord. Jarlaxle was quite enamored of his current life.

"You will tell me everything Kimmuriel learns," the archmage said at length. "And when he returns, you will deliver him to me immediately."

"Deliver him?" Jarlaxle shrugged and offered a meek smile.

"What?" Gromph demanded.

"Kimmuriel is a leader of Bregan D'aerthe, dear Gromph, and as such, he is free to make his own choices," Jarlaxle explained. "I will inform him of your desire to speak with him, but . . ."

Gromph's nostrils flared and for a heartbeat, Jarlaxle feared that he might have gone a bit too far in his overt backtracking. But Gromph quickly calmed—no doubt he reminded himself that he needed Bregan D'aerthe right now more than they needed, or feared, him. Jarlaxle could get word of Gromph's whereabouts to Matron Mother Baenre very quickly, after all, and the mercenary leader had a good idea that Quenthel and Gromph were not on particularly good terms at this time.

"I wish to speak with him," Gromph said calmly.

"Perhaps it would help if you would tell me why," Jarlaxle offered.

"Perhaps I might burn my explanation onto your naked back and leave you face down and dead on the floor for Kimmuriel to read."

"A simple no would have sufficed."

"Jarlaxle doesn't take no for an answer."

"Hmm," the mercenary leader snorted, and he shrugged, tipped his hat in concession, and walked away, muttering as he made his way through the haunted corridors of Illusk.

Now he knew, without doubt, that Gromph blamed Kimmuriel for Demogorgon. "Ah, my tentacle-loving friend, what have you done?" Jarlaxle asked himself, but the question carried back no answers in its echoes.

◆ ◆ ◆

THE PRIMORDIAL CHAMBER had been fully redone in the time Drizzt and Catti-brie had been away from Gauntlgrym. The altar block used by Matron Mother Zeerith had been efficiently removed by a team of dwarves, Bruenor centering them, who had merely pushed it into the pit to be devoured by the primordial beast. The webs were gone, the giant jade spiders rudely dismantled, and jade jewelry was all the rage in Gauntlgrym.

Another table, more a bathtub, rested where the drow altar had been, this one bound in mithral as if it were some altar for Bruenor's homeland—though, of course, any altar shaped like a bathtub seemed out of place in a dwarven chapel. Still, in a sense, it was just that. The metal tub had been placed there for the most reverent and somber of circumstances: to commit the dead to their unique coffins.

Below the tub, the dwarves had dug a narrow tunnel. Using a mithral drill and crank, they had driven the channel deep into the stone, angling it toward the primordial pit, where it had broken out just below the swirl of the water elementals. Heavy plugs had been bolted into place—the primordial would not get up through this shaft unless called upon.

They laid Thibbledorf Pwent out to rest in that bowl and Catti-brie began her work, covering Pwent in the special shroud, one heavy with metals that would strengthen the lava. Her assistant dwarves removed the tunnel plug and the priestess reached through her ring to coax the beast forth.

The process would take a full day of labor, bringing forth a bit of lava, magically easing it into place, and then summoning the next molten spurt. It was painstaking and heavy work, but Catti-brie did not tire and paid attention to every last detail. This was Pwent, once her friend, and dear to her Da, and she considered this work to be as much a piece of art as a sarcophagus.

"Have you told him yet?" a voice asked late in the day, startling her when she thought she was alone.

She spun to see Jarlaxle standing in front of her.

"I apologize for surprising you," the mercenary leader said, bowing low. He walked over and peered into the tub. "It is beautiful, a fitting tribute to a most heroic dwarf."

Catti-brie's first instinct was to snap at the uninvited drow—what would he know of Thibbledorf Pwent's true heroism, after all? But she bit it back and reminded herself that Jarlaxle had been a major player in the fight in Gauntlgrym those decades ago when Pwent had fallen to his state of undeath. The mercenary drow and his dwarf companion Athrogate had come into Gauntlgrym with Bruenor and Drizzt to put the primordial back in its pit. Jarlaxle had witnessed the fight when Pwent and Bruenor had defeated not only a pit fiend, but the vampire that had ultimately infected Pwent.

Jarlaxle had been a hero to Bruenor that day, no doubt.

"How did you find me? How did you get in here?" Catti-brie asked, but not sharply. She glanced about, her gaze settling on the lava-filled antechamber across the way, where Archmage Gromph had set up his teleportation room.

"I have a friend who told me where to find you," Jarlaxle replied. "He let me in."

"Drizzt?"

"Shorter," the drow replied, winking the eye that was not covered by a patch.

"Athrogate," Catti-brie said, shaking her head. "Athrogate was supposed to be putting Bruenor ahead of you. So it's not to be, then? Me Da will be interested in that bit of news, now won't he?"

"Pray don't tell him. Athrogate understood my purpose and so he thought allowing me in here to be the best course in serving King Bruenor's interests, given the current situation."

Catti-brie nodded for him to continue.

"You haven't told King Bruenor?"

The woman sighed. "It is not so easy a thing, to tell a dwarf king that his newly reclaimed kingdom will soon be destroyed."

"Then perhaps we should not allow that to happen."

"It is daunting," the woman admitted.

"You have Gromph Baenre."

"Archmage Gromph, the Harpells, my own powers . . . will any of it, will all of it, be nearly enough? The Hosttower was physically obliterated, and its magic is older than any living memory."

"That is not necessarily true," Jarlaxle replied. "And I have a few more avenues we may search to find greater clues. Life is daunting, my dear girl, but it is also wondrous, is it not?"

Catti-brie looked at him incredulously.

"Yes, I am in a fine mood," Jarlaxle added. "And believe me, your course is not the most daunting before me right now, nor the most dangerous."

"Perhaps you should find a place to rest."

"Perhaps I love the adventure."

"And the danger?"

Jarlaxle smiled.

"Do you mean to be beside me when I tell King Bruenor?" Catti-brie asked.

"If you would allow it."

"I would welcome it."

Jarlaxle's smile was genuine. In that moment it occurred to them both that there was nothing out of place with Jarlaxle being allowed unescorted into this room. He was indeed a friend of the king—and of them all.

"Let me gather the dwarves so they can bring Pwent to his resting place in the audience chamber," Catti-brie said. "They have to place him and properly pose him before the stone hardens fully."

"First, though, I believe our black-bearded friend awaits you beside the Great Forge," Jarlaxle said. "He said that he has something for you, and more importantly, that you have something for him."

Catti-brie nodded and grinned and moved over to her pack, producing a heavy leather girdle that Jarlaxle had seen before—and with recognition, the mercenary drow's eyes widened indeed.

"His belt?"

"Athrogate let me borrow it these last tendays," the woman explained.

"You had something heavy to lift?" Jarlaxle quipped. He understood the magic of that belt, which offered great physical strength to the wearer.

"To study it in Luskan," Catti-brie replied with a laugh.

Jarlaxle shook his head, hardly believing the sight in front of his eyes.

"He said he was a friend of King Bruenor's, loyal to the last," Catti-brie reminded. "He took the oath of kith'n kin more solemnly than any, so the whispers say."

"You mean to make such a girdle for Bruenor?" the mercenary asked. "You are capable of making such a girdle?" Clear excitement filled Jarlaxle's voice with that second question, as if he were seeing some real possibilities.

But Catti-brie laughed those away. "Someday, perhaps," she said. "But no, a girdle of this quality is rare and filled with an older magic I fear broken by the Spellplague."

"The Spellplague is gone."

"But the Weave is not fully regained, and the Art of the time before is . . . well, this is our trial in trying to rebuild the Hosttower."

Jarlaxle conceded that and preceded Catti-brie into the Forge room, where Athrogate stood waiting by the Great Forge of Gauntlgrym.

How his face brightened when Catti-brie handed him back his magical girdle, which he wasted no time in securing about his ample waist.

"And for me?" Catti-brie asked.

"Already in the oven," the dwarf explained. "Ye got yer spells ready?"

Catti-brie nodded and motioned to the glowing oven, and Athrogate gathered up his tongs, set the heavy leather apron over his head, and leaned in.

Jarlaxle watched it all from behind, and his curiosity only heightened when the dwarf pulled forth, and quickly dipped in the water trough, a mithral piece, octagonal and about the size of Jarlaxle's palm.

Athrogate drew it back out and held it up in front of Catti-brie's eyes, the woman already deep in spellcasting. A blue mist curled out of the sleeves of her multicolored, shimmering blouse.

Jarlaxle edged closer, trying to get a better look. "A belt buckle?" he whispered under his breath. He noted a carving on its face of a bow, and one that looked like a tiny image of Taulmaril the Heartseeker, once Catti-brie's bow, but now carried by Drizzt.

Catti-brie finished her spell and raised her hand to touch the item, and when she did a blue spark burst forth, sizzling in the air, and the woman fell back.

"Supposed to do that, is it?" Athrogate asked.

"I hope," Catti-brie said with a laugh. She bit it back quickly, though, and turned to Jarlaxle. "If you tell him, you and I will have a problem," she warned.

"Tell him? Tell who? And tell him what?"

The woman smiled and nodded. "Good," she said, and took the buckle from Athrogate and dropped it into her pouch.

"Did you get the rest?"

"The blood? Aye. Amber's got it. She'll get it to ye shortly."

"The blood?" Jarlaxle asked.

"The less you know, the better the chances that we will remain friends," Catti-brie pointedly told him. She pointed to the other end of the room, where the solemn procession of dwarves had begun. The trio fell in with them as they made their way to the highest level of the complex. They found Drizzt in the throne room, then went with him to find King Bruenor in his upper war room, not far away. He was meeting with Ragged Dain, Oretheo Spikes, the Fellhammer sisters, and the other dwarf commanders around a table set with a detailed map of the complex.

"Ah, time for a ceremony, then," Bruenor said upon seeing them.

Catti-brie held up her hand. "Not just yet, me Da," she replied. "Might we be speakin' with ye?"

Bruenor glanced all around and nodded. "Aye."

"Alone?" Catti-brie asked.

Bruenor glanced around again. "It is about the hall, then?"

The woman nodded.

"Then here and now," Bruenor said, motioning for the other dwarves to rest easy. "Any word o' the hall is a word for all gathered to hear. We're four clans in one here, aye?"

"Aye," said Shuggle Grunions of Mirabar, who led the Mirabarran members of Bruenor's new kingdom. The others all nodded, as did Catti-brie's companions. They had to know, after all, and better if they knew before they began emptying the halls of Mirabar, Adbar, Felbarr, and Mithral Hall as more and more flocked to the Delzoun homeland of Gauntlgrym.

"We intend to rebuild the Hosttower of the Arcane in Luskan," Catti-brie stated.

"Aye, ye been whisperin' as much," Bruenor replied.

"Archmage Gromph has agreed to aid us," Jarlaxle added.

Bruenor didn't seem overly pleased by that. "Yer city," he said. "Do what ye will. But be warned, drow, if ye're thinking o' rebuilding the tower as part o' some plan to make me beholden . . ."

"We're rebuilding it to save Gauntlgrym," Catti-brie blurted. "Only for that."

"Eh?" Bruenor and several others all said together.

"The power of the Hosttower brings forth the water elementals," the woman explained. "Only their combined power keeps the beast in its pit."

"Aye, and they're swirling thick in there," Bruenor replied.

"The residual magic is strong," Catti-brie explained. "But it is only that, residual. And already it is thinning."

"What're ye saying?" Ragged Dain asked breathlessly.

Catti-brie took a deep breath and was glad indeed when Drizzt squeezed her hand. "If we canno' rebuild the Hosttower and bring forth its magic once more, ye're not to have many years in Gauntlgrym. The magic will diminish and the water elementals will sweep away."

"And then the beast is free," said Drizzt. "And we have seen that before."

Bruenor grumbled indecipherably. He looked as if he was chewing on a pile of sharp rocks.

"How many years?" he finally asked, and all eyes turned to Catti-brie.

"I do'no know," she replied. "Less than yer life, to be sure, and suren less than me own."

"And ye know this?"

"Aye."

"Because the beast telled ye?"

"More than just that, but aye."

"And so ye'll fix the durned tower," Ragged Dain stated more than asked.

Catti-brie kept looking at Bruenor.

"Well?" the king of Gauntlgrym finally asked her.

"We are going to try, good King Bruenor," Jarlaxle unexpectedly interjected. "Between your daughter and the Harpells, and all the forces I can muster, we will try."

"And what's yer play in this?" Bruenor demanded.

"You know my stake in Luskan. I have not hidden that from you."

"So ye're thinkin' the volcano'd blow that way, are ye?"

"I have no idea, and suspect that Luskan is far enough out of its reach in any event," Jarlaxle replied. "And no, I'll not deny that rebuilding the Hosttower will be of great benefit to me, and in part because it will keep you here in Gauntlgrym, and that, good dwarf king, I prefer."

Bruenor looked for a moment as if he would question that claim, but he rocked back on his heels and let it go with a nod.

"But to do this, we will need your help," Jarlaxle added. "Send a thousand of your best builders to the City of Sails, I beg, that we can put them to use in physically reconstructing the Hosttower."

"A thousand?" Bruenor balked.

"We got walls to build here," Oretheo Spikes protested.

"Aye, and tunnels yet to secure," added Ragged Dain.

"And to what point might we be doin' that if the damned volcano's to blow?" Mallabritches Fellhammer said above them all, and indeed, that quieted the ruckus before it could gather momentum.

"Ye're askin' me to walk a thousand o' me boys into a city o' pirates and drow?" Bruenor said.

"I will guarantee their safety, of course. Indeed, I will build barracks and all accommodations right there on Cutlass Island, which cannot be reached by land except by going through Closeguard Island, upon which sits the fortress of High Captain Kurth."

"Yer boy?"

Jarlaxle confirmed that with a nod.

Bruenor looked around the room, and each dwarf in turn came to nod his or her agreement.

"And we might find that we will need more than a thousand," Jarlaxle warned.

Bruenor's nostrils flared, but Catti-brie interjected, "If we fail in this you will have no halls worth defending. Not here, at least.

"But if we succeed . . ." she added, as the dwarves began to grumble. "The primordial is secure and we will understand so much more of the magic that built Gauntlgrym. It might well be that the Hosttower's the secret to getting the magical gates up and running, too."

That ended the meeting on an upbeat note, as Catti-brie had hoped, but by the time Bruenor and the other dwarves emerged from the war room into the throne room for the ceremony committing Pwent's statue, they wore dour expressions once again.

Bruenor went right to the throne and hopped upon it, settling back with his hairy chin in his hand as he stared at the sarcophagus of Thibbledorf Pwent being set in its final, heroic pose on the wall a dozen strides away, about ten feet above the floor on a shelf the dwarves had carved. From there, Pwent would look over the hall, a guardian just above the fray, overlooking and protecting his king.

King Bruenor did gain some comfort from that sight, and was comforted, too, by the sensations of the godly throne. He had the distinct feeling, as clear as a whisper in his ear, that the sentient spirits within the Throne of the Dwarven Gods agreed with his decision to aid in the reconstruction of the Hosttower.

Between that and looking at Pwent, Bruenor felt strangely calm, given the shock of this day's news. He knew that he was not alone here, and that his friends, even including Jarlaxle, were no small matter.

He let other dwarves speak of Pwent at the dedication, and hardly listened. He did not need to hear tales of Thibbledorf Pwent to know the truth of that most wonderful shield dwarf. When they were done

Bruenor brought the cracked silver horn up to his lips on impulse and blew a discordant note, summoning the battleraging specter of Pwent.

As always when there was no enemy apparent, the defending spirit hopped about wildly, scouring every shadow and nook.

The others thought nothing of it and turned their attention to Bruenor, who led them in a toast to Pwent.

Except for Jarlaxle, who watched the spirit and noted that this thing, supposedly unconnected to Thibbledorf Pwent's actual spirit and soul, supposedly a simple and little-thinking manifestation of a bodyguard, paused and let its stare linger on the sarcophagus statue that had just been set on the wall.

And in those nearly translucent eyes, Jarlaxle noted something.

Recognition?

Chapter 2 ◈

House Do'Urden

S SHE COMING FORTH?" SARIBEL ASKED WHEN TIAGO RETURNED FROM Matron Mother Darthiir Do'Urden's private chambers.

"She is barely awake, as usual," the warrior spat in reply, his voice full of contempt, as it always was now when he spoke to his wife. Saribel had become more resolute and forceful of late, particularly concerning Tiago's disastrous obsession with the rogue Drizzt Do'Urden, and clearly that had not set well with Tiago.

Because he thought her his lesser, Saribel knew, despite the fact that she was a woman and a high priestess. She was not a Baenre by blood, and that, to Tiago, was all that mattered.

He would learn differently, Saribel mused.

"Ravel and the others await us in the chapel," Saribel said. "We are quite tardy."

"Is Braelin Janquay in attendance?" Tiago asked, referring to the newest noble of House Do'Urden, gifted by Matron Mother Quenthel Baenre to serve as the garrison commander.

It was not a gift that Tiago had appreciated, nor Saribel for that matter. Braelin had come to them from Bregan D'aerthe, reputedly as a stand-in for Jarlaxle himself, who was now nowhere to be found. Much of House Do'Urden's cobbled-together garrison was composed of Bregan D'aerthe soldiers. In that reality, how much power might the newcomer wield?

Too much, likely, as far as Tiago and Saribel were concerned.

When the couple entered the chapel to find the other House nobles waiting, Saribel was greeted by another of the new leaders, one whose arrival had greatly mitigated her fears of Braelin Janquay—and also exacerbated Tiago's misgivings.

"It is good to see you once more," Jaemas Xorlarrin, Saribel's cousin, said with a bow. He took her hand and kissed it.

Saribel looked past Jaemas to her brother Ravel, a fellow wizard and good friend of Jaemas. It was clear that Ravel was glad that cousin Jaemas had joined House Do'Urden.

"Is Faelas to number among our ranks soon, as well?" Saribel asked.

"Shall we rename Do'Urden to Xorlarrin, then," Tiago answered before Jaemas could, "that we might suffer the same grim fate as that doomed and fallen House?"

"Ah, well met again, young Master Baenre," Jaemas said, and he pointedly left it at that, turning his attention immediately back to Saribel.

"Matron Mother Zeerith and High Priestess Kiriy send their regards and trust that you are well," he said.

"I am," she replied, though she couldn't help but give a little wince at the mention of Kiriy, the highest ranking priestess of House Xorlarrin, just below Matron Mother Zeerith. Whispers spoke of Kiriy, who was also Matron Mother Zeerith's eldest daughter, possibly joining House Do'Urden as well, in which case, so much for Saribel's designs on ascending to the position of Matron Mother of House Do'Urden.

"Where are they now?" Tiago asked.

"Quite well and quite safe," said Jaemas. "Planning the next moves of House Xorlarrin, of course."

"You mean, of what is left of House Xorlar—"

"Do not think that we suffered great losses when the dwarves came for Gauntlgrym," Jaemas interrupted.

"None but your city."

"For now. But we are stronger." He looked back at Saribel and offered just enough of a wink to let her know that he made these claims just to anger Tiago. "Much stronger. So many wondrous items came from the Forge before we were forced back because of the failures in the Silver Marches.

"The dwarves emptied their citadels and swept across the land," he continued, somewhat dramatically. "It would have taken much of Menzoberranzan's combined strength to hold them off, as they were led by King Bruenor Battlehammer himself, and by that rogue from this very House."

"Drizzt?" Saribel asked, and she glanced at her husband. When Tiago and Doum'wielle came tumbling back into House Do'Urden at the end of one of Archmage Gromph's teleport spells, Tiago had told her that the half-drow Doum'wielle had stolen his kill, and so had slain Drizzt back in Gauntlgrym.

"He is dead," said Tiago.

Jaemas laughed. "Nay, he is quite alive. Indeed, it was he who defeated the demons Marilith and Nalfeshnee, with the help of his black panther. I witnessed it myself in the battle for the lower halls of Gauntlgrym."

"You are mistaken!" Tiago insisted.

Saribel shook her head at the anger evident in Tiago's voice. Such obsession would never end well.

"Braelin Janquay can confirm, I expect," Ravel chimed in, turning to Braelin, who remained silent. His position as a known associate of Jarlaxle, who was almost certainly still loyal to Jarlaxle, did not encourage him to speak.

"Jarlaxle was in the cavern during that fight," Jaemas confirmed, instead. "Indeed, it was he and Kimmuriel Oblodra who suggested that it was time for a withdrawal, and with good cause. Both of them knew of Drizzt Do'Urden's presence in the battle."

All eyes turned again to Braelin Janquay, with Tiago's gaze predictably intense.

"I was instructed by Jarlaxle to report to House Do'Urden, and it was made clear to me that my time in Bregan D'aerthe had come to its end," he answered, to a few snickers.

But Tiago wasn't laughing. He strode defiantly up to Braelin, his eyes flaring threateningly. "What do you know?"

Braelin matched his stare. "I just told you."

"Perhaps your corpse would tell my priestess wife differently."

"Surely such an event would tell much to Jarlaxle."

"You think I fear Jarlaxle?"

"I had always assumed you to be intelligent."

A little snarl escaped Tiago's lips and his hand went to the hilt of Vidrinath. But another hand, Ravel's hand, settled on his forearm. When Tiago turned to the House wizard, he found Ravel shaking his head. Jaemas similarly warned Tiago away from this dangerous course.

"I know what I saw, and what I saw was surely the rogue named Drizzt Do'Urden," Jaemas said. "Faelas will confirm. Drizzt was there, very much alive, in the battle of the lower chambers. There is no reason to believe him dead, no reason at all, whatever you might have seen when you were removed from Gauntlgrym."

Saribel scrutinized her husband carefully now, watching his expression go from murderous rage to something else. Intrigue, perhaps.

The high priestess shook her head, knowing where this new path would soon enough lead. She half expected Tiago to run from the House right then and charge off for Gauntlgrym in pursuit of the rogue.

"You do understand that Demogorgon cut a swath of destruction across Menzoberranzan before departing to the open Underdark?" Ravel remarked, which told Saribel that he, too, had noted Tiago's rather naked intentions. "And that the Prince of Demons is out there in the tunnels, likely not far?"

"And so many other demons, as well," Braelin Janquay added, "including other demon lords if the reports are to be believed."

"Do you purport to instruct me?" Tiago asked with a derisive snort of incredulity.

"No, but now is not the time," Ravel bluntly stated.

Saribel did well not to sigh out loud with relief that her brother was taking the lead. Tiago would listen to him, and no one else in this room.

"Matron Mother Baenre is vulnerable because of the disaster wrought by Archmage Gromph—or at least, one that is being attributed to him," Ravel reminded them all. "And if she is vulnerable, then so are we."

"You think House Baenre vulnerable?" Tiago scoffed.

"I think that they need to close up and concern themselves with their own situation right now," Ravel argued, and from his tone it was clear that he, like so many others, was becoming quite weary of Tiago's obsession. "Matron Mother Baenre did not construct House Do'Urden with such distinguished nobles as we see here in this very room in order for us to rely upon her for our own security. Our eyes must be turned nowhere but to the corridors and walls of House Do'Urden in this dangerous time. We have been graced by the matron mother in adding Jaemas Xorlarrin and Braelin Janquay to our ranks, one a Master of Sorcere and the other a senior member of Bregan D'aerthe and confidant of mighty Jarlaxle and Kimmuriel. Our foot soldiers here once knew loyalty to Bregan D'aerthe, and they are an ally that will serve us well now.

"But only," he continued, quite animatedly, "if we as the leaders of this House properly take and execute control of the situation and inspire confidence in our cobbled-together garrison."

"Faelas Xorlarrin is not far afield of us," Jaemas added before Tiago could angrily retort, as his expression showed him most certainly preparing to do. "And there are others at Sorcere who would quietly support us if the need arises. When House Xorlarrin set off to create Q'Xorlarrin, we did not cut ties to the Academy. And now that that House—my House—wanders unmoored, it is likely that more of our resources will flow House Do'Urden's way."

Though his words were aimed at Tiago, Saribel did not like the sound of them, either. Any members of Xorlarrin that joined Do'Urden would only bolster High Priestess Kiriy and Matron Mother Zeerith's plans. Plans that she knew would move Saribel away from the throne. She did not believe Dahlia, that abomination known as Darthiir Do'Urden, would live long in this tumultuous time, and Xorlarrin resources made her earlier calculations more urgent.

She looked to Tiago and saw that he could not suppress his wince at what amounted to a dangerous warning from Jaemas. None in the fledgling House now, other than perhaps a few minor soldiers in the garrison, had any ties to House Barrison Del'Armgo.

Indeed, House Do'Urden had become a de facto combination of House Xorlarrin and Bregan D'aerthe, with only Tiago Baenre holding any other direct in-House influence. The moment of joy that left Saribel thinking she might have gained the upper hand against Tiago was tempered only by the fact of Tiago's family name, Baenre, and his noted standing with Matron Mother Quenthel.

"That will be up to the discretion of the matron mother, of course," Tiago said coolly, composed again. "It is well known that Matron Mother Zeerith wisely seeks the counsel of Matron Mother Baenre at every turn, that she went to build her failed city at Matron Mother Baenre's behest, and that it was Matron Mother Baenre's decision to send the demon army to Q'Xorlarrin to allow Matron Mother Zeerith her retreat with most of her House intact."

He turned to Braelin, his expression perfectly awful, as he finished with confidence, "Bregan D'aerthe's tribute soldiers and House Xorlarrin's attempt to rejoin the ranks of Menzoberranzan will be orchestrated by the will or whim of the matron mother."

Tiago spun about and motioned to Saribel for her to follow as he strode out of the chamber.

"Drizzt alive!" he said to her when they were alone. "I had him! His head should stand on a pike outside this, my House, as a warning to all who would go against Tiago Baenre."

"*Your* House?" she dared remark, and Tiago spun on her, eyes wide. "Your obsession with the rogue Do'Urden wounds us all," Saribel pressed, and for a moment, she thought Tiago would strike out at her. "Ravel has tired of it, or could you not hear that clearly in his warnings to you?"

"Drizzt Do'Urden will fall to me," Tiago promised. "And this is already *my* House, do not doubt. On a word from me, Matron Mother Baenre would cast out any of you."

"There is a matron mother in the other room," Saribel reminded him, motioning toward Matron Mother Darthiir's private chambers.

Tiago scoffed.

"She sits on the Ruling Council," said Saribel, as convincingly as she could.

"She is a useful puppet for Matron Mother Baenre," Tiago replied. "And to me."

"I know what she is to you, husband."

"Do you, truly?" His laugh sent a chill to her bones.

"I am the future Matron Mother of House Do'Urden," Saribel proclaimed. "You would do well to never forget that."

Tiago laughed at her, and Saribel felt a scream of rage boiling up within her.

"Or perhaps the future Matron Mother of House Do'Urden will be borne by Matron Mother Darthiir," Tiago retorted, and then, lewdly, he added, "by the beautiful Dahlia."

"You disgust me."

Tiago laughed and started away, and he pointedly unstrapped his weapon belt before he had even reached the door to Dahlia's private quarters.

Saribel glanced around, feeling trapped. She wanted to go to Ravel or Jaemas, or perhaps even to Braelin Janquay, to see if she could build some support against Tiago. She understood the driving power of ambition—she was full of it herself, and indeed, was surprised by that, since she had always been the least of Matron Mother Zeerith's children in the eyes of all around her, even in her own eyes. Her oldest sister Kiriy was the High Priestess of House Xorlarrin, but the next eldest child, Berellip, had always been presumed to be the truly ascendant daughter. Even her brother Ravel ranked higher in Matron Mother Zeerith's eyes than she, Saribel had always understood, but had privately never accepted. She hadn't even realized that until her marriage to Tiago, until she had been given the surname of Baenre. With the power of that House behind her, why would she not assume the mantle of House Do'Urden upon Dahlia's surely-impending demise?

She would be the matron mother and her husband would serve as patron and weapons master.

But now it seemed that Tiago was both her ladder and her anchor. Could she rally the others against him?

She wanted to believe that she could, and tried to talk herself into that belief. But she was shaking her head the whole time she was trying to formulate some plan.

In the end, Tiago was a Baenre, and a shining light in the eyes of the matron mother. That mattered. In fact, Saribel's best chance at her own ascent, particularly in light of the possible arrival of Kiriy or even Matron Mother Zeerith, rested wholly on her husband's lineage and her new surname.

Tiago was a Baenre. Saribel was now a Baenre. That mattered above anything House Xorlarrin, Matron Mother Zeerith, or Bregan D'aerthe might desire.

Saribel's private contemplations were stolen by a soft whimper from the other room, where Tiago was claiming ownership of the seed of succession.

Or was he fooling himself?

Saribel found some hope in the scene when Tiago had returned through Archmage Gromph's gate. The mighty Gromph, in that event, clearly revealed his feelings for a half-drow abomination by casting Doum'wielle Armgo to the side of a distant mountain to die in the cold. Considering Gromph's bold action against a member of House Barrison Del'Armgo and the lack of any response from the Second House in retaliation, was it likely that Matron Mother Baenre would let a half-*iblith* child assume the throne of House Do'Urden?

Even with the consideration that Tiago was her ladder to success, the knowledge that others would not tolerate Dahlia for long gave Saribel some comfort. She wanted Tiago to fail even more than she wanted herself to succeed. A sound from the room, the soft but sharp cry as Tiago violated Dahlia, only crystallized those feelings.

◆　◆　◆

Matron Mother Quenthel Baenre reclined calmly on her divan, one leg freed of her decorated dress by a slit that reached to her hip.

She clicked her long fingernails together and played with the multiple golden bangles on one slender wrist, all the while wearing an expression of complete boredom.

Tiago Do'Urden moved from foot to foot in front of her, barely able to contain his explosive temper.

But he had to contain it. The matron mother had cut him short at the utterance of his first word, informing him that she was not quite ready for what had been proposed in the meeting he had demanded. Now it had become a test to see if he could properly adhere to the lead of the matron mother. Quenthel had silenced him with an upraised finger, and was letting it stretch out interminably, just to prove that she could.

"You are wasting my time," she said some time later, turning a glare that was both bored and threatening over the upstart weapons master.

"Matron Mother?"

"Yes, I am, as you must never forget. You requested this audience and I have granted it."

"But you . . ." Tiago started to protest. He thought better of it and said instead, "I did, but only because it is a most urgent issue."

Quenthel swung about on her jeweled and silken divan to place her feet flat on the floor, facing him directly.

"House Xorlarrin . . ." Tiago explained, shaking his head as if trying to sort it all out as he blurted the words. "They grow bold under the banner of Do'Urden."

"They?"

"Saribel and . . ."

"High Priestess Saribel?" Quenthel interrupted, her correction a clear warning.

"Yes, my wife."

"No," Quenthel corrected. "She is not your wife. You are her husband, the mate of High Priestess Saribel Xorlarrin Baenre Do'Urden. Do you understand that distinction?"

Tiago could barely spit out a response. Where was this sudden attitude shift coming from? He had been the leader of the Xorlarrin expedition to claim Gauntlgrym as a drow city, even above High Priestess Berellip herself. Tiago had held no small measure of sway in every movement and decision of that expedition, because of the insistence of Matron Mother Quenthel. Now she would side with dimwitted Saribel Xorlarrin over him?

He knew he had to take a different tack. "Her . . ." He paused again, wanting to keep Saribel completely out of the reference. "Ravel Xorlarrin," he corrected, and then again, "Ravel Do'Urden has been joined among the House nobles by his cousin Jaemas and other wizards of House Xorlarrin."

"They are without a home, of course," Quenthel replied. "And House Do'Urden must fend for itself against treachery that may yet come."

"I understand . . ." Tiago started to reply.

"I do not care if you understand or not," Quenthel scolded. "Why would I? You are the weapons master of House Do'Urden, answering thus to the Matron Mother of House Do'Urden."

"She is . . ." Tiago started to retort. But when Quenthel's hand came up, holding her vicious, snake-headed scourge, Tiago wanted no part of that. Favored nephew and noble or not, he was, after all, just a male, and had felt the bite of such punishing tools far too many times in his short life. He sucked in his breath and fell to his knees in supplication.

"Stand up, you fool," Quenthel commanded, and he did, quickly, and dared look into her eyes.

"You are Baenre," she said. "You know the way of things. Are you so bound up in your pride that you do not understand the opportunity before us now? House Xorlarrin has been dislodged from Q'Xorlarrin, and we'll not march against that fortress to drive out the dwarves. Not now, not anytime soon."

"Drizzt Do'Urden is there," Tiago dared to whisper.

The matron mother's scourge snapped and Tiago recoiled in fear as the snake heads hissed and spat and bit in the air just in front of his face.

"Do not ever speak that name to me again," Quenthel told him. "He is an inconsequential tick, and every time you speak of him or consider him, he bloats on the blood of House Baenre. The dwarves have reclaimed Gauntlgrym. The tunnels between us and them are thick with demons, including major demons, including demon lords. Shall I march an army through such a force to do battle with entrenched dwarves? Would that satisfy your hunger?"

"No, Matron Mother," Tiago said weakly.

"I choose not to protect House Do'Urden at this time, and know that you have enemies," Quenthel bluntly stated.

That declaration hit Tiago hard. This wasn't a choice, he knew, but a necessity. Only then did he realize how much damage Archmage Gromph's recklessness had truly wrought, not necessarily to Menzoberranzan but surely to House Baenre. Quenthel wouldn't help defend House Do'Urden because she couldn't help, because she was feeling the pressure of the other Houses, all outraged over the arrival of Demogorgon in Menzoberranzan at the hands of the archmage, the Elderboy of House Baenre and the arcane extension of Matron Mother Baenre.

Tiago pieced some things together then, and he did well not to gasp aloud as truths became clear to him. Jarlaxle had told the Xorlarrins to leave, so Jaemas had declared. Jarlaxle had arranged the truce with King Bruenor that had allowed Matron Mother Zeerith and her family to escape, Tiago had learned from Ravel soon after that meeting in House Do'Urden's chapel. And Bregan D'aerthe answered, most of all, to Matron Mother Baenre. Was it possible that Matron Mother Quenthel had surrendered the city of Q'Xorlarrin to pull back reinforcements she feared she would need for the security of House Baenre?

"Matron Mother Zeerith's troubles may well save your House," Quenthel explained. "So yes, Jaemas Xorlarrin is now Jaemas Do'Urden. As is Faelas, though he will retain his proper surname while he serves as my eyes in Sorcere."

"Until Gromph returns?"

Quenthel laughed at that. "Was Gromph obliterated by Demogorgon? Devoured?"

"He is the Archmage . . ."

"He *was* the Archmage," Quenthel corrected.

Tiago felt as if he couldn't breathe. This was too much, too quickly. He calmed by reminding himself that times of chaos were times of opportunity.

"So, Faelas . . ." he said leadingly, thinking he had sorted it out.

"Is a Master of Sorcere."

"Sorcere will need a new archmage."

"Worry about your House," Quenthel warned.

"I could do more to prepare House Do'Urden carrying the imprimatur of the matron mother."

"You are the weapons master of House Do'Urden. Only that. I thought I had made that clear."

"Yes, Matron Mother," he blurted, and lowered his gaze as he saw the scourge coming up once more.

"High Priestess Saribel will understand the way forward. That is all you need to know, and that is what you have no choice but to trust."

"Yes, Matron Mother," Tiago replied, and he was fuming then, but wise enough to make sure that he did nothing to make that apparent. Quenthel waved him away, and he was glad to be gone, and quickly.

◆ ◆ ◆

As soon as he exited the room, Quenthel waved her hand and slammed the door behind him, an exclamation point to the finality of his obsession with Drizzt Do'Urden.

"I told you," Quenthel said to Minolin Fey as she came out of the room's side door, having heard the entire conversation. "He is possessed of the same dangerous hubris as Gromph."

"A fatal hubris, no doubt," said the young woman accompanying Minolin Fey.

Quenthel, still not looking over, swallowed hard. She didn't want to look upon Yvonnel, especially now that Yvonnel was physically entering young adulthood, and was so beautiful, so physically, magically, painfully beautiful, that her appearance alone mocked any who thought themselves her equal.

"You did well, my daughter," Yvonnel said, and she giggled and added. "My aunt."

Both of the older women wore sour expressions at that comment, which only made young Yvonnel dance a bit more and smile a bit wider.

"Even with Tiago properly settled in House Do'Urden, we must move quickly now," Yvonnel said more seriously, moving up to stand in front of Quenthel. "Convene a Council."

"They will not likely come," Quenthel replied. "The Houses have gone into defensive crouches—it grows increasingly difficult to pry soldiers from them for the patrols beyond our cavern. All expect some fighting soon, House against House, or with demons coming forth. We know not if Demogorgon haunts the ways just outside the city."

"Some are surely trying to determine when a rival will be properly weakened by serving on such a patrol," Minolin Fey said, and both of the others turned unappreciative glares her way, a not-subtle reminder of her lowly place in such powerful company.

49

"The seats will suffice and the votes will be binding, by the word of Lolth," Yvonnel said.

Quenthel considered that for a moment then nodded. She, Sos'Umptu, and Matron Mother Darthiir would be easy enough to arrange, of course.

"We cannot outlaw secretive internecine war," she replied. "Without personal instructions from a handmaiden or communion with Lolth herself, none would accept our authority to make such a dramatic change in the customs of Menzoberranzan."

"But we can demand that all participate in the defense of Menzoberranzan," Yvonnel said. "And we must shut the city down, and quickly, both physically and magically. No dimensional doorways, no divination from without. The physical ways in are few, and we can defend them, but we deal with demon lords now, and so must defeat any of their magical attempts to breach the city before they even try."

"That is a tremendous task."

"It is, and it will require diligence and great attention from all priests and wizards alike."

"And so we name Tsabrak Xorlarrin as Archmage of Menzoberranzan," Quenthel reasoned, nodding.

"Tsabrak, who holds close ties to House Do'Urden now," Yvonnel agreed. "His sister, his brother, his cousins. Have you found any contact with Matron Mother Zeerith?"

"She is with Bregan D'aerthe, I am certain. An associate of Jarlaxle's, Braelin Janquay, delivered the message that High Priestess Kiriy Xorlarrin might be interested in returning to the city if a proper position in a fitting House could be found for her."

"High Priestess of House Do'Urden, of course—or eventual matron mother."

"I prefer her younger sister Saribel," Quenthel said. "Tiago will keep that one close and she is more easily controlled. I have never been fond of Kiriy. She is headstrong and convinced that her heart is ever in league with the wishes of the Spider Queen."

Yvonnel smiled and nodded. "We are blessed," she said with uncharacteristic kindness. "The illithid has given us both insight to the ways and memories of the Eternal. Mine is more pure, of course, but I am pleased by the insights of the Matron Mother of Menzoberranzan."

Quenthel leaned away a bit, staring skeptically at the beautiful young woman, even shaking her head in denial.

"I thought I was to serve you," Quenthel dared to say "perhaps even from the halls of Arach-Tinilith in the Academy."

"We are stronger right now with you as matron mother," Yvonnel replied. "We, House Baenre, and the city we control. Call the Ruling Council together—make it not a request, but a command. Demand unity in securing the city and so execute that unity. Declare the new Archmage Tsabrak, and remind any who balk at the proclamation that he was the voice of Lolth in darkening the skies above the Silver Marches."

"There will still be an attack on House Do'Urden," Quenthel warned.

"Hunzrin and Melarn," Yvonnel replied. "Undoubtedly. And I am counting on it."

She laughed again and skipped out of the room, Minolin Fey in her wake, leaving Quenthel dumbfounded and off-balance, which had been the whole point, Quenthel realized after a moment of reflection.

◆ ◆ ◆

BACK IN HER own chambers, Yvonnel dismissed Minolin Fey, secured her room with multiple glyphs and wards, and fell into a deep communion with the Abyssal Plane, using the imparted memories of Yvonnel the Eternal to formulate a demonic name.

She watched the summoned form materialize in front of her, like a great, half-melted candle of mud, tentacle arms dripping with Abyssal goo.

Yvonnel, so gloriously groomed and perfectly formed, winced at the grotesque handmaiden, and even more so when the yochlol said, "You summoned me, daughter of House Baenre?" in that watery, gurgling, mud-like voice.

"Could you not assume a more . . . pleasing form, Yiccardaria?" Yvonnel asked.

The handmaiden giggled, which sounded very much like water bubbling through a thick muddy puddle, and waggled her tentacles about as she turned, spinning round and round. Faster and faster she twirled, and the movement seemed more blurry still from the sheen of brown mist the handmaiden left in her turning wake. The brown cloud settled as she stopped, and now she was a drow woman, beautiful in form, delicate and naked and with long, thick white hair that hung to her waist.

"Do you approve?" Her voice was no longer muddy, but clear as a shining silver bell.

"I do," Yvonnel said. "And you have my appreciation, Handmaiden, both for the transformation and for coming to my call."

"I would not have come, were it not the will of the Spider Queen."

Yvonnel bowed again.

"We have much to discuss," Yiccardaria said, moving over and running the back of her fingers gently over Yvonnel's soft cheek.

It was a test, Yvonnel knew, to see if she could sort through what her eyes and nose and skin were telling her—to hold onto the truth that this was a lump of smelly goo teasing her.

"I had much I wished to discuss with you," Yvonnel replied, taking the yochlol by the wrist and moving her hand aside. "That is why I requested your presence, after all. But it would seem that you come with information that you believe I should know."

"Astute," the yochlol said, pulling away with a giggle. "I approve of your transformation and will relay my pleasure to the Spider Queen. Perhaps more so . . ." She reached to touch the beautiful young drow woman again.

"It was Gromph who brought Demogorgon to Menzoberranzan," Yvonnel said, trying to keep focused on the matters at hand. She had never known a handmaiden to behave like this, and wasn't quite sure what it might be about, beyond her initial inkling that the spy for Lolth—every handmaiden was a spy for Lolth, first and foremost—was testing her.

And she couldn't deny her body's reactions to the exquisite creature.

She thought the yochlol was trying to seduce her as a test of her will-power—a ridiculous challenge indeed for one of Yvonnel's understanding and intelligence. But then she understood: The handmaiden was testing her corporeal body, not her willpower, to see if this form Yvonnel wore was real or illusion. The physical reactions, involuntary and ignorant of willpower, would reveal that to the spy.

The handmaiden laughed again and danced away, staring knowingly at the young Yvonnel, whose nipples had visibly hardened under the soft shirt.

"Gromph summoned Demogorgon," Yvonnel said again, this time more sternly.

"Not without help," Yiccardaria replied. "Great help, and of most of which the Archmage remains unaware. Understand that Gromph Baenre did more than summon Demogorgon." She laughed again, and Yvonnel had to force herself not to lean forward too eagerly.

"Let me tell you of the Faerzress," Yiccardaria said.

"I know . . ." Yvonnel started to interrupt, but the handmaiden didn't slow.

"Of what it was and what it is, and of the demon lords who have come through. The Lady of Chaos wishes you to know these things, and the source of the ritual Archmage Gromph performed."

"And of how it might benefit . . . me," Yvonnel said with a wicked grin, and now it was the yochlol's turn to offer a respectful bow.

Yiccardaria spoke for a long time after that, revealing Lolth's brilliant deception of Kimmuriel Oblodra, and thus, Kimmuriel's subsequent deception of Gromph.

"The barrier of the Faerzress is wounded," she explained, "and so the demon lords have passed through, though they'll not so easily return. And if they do return . . ." she paused and laughed and let Yvonnel sort out the logical conclusion.

It was not a difficult maze to navigate. With the demon lords playing on the Material Plane in Faerûn's Underdark, Lady Lolth would fashion the Abyss more favorably to her own demands and desires.

Yvonnel found herself quite in awe of the Spider Queen at that moment, as she reflected on the events of the last few decades. After the murder of Mystra and the advent of the Spellplague, Lolth had made a play for the Weave in a failed effort to create the Web of magic. Then Lolth had lent her support to the chromatic dragons in their attempt to resurrect the catastrophe of Tiamat, weaving that grander purpose into a useful war in the Silver Marches.

And now, even as all of that, too, had fizzled, Lolth had done this next thing, perhaps the greatest upheaval of all.

How beautiful was this goddess, the Spider Queen, to so willingly and agilely assault the stability of the planes, to weave new upheavals even as the last ones were falling back to previous normality?

"The Spider Queen?" Yiccardaria teasingly asked.

Coming out of her contemplation, Yvonnel realized she had worn her thoughts too near the surface, and the handmaiden had read them all too easily. She looked at Yiccardaria with puzzlement for just a few moments, trying to decipher the question.

"You so easily name any of Lady Lolth's ploys as failure," the yochlol remarked. "Perhaps the failure is in you."

It took a moment for Yvonnel to decipher those last two remarks in the context of each other, but when she did, a wide smile spread over her face, and more beautiful still did Lady Lolth seem to her.

"No, not the Spider Queen," she said, "the Lady of Chaos."

"Good, good," purred Yiccardaria. "I came to teach you a lesson and you are a fine student indeed."

"I requested your presence because I am in need of information, Handmaiden," Yvonnel replied.

"Yes, and I leave you with one who will better serve your desires, and who will remain at your side and at your whim until you decide otherwise."

With that, the yochlol-turned-drow began to transform again, not as dramatically as before—not physically, at least, but more fully, Yvonnel realized when she sensed the life energy of the yochlol departing.

But still, a naked drow woman stood there in Yiccardaria's place, though only for a moment before the tiny, emaciated creature tumbled to the floor, seemingly too weak to even stand.

Yvonnel moved over and prodded the wretched and dirty drow with her foot, rolling her over just enough to look upon her face.

From the memories of Yvonnel the Eternal, this young Yvonnel knew this drow. Her first reaction was one of near murderous fury.

"K'yorl Odran," she mouthed, hardly able to spit out the name in her abject shock.

CHAPTER 3 ◈

The Recruiter

T HE WOMAN CHANTED SOFTLY, HER EYES CLOSED. SHE DIPPED HER fingers into the small bowl Ambergris had given her and pulled them forth dripping with ogre's blood. Gently she stroked the black leather belt, singing to it, the blood streaking it and melting in, disappearing without a trace. Over and over she dipped and ran her bloodied fingers across the enchanted material. This item was for her beloved husband, a secret gift, and one she hoped would keep him alive.

A long time later, Catti-brie collapsed onto the floor in exhaustion, the belt still hanging from the rack where she had imbued it with its powers. The mithral buckle glistened in the torchlight.

The woman slept the night away, her creation above her.

The next day, Catti-brie wore her simple white robe and a black lace shawl, its loose hood upon her head, framing her face. She sat on the altar stone in the primordial chamber and stared up at the water pouring in from the tendrils above: living water, carrying the essence of the Elemental Plane of Water in the form of elementals to hold back the mighty primordial from the Plane of Fire. These were the roots of the distant Hosttower of the Arcane, the residual magic holding strong—for now.

The constant steam in the room felt wonderful and she inhaled it deeply, feeling rejuvenated after the powerful enchanting the day before. There was a great equilibrium to be found here, a profound reminder to her of the balance of Toril itself: the give and take of the seasons, the undulations of the tides. What a wonderful gift was this home, this world.

And what a wonderful creation was Gauntlgrym, built by dwarves and almost surely by elves. What other race could have powers great enough to forge the Hosttower of the Arcane and devise this elaborate subterranean aqueduct, enchanting the water with the stuff of that elemental plane all along its hundred-mile journey to this place?

She could not hope to replicate such a masterpiece, of course, even with the help of Archmage Gromph and the Harpells, and any and every other wizard or priestess they might pull in from thousands of leagues around. Magic was no longer as pure as in the long-lost days of Faerûn, and ancient secrets were deeply hidden from the folk of the modern world.

But Catti-brie didn't have to replicate the grandeur of the undertaking that had made Gauntlgrym possible, she reminded herself. She just had to repair it.

"Give me the wisdom, Goddess," she whispered.

Someone cleared his throat behind her, and the woman twisted around. Jarlaxle was into his respectful bow before she fully recognized him.

"Again?" she asked in disbelief. "How long have you been there?"

"You looked serious," he said. "I did not want to disturb you."

"But now you have."

The drow mercenary laughed and bowed again.

Catti-brie apologized. "The task before me is daunting," she admitted.

"We'll find you allies in the undertaking," Jarlaxle promised. "Do not underestimate the knowledge and power of Archmage Gromph. And the Harpells, for all their eccentricity, have been known to deliver well in those moments of dire need. And there are others."

"Do tell."

"A thousand dwarves."

"Masons! That's the easy part, even for a structure as beautiful and intricate as the former Hosttower."

"There are many who would not wish to see the primordial escape its bindings," the drow replied. "And I speak not of fools like Lord Neverember, or any other of the local nobles, who cannot see far enough past their own mirror to even realize there is a wider world out there."

"More drow?"

"There are a few I would welcome," Jarlaxle replied without hesitation. "And with House Xorlarrin wandering about, there are some fine wizards to be found to lend a hand. House Xorlarrin plans to retake Gauntlgrym in the distant future, of course, and so they will be most eager to help with keeping the beast in its pit."

"Fine allies," the woman said dryly.

"Common goals—for now."

Catti-brie heaved a sigh, shook her head, and faced the pouring water again.

"But no, I wasn't speaking of drow," Jarlaxle said, walking over to stand beside her. "We already have the most learned of all the drow wizards in the person of Gromph. But there are others with knowledge of the ancient ways and magic. We will find them."

He put his hand comfortingly on Catti-brie's shoulder and she turned her head to regard him. She even managed a slight hopeful nod at his welcomed optimism.

Truly this was a daunting task!

"You will find these others, then, as we go about our work?"

"I hope. It is not in my best interest to let Gauntlgrym fall to the primordial, even beyond my friendship . . ." He paused and let that hang for a moment, staring hard at the woman.

"Is that the appropriate word?" he asked at length. "Am I considered a friend to the Companions of the Hall? To King Bruenor of Gauntlgrym?"

"You know the answer to that."

"But I want to hear it from you," he said. "And of you. Am I your friend, Catti-brie?"

The woman put her hand up to cover Jarlaxle's, but turned back to watch the waterfall. "You perplex me," she admitted. "I am never quite sure of your motives or your goals, and yet, those have aligned with my own enough times now that I have come to trust you."

"As a friend?"

"Yes." She was surprised by her quick admission, but even in reflection, she couldn't deny that she did indeed consider Jarlaxle a friend. He always had ulterior motives, of course, but he had never given Catti-brie or any of them any reason to believe that he would betray them. She remembered that day, long, long ago, when she, Drizzt, and Entreri were trying to escape Menzoberranzan only to find Jarlaxle and his band waiting for them in the tunnels.

He had them caught, but let them go.

Certainly Drizzt was fond of the mercenary leader—with caution, of course.

"I have a grand stake in the matter of King Bruenor remaining in control of this wondrous place," Jarlaxle said with a smile. "I will endeavor to make sure that the drow of Menzoberranzan do not try to displace him, and the trading opportunities this arrangement presents for me . . . well, let me just say that I am quite pleased that the dwarves have retaken Gauntlgrym."

Now Catti-brie looked at the mercenary a bit more cautiously. Jarlaxle was ever the opportunist. Could he really facilitate the movement of goods from Menzoberranzan and the surface through Gauntlgrym? Menzoberranzan and Mithral Hall had been mortal enemies—indeed, was it not Menzoberranzan that had spurred the most recent war in the Silver Marches? It was King Bruenor himself who had cleaved the head of Matron Mother Baenre in the Time of Troubles, cementing their enmity.

She stared at Jarlaxle for a long while, and finally understood that he really was thinking of such possibilities. In the end, she just shook her head. If anyone could accomplish such a ridiculously improbable thing, it would be Jarlaxle.

"Where is my husband?" she asked, thinking it time to change the subject—and why had Jarlaxle come here to see her?

"I was told he is patrolling the lower tunnels, as the dwarves attempt to widen their borders."

Catti-brie nodded. That fit her expectations, though she hadn't seen Drizzt since they'd split up earlier that morning.

"There are no Xorlarrins out there to concern you," Jarlaxle added.

"You have seen to that?"

"To some extent, yes. Let us just say that I showed them a better opportunity at this time than some foolish attempt to retake what King Bruenor has secured. I cannot speak for any demons, however. It is my understanding that the Underdark has become thick with the wretched things."

"What news, then, of the Hosttower?" Catti-brie asked.

"No news," the mercenary replied.

Again Catti-brie studied him carefully, and when she found no clues there—Jarlaxle stood quite at ease—she bluntly asked, "Why have you come to this place? There is nothing here that concerns you."

"I disagree, good lady. There is plenty here that concerns me greatly."

"Me? If so, then perhaps you should get to the point of your visit."

"More than that," Jarlaxle said, and he walked over to the edge of the primordial pit, staring down into the watery swirl and to the fiery eye of the beast below the water elementals.

"Perhaps you should stop speaking in cryptic riddles."

Jarlaxle turned to face her. "Do you know why Artemis Entreri is still alive?" he asked.

The question gave Catti-brie pause. "I do not know why I am still alive," she replied after a few moments. "Why would I know the cause or purpose of that one's existence?"

"He was cursed, so we all believed, with his life-force tied to a most wicked and powerful item."

"The sword, yes," the woman replied. "Drizzt came with him and Dahlia to this very place, so that Entreri could throw the weapon into the pit to be devoured by the primordial."

"Believing he would also be destroyed."

"But he was not," said Catti-brie. "So it was not the sword after all."

"Unfortunately, I believe it was," said Jarlaxle.

"The sword was destroy—" Catti-brie's declaration caught in her throat and she walked over to stand next to Jarlaxle.

"Was it?" he asked.

Catti-brie looked into the pit, and viewing the orange glow at the bottom, she could keenly feel the insatiable hunger of the great fiery beast. With hardly a thought to the movement, she ran the tips of the thumb and index finger of her right hand over the band she wore on her left.

"If not, it is irretrievable in any case," she said, "swallowed by the molten stone that gives the primordial form."

"Are you sure?" Jarlaxle asked.

"What are you proposing?"

"Have you ventured down there?" the drow asked. "You have a bond with the great beast, it is clear. It speaks to you through the ring you wear, and in the voice of the Elemental Plane of Fire, which you understand. So have you gone down there to be near the beast, to better see it, to better know it?"

Catti-brie balked and stepped back from the ledge, but kept her incredulous stare on Jarlaxle. Down there below the water elementals, she would be at the mercy of the primordial. Whatever protective magic she might don, the mighty creature could still swallow her and force her deep into its molten gullet.

"It wouldn't kill you, though, would it?" Jarlaxle asked. "Not while you wear the ring. You have given the trapped primordial an outlet for its frustrations. It has shown you its secrets and lent you wisps of living flame. It led you to the ancient portal and helped you turn that staff you carry into something more potent."

"And perhaps it knows that I am trying to keep it forever sealed in its hole," she retorted.

Jarlaxle shrugged. "Perhaps. But how can you remain so near to such beauty and preternatural power and not be curious?"

"I never said I wasn't curious."

"You are not a coward. Of that I am certain."

"Enough of your games, Jarlaxle!" the woman demanded. "What do you want?"

The mercenary drow reached into a belt pouch and pulled out a large gauntlet, one that seemed far too large to have fit in the pouch, which of course must be magical. Was anything on or about Jarlaxle not magical? Catti-brie wondered. He showed it to Catti-brie, then tossed it to her.

"This is a sister item to the sword Charon's Claw," he explained. "Necessary protection from the deadly magic of the weapon."

"You expect me to go down into that pit and retrieve the sword, which is almost certainly not there?"

"If it is not there, then at least we will know, and then Entreri can rest easy that his longevity is not tied to the sword."

Catti-brie tossed the gauntlet back. "You are not without magic. Go and get it yourself."

"It is Catti-brie who has bonded with the primordial. Catti-brie who understands the beast. Catti-brie who has determined that we must act to keep the volcano dormant and what that action must be to achieve such an end. It is Catti-brie, not Jarlaxle, who carries a gift from the primordial, and who coaxes elementals from the flames of the beast's tendrils."

"And it is Catti-brie who is wise enough to respect the power of the beast," she said.

Jarlaxle laughed and bowed. "There is another reason for my request, I admit," he said, and he tossed the gauntlet back to her as she looked at him curiously. "You claim to know the beast—we are all counting upon your judgment to guide us to a solution for the future dangers you have foretold—but how certain are you of what you have determined? How well do you really know this creature, this living volcano? You have met its offspring and touched its outer edges, but you have not faced it directly. I have spoken to Archmage Gromph about this and we are in agreement. You should face the primordial directly. You should stand before it and let it reveal to you more of its secrets. It may be our only hope in reconstructing the magic that will keep it in place."

Catti-brie fumbled over her thoughts in light of the dramatic request. "And if I reveal to it my own intentions?" she asked. "Will this great and ancient beast not merely consume me and be done with it? Surely the primordial desires release."

"We cannot know what such a creature desires," Jarlaxle said.

Catti-brie had to concede that point. This was not a creature of similar mind to any living being walking the ways of Faerûn. This was an ancient, devouring magic, whose goals were unknown and perhaps unknowable to a human or a drow.

"Perhaps there are other ways the beast might find that release," Jarlaxle offered. "Ways less devastating than a volcanic eruption. Ways that afford us all, even the beast, what we desire. And you are a Chosen of Mielikki, who would understand such a natural catastrophe as a primordial of fire better than perhaps any other god. Surely you can use that discipline and standing to direct the conversation with the primordial in a manner of your own choosing."

Catti-brie held up the gauntlet. "And since I will be down there anyway . . ." she said dryly.

"I would be forever grateful," Jarlaxle said. "Indeed, I will make it worth your while many times over."

"I am the daughter of a dwarven king," she reminded him. "Your riches do not interest me."

Jarlaxle's smile said otherwise. "I do not speak idly, my good lady. It is a small thing I ask of you, and that in accord with a short journey that may well help us all."

Catti-brie looked down, her expression doubtful. Even with her magical ring, she could feel the heat of the primordial's fiery breath, but still she began to cast a spell, using her divine powers to protect her even more from the heat and the flames.

"How am I to even get down there? Where am I to stand in a sea of liquid stone?" She turned back to Jarlaxle as she asked the second question, to find the mercenary holding out to her some black cloth, a folded garment perhaps. Catti-brie looked at it, then at Jarlaxle, for just a moment, then took it and unfolded it to find a shimmering black cape with a high, stiff collar.

"This was worn by Kensidan, who was once long ago called High Captain Kurth. It passed from him to his descendants—to Dahlia, surprisingly. Drizzt knows this cloak. Put it on. You will understand."

The woman swept the cloak around her back and found the ties.

"It perfectly complements your outfit," Jarlaxle said with a nod of approval. "So beautiful."

"A statement of fashion?" she asked skeptically.

"Much more than that," he replied. "Let it speak to you."

With a final doubtful look at Jarlaxle, Catti-brie closed her eyes and let her thoughts drift to the cloak. Like so many magical items, this garment, the Cloak of the Crow, seemed to want its wearer to understand its properties. It was one of the more curious aspects of magic, Catti-brie often thought, that even the insentient magical items wanted their magic to be used.

She let her thoughts reach deeper into the cloak and lifted her arms out wide—to find that they were not arms any longer, but shining black-feathered wings. She could feel the updrafts of heat from the pit more acutely then, playing among her feathers. So sure was she that she didn't question Jarlaxle further, nor did she cast any contingency spells in case the cloak should fail. She just leaned forward and let the updrafts lift her from the ground.

Down went the giant crow, cutting tight circles within the encircling and swirling dance of the water elementals. Even with her ring and the additional spells, Catti-brie could feel the heat growing as she neared the bottom of that watery barricade.

She broke through, under the wetness and the mist, and it seemed to her as if she had gone to another plane of existence, or another world perhaps, or to Toril in the earliest days of its formation.

Yes, that was it, she somehow understood. This molten field of bubbling magma and powerful stench—she felt as if she had been thrown into a boiling cauldron of rotten eggs—this was the way the world had been in the earliest days, before the elves even, perhaps before all life on Toril.

She drifted in the orange glow for just a moment before spotting and then landing on a solid block of veined stone. She touched down tentatively, ready to fly away if the stone proved too hot for her multiple dweomers of protection to counter. But to her relief, she felt no burning pain.

With a thought and a shrug, Catti-brie came out of crow form, and paused a moment to ponder her earliest days in this second life she had found, when the spellscar of Mielikki had granted to her shape-shifting powers. How often had she flown over the plains of Netheril in the shape of a great bird. How free she had been on the updrafts with the world spread wide below her.

All those thoughts blew away on a hot breeze when the primordial's voice came into her thoughts, seeping through her ring. She sensed the creature's confusion—dangerous confusion—and so she answered back in the language of the Plane of Fire, whispering assurances and seeking common benefit.

The primordial responded to her with sensations. She felt the beast stretching its tendrils to the Forge, to the inactive portal, to the spouts she had found when they had retaken the complex, like the lava mound where Catti-brie had transformed her staff.

On impulse she banged her staff on the stone, shifting it to its fiery form. She felt the pleasure of the primordial.

Then she began to probe. She looked up and focused on the water elementals, and she felt the primordial's frustration and anger—but it was not as burning an anger as she had imagined. And she was glad. Perhaps there were ways to lessen the preternatural desires of the beast, ways to siphon off some of its explosive and deadly energy.

For a long time, Catti-brie stood there in communion with the primordial, viewing Gauntlgrym from its perspective, and in that mental bonding she gained some insights into the magic that had put the beast in the pit and kept it there, insights she knew would aid her in the repair of the Hosttower of the Arcane.

She did well to keep those thoughts properly suppressed. If the primordial so desired, she would be dead, buried in lava and burned to nothingness long before she could get near to the protection of the water elementals.

But the primordial wasn't going to do that. It seemed to her that the beast almost enjoyed the company.

No, that wasn't it. Creatures like this didn't harbor such emotions. But still, there was no displeasure revealed. Clearly the beast understood that it was in control and that she was no threat, and so it tolerated her. It accepted the diversion with some modicum of pleasurable distraction.

On recognizing that, Catti-brie would have liked to remain, but the thought was accompanied by a stumble, a near swoon, that would have dropped her into the lava. It wasn't the heat but the smell, the lack of breathable air. She knew then that she had to be attentive to her task and quickly away.

She put the gauntlet on her hand and held it out in display to her godlike host. She didn't know whether it was the gauntlet or the beast, but she sensed something not so far away.

Becoming a crow again she fluttered over to another mound of stone, quickly reverting to her human form. She stared down into the bubbling, popping red magma. Dare she reach in? The woman shook her head before her hand even moved, certain that the molten stone would incinerate the glove and her hand, whatever enchantments she might try.

But still she stared, leaning low, mesmerized by the bubbling red lava.

And something substantial came forth, rising up from the magma. Catti-brie recoiled, taken aback by what appeared to be the skull and bleached bones of a small humanoid skeleton: a backbone and ribcage to a pelvis with boney legs spread wide to either side.

The item rose a bit more, bobbing in the heavy liquid, and Catti-brie gasped as she realized this to be the hilt and crosspiece of a sword, the slender, etched blade shining red in the glow of the lava.

With her gauntleted hand, she grasped the backbone hilt inside the basket of the ribcage and drew forth the sword, holding it up in front of her astonished eyes.

She felt the power of Charon's Claw. She felt its wickedness and had to work hard to resist the urge to throw it back into the magma.

The molten power of the primordial had not eaten Charon's Claw, had marred that perfect blade not at all.

Catti-brie called upon the cloak again and shifted to the crow. With a cursory telepathic salute to the primordial, she lifted away, beating her strong wings to circle once more inside the elemental swirl. Rising, she broke through on the other side and lit on the ledge near the sarcophagus stone. Jarlaxle was patiently waiting for her there.

"I knew it," he said, his eyes sparkling, when Catti-brie reverted to her human form, revealing the treasure she held in her gauntleted hand.

The woman examined the sword again and realized it wasn't the lava that had given Charon's Claw its red hue. The blade itself was red, with a black blood trough running down the center. She marveled at the workmanship, at the masterful etchings of hooded figures and tall scythes all along the blade.

"It has few equals in the world," Jarlaxle said, startling her. She looked over at the mercenary.

"A most remarkable blade," he said.

"And full of evil intent," she replied.

"A thirst for blood," he admitted. "Is that not the purpose of a weapon?"

"There is a power here . . ." She shook her head, nearly overwhelmed. She had once wielded Khazid'hea, the blade that now hung on Jarlaxle's belt, but even that marvelous weapon of destruction seemed to pale beside the wicked magnificence of this creation.

"Weapons are designed to kill, my good lady," Jarlaxle motioned to the floor and pointed to the gauntlet. "Do not touch the sword without it," he warned.

Catti-brie set the sword on the stone and pulled off the gauntlet, handing it over. As Jarlaxle set it upon his hand, the woman moved to remove the cloak, but Jarlaxle held up his hands and shook his head.

"My gift to you," he said.

Catti-brie nodded. "A worthwhile trade, then."

"Oh, it is no trade," he replied. "The cloak is my gift to you. Your reward for the sword is yet to come, and I promise you, it is a far greater gift."

He picked up the sword and saluted Catti-brie with it then smiled, bowed, and turned, moving back to the tunnel to Forge.

Catti-brie considered him for a long while, but did not follow. She found herself at the ledge once more, looking down into the pit, past the watery swirl to the fiery eye.

The beast had allowed her into its presence, and had not consumed her.

Strangely, she felt blessed. And Catti-brie knew she would return to the bottom of this pit again, perhaps many times.

Chapter 4 ◈

Petty

T
HEY HAVE NO ALLIES," HIGH PRIESTESS CHARRI HUNZRIN REMINDED her mother, Matron Mother Shakti. "They look down upon the whole of the city from the recesses of the West Wall, high above. They huddle behind their driders and sneer at all who are not Melarni."

"I am well aware of the zealotry of Zhindia Melarn," Shakti replied. "And true, it would be hard to name any as allies of this precocious young House. But Matron Mother Mez'Barris Armgo is no enemy to the Melarni, in these times."

The mention of the Matron Mother of the Second House quieted Charri. Barrison Del'Armgo had been House Hunzrin's most important ally for many decades. House Hunzrin thrived through trade and by controlling most of the agriculture in Menzoberranzan. Under the stern and disciplined leadership of Shakti, the family Hunzrin had greatly advanced in wealth and a subtle stature. Their ranking had not changed, and they remained the Eleventh House, cheated from ascension by the insertion of House Do'Urden onto the Ruling Council after the abdication of Matron Mother Zeerith and House Xorlarrin. Surely the other Houses held in check by that unusual, indeed unprecedented, creation by Matron Mother Quenthel had been simmering in outrage ever since, particularly House Duskryn, the Ninth House, whose ambitious matron mother openly coveted a seat on the Ruling Council and had been denied yet again.

But such formalities had never impressed Shakti Hunzrin. She was more concerned with actual power and wealth over ceremony and formality. Her family was often ridiculed as "stone heads" because of their work with the farms, but to her and the other nobles, that underestimation offered opportunity more than it wounded pride.

Past a bend in the avenue, rounding a large stalagmite mound, the two women came in sight of House Melarn, unmistakable because it was fashioned with the most unusual architecture in the City of Spiders. Melarn was the newest of Menzoberranzan's major Houses, formed of a union between House Kenafin and House Horlbar, a joining of purpose and spirit that arose from the ashes of war a century before, where the two allied Houses battled against House Tuin'Tarl, then the Eighth House. Tuin'Tarl was destroyed and the combined Houses, under the name of Melarn, replaced the deposed Matron Mother of House Tuin'Tarl on the Ruling Council. Among the new Melarni were many drow left orphaned by the fall of the sister city of Ched Nasad, a community distinguished by its web-like walkways.

Those refugees had brought Ched Nasad's unique architecture with them to Menzoberranzan, and it was clearly on display here in the gracefully swaying bridges of spiderwebs that filtered back and forth, climbing the west wall of the cavern to the Melarni front door, a hundred feet and more from the cavern.

Matron Mother Shakti held her daughter back with an upraised arm, and quietly uttered a minor spell. A magical hammer appeared in the air across the way, just to the right of the lowermost web pathways of the facade of House Melarn. On Shakti's command, the hammer tapped against the wall, once and then again.

Then it disappeared, and Shakti motioned for Charri to follow. By the time they neared the area, the cracks of a concealed doorway were evident in the wall, and the stone fell away as they approached, revealing a tunnel. Within stood First Priestess Kyrnill Melarn, who bowed in proper deference to Matron Mother Hunzrin and bade her to follow. This was no ordinary first priestess, Shakti prudently reminded herself. Normally, that title was held by the eldest daughter of a noble family, but Kyrnill was not related to Zhindia. Zhindia was the eldest daughter of Matron Mother Jerlys of House Horlbar, and Kyrnill had been the Matron Mother of House Kenafin. When the two Houses merged into House Melarn, Kyrnill Kenafin had allowed Zhindia to become matron mother of the new House Melarn. It was a strategic move, the other matron mothers knew, because the too-clever Kyrnill had expected that the first matron mother of the new House would surely be killed in the chaotic aftermath of the joining. But Zhindia had survived, and Kyrnill had accepted her role as first priestess—though surely she was more than that.

Deep and down the trio traveled, far into the western wall and far below the compound of House Melarn. They passed many guard stations on their journey, manned by beastly driders. No House was more enamored of and protected by the horrid half-drow, half-spider abominations as the zealots of House Melarn, who celebrated the torture of morphing a drow into a drider like other families might celebrate the birthday of a favored daughter.

In a deep and secret room, protected by hundreds of feet of solid stone and magical wards, both arcane and divine, the two Hunzrins were presented to Matron Mother Zhindia Melarn, the youngest Matron Mother of Menzoberranzan, and by far the youngest member of the city's Ruling Council—if one ignored the presence of the *iblith* Matron Mother Darthiir Do'Urden, and none was more pleased to ignore that abomination than Zhindia Melarn. The circular chamber was ringed by a raised walkway upon which stood drider guards, looking even larger because they stood several feet above the lower floor. All clutched adamantine long spears, and all seemed eager to put those deadly weapons to use.

"I am pleased that you answered my call," Matron Mother Zhindia said to her guests, and she motioned for the visiting Hunzrins to sit around the small, rectangular table, as Kyrnill took her place to the right of her matron mother.

"You insisted that your information was important to my family," Shakti Hunzrin replied. "And my prayers to the Spider Queen assured my safety."

"Indeed, to both," Zhindia replied. "You are aware of the events in Q'Xorlarrin?"

"That the dwarves reclaimed their complex and expelled Matron Mother Zeerith?"

"Yes, and the present disposition of Matron Mother Zeerith and her family?"

"Her powerful family," Shakti remarked.

"Her heretical family," Kyrnill corrected with a sneer.

The remark surprised the Hunzrin guests. By all estimates, House Melarn was in no position to engage powerful House Xorlarrin, even if Matron Mother Zeerith's family had been wounded by the advance of the dwarves.

"You are pleased by this development, no doubt," Matron Mother Zhindia said bluntly.

Matron Mother Shakti stared at her counterpart curiously, with more than a little trepidation. She wasn't about to admit to any such thing, particularly given House Xorlarrin's close alliance with House Baenre.

"It is no secret that House Hunzrin feared the creation of the city of Q'Xorlarrin," the always blunt and brutal Zhindia stated. "City," she said again, and she spat upon the floor. "It was a servile satellite of House

Baenre, of course, created so that House Baenre could take from you the most profitable trade to be found."

"The point is moot. Q'Xorlarrin is no more," said Matron Mother Shakti, and she nudged her daughter under the table, warning the volatile Charri against saying something they might both regret.

"But did Matron Mother Baenre lose?" Zhindia Melarn asked slyly.

"She sent the demons forth, and the demons were defeated by the dwarves, so say the reports."

"And so the dwarves reclaim Gauntlgrym, and fire anew the Great Forge," Zhindia agreed. "But these particular dwarves are known associates of Jarlaxle and Bregan D'aerthe."

Despite her great and practiced discipline, Shakti Hunzrin couldn't help but fidget at the mention of Jarlaxle. Bregan D'aerthe had long been a thorn in the side of ide of House Hunzrin and a threat to Shakti's plans for trade dominance beyond Menzoberranzan. Bregan D'aerthe's loyalty to House Baenre could not be doubted.

"Your easiest route to the World Above is no more," Zhindia said. "Your caravans will not get past the armies of the dwarves. But if Jarlaxle is able to secure an agreement between House Baenre and the new kingdom of Gauntlgrym . . ."

She let it hang there, tantalizingly.

"The Spider Queen would abandon her," Shakti said, because she really had no other retort.

"Are you going to tell her that?" Zhindia asked with a laugh.

Shakti stared at her hard. "Among all the Matron Mothers of Menzoberranzan, are you not the one who claims closest communion with the Spider Queen?" she asked very seriously. "Would Lolth accept such a move by Matron Mother Baenre?"

"The same Matron Mother Baenre who instituted a *darthiir*, a wretched elf, as a matron mother with a seat on the Ruling Council?" Zhindia countered. "Who put Matron Mother Do'Urden ahead of you on the ladder of Menzoberranzan's hierarchy?"

"Your insults are uncalled for," Charri Hunzrin remarked.

"No insult," said Zhindia. "Simple truth, and unpleasant to both of us. Perhaps, though, this abomination Matron Mother Do'Urden is a test, not for Quenthel Baenre but for the rest of us. Do we allow the *darthiir* to continue as a voice on the Ruling Council?"

"Or do we tear her down?" asked Shakti. "We are back to this, then. Did we not just see this play with the demon assault on House Do'Urden? That failure strengthened Matron Mother Do'Urden's reputation and strengthened Matron Mother Baenre's hand."

"So you are accepting of an agreement between Matron Mother Baenre and Bregan D'aerthe to move goods through the dwarven city?"

"I do not believe that such an agreement exists."

"Oh, it exists," Matron Mother Zhindia said confidently. "Jarlaxle's influence is clear to see, and who would benefit more from such an agreement than that opportunist heretic mercenary and his filthy band of male rogues?"

The leader of House Melarn turned to the side and motioned to a drider guard, who put a hand against a concealed plunger on the wall and pressed. Unseen stones slid and a secret door fell open. To Shakti and Charri's surprise and fear, an impressive drow female strode out from the darkness. She wore the robes of a high priestess, indeed those of a First Priestess of a House, and her emblem was well known.

Kiriy Xorlarrin, Matron Mother Shakti's fingers signed to her daughter.

The newcomer moved to the table, summoned a magical disc—a circle of blue light hanging in the air at about waist height—and sat down upon it.

"We were speaking of male rogues," Matron Mother Zhindia said.

"A redundant description," Kiriy replied, with no small amount of contempt behind her words.

The Hunzrin matron mother and daughter glanced at each other, somewhat confused. Wasn't House Xorlarrin known as the House most lenient with, and most deferential to, its men? House Barrison Del'Armgo and House Xorlarrin had long been the two Menzoberranyr Houses known to promote men high into the House hierarchy, but with Barrison Del'Armgo, there had never been any doubt that the highest ranking male noble, usually the weapons master, remained subservient to the lowest of the high priestesses. In House Xorlarrin, such was not always the case.

"You know First Priestess Kiriy Xorlarrin," Matron Mother Zhindia said, and the guests at her table nodded.

"I am soon to join House Do'Urden," Kiriy informed them. "My sister, my brother, and many of the male cousins are already there, strengthening the ties between House Do'Urden and Sorcere."

"And the ties with House Baenre," Shakti dared to remark.

Kiriy snorted dismissively.

"Saribel, your sister, is presently the First Priestess of House Do'Urden, is she not?" Shakti pressed. "Will you displace her?"

"For a time."

"You mean to become Matron Mother Do'Urden," Shakti reasoned.

"And again, I may wear that title for a time, perhaps," Kiriy replied. "And then I mean to destroy House Do'Urden and replace it with a reformed House Xorlarrin."

"You plot against your own mother," Shakti said sourly. She was looking straight at Matron Mother Zhindia as she made the remark, as if Zhindia should be ashamed of herself for even entertaining such a thought. Matricide was not well-received in Menzoberranzan, and particularly not welcomed at that moment, when Shakti sat in conference with her eldest and most powerful daughter seated right beside her.

Of course, Matron Mother Zhindia didn't have that particular problem.

"Matron Mother Zeerith has traveled too far along the road of heresy," Matron Mother Zhindia stated. "Too much influence has she given to mere males. This is not the way of Lolth."

"Her sacrilege rained doom upon Q'Xorlarrin," Kiriy added. "There was no proper order of things awaiting the demon army in our city, to keep them in line when Matron Mother Baenre sent them to us to defeat the dwarves. It was clear to me from the outset of the dwarven invasion—even before that, when so many of our House were killed in the far-off fields of the Silver Marches—that House Xorlarrin was losing the favor of the Spider Queen."

"You will betray Matron Mother Zeerith," Shakti said.

"She will not return to Menzoberranzan in any case!" Kiriy shouted. "I will save House Xorlarrin! We will not become an extension of Bregan D'aerthe, to be used at the whim of Matron Mother Baenre. I will never allow that. Our place is here, with an independent Matron Mother Xorlarrin sitting on the Ruling Council."

"I have asked you to accept a lot of startling information here," Matron Mother Zhindia apologized to her Hunzrin guests.

"You have hinted at a daring plan," Shakti replied. "One that pits us against Matron Mother Baenre and her cadre of powerful allies."

"Not so!" Zhindia argued. "She is far too engrossed now in matters beyond the fate of House Do'Urden. The demon lords walk the ways of the Underdark, and in no small part because of the foolish actions of her own brother! Before the coming of Demogorgon, Matron Mother Baenre went to great lengths to fortify this phony House she has constructed, and so she expects them to stand on their own. Indeed, they must. Many others—House Barrison Del'Armgo and some of Matron Mother Baenre's closest allies—are watching with wary eyes. Lolth will decide the fate of House Do'Urden, not the army of House Baenre."

"And Lolth is surely with us," Kiriy added.

After a long paused, Shakti replied to Zhindia, "Your claims are extraordinary."

"Then I will prove them to you."

Shakti nodded.

"I trust in your confidence in these matters until I can make my case fully to you," Zhindia said. "And do understand that if I am correct in my suspicions—and I assure you that I am—any betrayal of me to Matron Mother Baenre will also provide her with the excuse she needs to sublimate your House. You came here, after all, willingly and alone in trust, to a known rival of House Do'Urden. And do not doubt that Matron Mother Baenre understands that Hunzrin demons were among the horde of fiends who attacked House Do'Urden.

"Waging war on House Melarn would bring a smile to the face of Matron Mother Quenthel Baenre, indeed," Zhindia went on. "But how much wider might that smile grow if she has an excuse to eliminate both our families, stripping Matron Mother Mez'Barris Armgo of the only allies she might have in her attempt to keep House Baenre from complete domination?"

Shakti Hunzrin spent a long while staring hard at her counterpart.

Matron Mother Zhindia motioned to her daughter, who went to the side of the room and pulled a blanket aside, revealing a small chest. She hoisted it and carried it back to the gathering, placing it in front of Matron Mother Shakti.

"Open it," Matron Mother Zhindia bade her. "But take care and do not handle any of the contents."

With a wary look to her daughter, Shakti carefully pulled back the lid of the chest, revealing a pile of beautiful gemstones set in fabulous pieces of jewelry. Despite the warning, her hand drifted for one piece, a tiara of brilliant rubies.

"Do not," Matron Mother Zhindia warned.

"What is this?" Shakti asked, and she closed the lid.

"A gift to you," said Zhindia. "One of faith and continued goodwill between our Houses in this most important battle we wage."

"Jewelry?"

"Goods for the World Above," Zhindia explained. "I trust you can find some way to deliver them to the proper . . . merchants."

"It is not our normal merchandise," Shakti said. "We trade food and exotics—items of the Underdark. There is no shortage of gems and jewels on the surface." She opened the coffer again and glanced in. "No doubt these have great value—they are very beautiful pieces. But these are not my usual wares, and it will be expensive and difficult for me to open proper channels to see them brought to market."

Zhindia, Kiriy, and Kyrnill exchanged knowing, smug looks, and Shakti and Charri realized that they were apparently missing some inside joke.

"So you do not want the bounty?" Zhindia asked.

"I will take them, with my gratitude, Matron Mother Zhindia," Shakti replied. "I will deliver them to the World Above and find a place to sell them. I only warn that the profit will be minimal."

"They are more exquisite than you realize," Kyrnill Melarn put in.

"Must everything be about coin?" Matron Mother Zhindia said.

Shakti looked at her curiously.

"Surely there are other reasons to ply your trade," Zhindia added.

Now Shakti was completely at a loss. She looked to her daughter, who could only shrug in confusion.

"You will be doing the work of the Spider Queen," Zhindia explained. "Those are not mere gemstones set in jewelry, Matron Mother Hunzrin. They are phylacteries, each possessing the spirit of a slain demon."

Shakti's eyes went wide and she opened the coffer again and peeked in, just for a moment, then closed it tight and put her hand on top of the lid to keep it closed.

"A nobleman or noblewoman wearing such a brooch, or necklace, or tiara, will come to find her thoughts darkened, her mind drawn to chaos, her soul possessed to demonic intent," Matron Mother Zhindia said with great relish.

"Do you still think it a minor gift?" Kyrnill put in snidely.

73

"I will see these to the World Above," Shakti said at length, her glare lingering on the former Matron Mother of House Kenafin. "For the glory of Lolth. As to the rest, your claims are extraordinary, as I have said. You see the Baenre alliance as fractured, and believe that our path to destroy Do'Urden is clear."

"And that Lolth is on our side," Kyrnill reminded her.

Shakti Hunzrin conceded the point with a nod. "It is often hard to discern the true intent of the Spider Queen." As Zhindia clearly tensed up in response, Shakti pointed at the zealous matron mother and added, "Even for her most devout disciples. Yet I do not doubt that Lady Lolth would approve of our plans, should they come to pass."

Matron Mother Zhindia relaxed and nodded.

"But as to the rest," Shakti finished strongly, "bring me proof." She motioned to her daughter, and the two wasted no time in departing the dungeons of the Melarni fanatics. All the way back to her own compound, Shakti mulled over the lack of choices available to her. The city of Q'Xorlarrin had posed a direct threat to the trade empire she had built, and she had not lamented the fall of Matron Mother Zeerith's trial city.

House Do'Urden didn't really matter to her. She didn't care much about the formal ranking of her House. In fact, she considered her lower position to be an asset as she went about growing her riches and building dependence to her network among the other Houses.

But the ability to trade beyond the borders of the city, to bring exotic goods to the matron mothers and to market their wares in places full of riches, was not something Shakti Hunzrin would surrender without a fight. If the Baenres were truly intent on dominating trade to the surface, that was indeed a direct threat to the standing and purpose of House Hunzrin.

The question then was whether Matron Mother Baenre desired all of it—all of the power, and all of the commerce.

◆ ◆ ◆

"NONE CAN KNOW that you are here," Matron Mother Baenre said to her guest. "It would cause great upset in a city that is already reeling from the march of the Prince of Demons."

She stared at Zeerith as she spoke, but the Matron Mother of House Xorlarrin was not looking back at her at all, and though she was nodding, it seemed to Quenthel as if Zeerith had hardly heard a word that she'd said.

Matron Mother Zeerith was distracted by the beautiful young woman sitting at the left end of the small table.

Not distracted, Quenthel silently corrected herself. Enchanted.

The young woman's hair was smooth and thick, a startling white contrast to her coal-black skin. It curled teasingly between her perfect breasts, which were barely covered by the plunging cut of her soft purple dress, a simple silk affair that clung to her body's every curve.

It took Quenthel a long while to realize that she too was staring hopelessly at the beautiful young woman.

"Who is this?" Matron Mother Zeerith practically demanded.

"The child of Gromph," Quenthel replied, and she hoped that putting the now-deposed archmage's name on Yvonnel would somehow lessen Zeerith's trance.

Even still, a long while passed before Zeerith was able to turn back to Quenthel. Even then it seemed as if Yvonnel herself had released Zeerith from the trance, as evidenced by a little giggle Yvonnel offered as Zeerith turned away.

"I did not know Gromph had—"

"And Minolin Fey, of House Fey-Branche," Yvonnel interrupted, an incredible breach of etiquette.

Zeerith's face screwed up with confusion as she swung back to view the young woman, who was surely near twenty years of age, if not older. Zeerith had known about Minolin's pregnancy. The visitation of the avatar of Lolth upon House Fey-Branche in the Festival of the Founding was common gossip that had followed House Xorlarrin across the Underdark. Zeerith knew that Minolin Fey was now in House Baenre—she had seen the high priestess while being escorted through the royal chambers to come to this very audience.

"The child of Gromph and Minolin Fey?" Zeerith asked Quenthel.

"Yes," Yvonnel answered, again out of turn, and this time interrupting the matron mother as Quenthel began to answer.

"She is an impetuous sort," Quenthel said dryly, and cast a glance at the young woman.

"And a distracting one," Quenthel added when she saw that Zeerith's eyes were once again held by the young woman.

"Yes," Zeerith said absently.

"May I go, Matron Mother?" Yvonnel asked.

"Please do," Quenthel replied, trying to sound sweet.

Yvonnel rose and Zeerith's eyes rose with her. Much of her leg slipped free from the high slit in her simple but elegant gown, and Zeerith gave a little gasp as she spun away and moved to the room's door.

She was barefoot, Quenthel and Zeerith both noted then, and somehow that seemed even more fitting for this one, like a promise of something unbridled and so very pleasing.

The door closed, but it took Zeerith a while to compose herself and look back at her host.

"She is quite . . . lovely," Matron Mother Zeerith said, and Quenthel understood well that her counterpart had to pause there to search for the right word, because "lovely" certainly didn't seem sufficient.

"Do you plan to tell them I perished in the fight?" Zeerith asked, and she shook her head and seemed removed from the enchantment of Yvonnel then, and apparently had forgotten all around the surprising revelation of that one's parentage.

Was Yvonnel's appearance that distracting, Quenthel wondered, or had the young witch cast a spell to remove thought from Zeerith's mind?

"I do not believe that to be our best course, if I may offer advice, Matron Mother," Zeerith rambled on.

Was Yvonnel powerful enough to do that so casually? To an accomplished matron mother of a powerful House?

Yes, she was, Quenthel realized with a sigh.

"If you have other designs . . ." Zeerith offered, somewhat sheepishly.

"No, no, my mind was other-where. So much has happened and so much is yet to come. You are correct, my friend, of course. Matron Mother Zeerith is not to be rubbed from the ranks of Menzoberranzan—hardly that! You will circle and reside outside the city and together we will find opportunity."

"While my children ascend," Zeerith added with her eyes sparkling.

"High Priestess Kiriy is in House Do'Urden?"

Zeerith nodded, then asked, "First Priestess?"

"Saribel is First Priestess," Quenthel corrected her, somewhat sternly. "And that is something Kiriy must understand and accept."

"Yes, Matron Mother," Zeerith said and respectfully lowered her eyes. It was no surprise. Though Kiriy was far more accomplished than Saribel, and much older, indeed the eldest daughter of the House, Saribel had something that Kiriy did not: a Baenre husband.

"When time for ascent comes, who will it be?" Zeerith asked.

"That is a discussion for another day," Quenthel replied. "I know that you favor Kiriy."

"Saribel is a bit of a dullard, I must admit," said Zeerith. "It pains me to say that, but would that Lolth had accepted her as my sacrifice instead of Parabrak, my third-born son."

"Pray to Lolth to forgive your words," Quenthel said half-jokingly— but only half.

"I wish I could join you at the Ruling Council," Zeerith said. "If only to see the face of the witch Mez'Barris when she is formally told that Tsabrak Xorlarrin will assume the mantle of Archmage of Menzoberranzan."

"You will witness the ceremony," Quenthel promised and Matron Mother Zeerith swelled with pride.

◆　◆　◆

"THEY ARE SUCH petty creatures," Yvonnel remarked to Minolin Fey in the anteroom, where the young upstart had enchanted a scrying pool so that she could look in on the conversation in the Baenre audience chamber. "They puff and preen over the most unremarkable and fleeting things."

Yvonnel gave a sigh and turned to her mother, who stood staring.

"How did you do that?" Minolin Fey asked. "How do you do that?"

"What?"

"All the time," the woman went on. "In there, with Matron Mother Zeerith. With all you see—or all who see you. Man and woman alike, taken aback, thrown from their guard, with a simple glimpse upon you."

"Why Mother, do you not think me beautiful?" Yvonnel coyly asked.

Minolin Fey could only shake her head and reply, her voice barely a whisper, "Many drow are beautiful." She kept shaking her head. She knew there had to be more to it than that.

"Your mother, Matron Mother Byrtyn," Yvonnel began, "she is a painter, yes? I have heard that some of her portraits hang in this very house."

"She is quite talented, yes."

"Get her, then. I wish to pose for her."

"I do not know that she—"

"She will," Yvonnel said. "Tell her the matron mother insists upon it, and that she will be well rewarded."

Minolin Fey seemed off-balance then. Matron Mother Byrtyn had not even seen this child yet, her granddaughter, who should be no more than a toddler.

"Matron Mother Byrtyn was told of me by the avatar of Lolth in the parlor of her own House," Yvonnel reminded Minolin Fey. "Tell her that she will come to House Baenre the day after tomorrow, after Tsabrak is named as Archmage of Menzoberranzan, and she will begin her work. And she will return every day thereafter until it is completed."

Minolin Fey stared blankly.

"I am not asking you," Yvonnel warned. She turned back to the scrying pool, then sighed with disgust and cleared the image from the water with a wave of her hand.

"So boring and petty," she said as she pushed past Minolin Fey and skipped to the door at the far end of the room.

"You speak of the Matron Mother of Menzoberranzan," Minolin Fey reminded her.

"Yes," Yvonnel answered. "And why?"

She shrugged, winked, and exited, leaving Minolin Fey to stand there dumbfounded with that simple yet devastating question hanging over her. She glanced back at the unremarkable water in the bowl. Minolin Fey couldn't begin to cast a clairvoyance dweomer powerful enough to get past Quenthel Baenre's wards, as Yvonnel had so easily done. She considered the conversation in the other room. The incessant plotting and conniving, the desperate pursuit of a goal that would often be nothing more than the platform from which to pursue another goal.

"Why?" she whispered through her own frown.

◆ ◆ ◆

From the balcony of House Do'Urden, the Xorlarrin sisters watched the ceremony across the way. Ravel and Jaemas were there, on the grounds of Sorcere, as was Tiago, whose presence had been commanded by the matron mother.

"It was always Matron Mother Zeerith's dream, of course," Saribel said when a great burst of fireworks exploded up by the ceiling, shooting from the alcove of Tier Breche, the raised region that held the three Houses of the drow academy. "To see a Xorlarrin rightfully in place as the Archmage of Menzoberranzan . . ."

"Better in these times than not at all, I suppose," said a less-than-enthusiastic Kiriy.

"Better regardless," Saribel corrected. "Why would a Xorlarrin noble-woman wear such a frown on this day?"

"Dear sister, shut up."

Saribel sputtered for a moment before declaring, "I am the First Priestess of House Do'Urden."

Kiriy turned slowly to regard her and looked her up and down. If she was impressed at all, she surely didn't show it. "House Do'Urden . . ." she whispered quietly and dismissively.

"It was a terrible fight?" Saribel probed, trying to find the root of her sister's anger.

Kiriy looked at her with puzzlement.

"In Q'Xorlarrin," Saribel clarified.

"Hardly a fight," the older sister replied. She looked back to the distant ceremony. "More like a whimper and a retreat."

"Do you think Matron Mother Zeerith erred in surrendering the—"

"I think that if all the Xorlarrin nobles were in Q'Xorlarrin, as they should have been, and if Menzoberranzan had offered proper support instead of sending an army of demon beasts, too busy chewing the flesh of each other to understand our enemy, then you and I would not be having this conversation."

The blunt words and determined tone set Saribel back on her heels.

"So now here we are," Kiriy went on, "anointed nobles of the wicked joke that is named House Do'Urden."

"Whose matron mother sits on the Ruling Council," Saribel reminded her, and Kiriy snorted.

"Matron Mother Darthiir's reign will be short," Saribel added.

"Oh indeed," said Kiriy. She backed away a step and looked Saribel up and down, smiling as if she knew something her sister did not. "And you are First Priestess Saribel, whose tenure will be long, if you are wise."

Saribel felt very small suddenly, and very vulnerable. Her thoughts went back to her childhood, when Kiriy used to discipline her mightily and mercilessly and often—so often! Under Kiriy's stern guidance even the slightest infraction of etiquette would get the child Saribel beaten to unconsciousness, or bitten by a snake-headed scourge.

Just looking at Kiriy then made Saribel's blood burn with the memories of that awful poison, made her throat dry at the feeling of the fiery vomit burning all the way up her throat.

"Whose *tenure*," Kiriy had said, and not "whose reign."

Saribel's thoughts whirled in a hundred different directions. She wanted to speak with Matron Mother Zeerith, but she knew Zeerith would be secretly out of the city that same day and might not return for years, or decades even.

She thought she should go to the matron mother, but realized that Quenthel Baenre would more likely murder her than aid her.

Tiago might be the answer, she realized, and that thought troubled her more than any other. Her only path to the throne of House Do'Urden would be beside Tiago, and he, not she, would have to forge the trail. Saribel hated that thought, hated the notion that Tiago would hold sway over her even if she realized her highest ambition and became Matron Mother Do'Urden.

How many years would she have to suffer him beside her?

A loud boom shook the balcony, and the whole of the city, the final burst of celebratory fireworks for the appointment of Archmage Tsabrak Xorlarrin.

Saribel again glanced at Kiriy, whose eyes gleamed as she fixed them upon the distant ceremony. Saribel was not close to her brother Tsabrak in any way. He was older, the eldest of the Xorlarrin children, but only a few years senior to Kiriy. The two of them had been more parent than sibling to Saribel and Ravel, with Berellip in the middle, always pitting the older Xorlarrin children against the younger two, particularly against Saribel.

It occurred to Saribel only then that with Tsabrak's ascension and Matron Mother Zeerith's expected long absence, Kiriy had just gained a mighty ally.

Perhaps, Saribel thought, she would be wise not to covet the untimely demise of Matron Mother Darthiir Do'Urden.

CHAPTER 5 ◈

The End
Straightaway

THEY WERE OF CLAN BATTLEHAMMER. THIS HE KNEW AS HE SILENTLY slipped past the torn dwarf body. Stokely Silverstream had warned of this. They had found some of the Icewind Dale dwarves battered but alive in the tunnels immediately around the Forge Room and the chambers the drow House had taken as its home.

But for those deeper in the mines . . .

The Hunter looked at the ankle cuff binding the dwarf to the stone. The poor fellow had nearly torn his foot off trying to slip free of it.

Because he had known, as the Hunter knew now.

The tunnels were thick with demons.

Around a corner in the low lichen glow, the Hunter saw another dwarf victim, or pieces of the poor lass, at least. He slid Taulmaril back over his shoulder and drew out his scimitars. He wanted to see the beasts up close.

He wanted to feel the heat of their spilling blood.

This was the darkness of the Underdark, where Abyssal creatures were surely at home. But this was the home of the drow, too, and the Hunter was their perfect incarnation.

He caught a snuffling sound up ahead, around a left-hand corner, and recognized that some beast had caught his scent. The corridor ended at that corner, but went to the right as well, so going fast around it would expose his back to any allies of the creature.

He glanced back at the torn dwarf, and he cared.

He glanced ahead at the intersection, imagined the potential trap, and the Hunter did not care.

He went around the corner in a blur, hands working furiously before he ever came in sight of the creature, scoring a first hit before he realized the identity of this demon, a balgura, a dwarf-like thug two feet taller than the Hunter and thrice his girth, and that bulk all muscle and heavy bone.

Icingdeath dug into the demon's shoulder, and the brute howled when the scimitar bit at its Abyssal core. Around came the beast, a huge hammer swinging, and the Hunter dived back into a roll, disengaging his blade. The corridor shook violently under the weight of that blow. Stones and dirt tumbled from above.

And the Hunter realized the trap as he came around, noting a trio of emaciated manes ambling in at him. He started for the balgura but cut back fast, spinning and slashing, then boring ahead, his blades tearing and chopping with every step, sending bits of these least demons flying.

He went through them like a mole through soft dirt, burrowing and chopping and shoving aside the dying husks. He heard the heavy footsteps of the balgura behind him and thought to dive into a roll and bring forth his bow.

But no, this was personal.

He wanted to feel the heat of its spilling blood.

He stopped and spun, ducking so low that his bum touched the stone floor, the heavy hammer sweeping over his head to smash into the corridor wall once more.

Up came the Hunter, flipping his scimitars in his hands and digging their tips into the heavyset demon with overhand chops, walking them up the way he might use them to climb an ice sheet.

On pure instinct, before he was even consciously aware of the move, he threw his legs out behind him and up high, his form parallel to the floor, and the backhand swing of the lumbering demon swiped harmlessly below him.

His feet touched down and he quick-stepped forward, but threw his shoulders back tearing free the blades and rolling straight back to avoid another corridor-rattling swing.

The opponents paused and squared off and the Hunter saw pain in the balgura's black eyes, and saw the lines of blood streaming from the wounds, particularly the deep shoulder cuts. And the Hunter felt that blood on his own bare forearms, and he was glad.

In he charged as the balgura brought its heavy hammer behind it for an overhead chop. The Hunter's blades worked a dizzying blur, stabbing and slashing, and into the air he went, diving forward, scimitars crossed. He passed over the squat creature and tucked fast, setting the crook of his blades against the rising warhammer.

He lifted over the warhammer, twisting and pressing, and only finally releasing it as he spun to land lightly. Not so agile was the balgura, caught by surprise by the bold and speedy move, its balance and weight all askew. It hopped weirdly, barely able to still bring the hammer over its head, and it stumbled as it did, crashing shoulder-first into the corridor wall.

With a roar of protest, the demon bounced off that stone and whirled about.

"I wear no shackles!" proclaimed the Hunter, who was too close by then. In bore his blades, and this time, when Icingdeath found the Abyssal creature's throat, the Hunter did not retract. He pressed in all the harder, Twinkle working independently to keep the demon's grasping hand aside, and to repeatedly dart under the extended Icingdeath to stab at the arm that still held the warhammer.

Like a trained fighting dog, the Hunter would not let go. Icingdeath feasted, and the balgura howled.

And the balgura died.

With an angry twist of his wrist, the Hunter cut the demon's throat as it slumped to the floor.

A roar from behind, from the corridor where he had first turned, and the Hunter had his bow in hand, fitting an arrow so fluidly that it would have appeared to any onlookers that the missile had been set on the bowstring all along.

A second balgura bore down on him, crossing the perpendicular corridor.

But the Hunter held his shot. Out of that corridor came another form, a lithe form not unlike his own.

A slender blade led, plunging through the balgura's side. The demon howled and threw itself against the far wall, trying to turn and keep up as the second drow sped behind it, the blade working fast, thrust and retract, thrust and retract, and so cleanly and smoothly did it travel, deep into the demon's muscle and gristle with every plunge, that the Hunter could only watch in appreciation.

With undeniable skill and perfect aim, the drow drove the deadly weapon home again and again, and always was he one stride ahead of the turning, dying demon.

When at last it crumbled in death, the second drow was once more between the Hunter and the newest kill, and Drizzt recognized him by his outrageous hat before he even turned about and dipped a polite bow.

"Well met again, my old friend," Jarlaxle said, and he saluted with a sword Drizzt knew well: Khazid'hea, the sword more commonly known as "Cutter."

Curiously, though, another blade rested on Jarlaxle's hip where he would normally sheathe Cutter.

"I have searched long for you," Jarlaxle said. "Though not as long as I might have feared," he added with a chuckle, kicking at the balgura Drizzt had killed. "You do leave a trail of easily followed crumbs."

"As bait for the other demons," Drizzt explained. "Let them find me and make my hunt easier."

"There are some powerful foes down here," Jarlaxle warned.

"I have not yet even brought Guenhwyvar to my side. I will save her until I find another marilith, perhaps."

Bigger foes, Jarlaxle thought but did not say. He had been apprised of the events in full and believed that several of the demon lords had come into the Underdark, with hosts of major demons with them.

"You came to join in my hunt, then," Drizzt said. "I am glad for the company."

"You came to find any more survivors from Icewind Dale."

Drizzt solemnly shook his head, certain that none would be found alive.

"So you stay to exact vengeance."

"To clear the corridors for King Bruenor's people," Drizzt corrected, though the thoughts were not mutually exclusive, and both were true.

"I will join in your hunt, then, if you will have me," said Jarlaxle. "But that is not why I have come, my friend."

Drizzt looked at him curiously, not sure what to expect.

"I have tidings, many, both dark and hopeful, from the lower tunnels," Jarlaxle explained. "Come, let us be gone from this fetid place. I will set us a fine dinner."

"A dinner? Down here?"

"The growl you hear is no demon, but my belly, and I am sure I will die of starvation before I find my way back to Bruenor's halls, even if my path is clear all the way. Come."

Drizzt shook his head, reminding himself never to be surprised by Jarlaxle—and found himself, yet again, quite astonished. As Jarlaxle turned, Drizzt caught a better view of the sword that hung on his belt. It was a sword Drizzt knew well: Charon's Claw, the blade Drizzt had watched Artemis Entreri throw into the primordial pit.

"How?" he blurted, and Jarlaxle swung back, then followed Drizzt's gaze down to the distinctive skeletal hilt and red blade of that most wicked weapon.

"Surely you know me better than to expect me to leave such a treasure as Charon's Claw lying in the hot stones of a pit," Jarlaxle innocently replied.

"You went down there to retrieve . . ."

"No," Jarlaxle said casually, and he turned back and started away, "your wife did."

Drizzt stood there stunned for a few moments. He scrambled and caught up to Jarlaxle around a bend in the corridor and into a side chamber, where the mercenary was already preparing his banquet. From a magical pouch came a table, cleverly folded so that it opened, again and again, to become a rectangular table as long as Drizzt was tall, and half that width. Chairs followed and a fine linen tablecloth as well, with plates and fine silver, large drinking goblets, and all from a pouch barely larger than the one Drizzt wore to hold the onyx figurine that summoned Guenhwyvar.

From some secret pocket inside his cloak, Jarlaxle produced a wand, and from it came a meal fit for Bruenor's table on the highest holiday of the dwarven year.

"Sit," Jarlaxle bade Drizzt. "And eat. We have much to talk about."

A groan back in the corridor alerted them that they were not alone. Drizzt turned and reached for his blades, but Jarlaxle held his hand up to stop him then reached his other hand to the huge feather stuck into the band of his grand hat. He threw it down, summoning a gigantic flightless bird—a diatryma—with a huge beak that could break through a skull with ease and massive legs that would make fine drumsticks for the gods of the giants.

Off it went with a squawk that echoed about the stones. Barely had it turned the corner into the corridor when the first demon manes let out a great gasp, a burst of air flying from its suddenly torn lungs.

Jarlaxle motioned for Drizzt to sit, and took his own seat opposite, carefully laying Khazid'hea onto the table.

Drizzt did likewise with his bow, and put the onyx figurine of Guenhwyvar within easy reach as well.

Jarlaxle tore a leg from the beautifully browned turkey set on a silver platter, and hoisted his large mug, filled with fine ale, in toast. "To friends!" he said.

Drizzt lifted his own mug and nodded his agreement.

"You understand why the dwarves won so easily, do you not?" Jarlaxle asked. But then he paused, held up his hand to prevent a response, and shook his head, his expression one of disgust as he considered the tumult coming from the hallway. He reached for his belt pouch again, then reconsidered and went for a second pouch instead.

He brought out a tiny stringed instrument with an even smaller bow, and he tossed it into the air.

And there it hung, and it began to play.

"Much better!" Jarlaxle said when the music drowned out the noise of ripping and tearing flesh out in the corridor, and Drizzt could only shake his head helplessly and laugh.

"Now, to the point," Jarlaxle went on. "You understand why the dwarves so easily won?"

"The hundreds of dead might not agree with that description of the victory."

"True enough," Jarlaxle conceded. "Nor do I mean to minimize your own struggles, particularly with the great demons you defeated in the main chamber of the lower level. Truly that was a fight to remember. I don't know that I have ever seen you fight better, and I have witnessed many of your battles over the years."

"I fought with grand allies," said Drizzt. "And that is why the dwarves won."

"Indeed, and they would have prevailed in any case."

"But not as easily?"

"Must I remind you of the power of a drow noble House? Surely you remember, and this was House Xorlarrin, my friend, thick with deadly wizards more than ready to send a thousand of Bruenor's kin to the grave in short order."

"But they did not," said Drizzt, catching on, "because of . . ."

Jarlaxle smiled.

"I have known Matron Mother Zeerith most of her life," the mercenary explained. "She is a most reasonable creature. I know that's hard for you to believe, but I ask that you trust me on this observation."

"You convinced her to depart, and to surrender," Drizzt replied. He knew much of this already, from the surrender of Matron Mother Zeerith in the primordial chamber, when she had returned the Harpell prisoners and Stokely Silverstream in exchange for her own exit into the Underdark.

"Have you seen any signs of them?" Jarlaxle asked. "Of any drow?"

Drizzt shook his head.

"Why not, do you suppose? The tunnels are thick with demons—surely a matron mother of a drow House and her high priestesses could convince more than a few to go and cause havoc among the dwarves as they settle into their new home."

"How do I know they have not?" Drizzt replied. "Demons are all around, perhaps at Matron Mother Zeerith's behest."

"They have not," Jarlaxle assured him. "House Xorlarrin is far removed from this place and will honor the terms of their surrender. And yes, my friend, because of my efforts."

"Then I lift my flagon in honor of Jarlaxle," Drizzt said, and he did just that.

"At great expense," Jarlaxle added.

"No doubt."

"And now I wish something from you."

"You did this as a requisite for a favor?" Drizzt asked. "Then truly you wound me."

"Why did you think I did it?"

"Out of respect and friendship, I dared to hope. Was I wrong?"

Jarlaxle laughed, and now it was his turn to salute Drizzt.

"Then I ask you as a friend, and because it is the right thing to do," Jarlaxle said after a big gulp of ale and a large bite of delicious turkey. "I need you to come with me."

"Where?"

"Home."

"I am home," Drizzt said, mostly because he simply had to deny what Jarlaxle seemed to be hinting at.

"Matron Mother Baenre has reconstituted House Do'Urden."

"They are no kin to me, no blood, and no family."

"Of course not," Jarlaxle agreed. "They are mostly Xorlarrins now, and my own soldiers."

"She did it to sully my name, I expect, given the liberal use of the House name in the War of the Silver Marches. I can think of nothing more pathetic, and I hardly care."

"Nor should you! You are far removed from that House and that city. But," Jarlaxle said, leaning forward and prodding Drizzt with the half-eaten turkey leg to emphasize his point, "you should care about the new Matron Mother of House Do'Urden. She is someone well known to you, and someone desperately in need of your help."

Drizzt stared at his counterpart blankly, his thoughts dancing about the decades as he tried to recall the fate of all those priestesses he had known in Menzoberranzan. The only one he could think of who would remotely satisfy Jarlaxle's claims was his sister Vierna. But Vierna was dead, long dead, Drizzt knew all too well. He had killed her with his own blade.

"Dahlia," Jarlaxle said, and Drizzt found it hard to breathe.

"Yes, it is true," Jarlaxle assured the incredulous ranger.

"Dahlia is no drow!"

"She is *darthiir*—a surface elf, and indeed, that is the name Matron Mother Baenre has given to her. Matron Mother Darthiir Do'Urden."

Drizzt shook his head in disbelief, stumbling over words he could not find.

"She is no more than a puppet, of course," Jarlaxle explained. "Baenre uses her to insult the other matron mothers. Indeed, Dahlia sits on the Ruling Council, her mind too broken for her to serve as anything more than an echo for whatever Matron Mother Baenre declares. She will not survive long, of course—already, several of the other matron mothers have tried to murder her. They will succeed eventually, or Baenre will grow tired of her and will destroy her."

"This cannot be."

"I have no reason to lie to you," Jarlaxle said. "Dahlia is a pitiful and broken thing, but her soul is still in her corporeal form, trapped in a web of ultimate confusion wrought upon her by Matron Mother Baenre's pet illithid. Kimmuriel has looked inside her thoughts, and yes, I insist again, she is still in there. She understands her plight, and she is quite terrified, every moment of every day."

"And you want me to go back to Menzoberranzan beside you to rescue her?" Drizzt asked with intonations of utter disbelief dripping from every syllable.

"I have a plan."

"Make a better one."

"Tiago Baenre is the weapons master of House Do'Urden," Jarlaxle said.

The mere mention of his name brought a sneer to Drizzt's lips, and brought another thought to him. "What of Doum'wielle?"

"Cast out by Gromph. She is alive, I believe. I have agents searching for her. I do expect that rescuing that one will be more difficult than the hunt for Dahlia. Not physically, of course, but if Dahlia is a confused soul with a battered mind, then Doum'wielle is a truly broken and fallen sort. There is not enough water washing against the Sword Coast to clean the blood from Doum'wielle's young hands."

Drizzt dropped a wing bone to his plate, propped his elbow on the table and put his head in his hands, staring at Jarlaxle all the while.

"Tiago will come for you again, of course," Jarlaxle said. "His obsession is complete and undaunted. And he will bring many friends, truly powerful friends."

"So you want me to go to him instead?"

"The look on his face alone will be worth the journey, I expect."

"Forgive me for not agreeing with that assessment."

"Dahlia will not survive long," Jarlaxle said flatly. "Already, she is wearing out her usefulness to Matron Mother Baenre. Her death will be most unpleasant, if they even allow her to escape into the peace of death."

"You have many resources at your fingertips," Drizzt reminded him. "Why do you need me?"

"There are many reasons, but they are my own," Jarlaxle replied. "All you need to know is that I do need you, and that we can do this. Dahlia can be free and the threat of Tiago removed. Then my psionicist friend can repair her broken mind. So I ask you as my friend to stand beside me—and yes, I offer in exchange my own work in helping your friend King Bruenor regain this place and my continuing efforts to make sure he holds it—from the drow and from the primordial. And that is no small thing."

Drizzt could hardly wrap his mind around any of this. All the memories of Dahlia, once his lover and traveling companion, came flooding back to him. They had been close, very close, and though he had never grown to love her as he had loved, and once again loved, Catti-brie, Drizzt could not deny that he still cared for Dahlia, or at least that he cared what happened to her.

Of course, he also couldn't deny that she had attacked him on the slopes of Kelvin's Cairn, and had inflicted a wound that would have surely proven mortal had not Catti-brie and the others found him up there, dying under the stars.

"And it will be a great service to another you have come to know as a friend," Jarlaxle went on.

Had his thoughts been focused on Jarlaxle's words, Drizzt would have easily guessed that Jarlaxle referred to Artemis Entreri, particularly given the weapon hanging at his hip.

But Drizzt wasn't focusing on much at that stunning moment, his mind bouncing from past to present and back again, as all the years of his journey compressed into this one moment.

He could go with Jarlaxle, but what if he did and they failed, and he was caught in the city of his birth? What if he was slain trying to rescue a former lover, and so was taken from his beloved wife for the sake of Dahlia?

"Catti-brie is engaged in her own struggle," Jarlaxle said as if reading his mind—which Drizzt realized would be no great feat. He was surely echoing every thought with his expressions. "Archmage Gromph assists her only because of me, of course, and because of my stake in Luskan, which offers to him, and to King Bruenor and all his designs, the only true hope."

"Again you hint that I owe this—"

"No, no," Jarlaxle said, holding up his hands and shaking his head emphatically. "I only hope that you see me as I see you. As a friend, and one to be trusted."

Before Drizzt could digest the words, before he could respond, there came a louder roar from the corridor, followed by a shriek of Jarlaxle's monstrous pet bird, one that told the pair that their meal was about to be interrupted.

"Come," Jarlaxle said, leaping up, taking up Khazid'hea, and drawing Charon's Claw as well. "To the play!"

Drizzt and Jarlaxle went out together, side-by-side, Guenhwyvar close behind. They found a cluster of a dozen demons—balgura; manes; and even a pair of gigantic, four-armed glabrezu—waiting for them.

The demons were sorely outnumbered.

◆ ◆ ◆

"Ye canno' begin to be thinking o' such a thing!" Catti-brie said, and her reversion to that thick Dwarvish brogue warned Drizzt to tread lightly. Aye, but she had that look in her eye, and when it came to this, her tongue could be a greater weapon than the scimitars on his belt.

"Have ye lost yer mind then, ye durned fool?" she lashed out.

Drizzt started to reply, to explain that Jarlaxle was doing a great service to the dwarves, and that he was deserving of their trust, even in this seemingly suicidal mission. But the ranger gave up after a few whispered words, realizing it was futile.

He had just hit his wife with his intention to stroll into the City of Spiders. She deserved to express a few moments of outrage.

"Oh, but ain't we a couple o' sly and clever dark elves, me and me friend Jarlaxle?" Catti-brie went on, imitating Drizzt's posture and striking a most unflattering pose. "Just walking into Menzoberranzan so casual and easy that they'll think we belong and won't be cutting our heads off. Bah! But if I e'er heard a more stupid plan, then I'm not for rememberin' it!"

"I remember one time when you walked into Menzoberranzan alone," Drizzt said, and as soon as the words left his mouth, he wished he could have taken them back. On that dark occasion, she had done so only because of his own foolishness.

Catti-brie slugged him in the shoulder. "Ye're a damned fool," she said, her voice suddenly more resonant with fear and sorrow than with anger.

"Ye canno' go," she decided, and crossed her arms over her chest.

"Did you not just float into the pit of a primordial beast of fire?"

"Not the same thing."

"No, worse!"

"Not so!"

"Of course it is so!" Drizzt argued. "For all your tricks and magic, and that ring I gave you, you cannot know the heart of the primordial! And for all your wards, for all your power, we both know that the beast could have incinerated you"—he paused and tried to assume a more understanding and sympathetic posture, but still indignantly snapped his fingers in the air—"like *that*!" he said. "And you would have been no more than a charred pile of bones to be swallowed by the magma. I would not even have known, nor would Bruenor nor anyone else, unless Jarlaxle chose to share the information—and would he have admitted it to us, had he caused your fiery death?"

"Ye just said ye trusted him."

Drizzt couldn't hold his stern expression in light of the way Catti-brie had made the off-hand remark. Despite it all he giggled just a bit, and so did Catti-brie, and she threw her arms around him and wrapped him in a hug.

"I'm just scared," she whispered in his ear.

"I know," he said with a growl. Then, "I know," in a more conciliatory and understanding tone. "How do you think I feel knowing that you'll be working beside the mighty and merciless Archmage of Menzoberranzan, trying to reignite some ancient magic that is . . ." He sighed and buried his face in her hair.

"But I'm trustin' ye," Catti-brie said.

Drizzt pushed her out to arms' length, locked her rich blue eyes with his lavender ones, and slowly nodded his understanding and acceptance.

"I'm not wantin' to go through this life without ye," the woman said.

"I have already seen life without you," Drizzt replied. "It is not something I wish to experience again."

Catti-brie hugged him tighter. "Do ye think ye can save her? Dahlia?"

"I don't know," Drizzt admitted. "She is in the spidery claws of Matron Mother Baenre."

"So were you once," Catti-brie said, and Drizzt squeezed her a bit tighter.

"I have to try," Drizzt said. "I . . . we owe this to Jarlaxle, and I owe it to Entreri."

"I'm not thinking ye're owing anything to that one. Ye spared him his life on more than one occasion, and that's better than he's deserving."

Drizzt really had no retort, even though he disagreed. So complicated was his relationship with the former assassin! And indeed, despite everything that had occurred, both ways, he did feel that he owed it to Entreri to make this try, desperate as it seemed.

"And are ye thinking ye owe it to Dahlia?" Catti-brie asked.

Drizzt pulled back and shrugged. "She does not deserve this fate."

"Ah, me husband, righting all the wrongs o' the world."

Drizzt shrugged again, searching for an answer.

"And that is why I love you," Catti-brie said slowly and clearly, and she came forward again and gave Drizzt a deep and long kiss. "You go free her, and bring her home, and if there is anything I can do to help heal her broken mind, you'll need not even to ask."

Drizzt felt as if his heart would explode at that moment. He pulled Catti-brie tight, so tight. He wanted to join with her then, as if he could somehow merge their souls into one brighter being, and he held her for a long, long while.

He stepped back after a few moments, recalling another issue, and an important one. "Here," he said, pulling the magical necklace with the unicorn head and golden horn over his head and handing it to her. "I'll have no need of Andahar in the Underdark, and not in

Menzoberranzan, where the brilliant essence of a unicorn would surely announce my arrival."

Catti-brie took the gift and nodded. She slipped it over her head, her hand touching the beautiful sculpture hanging upon her chest.

"And here," Drizzt added, reaching into his pouch to bring forth the onyx figurine of the panther Guenhwyvar.

Catti-brie's eyes widened in shock. "I'm thinkin' ye'll be needin' that one!" she argued, holding forth her palm in denial of the gift.

"I've thought long on this," Drizzt assured her. "I am not bringing Guenhwyvar back to Menzoberranzan. She was created in Myth Drannor, so says the tale, but she was long in the city of drow. Many know of her and many coveted her, including the family of those from whom I took her. I cannot risk it."

Catti-brie started to protest, but Drizzt put his finger over her lips to silence her.

"If I am to die, then so be it," he said. "This is the life I have chosen and the code of behavior that I must follow. I can accept that. But I cannot accept Guenhwyvar in the hands of a dark elf. I cannot reduce my dear companion to an existence as a tool of murder and chaos. She deserves better. If I am to die, then she deserves nothing less than you."

"I'm thinkin' ye're more likely to die without her at yer side!"

Drizzt didn't disagree, but neither did he retract his hand. "I am with fine allies. Worthy fighters, both, and Jarlaxle with a million tricks I have not yet witnessed. If we are captured, he may be able to somehow buy us out of our dilemma, but never would we be allowed to take the precious Guenhwyvar with us."

He motioned the figurine toward her.

"I cannot."

"You must. I go with a heavy heart, but I accept that because I must do this. And because I know that if I am to perish in the City of Spiders, then so be it, because I say with all hope and faith that my friends are safe and thriving without me, that Bruenor will sit on his throne and you will secure that seat. That Wulfgar and Regis have found adventure and enjoyment in the distant land of Delthuntle, and that Guenhwyvar . . . Aye, there's the rub. I cannot accept that my grand risk might condemn her to such an existence." He pushed the figurine at Catti-brie again and nodded more than once until she at last took it from him.

93

"Keep her safe," he said.

"If I have to come get you, then know that Guenhwyvar will be by my side," Catti-brie said, a clear reference to the last time Drizzt had walked into Menzoberranzan.

"With ten thousand dwarves around you, I hope."

"Aye," she replied with a grin.

He offered her his hand and started away, but Catti-brie tugged back hard, halting him.

"One more thing," she said when Drizzt turned back to regard her curiously.

She paused and he shrugged, confused.

"Taulmaril," she said.

Drizzt looked at her curiously.

She held up her free hand and beckoned with it. "The bow. It is a hindrance to you as you flee about the tunnels. It was mine. I took it in Mithral Hall and so Bruenor, and so you all, gave it to me then. I would like it now."

Drizzt stared at her incredulously, but she just smiled calmly and beckoned again.

Drizzt let go of her hand and stepped back. "The bow . . . has been of great help to me . . . in the tunnels," he stammered.

"And I will have it," Catti-brie demanded. She motioned to the bow with her hand again. "You said you were with fine allies."

"And better to keep enemies at bay," Drizzt argued.

"And so I shall, if it comes to that," the woman said evenly. "And Jarlaxle will do the same for you, no doubt."

"You would take . . ." Drizzt stammered and stuttered and shook his head when he found he had no response. He pulled Taulmaril over his shoulder. "I have used this in my adventures against the demons in the lower tunnels off of Mithral Hall," he explained again.

"Aye, and you used Guenhwyvar, too."

"Not the same . . ." the confused drow ranger replied. "Are you trying to dissuade . . . ?"

"No!" Catti-brie said with finality, then more gently, "No."

The woman beckoned again. "Trust me."

Now Drizzt's expression turned to one of curiosity, as he caught on that she had something in mind. He handed over Taulmaril then reached around and removed the magical quiver that would afford him an endless supply of arrows to be enchanted and loosed by the magic of the great bow.

Catti-brie nodded and slung the bow and quiver over her shoulder.

They said no more then. There was nothing more to say. She would trust him as he trusted her. That was their unspoken agreement,. They did not inhibit each other's journey, but rather trusted and encouraged those choices.

But Drizzt knew there remained a loaded weight in that level of trust. It implied that he would make his choices well. And on the surface, this particular choice to travel beside Jarlaxle to Menzoberranzan could not seem a wise decision. Even for the sake of Dahlia.

And still, Drizzt knew that he was walking the right road. There was something more, something nagging at his very soul, some whispering notion that this road would prove an important part of his own journey, a measure of closure that he needed so that he could honestly go on with his life as planned.

This was fated, he felt, though Drizzt had never been one to believe in fate, or in the pre-planning of the gods, or any other such notions. He believed in free will and reason above all—he lived his life by that credo. Even in matters of faith, Drizzt placed his moral compass above any external edicts, and indeed, Mielikki was merely a name to what he knew was in his heart—though he had come to doubt that label of late.

Still, this offer of adventure Jarlaxle had placed before him felt to him more like some road to lasting peace. If he succeeded, he suspected he would finally and forever put Menzoberranzan behind him, or at least lock his awful experiences in that dark cavern into proper perspective.

And yes, it was a great risk.

Perhaps he would be slain, perhaps turned into a drider, perhaps sent into the Abyss to serve as a slave to Lolth forevermore.

But even in the face of those grim possibilities, he had to do this.

He and Catti-brie spent a long time alone then, expressing their love and respect as if it might be the last time.

They went together, and found Jarlaxle to bring along, to tell King Bruenor, whose excited response was, of course, perfectly predictable.

"Call out the boys!" the dwarf proclaimed. "Oh, but we'll march with ye, elf, all of us, and we'll tear down every drow House and put a blade up every ugly, skinny drow bum!" He paused in his rant and looked at

Jarlaxle. "Well, exceptin' those ye tell us to let be, and then we'll be lettin' 'em be only if they keep them skinny bums out o' our way!"

"Bruenor, no," Drizzt was finally able to say, and forcefully enough to halt the dwarf's momentum. Standing on the Throne of the Dwarven Gods then, King Bruenor looked at Drizzt curiously and said, "Huh?"

"You have your work here," Drizzt said. "No less important. The tunnels are full of demons, the drow may return to Gauntlgrym, and the Hosttower must be rebuilt or it is all for naught anyway."

"Bah! But ye think I'm to let ye walk off along to Menzoburysomedrow?"

The play on the name gave Drizzt pause, enough for Jarlaxle to verbally wade into the conversation with, "Yes, that is exactly what we think, and what we demand."

All around the group, dwarves gasped at the dark elf visitor's impertinence, especially with King Bruenor standing atop the throne.

"Were you to empty your halls, indeed all the halls of the Silver Marches, you'd not win a fight with Menzoberranzan, good dwarf," Jarlaxle explained. "Not there, not where all the Houses would unite against you. You'd not get near to our goal."

"Trust them, me Da," Catti-brie said. She looked over at Drizzt and nodded. "They will not fail in this."

Bruenor was clearly unable to come up with any answer that satisfied him or assuaged his all-too-obvious fears. He slowly melted back into the throne and heaved a great sigh.

"We're almost there, elf," he said quietly. "Can ye no feel it?"

"I do," Drizzt said. "And we are. To that place we've talked of since our days together on Kelvin's Cairn. Almost there. The winding road shows the end straightaway."

"The door to home's in sight," Bruenor said.

Many hugs later, Drizzt and Jarlaxle walked together into the Underdark, side-by-side. Oftentimes, Jarlaxle lifted a hand to put it comfortingly on Drizzt's shoulder, and more than once, the mercenary whispered Bruenor's last words, "The door to home's in sight."

CHAPTER 6 ◈

Amber Eyes

WITH A THOUSAND DWARVES MARCHING BEHIND HER, CATTI-brie, astride the mighty unicorn Andahar, led the way to the gates of Luskan. Athrogate and Ambergris rode at her side, the two of them assigned by Bruenor to serve as her personal bodyguards. Many threatening looks came at the woman, and particularly at her entourage, from the scalawags serving as gate guards—rogues in the service of one or another of the five competing Captains of Luskan. But Jarlaxle's hold on the city was so powerful not a single word was spoken, not even a request for the leaders to identify the approaching army.

The gates were pulled open without a word, and Catti-brie led the way into the city.

"Take me to the Hosttower," she ordered one of the nearby guards, a woman so dark from the sun and dirty from the streets she looked as if she had the shadow of a beard.

Still without a word of response, she escorted them up Reaver's Run, the main boulevard that led all the way to the city's main market. Beyond that lay the bridge to Closeguard Island, which housed the Ship of High Captain Kurth, who was of course Jarlaxle's lieutenant, Beniago.

Indeed, Beniago waited at the far end of the bridge, bidding the newcomers to cross. He took up beside Catti-brie and led the way to the next bridge, from Closeguard to Cutlass Island, where once had stood the Hosttower of the Arcane. Large tents had already been constructed all around the ruins of that once-grand structure.

"Food will be brought to you daily," Beniago assured Catti-brie.

"Enough to keep me belly fat?" Athrogate demanded.

Beniago, who knew Athrogate well, merely laughed and nodded.

"Aye, better be," the dwarf grunted.

Catti-brie moved over to the roots of the ruined structure as the dwarves settled in. The devastation had been so complete that she could look down into what had once been the basement of the tower, and even below that broken stone and metal to the deep roots trailing down into the Underdark. These were the roots that ran to Gauntlgrym, delivering seawater to the elementals that held the fire primordial in its pit.

She looked up at the darkening sky. The sun had slipped below the horizon, but only recently. The clouds to the west flared pink and orange in the dying light. The wind was off the water, wet and chill in her face, and Catti-brie pulled her black cloak—the cloak Jarlaxle had given her—tighter about her.

"A daunting task," Gromph Baenre said and the woman jumped—and nearly transformed into a raven and flew away. The drow was suddenly there, out of nowhere it seemed, standing perfectly calm beside her.

She gave him an incredulous look, and he returned a smile that reminded her of their respective powers. She knew Gromph's appearance and demeanor was meant to intimidate her so she calmed herself quickly and presented herself more forcefully.

She did a good job of hiding the winding line of terror that continued to twist inside her. Catti-brie trusted in her powers and her relationship with Mielikki. She had returned to this world with clear goals, and that guiding purpose had dominated her existence over the more than two decades of her second life. She had trained with powerful wizards, studied in the extensive library of the Harpells, communed closely with a goddess . . .

But this was Gromph Baenre, recently the Archmage of Menzoberranzan. He had magically appeared right beside her without a hint of warning or a tingle that anything was amiss.

Catti-brie understood that he could very likely destroy her just as easily and unexpectedly.

"I have examined pieces of the fallen tower already," Gromph explained. "All the materials are available. We have paintings and have uncovered design sketches of the tower in the bowels of Illusk, below this city. The dwarves should have no trouble replicating the physical structure."

"That is the easy part," Catti-brie said.

Gromph stared at the hole in the ground and nodded.

"Why are you doing this?" Catti-brie asked bluntly, and he looked up to match her blue eyes with his amber orbs, the two locking stares intently.

"If I wished you to know—"

"Amuse me," she heard herself saying, and couldn't believe the words as they came forth.

Gromph was the one who seemed amused, and he looked back to the hole.

"You intend to inhabit the tower when it is rebuilt," Catti-brie said in a voice that sounded far too accusatory.

"If it suits me," Gromph answered. "I intend to live wherever I desire to live. Would you wish to try to stop me?"

"In this city, run by drow?"

Gromph looked up at her again and flashed a wicked smile. "Here or anywhere," he clarified.

Catti-brie swallowed hard, but she did not allow herself to blink and did not look away.

"You fear for the dwarves," Gromph surmised. "You fear that if I am in control of the new Hosttower, I might use that position against the magic that preserves Gauntlgrym."

Catti-brie saw no need to answer.

"It is a reasonable fear, of course," said Gromph. "Or it would be, except for two important matters. First, the magic of the Hosttower isn't enacted like that of a wand. I will not call upon the tower to fuel the elementals enslaving the primordial any more than I can tell the tower not to do so. I expect you will understand this as we go through the process. Surely no instrument of such power would have ever been left to the whims of whomever happened to be serving as the leader of the Hosttower at any particular time in its millennia of existence, particularly not since the dwarves helped build the original tower, from all that I can tell.

"And second, I am not a simple and capricious murderer. What reason would I have to destroy Gauntlgrym, even if that was within my power?"

"Why did the drow attack Mithral Hall? Why does Tiago pursue Drizzt? Why—?"

"Gauntlgrym in the hands of a dwarf king serves me well at this time," Gromph stated.

"And if that changes?"

"I assure you, human woman, I am not one you wish to anger. And I do not need a Hosttower beneath my feet to rain destruction, wherever I choose."

"You say such things and expect me to trust you in this most important endeavor?"

"I speak the simple truth, and know that you have no choice in the matter. If you believe that you can reconstruct the Hosttower of the

Arcane without my aid, then you prove the drow matron mothers correct when they proclaim the stupidity of humans."

Catti-brie was very relieved at that moment when Beniago walked up to stand beside her. Jarlaxle and his many henchmen would protect them all from the wrath of Gromph.

"Braelin Janquay has returned to serve in House Do'Urden?" Gromph asked in the drow tongue, and Catti-brie was glad to learn that she could still understand the language well enough to keep up with the fast-speaking wizard.

A mixed blessing, she realized, when Beniago answered in perfect drow, *"Yes, uncle."*

Uncle.

The web around her was daunting. Catti-brie walked away, to a tent she had taken as her own. As she neared the closed flap, she shut her eyes and pictured again the hole in the ground that had been the grand and wondrous Hosttower of the Arcane. She tried again to picture that magnificent structure with its branching tendrils—it seemed as much a living thing as something built by elves and dwarves.

The image proved fleeting, replaced by something else, something that surprised Catti-brie: the amber eyes of Gromph Baenre, staring at her, measuring her, devouring her.

She glanced back to find Gromph looking back at her from the base of the Hosttower.

Shaken, the woman retired to her tent.

◆ ◆ ◆

"IGNORE THE GHOSTS," Jarlaxle told Drizzt as they wound their way through ancient, cobweb-filled halls and corridors, many with stone statues and bas reliefs so covered by the dust of centuries that they had become unrecognizable.

Still, Drizzt understood the design of the place and the architecture and statues enough to suspect that he and Jarlaxle had come into Illusk in their underground meandering.

"The spirits have been rendered benign by my associates," Jarlaxle explained. "At least, benign to those strong enough of mind and will to ignore them—I would expect you are among that group. Such creatures feed and strengthen on fear."

Several of the specters appeared, their faces stretched and elongated as if frozen in some exaggerated, truly horrified scream. The long-dead of Illusk floated about the sides of the wide hall Drizzt and Jarlaxle traversed. They leered at them from every shadow, it seemed. And they whispered in Drizzt's mind, telling him to flee, offering him images of some gruesome impending feast upon his warm flesh.

Drizzt looked at his companion, then steeled himself against his budding terror. Trust Jarlaxle, he silently reminded himself. The drow mercenary's casual gait comforted him, reminding him that he was traveling with one of the most capable people Faerûn had ever known.

So Drizzt found his center and his heart, and in his fortified emotional state, the ghosts became no more to him than moving decorations, like a rolling animation of Illusk's ancient secrets and history.

They came to an area less dusty and forlorn, and with other dark elves of Bregan D'aerthe moving about, all pausing to tip a nod to their leader, and to Drizzt. At one door, Jarlaxle paused and held his hand up to halt Drizzt. "Pray wait here," the mercenary instructed. "I will return in a moment."

Drizzt moved to put his back up against the wall, and tried to appear relaxed, though he surely didn't want to be in this place without an escort. But no sooner had Jarlaxle gone through the door than he came back out, shook his head, and apparently reconsidered,. He motioned to Drizzt to follow.

It was a small chamber with a single bed, a single desk, and a single chair, now filled by a lone man, a human, sitting back with his soft boots up on the table.

A man Drizzt knew well.

"Drizzt has agreed to join our quest," Jarlaxle explained, and Artemis Entreri nodded.

"You will risk the ways of Menzoberranzan for the sake of Dahlia?" Drizzt asked the assassin.

"You will?" Entreri returned with equal skepticism. "Will not Catti-brie burn with jealousy?"

"She knows I have no interest in Dahlia in any way that is threatening to her," Drizzt replied. "I seek to aid an old companion, nothing more." He paused and stared hard at Entreri, beginning to decipher more regarding this unexpected valor from the assassin. "Do you understand that?"

After a pause, Entreri offered a slight nod and said convincingly, "I am pleased to have you along."

Jarlaxle dropped a mask on the table beside the assassin's legs, and Drizzt recognized that magical item. Jarlaxle had gotten it from him after he had taken it from a banshee named Agatha. It appeared as a simple white stage mask with a tie to hold it in place, but it was so much more.

"You will walk as a drow," Jarlaxle told Entreri. "Every step of the way from this place to Menzoberranzan and back again. We do not know what eyes will be upon us when we leave the wards my friends have enacted as protection around Illusk."

Entreri picked up the mask, rolled it over several times with his fingers, and at last managed a nod, one clearly of great reluctance.

"We can afford no mistakes," Jarlaxle explained. "So we will take no chances."

"Would not a simple spell of illusion suffice?"

"Ah, but that is the beauty of Agatha's Mask," Jarlaxle explained. "Neither it nor the changes its wearer enacts can be detected with magic."

As he explained things to Entreri, Jarlaxle turned sidelong, his gaze sweeping out to include Drizzt in his warning. Drizzt was looking past Jarlaxle, though, to this enigma he knew as Entreri. He noted the assassin's eyes widening with clear shock, a profound scowl coming over him. Drizzt didn't even have to follow Entreri's gaze to realize he had noted the red blade Jarlaxle wore at his hip.

Entreri seemed as if he would melt there and then. His lips moved as if he wanted to say something, but no sound came forth.

"It was not destroyed," Jarlaxle said, obviously noting the same thing as Drizzt.

"Throw it back in the pit!" Entreri demanded.

"You still do not know if your longevity is tied to the blade."

"It is," Entreri stated flatly. He spat both words, and spat before and after for good measure.

"Well, so be it, then," Jarlaxle told him. He drew the blade, laid it on the table, then pulled off the magical gauntlet and put it down beside the sword.

Entreri shied away, sliding his chair back. "Throw it back into the pit," he whispered again, seeming on the edge of abject desperation.

"No one will hold Charon's Claw over you now," Jarlaxle assured him. "I give it to you. The Netherese are a fading memory—they'll not hunt the blade now."

"I do not want it," Entreri said with a sneer. "Destroy it."

"I am sure I have no idea how that might be done," said Jarlaxle. "Nor would I deign to do so if I did. You have long demanded of me that I help you retrieve Dahlia from Matron Mother Baenre, and so I . . . so *we* shall."

"Not with that," Entreri insisted, his hateful stare never leaving the bone-hilted, red-bladed, diabolical sword. "It's not possible."

Drizzt could feel the pain emanating from Entreri's every word. This sword, Charon's Claw, had enslaved him. And with it, the Shadovar Lord Herzgo Alegni had tortured the man for decades. All of those awful memories resounded clearly now in Entreri's tone. This was not a man used to being submissive, but the obvious level of his fear now truly touched Drizzt. Entreri really had expected to die when he threw Charon's Claw into the primordial pit, and yet he had demanded that the sword go in. He, Drizzt, and Dahlia had ventured through danger to the bowels of Gauntlgrym for exactly that reason: to destroy Charon's Claw, and with it, to destroy Artemis Entreri.

It would seem that Entreri hated Charon's Claw more than he valued his own life. The question, then, Drizzt knew, was whether or not Entreri hated the sword more than he cared for Dahlia—and that, Drizzt now suspected from Entreri's hesitance and twisting expression, was a different matter entirely.

"Do you not believe you can dominate the blade?" Jarlaxle asked.

"I want nothing to do with it."

"But it is here, and not destroyed," said Drizzt, "and if Jarlaxle had not retrieved it, then someone else would have. Surely such a powerful magical sword would have soon enough found a worthy wielder, and since Charon's Claw knows you and is tied to you . . ."

"Shut up," said Entreri.

"The choice is yours," said Jarlaxle. "Who is the master and who the slave?"

Entreri's scowl showed that he wasn't buying into that particular line of reasoning.

"An excuse," Drizzt interjected, rather harshly, and the other two stared at him curiously.

"What do you know?" Jarlaxle asked.

"I know that I am looking upon a coward, and that I never expected," Drizzt stated. He didn't blink as he locked Entreri's gaze with his own. "Our human friend uses the sword to shield his deeper anger."

Entreri shook his head, his expression caught somewhere between outrage and doubt.

"You loathe Charon's Claw so you won't have to loathe yourself," Drizzt accused. "Isn't that always your way? There is always some external reason for your anger, so you claim, but in truth that reason is . . ." He waved his hand dismissively and swung about for the door.

"You dare?" Entreri muttered.

"If we are to be done with this, Jarlaxle, then let us be on with it now," Drizzt said. "I miss my wife already."

He paused and gave a derisive snort, and without turning, addressed Entreri, "If you mean to run up and attack me, you should do so now, while my back is turned."

"Shut up," Entreri said again.

"Because you cannot bear to hear my words?" Now Drizzt did swing around to face the man.

Entreri stared at him hard, and for a moment it seemed he meant to leap across the room and attack Drizzt. But then he just laughed helplessly and whispered, "Yes."

He lowered his gaze to the table and stood there studying the vicious sword that had for so long been the instrument of his torture.

"Who is the slave and who the master?" Jarlaxle asked again.

"That choice is wholly your own, Artemis Entreri," Drizzt said. "That sword, powerful as it may be, cannot compel you in any way—if you are your own master first."

Entreri chewed his lip for a moment, never taking his gaze from that cursed blade. Then he moved swiftly, sweeping the glove from the table and sliding his hand into it. With a growl, he took up Charon's Claw and raised the blood-red blade up before his eyes. It seemed to Drizzt that Entreri and the sword shared a private moment then, a private battle, and if Charon's Claw had any hold over him, then it would be proven only if Entreri held it without the protective gauntlet.

"Let us be done with this," Entreri said, and he slid the sword into his belt. "And quickly, for surely I will be driven mad with the echoes of Drizzt Do'Urden—who has appointed himself as my conscience—sounding about me."

Drizzt smiled warmly at that, and even patted Entreri on the shoulder as he moved past with Jarlaxle. For all of the assassin's grumbling and complaining, Drizzt noticed that Entreri didn't flinch at his friendly touch.

Not at all.

◆ ◆ ◆

MINOLIN FEY GASPED and put her hand to her mouth, thinking that such a sound probably wasn't a good idea with Yvonnel posing naked save a string-of-pearls belt with a tassel of gemstones cascading down over her right hip, that leg demurely crossed over her left.

She wasn't gasping at Yvonnel, who looked very beautiful and had been sitting like this for long stretches over the last several days—well, in a sense she was. The reaction came from the image on the canvas in front of her, the portrait of Yvonnel now being finished by Minolin Fey's mother, Matron Mother Byrtyn Fey.

Matron Mother Byrtyn was a noted artist, her work always a pleasure to behold, and her best work manifested in portraits.

But Yvonnel had demanded no interpretation. She had explicitly instructed Matron Mother Byrtyn to paint her exactly as she appeared. And Yvonnel, this little tyrant who had sprung forth from Minolin Fey's loins, had gone further when explaining things to Minolin Fey. If Byrtyn failed at this task, Yvonnel meant to turn her into a drider.

Looking at the painting now, undeniably beautiful, but surely quite different from the living Yvonnel sitting on the divan in front of them, Minolin Fey believed her mother doomed.

Matron Mother Byrtyn nodded and stepped back, looked at Yvonnel, then back at the painting, and she nodded again.

"Grand!" Yvonnel exclaimed, and she leaped up from her seat.

"No!" Minolin Fey cried, drawing a surprised look from her mother and a knowing smile from Yvonnel. "No," she said more calmly. "It must be presented formally, touched up to perfection and unveiled from beneath a proper cloth."

Yvonnel said nothing, just kept smiling. She didn't bother to collect the robes lying beside the divan, but padded on bare feet toward the canvas.

Minolin Fey reflexively went for the canvas.

"Do not touch that," Yvonnel warned. She kept coming, and now her smile was dangerous indeed, one that chased Minolin Fey back from the canvas. The wife of Gromph, the mother of Yvonnel, held her breath as Yvonnel, naked as a baby but so deadly, came around the edge of the canvas.

And there stood Matron Mother Byrtyn, smiling proudly, oblivious to the fate that was about to befall her. Minolin Fey closed her eyes.

"Brilliant!" Yvonnel shouted, and Minolin Fey jumped back and stared dumbfounded—the painting was beautiful and yes, brilliant, but it hardly resembled the naked woman standing next to it.

"It feels as if I'm looking into a mirror," Yvonnel went on. "Truly your talent exceeds what my mother claimed."

"Your mother?" Matron Mother Byrtyn replied. "And which Baenre . . . ?"

"Your daughter," Yvonnel said, "my mother, Minolin Fey Baenre."

Matron Mother Byrtyn stared at the woman curiously, and with a bit of ire, clearly. Though this was a Baenre daughter, and one who had paid Matron Mother Byrtyn well, she did not have leave to speak to a matron mother of a Ruling House in such a manner.

But Byrtyn's expression didn't hold when she turned to regard Minolin Fey, who nodded sheepishly.

"Ah, I see you have much to talk about, Mother," Yvonnel said in a tease, "and Grandmother."

She tapped the edge of the painting and walked away, laughing. She didn't even pause to scoop up her discarded robes, just walked out naked into the hallway and closed the door behind her.

Minolin Fey stared at the painting, well aware that Matron Mother Byrtyn's stern gaze was upon her. Perhaps she should have warned her mother—she just wasn't sure of her proper place around Yvonnel.

Now she had to explain, in any case, but even that urgency could not tear her eyes from the painting. She had seen Matron Mother Byrtyn's work many times in her life, and the discrepancy between the painting and the flesh of Yvonnel seemed so very odd to her, so very unusual. Even Yvonnel's hair was cut differently than the woman pictured. And her breasts were very different, not nearly as large as Byrtyn had painted.

Minolin Fey ran her hands over her face and through her own white hair, unable to reconcile the scene in front of her, as she so often was where her unusual daughter was concerned.

◆ ◆ ◆

"I WAS BEGINNING to wonder if you would forget a courtesy visit and already be on your way," Catti-brie said when Jarlaxle at last caught up to her in her tent beside the ruins of the Hosttower. There was no mistaking the edge in her voice, a purposeful reminder to Jarlaxle that she wasn't very happy with him pulling her husband back to the city of his birth.

"My associates are gathering supplies. It is a long journey, and not one where scavenging for food and water is advisable." He ended with a wink and a smile, but it was clearly lost on the woman. Jarlaxle merely shrugged then, and placed a stack of parchments and scroll tubes down on the table between him and Catti-brie.

"Gromph has translated the Illusk references to the Hosttower so that you might easily peruse them," he explained.

"How generous of him," the woman remarked sarcastically. "For alas, he would believe, wouldn't he, that such simple spells of translation are beyond me."

"I recognize and accept your anger," Jarlaxle told her, and he offered a gracious bow.

"You have no right to ask this of Drizzt."

Jarlaxle rocked back on his heels, which was not a typical response from the ever-wary mercenary.

"Look around you," he replied. "Do you believe all of this happened by good fortune? Or some spontaneous act of the gods? Those parchments on your table—do you understand the lengths I traveled to uncover them and decipher them?"

"I do understa—"

"I have delivered Archmage Gromph to you!" Jarlaxle interrupted. "The Archmage of Menzoberranzan, the most powerful drow wizard in Faerûn! And one who can destroy me, utterly. You do not understand, good lady. Oh, certainly you comprehend the basic details of what I have done, but you do not begin to understand the risks I have placed upon myself."

"And upon my husband!"

"Yes, and upon you! Do you wish to secure Gauntlgrym? If so, then this is how. It is not an easy task, for any of us. And yes, I understand how the idea of Drizzt walking back into Menzoberranzan terrifies you. But make no mistake here, Catti-brie, your own course is no less dangerous, nor is mine. The victory we won to initially reclaim the dwarven halls might well prove the easiest one of all."

"What does Drizzt returning to Menzoberranzan have to do with securing Gauntlgrym?"

"Nothing," Jarlaxle answered, and he managed a smile. "And everything. This is not a journey to simply rescue his old companion. This is a quest to placate the archmage and to give to him, and to me and to all the other drow associates who now stand with your father, a measure of hope and respect."

Catti-brie stared at him incredulously, and clearly she could not sort out those cryptic references.

But Jarlaxle didn't back down under that scouring gaze. He stood resolute, and even nodded to reaffirm his position.

"I must admit that it is an impressive assemblage you have gathered here," said Catti-brie. "Myself and Gromph and the Harpells, and a thousand dwarves and Luskan helpers besides."

"We will rebuild this tower."

"Why?" Catti-brie asked. "Why is this so important to you?"

"Why is it so important to you?"

"King Bruenor is my father."

"And my friend," Jarlaxle said, but Catti-brie was shaking her head even as he answered.

"Is it for your own power here in Luskan?" she asked. "Do you think the renewal of the Hosttower will strengthen your mercenary band? Or that it will perhaps offer more independence for you from the demanding and demeaning calls of the Matron Mothers of Menzoberranzan?"

"It is all of that," Jarlaxle admitted.

"Archmage Gromph?"

"Yes, him too. I have many interests here, some my own, some for Bregan D'aerthe, some for Luskan, some for Gromph. I do not deny any of that. But I also have interests here for King Bruenor, and for you. And, of course, for Drizzt, whom I have come to love as a brother."

"Strong language."

"I consider my every word carefully before I speak," Jarlaxle replied.

Catti-brie nodded, and Jarlaxle was glad that she would let it go at that. He wasn't really sure exactly what he was looking for beyond a few immediate gains. But there was something more, Jarlaxle knew in his heart, though he couldn't bring himself to admit it or express it.

It went back to Gromph, and to Matron Mother Zeerith, the only matron mother who had ever—to his knowledge—truly appreciated the plight of Menzoberranzan's male drow. Jarlaxle held no illusions that he could transform drow society, but he was determined to begin that shift at least, and in doing so, to bring himself a level of greater autonomy from the matron mothers of that city, particularly from his ridiculous sister, Matron Mother Quenthel.

"It is an awesome force we have assembled here," Catti-brie admitted, walking to the tent flap and looking out at the dwarves, who were already hard at work gathering together any surviving pieces of the shattered tower. "And yet I fear our task will still be above us. I have looked at the parchments you earlier provided." She snorted and shook her head. "I feel like a child trying to decipher the treatises of the great philosophers, or like a dimwitted goblin reading the spellbook of Elminster!" She turned back and offered a sheepish grin. "But I am not alone," she said with a determined nod. "We will get this done."

"You are right to feel that way," Jarlaxle replied. "We haven't gathered nearly enough of the information to accomplish the task before us. We have a Chosen of Mielikki, a great accomplished drow mage, a cadre of lesser wizards, and an assemblage of the greatest dwarf masons and builders of this era. Also, and of no small importance, my associate communes with an illithid hive-mind. But still, there remain missing pieces."

Catti-brie studied him carefully. "But you know how to find those pieces," she stated instead of asked.

Jarlaxle laughed. "All of the elder, great races partook in the creation of the Hosttower of the Arcane, I believe, so yes, I have some ideas. Tazmikella and Ilnezhara will arrive shortly."

"The dragon sisters?"

"Dragon magic is among the most ancient, most powerful, and most lasting."

Catti-brie nodded her agreement.

"And we'll not stop there," Jarlaxle explained. "And so I bid you to leave this place today. I have already spoken with Kipper Harpell and he has agreed to send you on your way." He smiled wider as he finished, "I need an ambassador."

"To where?"

"A place you know well," he replied. "Or . . . knew well."

With that, Jarlaxle tipped his hat. "This is my last work here at this time, perhaps for many tendays. My associates—your husband among them—await my return, and so I bid you farewell, Catti-brie."

He offered that typical disarming smile and started to turn, but Catti-brie held him with her look. She bent down and picked up a bag that had been sitting at her feet, pulled it open, and produced a most remarkable black leather belt, set on one side with a brown cylindrical pouch, and possessed of a striking mithral buckle that Jarlaxle had seen before, shining silver and with the relief of a slightly recurving longbow on its face. That raised image had been cut out when Athrogate had taken the item from the Great Forge.

"What is it?" he asked, taking it and studying the carving more closely. "It resembles the Heartseeker."

"A memento," Catti-brie replied. "You will give it to Drizzt?"

The mercenary nodded.

"On your word?"

Another nod, and a reassuring smile. "May Mielikki walk with you these difficult days and guide your steps toward what is best for you, for your father, and . . ."

"And for you," she finished.

Jarlaxle laughed, stepped forward, and kissed her on the cheek.

"Yes," he admitted. "And is it not a wondrous thing that all of our interests are so perfectly aligned? We are, it would seem, of like heart!"

He tipped his hat again and strode out of the tent, making a straight line for the bridge to Closeguard Isle, which would bring him to another bridge to the mainland and the entryway to Illusk and the deeper Underdark, where Drizzt and Entreri waited.

◆ ◆ ◆

SOON AFTER, CATTI-BRIE stood in a familiar garden, sheltered by rocks from the great brown plain of Netheril.

She lingered some time there, feeling the soft petals of the plants, rubbing her hand along the smooth back of the same young cypress tree that had given her the limb for the staff she now carried. She couldn't come to this place without being transported back in time, to her earliest days in this second life she now enjoyed. This was her secret garden, her secret refuge, the place where young Ruqiah had come to understand that Mielikki was with her still, and that the goddess would help her on her difficult journey.

On a sudden impulse, Catti-brie took out the onyx figurine of Guenhwyvar and called for the panther. She wanted Guenhwyvar to see this place, to know this place.

The gray mist became a black panther. Guenhwyvar went off her guard almost immediately, and Catti-brie was glad. The gentleness of this garden refuge she had created could not be denied—not even by the blood that had been spilled here. The sense of peace permeated the air and filled her nostrils, and so filled Guenhwyvar's, too.

"Let me tell you a story, Guen," Catti-brie said, sitting down among the flowers. "Of a little girl named Ruqiah and the wonderful friends she once knew."

Guenhwyvar seemed to understand—of course she did!—and she settled in front of the woman, lying down and stretching, but never taking her large eyes or her attention from Catti-brie.

Sometime later, Catti-brie moved out from the rocks, and climbed atop a large one to afford herself a look over the land.

Shade Enclave, the grand floating city she had once called home, was no more—not up in the sky to the north, at least—indeed, not up in the sky at all. The magic had been stolen by the advent of the Sundering, and the great city and the floating stone upon which it sat had fallen from the sky to crash upon the ground.

Thousands had died in that cataclysm, so Kipper had told her—after Jarlaxle had explained it all to him, apparently. The carnage had been tremendous, both for those living in the floating city and those living on the ground in its shadow.

But they had not all died, and so up there, amid the broken stones and fallen towers, an enclave of Netherese remained, and thrived anew.

"Lord Parise Ulfbinder," Catti-brie quietly muttered, and not for the first time, as she strove to commit that name to memory, or to search her own memories to try to recall anything she might have learned of the great man in her days in Shade Enclave.

He was alive, so Jarlaxle had relayed through Kipper, and it was up to Catti-brie to convince him to journey beside her back to Luskan.

A strong wind blew down from the north, carrying stinging sand. Catti-brie pulled her black cloak tighter about her as a shield. Then she pulled it tighter still, so much so that its magic began to tingle all around her, as she and the cloak became as one.

The woman-turned-crow leaped off and spread her wings, the strong winds lifting her higher and higher.

She beat her wings and bucked the headwinds, making her way to what remained of Shade Enclave, and looking, too, for something else, for somewhere else.

For a home more dear.

PART 2 ▣

Ghosts

Who is this maestro, this puppet master, pulling the strings of so many marionettes?

Including my own!

Jarlaxle's maneuvers reach far into the shadows and involve great powers—and these are merely the plots of which I am aware. No doubt he reaches much farther still, to the darkest shadows of Menzoberranzan, to the heart of dragonkind, to the hive-mind of the illithids, to places I can only imagine, or dream rather, in my worst nightmares.

Who is he to wrangle together my wife, the Harpells, a thousand dwarves, and the Archmage of Menzoberranzan in an effort to resurrect a structure of such ancient power?

Who is he to secretly control the city of Luskan, through great deception and great hidden power?

Who is he to goad me and Artemis Entreri to Menzoberranzan, to rescue Dahlia, to assault House Do'Urden and thus invoke the wrath of the Matron Mother of the City of Spiders?

Who is he to convince Matron Mother Zeerith of House Xorlarrin to surrender Gauntlgrym to Bruenor?

Who is he to bring dragons onto the field of battle in the Silver Marches?

Who is this maestro, turning the wheels of Faerûn, playing the music of fate to the ears of all who would listen?

I call him a friend and yet I cannot begin to decipher the truth of this most interesting and dangerous drow. He moves armies with silent commands, coerces alliances with promises of mutual benefit, and engages the most unlikely companions into willing adventures that seem suicidal.

He elicits a measure of trust that goes beyond reason—and indeed, often runs headlong against reason.

And yet, here I am, walking the ways of the Underdark beside Jarlaxle and Artemis Entreri, bound for the city of my birth, where I am perhaps the greatest fugitive from Lolth's damning injustice. If I am caught in Menzoberranzan, I will never see Catti-brie or Bruenor or the sunlit world again. If Matron Mother Baenre finds me, she will turn my two legs into eight and torment me as a drider for the rest of my wretched life. If Tiago and his allies discover me, he will surely deliver my head to the matron mother.

And here I walk, willingly, to that possible fate.

I cannot deny my debt to Jarlaxle. Would we have won in the Silver Marches had he not arrived with Brother Afafrenfere, Ambergris, and the dragon sisters? Perhaps, but the cost would have been much greater.

Would Bruenor have won out in Gauntlgrym had Jarlaxle not convinced Matron Mother Zeerith to flee? Likely, yes, but again only with horrific cost.

Could we rebuild the Hosttower of the Arcane, and thus preserve the magic that fuels Gauntlgrym's forges, and indeed, contain the violence that would blast the complex to rubble, without the efforts of Jarlaxle and his band of rogue dark elves? I find that very unlikely. Perhaps Catti-brie, Gromph, and the others will not succeed now in this momentous endeavor, but at least now, because of Jarlaxle, we have a chance.

None of us, not even Gromph, can deny our debt to the maestro.

I must admit, to myself if no one else, that there is more driving me now than that simple debt I know I owe to Jarlaxle. I feel a responsibility to Dahlia to at least try to help her in her desperate need, particularly when Jarlaxle, ever the clever one, assures me that we can somehow manage this rescue. And so, too, do I feel that responsibility to Artemis Entreri. Perhaps I will never call him "friend," but I believe that if the situation was reversed, that if it was Catti-brie trapped down there, he would venture with me to rescue her.

Why in the Nine Hells would I believe that?

I have no answer, but there it remains.

Jarlaxle has hinted, too, that all of this is connected to a higher goal, from the defeat of the drow and their orc minions in the Silver Marches to the taking of Gauntlgrym to the surrender of Matron Mother Zeerith to the rebuilding of the Hosttower to the rescue of Dahlia.

Bruenor's Gauntlgrym is Jarlaxle's buffer to Luskan, allowing him a refuge for male drow, and one housing the former Archmage of

Menzoberranzan in a tower to rival the power of Sorcere. Jarlaxle's treachery against Matron Mother Baenre in the Silver Marches facilitated not only a rebuke of the high priestesses of Menzoberranzan, but a stinging rebuke of the Spider Queen herself. And so, too, will the web of Matron Mother Baenre be unwound when Dahlia is taken from her grasp.

And Jarlaxle uses me—he has admitted as much—as a beacon to those drow males oppressed by the suffocating discrimination of the female disciples of Lady Lolth. I escaped, and thrived—that is my heresy.

Matron Mother Baenre proved that point all too well when she reconstituted House Do'Urden, and tried to use that banner to destroy my reputation among the people who had come to accept me in the Silver Marches. I am not arrogant enough to believe that I was the only reason for Menzoberranzan's assault on the Silver Marches, but in so absurdly trying to stamp my name and my coat of arms upon the invasion, the drow priestess tipped Lolth's hand for all to see.

And in that hand is the revelation that Jarlaxle's maneuvers frighten the powers that rule in Menzoberranzan.

And in that fear, I cannot help but see hope.

Even aside from all that, from the debt to friends and companions and the greater aspirations of an optimistic Jarlaxle, if I cannot admit that there is something else, something more, luring me to continue this journey, then I am lying to myself most of all. Yes, I deny Menzoberranzan as my home, and hold no desire to live there whatsoever. Nor am I returning, as I so foolishly did once before, to surrender to the darkness. Perhaps, though, I will explore that darkness to see if light is to be found, for I cannot so easily eliminate the memories of the decades I spent in the City of Spiders. In Menzoberranzan, I was trained to fight and was taught the ways of the drow, and it is precisely the rejection of those mores and tenets that have made me who I am today.

Menzoberranzan shaped me, mostly by showing me what I did not want and could not accept.

Does that not put upon me a debt to my people, to the Viernas and the Zaknafeins who might now reside under the suffocating abominations of the Spider Queen?

My sister Vierna was not evil, and Zaknafein, my father, was possessed of a heart similar to my own.

How many more of similar weal, I wonder, huddle in the shadows because they believe there is no escape? How many conform to the expectations of that cruel society because they believe that there is no other way possible for them? How many feel the bite of the snake-whips, or look upon the miserable driders, and so perform as expected?

Is it possible that my very existence, that my unusual journey, can bring even a bit of change to that paradigm? Jarlaxle believes so. He has not told me this bluntly, but as I piece together the strands of the web he is building, from Gromph in Luskan to Matron Mother Zeerith—whom he assures me is unlike the other matron mothers in this important regard—I can only conclude that this is his play.

Given that, given Jarlaxle's machinations, is it possible?

I know not, but am I not duty-bound by those same principles and ethics that guide my every step, to at least try?

And am I not, for the sake of my own reflection, duty-bound to confront these ghosts that so shaped me and to learn from that honest look in the mirror of my earliest days?

How might I truly understand my life's purpose, I wonder, if I cannot honestly confront who and what placed me upon this road I walk?

—Drizzt Do'Urden

CHAPTER 7 ◈

Some Things We Knew

K'YORL, THE FORMER MATRON MOTHER OF HOUSE OBLODRA, HAD lost track of the decades she'd spent in the Abyss as a slave to Errtu. She had endured torture beyond what any mortal could expect to survive. In many ways, it had broken her. Physically, she could barely stand. Emotionally, she existed on the edge of disaster, cowering at every movement, trembling at every sound. She was not K'yorl Odran as K'yorl Odran had been, but a hollowed-out creature, thoroughly battered. Still, there was enough left of her to occasionally see beyond her safe hiding places and recognize those around her.

Amazingly, her decades of training in the psionic disciplines had allowed her to keep some portion of who she once was locked in safe rooms she had carved out in the corners of her mind.

This creature, this young drow priestess, was far more than her match. K'yorl knew that beyond doubt, felt she knew this little beast who called herself Yvonnel, and had a hard time distinguishing her from the Yvonnel Baenre K'yorl had known and hated.

This one looked so different, though, and was far too young. The psionic K'yorl knew beyond any doubt that this was no illusion. Was it another drow, or had the old matron mother found a way to revitalize herself?

An illithid, its head grossly misshapen—even more than usual—stood by the door at all times. The creature maintained boundaries in K'yorl's mind, preventing her from gaining a solid mental foothold on reality while constantly trying to get into her thoughts. She had to be ever vigilant against that, and then hope that her vigilance would be enough to keep the mental intruder at bay.

K'yorl Odran was free of the Abyss for now, for the first time in more than a century, perhaps, but she remained in a cage.

Caged by this one impossibly beautiful young drow woman who called herself Yvonnel—the name of K'yorl's most hated adversary, hated more than even Errtu. Yvonnel, the matron mother who had ruined K'yorl's

117

life and had torn asunder the stone roots of House Oblodra, dropping the structure, and most of K'yorl's family, into the chasm known as the Clawrift. Whether this was the same Baenre or someone new, K'yorl already hated the witch.

And she knew, beyond any doubt, that there was nothing she could do about it. If Yvonnel made a mistake, K'yorl could strike . . . but this one didn't make mistakes.

◆ ◆ ◆

"I KNOW NOT," Jarlaxle replied, holding the black leather belt out to Drizzt. "She fashioned it."

"You would have me believe that you were presented with a magical item and did not bother to try it?" Drizzt said as he took the belt.

"I do not even know if it is magical," Jarlaxle replied, and now it was Artemis Entreri's turn to offer his doubts, in the form of a chortle.

"Well," said Jarlaxle, "it has to do with that bow of yours, I expect, and I have no interest in bows. Most inefficient weapons, when a lightning bolt or fireball would better serve."

"Says the knife thrower," Entreri remarked.

Drizzt was only half-listening by that point. He set the belt about his waist, fastening it with the remarkable diamond-decorated mithral buckle. He felt somewhat stronger immediately, just a bit—and fortified, as if he had strapped on some armor. But there was more, he realized, focusing his thoughts upon it. This might be one of the many magical items that conveyed its powers to the user's thoughts.

If it even was magical, he realized when nothing else came to mind, and he wondered if his earlier sensations of strength and armor were merely his own expectations manifesting. Perhaps Catti-brie had fashioned this simply as a measure of goodwill for allowing her to regain possession of Taulmaril the Heartseeker.

Still nothing came to him. He adjusted the fit of the belt and fiddled with the curious cylindrical pouch at his hip, thinking it might serve as a sheath for a small wand. His hands went to the buckle, and he turned it up to consider the diamond gemstone image set upon it, a perfect likeness of the Heartseeker. He noted then that the buckle was double-layered, mithral upon mithral.

"Twist the top sheet," Entreri instructed—he too had noted the layers.

Drizzt grasped just the top plating and gave a slight turn, and the glittering gemstone design popped free, but it was not a tiny diamond item he held in his hand.

It was Taulmaril!

He felt the weight suddenly on his hip and understood before he even looked that the quiver had expanded as well, had become again the Quiver of Anariel, which would magically feed him arrows.

"Clever woman," Jarlaxle commented. "You'll better navigate some of the tighter tunnels without that longbow sticking up from your shoulder."

"What?" was all the shocked Drizzt could say.

"A buckle-knife," Jarlaxle replied. It was a weapon somewhat common among the rogues of Toril, a belt buckle that transformed into a deadly knife.

"A buckle-bow, you mean," said Entreri.

Drizzt couldn't resist. He drew an arrow from his quiver, set it to the string of Taulmaril and let fly, the missile drawing a silver line down the corridor before exploding in a torrent of sparks against the far wall, where the passageway bent to the side.

The report of the blast echoed, and in those rocky grumbles came the shriek of demons.

"Well played," Artemis Entreri remarked. "Perhaps you might shoot the next one straight up above us, to collapse the tunnel upon our heads and save the demons you alerted the trouble of rending us apart."

"Or perhaps I will simply shoot you so that I am less inclined to so readily accept death," Drizzt returned, and he sprinted off ahead to meet the charge.

Unused to being insulted, Entreri looked to Jarlaxle for support, but the mercenary just drew Khazid'hea and a wand, offered a wink, and came back with, "He has a point."

◆　◆　◆

THE ROOM OF Divination in House Baenre was among the most marvelous of constructs in all of Menzoberranzan. In this dark city knowledge was power. Mirrors lined three walls, the fourth being the massive mithral door, which gleamed almost as reflectively as the mirrors. The apparatuses holding the mirrors were set several strides from each other all along the way, but were bolted to metal poles running floor to ceiling, and not to the wall. Each apparatus held three mirrors, set on iron hangers, edge-to-edge-to-edge, forming a tall, narrow triangle.

In the center of the room sat a stoup of white marble, a round bench encircling it. Dark, still water filled the bowl. Deep blue sapphires were set in its thick rim, the angle of their reflection making the water within seem wider, as if it continued far under the rim, beyond sight, beyond the bench.

In a manner, it did.

Yvonnel gracefully stepped over the bench and sat facing the water. She motioned for K'yorl to sit opposite her.

The battered prisoner, so long tortured in the Abyss, hesitated.

With a sigh, Yvonnel waved to Minolin Fey, and the priestess forcefully pushed K'yorl into place on the bench.

"Put your hands up here on the rim," Yvonnel told the psionicist, and when K'yorl hesitated, Minolin Fey moved to strike her.

"No!" Yvonnel scolded the priestess.

Minolin Fey fell back a step in shock.

"No," Yvonnel said more calmly. "No, there is no need. K'yorl will come to understand. Leave us."

"She is dangerous, Mistress," Minolin Fey replied, using the title Yvonnel had instructed them all to use now, for Quenthel remained, to outside eyes at least, as Matron Mother of House Baenre.

"Do not be a fool," Yvonnel said with a laugh. She looked into K'yorl Odran's eyes, her grin disappearing, her own eyes flaring with threat. "You do not wish to be cast back into Errtu's pit."

The psionicist gave a little whimper at that.

"Now," Yvonnel said slowly and evenly, "place your hands on the rim."

The woman did as instructed. Yvonnel nodded at Minolin Fey to dismiss her, and the priestess hurried away.

"I do not wish to punish you—ever," Yvonnel explained to K'yorl when they were alone. "I will not ask much of you, but what I ask, I demand. Obey my commands and you will find no further torture. You may even purchase your freedom, once we are truly in agreement, mind and soul."

The psionicist barely looked up and seemed not to register the soothing words or the dangled carrot. She had heard it all before, Yvonnel assumed, and likely a thousand times during her time in the Abyss. Unlike Errtu, though, Yvonnel meant it, and she would convince K'yorl soon enough. After all, the psionicist was going to be in her thoughts, where deception was nearly impossible.

"Together we are going to find Kimmuriel," Yvonnel explained.

She put her hands on top of K'yorl's and uttered a command word. The rim of the bowl became less than solid, and the hands sank into the white marble, melded with the stoup. Yvonnel felt K'yorl's terrified tug, but she wouldn't let go. She had placed enhancements of strength upon herself in anticipation of exactly this, and the psionicist might as well have been tugging against a giant.

All around them, the mirrored apparatuses began to turn. The torches lighting the room went out and were replaced by a bluish glow emanating from the sapphires set in the rim of the stoup.

"You know Kimmuriel," Yvonnel whispered. "Find him again, but this time through the divination of the scrying pool. Let your mind magic flow into it, but do not send forth your thoughts to Kimmuriel unaccompanied by this scrying magic! Now, send forth your thoughts, K'yorl, Matron Mother of House Oblodra." She felt the psionicist tense up at the mention of the doomed House, and Yvonnel knew that reference would soon enough come to be her greatest weapon.

It took a long, long while—out in the cavern, the light of Narbondel diminished by half—but finally, Yvonnel felt her own thoughts going forth, following K'yorl's psionic call. They were joined by the magic of the stoup, their minds in perfect harmony, and Yvonnel could hardly contain her delight at that realization. The stoup had been built for Baenre priestesses, of course, so they could join in ritual scrying. Quenthel and Sos'Umptu both had insisted that Yvonnel's plan would not work here, that the stoup would not accept K'yorl's mind magic.

But they were wrong.

Through K'yorl's thoughts, Yvonnel could see the cavern in the waters of the stoup and reflected at every angle in the mirrors. She felt K'yorl's regrets then, particularly when they neared the Clawrift, wherein House Oblodra had been cast.

It proved to be too much for the fallen matron mother, and her mind-sight failed, casting her and Yvonnel back into the room.

The water cleared to still darkness.

The lights brightened, the torches reignited.

Yvonnel sat staring at K'yorl, their hands still joined within the marble.

K'yorl tried to recoil. She had failed and expected punishment, Yvonnel clearly saw.

"Wonderful!" the daughter of Gromph congratulated. "In one attempt, your vision fled the boundaries of this room! Did you feel it, Matron Mother K'yorl? The freedom?"

Gradually, the other woman's expression began to change; Yvonnel could feel her hands relaxing.

"I did not expect that you would get out of the room on our first session," Yvonnel explained. "Next time we will go farther." She pulled her hands out of the stoup, taking K'yorl's with her, and the rim appeared undisturbed.

"We will find him," Yvonnel said confidently.

Kimmuriel? she heard in her thoughts, the first time K'yorl had communicated directly to her.

"Yes. Yes, and soon," Yvonnel promised—promised K'yorl and herself.

◆ ◆ ◆

"ARE WE TO be fighting these beasts all the way to Menzoberranzan?" Entreri demanded two days later, when the trio had found yet another cluster of Abyssal beasts. The assassin slipped a quick side-step to avoid the overhead swing of a gigantic hammer, then stepped in quickly, Charon's Claw easily and beautifully sliding into the balgura's thick chest. The magnificent sword slowed when the blade hit a thick rib, the blade too fine to be chipped or snagged. Entreri's sigh revealed his pleasure at the power of the weapon. He hated this sword profoundly, but he could not deny its utility and craftsmanship.

Balgura blood flowed along the trough in the red blade, pouring over the demon's torso.

Entreri didn't merely retract the weapon. So confident was he in the power of Charon's Claw, he tore it out to the side, through skin and bone, leaving the dying demon nearly cut in half.

And this was a balgura, massively thick and heavy-boned.

"Do you truly believe I mean to walk all that way?" Jarlaxle replied with a laugh, and he too put his newly acquired sword to use. Khazid'hea decapitated one manes as Jarlaxle began his slash, bringing the vorpal blade across to cut deeply into a second enemy. "Your lack of faith disappoints me."

"When you're done talking . . ." Drizzt said from the side of the small oval chamber, where he held the door against the press of several demons, a mixed group of thick-limbed balgura, manes, and some other fiends Drizzt did not know: slender and with tentacle-like arms that they effectively used as stinging whips. Those tentacles, coming at him from behind a wall of allies, kept him moving and threatened to drive him back, which he did not want. He had the incoming monsters bottlenecked at the narrow entryway. One step back and the beasts would fan out to either side and the chamber would become a wild melee.

Drizzt ducked a snapping tentacle, but moved forward from a crouch, his scimitars working furiously to poke at a balgura, one, two, three, as he tried to drive the brute into a retreat.

But then it was Drizzt who was backstepping, and covering his head with his cloak. Out of nowhere, it seemed, a whipping wind came up, and stinging sleet pelted down all around him.

"Magic!" he warned, thinking it a trick of the demons, and unaware at that moment that they were taking the brunt of the ice storm.

"Left!" Jarlaxle called, and Drizzt slid that way—and just in time.

A glob of viscous goo from Jarlaxle's wand shot past him. It struck the floor right at the feet of the closest demons, but it didn't hold securely there. The floor was already a sheet of ice. The glob did stick to the front demons, though, who stumbled in futile attempts to maintain their balance. The momentum of the glob sent them skidding back into their allies.

A second glob came forth, hitting the ice again right in front of the first row of enemies and sliding in with great weight and force, taking the whole ball of demons back to the far wall of the corridor, where they struggled against the goo, stuck together as one.

Drizzt slid away his blades and let his left hand come to the belt buckle, his right to the small quiver, pulling forth Taulmaril and setting an arrow so fluidly that an observer might still be wondering where the scimitars went. The chamber and corridor filled with streaks of silver as the drow let fly. Drizzt's barrage pummeled the helpless demons as they rent and tore at the unyielding magical globs, and at each other. They were, after all, demons.

The ice storm had ended, and Drizzt battered the group in relative comfort, explosive arrows pounding home, every shot boring into demon flesh. But a sudden buzzing in the air was his only warning, before a swarm of horrid demons soared past the trapped group: chasme, like great houseflies with the head and face of a bloated human.

Drizzt managed to alter the angle of his bow enough to shoot the first of the flying demons from the air, but the second dived upon him, and a host of others were close behind, entering the chamber.

Or trying to.

A wall of ice appeared in that opening. It resounded with the impact of the third of the chasme, which collided with it full force. It shook again and again as the others crashed in behind.

The one in the room had Drizzt diving for the floor though, his bow flung aside and desperately going for his scimitars. Before he ever drew them, barely an eye-blink of time, he found he didn't need them. A red blade swept down in front of him, tearing the edge off the chasme's fly-like wings. As the demon spun and crashed, the great Netherese sword slashed in again, scraping the grotesque human face right off.

Entreri didn't remain in place to accept Drizzt's thanks, leaping away for the wall of ice. He stabbed Charon's Claw through one of the spider-web cracks, the shriek of a chasme telling them all that he had struck true.

"Well played," Drizzt congratulated Jarlaxle, thinking it he who had brought forth the ice storm and the wall.

But Jarlaxle shook his head and shrugged, his smile wide.

He turned away from Drizzt, and from Entreri, who was stabbing through the ice wall yet again, scoring another hit on a second of the flying beasts.

"Quite the hero," Jarlaxle said, addressing another dark elf who had come into the small chamber, though from where, Drizzt could not guess. He seemed about Drizzt's age and wore the robes of a wizard and the House emblem of Xorlarrin. A small silver chain closed the collar of his fabulous *piwafwi*, showing him to be a master of Sorcere, the drow school of magic.

"Be quick with your spell and remove us from this place," Jarlaxle instructed.

"Yes, do," Entreri added, speaking perfect drow, and looking very much like a Menzoberranyr soldier behind the magical disguise of Agatha's Mask.

MAESTRO

A quick look at the assassin revealed the source of the urgency in Entreri's voice. The ice wall was cracking more and more, pressed by the vicious and unyielding demons behind it.

"I cannot," the newcomer replied to Jarlaxle.

"Help our friend hold the door," Jarlaxle said to Drizzt, his tone for the first time less than calm. The mercenary pulled the newcomer aside and conversed silently in the hand code of the drow, shielding his fingers from Drizzt and Entreri.

Drizzt and Entreri met the onslaught side-by-side as the ice wall crumbled bit by bit and the demons pressed in. With Entreri beside him, Drizzt gave the beasts more leeway into the room. The pair were not afraid of being flanked.

Drizzt double-stabbed a balgura right in front of him, but quickly retracted the blades. He knew Entreri was coming by him, right to left. Drizzt rolled behind that rush, back to the right, coming in cleanly at a tentacle-armed demon distracted by Entreri's sudden departure, its confusion leaving Drizzt an opening he would not miss.

Icingdeath he buried nearly to the hilt into the fiend, the magic of the sword hungrily eating the demon's Abyssal force.

Twinkle Drizzt brought to the side, prodding the elbow of the balgura he'd just stabbed, preventing the brute from coming forward with its overhead chop. The demon let go with that hand, thinking to complete its attack with just one hand on the heavy hammer, but its other arm fell off—Charon's Claw swept across, above the crumbling demon Entreri had already dispatched.

Now they had room to maneuver again, and Entreri went forward, closing the bottleneck, and Drizzt fell back and gathered up Taulmaril once more. His first shot went over Entreri and the beast he battled, blasting another chasme from the sky. He called to his companion, directing Entreri's movements to provide openings through which the Heartseeker's deadly barrage could continue.

Soon enough, all that remained were the least of the demons, the zombie-like manes, and Drizzt brought his bow across, the item shrinking once more and becoming diamond as he set it in place on the mithral buckle. He drew his blades, and waded through the archway beside Entreri, out into the adjacent corridor and right into the midst of the mob of manes. Grasping, clawed hands never got near either of the two sword-masters, their speed and coordination too much for these least of demonkind to comprehend, let alone fight.

But in the midst of that slaughter, the companions noted a greater presence coming fast to the fray, a pack of gigantic and hulking four-armed, dog-faced glabrezu, each with two arms ending in giant pincers that could cut a drow in half. These beasts knew no fear and hunted as cleverly as a pack of wolves. Their claws snapped eagerly.

Drizzt and Entreri gasped and fell back, to be confronted by a shouting Jarlaxle. As one, they turned to protest, to tell Jarlaxle that they could not hold the door.

But their protests were lost in their throats. A third drow had joined Jarlaxle and the Xorlarrin wizard.

◆ ◆ ◆

THE DIVINERS ESCAPED the room more easily this time, their hands joined in the stoup, their thoughts entwined through the magic of the room and the powers of K'yorl's discipline.

Yvonnel guided her differently this time, not out into the cavern but just into the hallway adjacent to the Room of Divination, where sat Minolin Fey, awaiting Yvonnel's word. They hovered over the priestess, who was clearly oblivious to them. She was quietly singing, humming mostly, and to Yvonnel's delight, she could hear Minolin Fey quite clearly. The scrying was strong, both clairvoyance and clairaudience, washing away Yvonnel's fears that the injection of psionics would hurt the divine magic.

Yvonnel wondered how much the psionics might heighten the experience.

To her, Yvonnel imparted to K'yorl. *Into her!*

Together, they went to the seated priestess—close enough for Yvonnel to see the small flecks of black around the iris of Minolin Fey's red eyes. And closer still, so that one of the priestess's eyes filled Yvonnel's vision.

Then it shifted and they were looking across the hallway. Yvonnel's thoughts became so badly disoriented that it took the powerful drow many moments to realize that the shift had been more than a turn of their disembodied consciousness. They were seeing as she was seeing, and when she looked to the side, so did they.

Yvonnel tried to read the priestess's thoughts, and when that failed, she implored K'yorl to do so.

But that, too, failed, as did any messages or suggestions either of the two tried to impart upon Minolin Fey.

They still saw the outside corridor through her eyes, and better still, she seemed fully unaware of it. Intellectually, Minolin Fey was no Yvonnel, but she was a priestess of Lolth of some renown and achievement. And still she was oblivious to the scrying.

They lingered there for a long time, a very long time, until Yvonnel became convinced that there was no limit here, that they could have remained in Minolin Fey's head, seeing through her eyes for as long as they wished—and that Minolin Fey would never become wise to it.

Back in the Room of Divination, Yvonnel pulled her hands from the stoup and sighed profoundly.

"Maintain the connection to Minolin Fey!" she ordered. K'yorl hadn't yet returned. "See though her eyes!"

On impulse, Yvonnel rushed out of the room to the waiting priestess.

"What is it, Mistress?" a startled Minolin Fey asked.

Yvonnel merely smiled. Minolin Fey remained oblivious to the intrusion, and K'yorl remained in there, seeing and hearing Yvonnel exactly as clearly as was Minolin Fey.

Yes, Yvonnel thought, this will do.

◆ ◆ ◆

"Down!" Jarlaxle warned, and in the heartbeat it took Drizzt and Entreri to recognize the second newcomer, who was in the midst of casting, they surely did as they were told.

The lightning bolt went above them as they flattened themselves on the floor. They felt its radiating heat as it flashed into the hall, through the glabrezu, and into the far wall. The report jolted the stones so profoundly that both Drizzt and Entreri were able to regain their footing without even calling upon their own muscles to propel them upward. They spun around, blades ready.

But as the smoke cleared, the way in front of them was empty of enemies. Entirely empty.

Though they did see the glabrezu's feet, still side by side in the hall, smoke rising from severed ankles.

"Archmage," Entreri whispered, and Drizzt, too stunned by the display to find his voice, could only nod his agreement.

After a quick glance along the corridor to ensure that no more demons were about, the pair sheathed their weapons and Drizzt replaced his "buckle bow." Together they returned to join Jarlaxle and the two wizards.

"You cannot," Faelas Xorlarrin was saying to the mercenary leader when they arrived. "The matron mothers have sealed the city from magical intrusion. You cannot magically teleport into the city, or near to the city, or even use a simple dimensional door to breach one of the cavern's outer walls. Nor will clairvoyance or clairaudience afford you any insights. Under the inspired guidance of Matron Mother Baenre, they have been most complete and effective in controlling the flow of such spells."

"But you are here and mean to return," Jarlaxle replied.

"I was instructed by Sos'Umptu Baenre, Mistress of Arach-Tinilith and High Priestess of the Fane of the Goddess to report to Luskan with news of the changing rules in Menzoberranzan. If you or any of Bregan D'aerthe intend to magically return to Menzoberranzan, Jarlaxle, you must do so with the express permission of Matron Mother Baenre." He glanced at the other two. "She would not give such permission for these companions of yours whom she does not know, I am certain."

"Oh, she would know one of them," Gromph remarked, "and would welcome him with open fangs."

Jarlaxle threw a smirk Gromph's way, then shook his head and said to the archmage, "She suspects that I am in some way connected to your disappearance. No matter, then."

"The way is magically sealed," Faelas reiterated.

"There is always a seam in even the finest armor, even in the armoring spells the greatest wizard might conjure," Jarlaxle returned, grinning at Faelas, then turning to encompass Gromph as well.

But Gromph paid him no heed, Drizzt noted, and was instead staring hard at the fifth drow of the group, Artemis Entreri, and with the rare hint of puzzlement gnawing at the edges of his expression.

"You cannot detect the truth, can you?" an obviously-pleased Jarlaxle asked the archmage, clearly catching on to the same thing Drizzt had noted.

"That is your human toy?" Gromph asked.

Entreri snickered, but not too loudly, and none, not even Jarlaxle, were about to correct Gromph.

"I wish I could decipher the magic of Agatha's Mask," Jarlaxle lamented. "So many grand old artifacts we have seen. Ah, but to have known the greatest days of Faerûn's magic."

"We are rebuilding the Hosttower," Gromph reminded him. "Do you believe that I cannot unravel the magic of that simple mask should I try?"

"I ask that you wait until I am done with it," Entreri remarked.

"If you ever address me again, I will turn you into a frog and step on you," Gromph promised, his voice as steady and sure as anything Drizzt had ever heard.

Drizzt looked to his often too-proud companion and noted an almost involuntary twitch of Entreri's fingers. Surely the assassin wondered if he might get out his deadly dagger or that awful sword and put one or both to use on Gromph before the archmage could cast a spell.

"Faelas speaks the truth," Gromph confirmed. "The matron mothers and high priestesses have joined together in grand communal rituals, weaving their powers into a shield that has magically sealed off Menzoberranzan. They know that Demogorgon is about—or was—and his magical powers cannot be underestimated."

"The mere sight of him can drive a man to tear out his own eyes, I have been told," Jarlaxle replied, and he was staring at Gromph's eyes as he spoke. Drizzt nearly gasped when he looked closely at the archmage, to see the scratches that confirmed Jarlaxle had referenced the actions of Gromph himself.

Drizzt didn't know much about Demogorgon, though it was a name that he, like every adult of every sentient race on the face of Toril, had surely heard. Looking at Gromph, perhaps the most powerful wizard he had ever met, a wizard worthy of being spoken of in the same breath as the great Elminster himself, Drizzt suddenly realized just how profoundly he preferred to keep it that way.

"Even with the wards of the matron mothers, surely Gromph can break through the barrier and get us into the city," Jarlaxle said.

"No," Faelas answered, his subsequent sharp intake of breath and his expression clearly revealing that he had blurted it out before realizing that he was insulting the Archmage of Menzoberranzan . . . who was standing right beside him. "At the very least, such an intrusion would alert the matron mothers that Archmage Gromph was involved," he quickly added. "In that event, you would be compromised."

Jarlaxle sighed and seemed at a loss, though only for a moment, of course. He was, after all, Jarlaxle. "Kimmuriel," he said with a wry grin.

Faelas nodded.

"His magical abilities are apart from their wards," Jarlaxle reasoned. "In the days of House Oblodra, the greatest Houses always held a measure of fear and watchfulness for Matron Mother K'yorl, for she and her mind-magic minions could walk past their wards."

Thinking he had found the answer, Jarlaxle grinned more widely and nodded at his own cleverness. Until he got to the scowling Gromph.

"I will reduce him to ash," the archmage promised, and there was no compromise or debate to be found in his tone. "Yes, dear Jarlaxle, do go find him."

All four of the others took a cautious step back from the sheer weight of the threat.

"He was your instructor in what you most desired," Jarlaxle dared to reply.

"Was," said Gromph. "And he betrayed me."

"You do not know that."

Gromph glared at him.

"Am I to believe that mighty Gromph Baenre considers himself to have been used as a puppet by Kimmuriel?" Jarlaxle answered. "You think it was Kimmuriel who tricked you into casting a spell beyond your control, one that brought the great Demogorgon into the tower of Sorcere?"

"There are many times when Jarlaxle speaks too much," Gromph warned.

"But that cannot be," Jarlaxle pressed anyway. "How can Kimmuriel have had knowledge of that kind of power? To summon the Prince of Demons? Every matron mother in the city would have murdered her own children to find such a secret."

"Most matron mothers would do so simply for the pleasure of it," Entreri remarked under his breath, so that only Drizzt could hear.

"To summon a power that cannot be controlled?" Faelas asked doubtfully.

"Yes, because such a threat alone would elevate the summoner!" Jarlaxle insisted. "It matters not if House Baenre, or Barrison Del'Armgo, or Xorlarrin, or any of the others would also be consumed in the process.

A matron mother possessing the power to call forth the greatest of demonkind would dominate the Ruling Council by mere threat! Besides, such an act would be to the pleasure of Lolth, the Lady of Chaos. Is not Demogorgon the epitome of chaos, even among his own frenzied kind?

"No, it could not have been Kimmuriel," Jarlaxle finished.

"You deflect and dodge!" Gromph declared. Then he added with finality, "If I find your Oblodran stooge, I will destroy him."

When Jarlaxle started to respond, Gromph held up a finger, just a finger, and it was enough of a warning to lock Jarlaxle's retort into his throat.

"You should be leaving," Gromph said to Jarlaxle and his two warrior companions a few uncomfortable heartbeats later. "You have a long walk ahead of you."

"Your own journey will prove no less trying," Jarlaxle replied to his brother.

"Farewell. Perhaps we will meet again soon," Faelas said, and he began casting a spell that would transport him back to the waiting Sos'Umptu.

Gromph, too, began casting the spell that would return him to Luskan, but not until offering a derisive snicker at the trio of travelers.

"Always a pleasant one," Entreri said when the wizards were gone.

"It will be his death," Jarlaxle noted. "Someday."

"Not soon enough," Entreri muttered.

"The way is full of demons," Drizzt reminded them both.

"We'll be fighting every day," Entreri agreed, "and likely will find little rest when we pause our journey to eat or sleep. Would it have been too much trouble for Gromph or the other one to have magically brought us *nearer* to the city, at least?"

"The matron mothers are watching for such spells," Jarlaxle said as they started off once more. "Who knows how far their scrying eyes might extend?"

"Even here?" Entreri remarked, glancing around as if expecting the might of Menzoberranzan to descend upon him then and there. Drizzt, too, shuffled nervously, but when he looked at the nonchalant Jarlaxle he found some peace.

"This was the appointed meeting place," Jarlaxle explained to the others. "No one is more careful than Archmage Gromph, and no one is less inclined to have a visit with the matron mothers. I trust that we were properly warded from any prying eyes."

"But going forward?" Drizzt asked.

"They are looking for magic. We'll be using little, so it seems." Jarlaxle paused and turned his gaze aside, a sudden thought taking his attention. "We will eventually need Kimmuriel," he explained after a few moments. "And not just to help us get into the city—perhaps we can accomplish that on our own. But Dahlia's mind is twisted, her thoughts are wound like a writhing pile of worms. The only person who can hope to unravel that is Kimmuriel. Rescuing Dahlia without that resource would do us little good. Better in that event that we simply and mercifully end her life."

Drizzt glanced sideways at Entreri as Jarlaxle spoke and noted the man's profound grimace.

"So just call to him now then and let us be done with this," an agitated Entreri said. "And save us the pain of the march."

It wasn't about the march at all, Drizzt knew, or about any demons that might rise to block their path. Entreri had to get to Dahlia and had to learn if she could be saved. His tone suggested that he merely wanted to rid himself of the inconvenience, that he had better things to do with his time. But were that the case, why would he even be with them now?

"We are in less of a hurry than your impatience demands," Jarlaxle answered. "Let us search the tunnels about Menzoberranzan and devise our plans, perhaps?"

"Battling fiends all the way?" Entreri asked.

Jarlaxle laughed, but Drizzt caught something behind that dismissive gesture. And then it hit him: Jarlaxle didn't know how they were going to accomplish this mission. Jarlaxle, the maestro who prepared for every eventuality, who never stepped along the roads of a journey without complete preparation, was truly at a loss.

And had been since the beginning.

Jarlaxle took the point and started away, and Drizzt held Entreri back a bit so that he could ask, "Have you ever seen him like this? So unsure?"

"Consider where we're going," Entreri replied. "And consider that the whole of Menzoberranzan is on its highest guard right now. Would you believe his confidence if he pretended as much?"

Drizzt couldn't disagree with that. Menzoberranzan was shut down, the drow locking out the demons and monitoring every movement about the city. If their task to sneak in and steal Dahlia away had seemed difficult before, it surely seemed impossible now.

Foolhardy.

Suicidal.

Jarlaxle was uneasy—that much was clear—because he now lacked information about his adversaries. Lack of knowledge was never Jarlaxle's way.

They were still going, though, each putting one foot in front of the other on the winding way into the deeper Underdark. Perhaps Jarlaxle was already considering ways in which he might correct his lack of understanding and accordingly adjust his course. Perhaps he would find the solutions.

Drizzt had to believe that, had to hope for that, because he wasn't about to turn back either. His friendship to Dahlia, his debt to Jarlaxle, and surprisingly, his relationship to Artemis Entreri would demand no less of him that he try.

"We always knew this would be difficult," he said to Entreri as they made their way along in Jarlaxle's wake.

Up ahead, there came a demonic shriek, followed by a sharp whistle from Jarlaxle.

Already the fiends had found them once more.

"Some things we knew," Entreri corrected with an angry snort. But he drew Charon's Claw and his jeweled dagger and rushed ahead.

Chapter 8 ◈

A House Devout

RAELIN JANQUAY MOSTLY KEPT TO HIMSELF THAT DAY. HOUSE Do'Urden had been called out to supply a patrol group in the caverns outside of Menzoberranzan. By edict of the Ruling Council all such groups were to be headed by a noble of the House. However, like any rule in Menzoberranzan, it had translated to the various Houses as more of a suggestion than a literal command, and predictably, none of the Xorlarrins, nor Tiago Baenre, had been so inclined.

And so Braelin had been declared a noble of the bastard House. In House Do'Urden, it was as simple a matter as Tiago and Saribel claiming it to be so, apparently. There was no royal family, after all, with a Baenre and several Xorlarrins all laying claim to the title of noble, to say nothing of the surface elf who served as the Matron Mother of House Do'Urden. Or the two Armgos, Tos'un and the half-drow Doum'wielle, who had also been granted nobility.

Since Braelin had come to House Do'Urden at the wish of Jarlaxle, who was afforded great latitude in the matter by Matron Mother Baenre, and who, no doubt, would serve as a major noble in the House should he decide to reside there, it was only fitting, said Tiago and Saribel, that Braelin be given the honor in his stead.

Of course, the real reason the Houses were working around the edict of the Ruling Council was that none of the House nobles—indeed, few nobles in all the city other than perhaps that crazed Malagdorl Armgo creature—wanted any part of the extra-city patrols. The tunnels were thick with demons, and the ultimately deadly Demogorgon—and, if reports were true, other demon lords—hunted out there somewhere.

The mission was doubly dangerous for Braelin. He had no allegiance to any of his dozen Do'Urden companions, nor they to him. They were common soldiers from several different Houses, sent to serve in the Do'Urden ranks as several of the matron mothers tried to keep their eyes attuned to the happenings in Matron Mother Baenre's lackey House.

Braelin doubted that any of the soldiers accompanying him would make a move against him—no one outside his or her matron mother's protection would willingly invoke the wrath of Jarlaxle—but if the situation arose where a demon had gained the upper hand over Braelin, should he expect assistance?

He doubted that.

So he remained among the main group of his patrol, sending others out to walk point and envisioning an escape route with every corridor they traversed.

He also made a mental note to speak with Jarlaxle. He wasn't supposed to be a noble of House Do'Urden, and wanted nothing to do with such an "honor," as he truly wanted nothing to do with Menzoberranzan, a place he had escaped years before. He was of Bregan D'aerthe and the entire purpose of putting him in the House was to give Jarlaxle inauspicious eyes in the fledgling House, which would surely be in the middle of any excitement within the city.

Braelin reminded himself all the time that he just had to survive until Jarlaxle returned. He was confident that Jarlaxle would put the upstart Tiago in his place.

Fortunately, the House Do'Urden patrol encountered no monsters that day out in the wilds of the Underdark, and they returned to Menzoberranzan with not a blade drawn in alarm.

"Hold close until we reach the compound," Braelin ordered his soldiers when a trio of recruits started to break off from the main group.

The two men, of minor Houses, and a woman of Barrison Del'Armgo looked back at Braelin doubtfully, then ignored him entirely and moved off down a side alley leading to the Stenchstreets.

A flustered Braelin stood with hands on hips watching the mutinous commoners melt into the shadows. He thought to shout a warning that he would inform Tiago of their impudence, but he held his tongue. He wasn't a real noble of House Do'Urden, or of any House for that matter. He was a Houseless rogue, whose only claim to authority was because Jarlaxle had taken him into Bregan D'aerthe. In Menzoberranzan, at this troubled time, that meant he had no claim to authority at all.

He was reminded of that fact when the remaining commoners laughed.

Braelin sharply turned on one in particular, a young priestess formerly of House Fey-Branche, who had been offered to House Do'Urden mostly because she had been dismissed from Arach-Tinilith for her ineptitude and so had become an embarrassment to Matron Mother Byrtyn Fey.

"You think there will be no consequences?" he asked the woman as convincingly as he could manage. In fact, Braelin knew there would be none.

She just smiled at him and before he could further chastise her, another group, five of them this time, simply walked off the other way.

"Is there even a House Janquay remaining in the city?" the Fey-Branche woman asked, her eyes on the new deserters.

"Does it matter?" Braelin angrily retorted.

"Am I to expect Tiago or the Xorlarrins to take up your cause?" she replied without hesitation. "They appointed you out of convenience, and resent your presence in their House. They think you Jarlaxle's spy. And of course, you are."

"Then you would be wise to fear me," Braelin countered. "For that makes me valuable to Jarlaxle, does it not?"

The woman seemed less sure suddenly, as did the other three of the patrol group remaining with Braelin.

"You are confused, and with good cause," Braelin said to the four. He was trying to be somewhat conciliatory here, but also determined to show no sign of weakness. "What is this House Do'Urden? What future might it hold for any of us? Trust me when I tell you that I remain as tentative as any of you—we are pawns of powerful matron mothers, all of us. And our current abode, this House Do'Urden, is viewed as an abomination by many of the powerful Houses."

"But under the protection of Matron Mother Baenre," the young woman of House Fey-Branche reminded him. "That is no small thing."

"Allied with your House," another added, and he, along with yet another, nodded their agreement at the reminder of the matron mother's protective shadow.

"That is no small thing, true," Braelin admitted. "But for how long?"

"You should ask the matron mother," said the Fey-Branche priestess and she ended with a wicked smile. "I am certain that she will welcome your questions."

Another of the soldiers, the other female remaining, snickered, but one of the men seemed less amused and revealed that he was far more concerned with Braelin's point when he asked, "What of Bregan D'aerthe?"

"What of them?"

"Do you plan to continue to pretend that you are not of Jarlaxle's band?" the drow, an older warrior, pressed. "We all know."

"And we know, too, that the cadre of nobles of House Do'Urden do not look with favor upon Jarlaxle or his minions," said the other male.

"Tiago is Baenre, and House Baenre supports Jarlaxle's endeavors, of course," Braelin said. "And House Xorlarrin is not at war with Bregan D'aerthe."

"Not the Houses, but these particulars," the male replied. "Tiago is Baenre, true, but he has no love for Jarlaxle or any of Jarlaxle's band. None of them do."

"They would have cared not at all if you did not return to House Do'Urden," said the Fey-Branche woman.

"And so perhaps I will care not at all when Matron Mother Baenre looks away from them long enough to allow those who hate this incarnation of House Do'Urden to overrun their—your—compound," said Braelin. "And where will you turn in that event?"

"It depends what you are offering," said the older male fighter.

Braelin welcomed their obvious intrigue. He understood that many of the commoners of House Do'Urden would be looking for a way out if an attack came. They knew their own former Houses wouldn't help them. Any attack on House Do'Urden would surely result from a powerful alliance—likely one that included House Barrison Del'Armgo, second only to House Baenre. What might House Fey-Branche or the scattered refugees of House Xorlarrin do in that event?

He knew he had to let the matter drop, determined not to get too far ahead of anticipated events. He had planted a seed among these four. Let the whispers of a planned assault on the Do'Urden compound fester, and they would come to him, begging.

Bregan D'aerthe could offer them an escape route. All other roads would lead only to death, or worse.

Braelin looked at the older warrior and chortled. "The eight who deserted us assured their participation in the next Do'Urden patrol," he said.

"Deserted you, you mean," the Fey-Branche priestess said, and with a laugh she moved to the corner of a building, leaning into the alleyway as if she, too, was thinking of leaving.

Braelin didn't much like her. If it came to an escape with Bregan D'aerthe, he decided, he would invite that one along then kill her as soon as she believed herself free from the disaster of House Do'Urden.

"As you wish," he started to say, but he mumbled out the last two words as the priestess's expression changed to surprise.

The others noticed it, too. All eyes went to that Fey-Branche woman.

She sucked in her breath, eyes going wide, as she jerked back just a bit. Then the source of her discomfort became clear as the tip of a huge spear exploded out of her back, pieces of lung and heart still attached.

Into the air she lifted, her assailant still unseen, and with a flick of the spear shaft, she was flung from the weapon to bounce off the structure across the alleyway and flop grotesquely onto the boulevard.

And then came her assailant: huge and powerful, eight-legged and two-armed.

The four remaining drow gasped in unison at the sight of the mighty drider, and drew their weapons as one. But before any combat could be joined, the air filled with stinging bees—darts from hand crossbows. Braelin and the others, for all their agility, armor, and clever movements, could not escape the swarm.

Braelin was hit several times, and he felt the burn of poison immediately. Being of Bregan D'aerthe, he had been trained in resisting the sleep poison. Not so for one of his companions, who slid down onto the street.

"Form and run!" he told the other two. They started for him, the older male moving well, but the remaining woman strode sluggishly, fighting the call of the poison with every step. She surely wasn't moving swiftly enough to escape the drider.

It didn't really matter, though, Braelin realized. The trap had been well-coordinated and every route was blocked now by driders backed by drow.

"Melarni," Braelin mumbled under his breath. That House of vicious fanatics was known for its driders, and no fewer than four of the abominations skittered out around the trapped patrol.

Four driders backed by drow soldiers against three drow. Braelin glanced around, expecting a second barrage of poisoned darts, and saw just one possibility for escape, back the way they had come. Only a single drider and a single drow enemy had come out that way.

If they could move swiftly and decisively, he, at least, might be able to slip past and run free. He turned to his companions just in time to see the older warrior bring his sword to bear on the slumping, sluggish woman. Braelin realized the man had not been struck at all by any of the darts.

"Second House!" the older warrior cried to the attackers as he cut his companion down. "I serve Matron Mother Mez'Barris!"

And so Braelin Janquay knew he was alone.

He turned and sprinted at the lone drider, dived into a roll to avoid a flying hand crossbow dart, and came up into a sudden charge, his swords working together to turn the creature's thrusting spear aside, out to his left.

He disengaged his right hand from the parry and leaped up and ahead, stabbing furiously and finding some measure of satisfaction at least when his blade entered the belly of the large half-arachnid creature.

But Braelin was struggling even as he retracted the blade, as filaments filled the air around him and his opponent, magically coagulating into a web.

Braelin growled and rubbed his thumb across the ring on the index finger of his left hand, enacting the magic, just a small spark, but one that lit the web even as it formed. The Bregan D'aerthe scout, knowing what was coming, ducked under his protective *piwafwi*, and the drider shrieked in sudden stinging pain. Then shrieked again as Braelin scrambled across the beast itself, running along its bent spider legs, his second sword coming in hard to slash the drider's chest.

Braelin leaped away, thinking to sprint off into the shadows, but where he landed was not the boulevard, as he had expected, but a deep hole into which he tumbled, rolling and skidding to the bottom. Even as he managed to recover from that shocking descent, Braelin looked up to see the hole ringed by drow, half a dozen hand crossbows aimed his way, a trio of wizards and another two priestesses already into spellcasting.

He had nowhere to run.

"You are caught!" one drow warrior cried out, his red eyes flashing.

The older male of Braelin's group moved up beside that one, glanced down at Braelin, and snickered.

◆ ◆ ◆

"You will not replace her!" High Priestess Kiriy Xorlarrin said to her younger sister. Kiriy grabbed Matron Mother Darthiir by the arm and thrust her forward. The confused surface elf, looking as always as if she had partaken of far too much Feywine, stared blankly in Saribel's direction while not actually looking at the priestess.

"Save yourself the disappointment and dismiss that thought now," Kiriy finished. She spun Dahlia to face her and gently stroked the dazed elf's face. "She is pretty, is she not? The perfect plaything."

"She is the Matron Mother of House Do'Urden," Saribel managed to gabble.

"She is Matron Mother Baenre's toy and nothing more, you silly child," Kiriy corrected. "Is that why you are so stupid as to believe that you are destined to lead House Do'Urden, because you believe that this, this, this creature from the sunlit world is somehow taken seriously among the matron mothers?"

"Quite the opposite," Saribel said. "I believe it because Darthiir is not!"

But Kiriy laughed at her. "Then why do you suppose that you will replace her? Do you think the rules that apply to the other Houses have any meaning here in this abomination called House Do'Urden?"

"No, because they do not," Saribel argued. "I am the wife of Tiago Baenre, and so I am Baenre, and so I am favored . . ."

Kiriy's laughter stopped her.

"Understand this, my young and foolish sister, when Matron Mother Darthiir falls, as surely she will, it will be because Matron Mother Baenre is wise enough to no longer afford this *iblith* her protection. In that event, Matron Mother Baenre will have turned House Do'Urden over to Matron Mother Zeerith most of all, and which of us do you suppose our great mother might decide is most worthy to serve as Matron Mother of House Do'Urden in her continuing absence?"

Saribel didn't answer, but silently reminded herself not to put too much stock into Kiriy's predictions. Something was wrong here, and out of kilter. Saribel had not heard from Matron Mother Zeerith since the fall of Q'Xorlarrin—rumors said that Zeerith was hiding in the Underdark under the protection of, or at least with information supplied by, Bregan D'aerthe.

"If that is the case, then Matron Mother Zeerith will return," she said meekly.

"She will not," Kiriy taunted. "You will likely never see our mother again in this city. Her ways have long been gossiped about unfavorably by the other matron mothers, and now that Q'Xorlarrin has failed, more than one matron mother will think Matron Mother Zeerith a fine target for earning them the favor of the Spider Queen. Our path is to hide under the banner of Do'Urden—Xorlarrin is dead in Menzoberranzan. The sooner you understand that, the better your chances are of surviving." She paused and grinned wickedly, making sure that Saribel was listening very intently before clarifying, "Of surviving my rule."

Saribel left that meeting more shaken than she had been in many tendays. She had just started to find solid ground beneath her feet, had just begun to assert herself and press forward with daring plans to someday rule House Do'Urden.

And now entered Kiriy, her oldest sister, the First Priestess of House Xorlarrin, with a greater chance of ascension than she.

Saribel found herself wishing that Matron Mother Zeerith would return and assume command of the House. Surely that would destroy her own plans to become Matron Mother Do'Urden, perhaps forevermore, but better Zeerith and her even hand than the volatile Kiriy.

"You are a Baenre now," Saribel whispered repeatedly, trying to convince herself that she would survive the reign of Matron Mother Kiriy.

Or maybe, she thought, she could quietly whisper in Tiago's ear, and let Kiriy deal with his family should it come to that.

"I will be Matron Mother Do'Urden," she stated, nodding. She thought then that perhaps she should go out into the Underdark to find her mother—she could preemptively warn Matron Mother Zeerith that allowing Kiriy to assume the throne of House Do'Urden could bring dire ramifications to the remnants of House Xorlarrin.

But she shook her head at that unsettling possibility. She would throw in with Tiago, she decided. If Kiriy got in her way to the throne of House Do'Urden, Saribel would find a way to use Tiago to be rid of the witch.

Saribel was pondering the benefits of being part of three separate families—Xorlarrin, Baenre, and Do'Urden—when word came of an urgent meeting in the audience chamber. She rushed across the compound to find Kiriy, Ravel, Tiago, and Jaemas already in attendance, along with a couple of House soldiers who had recently returned from the outer corridor patrol. Matron Mother Darthiir was there, too, sitting in the back like an ornament—and what more might she be?

The patrol members were in the middle of recounting their tale when Saribel neared the group—they hadn't bothered to wait for her, clearly. She shot a sharp glance at Kiriy, who pretended not to notice.

Saribel sighed, but it was cut short when she finally realized the subject of the tale.

And the weight of it.

These drow, a formal patrol of House Do'Urden, clearly marked as such, had been attacked in the streets of Menzoberranzan!

"We must inform the Ruling Council immediately," Saribel blurted.

"Do shut up," said Kiriy, and when Saribel looked to Tiago, she found him looking back at her with open disgust.

"Likely rogues," Kiriy went on. "What of Braelin Janquay?"

The scouts shrugged and shook their heads—too conveniently, Saribel thought, as if they had been coached.

"Was it Bregan D'aerthe, then?" Kiriy asked Tiago.

"To what end?" Jaemas added, his skepticism clear.

"Jarlaxle hates Tiago—that is common knowledge," said Kiriy.

"Jarlaxle sides with the heretic Drizzt," Tiago added.

Saribel stared at her husband, trying to read him. Given his honest reactions and expressions to Kiriy's startling deduction that Bregan D'aerthe might have perpetrated the ambush, Tiago didn't seem to be in formal league with Kiriy, thank Lolth. But he was no admirer of Jarlaxle. And particularly not now, when he was convinced that Jarlaxle had played more than a minor role in foiling his attempts to kill the heretic in Gauntlgrym and elsewhere.

Equally intriguing to Saribel was Jaemas's reaction, though. He clearly wasn't buying this theory Kiriy had floated, and indeed, seemed more than a little suspicious of Kiriy herself.

That might be a lead worth following, she noted.

"We should use this to defer from any further patrol responsibilities," Kiriy said.

"We should prepare for an assault on our House," Jaemas countered. "This was a brazen attack in a time when the Ruling Council has forbidden such infighting."

"Bregan D'aerthe does not listen to the Ruling Council," Kiriy replied.

"If it was Bregan D'aerthe," Jaemas countered. "We have no evidence—"

"Who gave you permission to speak to me in such a manner?" Kiriy asked bluntly. "You are a nephew to Matron Mother Zeerith, and with no direct line to the throne of House Xorlarrin, yet you address the first priestess of your House with such familiarity?"

Jaemas shrank back. "Your pardon, First Priestess Kiriy."

"If it was Bregan D'aerthe, then they have Braelin, apparently," Ravel remarked. "In that case, they know much of our House defenses."

"A third of our warriors were culled from the ranks of Bregan D'aerthe," Tiago said. "They know everything of our defenses, and are inside our line already."

Despite his dramatics, the others really didn't seem too alarmed at his claim. Bregan D'aerthe had indeed supplied many of the House Do'Urden soldiers—in the beginning of the new House, Jarlaxle himself had been among that group. But Jarlaxle had slipped away and had replaced nearly all of his Bregan D'aerthe veterans with new recruits plucked from the Stenchstreets, Houseless rogues who offered little threat to House Do'Urden. Indeed, if it came to a fight with Bregan D'aerthe or anyone else, those new Do'Urden recruits who did not outright flee would almost surely fight for this House, their only House, their only real chance to survive with any dignity in what might come after.

Saribel found herself off-balance, as did Jaemas and Ravel, she noted. She would be wise to hold some private meetings with those two, perhaps.

◆ ◆ ◆

"AND NOW YOU serve me," Matron Mother Zhindia Melarn said to Braelin Janquay.

The beaten rogue stood naked, his arms stretched out to the sides by taut chains affixed to stout metal poles. Two of Zhindia's priestesses sat at the base of those poles, occasionally casting minor arcane enchantments: stinging jolts of lightning coursed the metal to Braelin's singed and smoking wrists.

They cast their little spikes of torture quite often—too often for them to be actually casting the spells. Likely they possessed magical items with the magic stored for easy access, such as rings or wands.

Or more likely, Braelin realized, the brutal Melarni had constructed this torture location right in their chapel, with such magic built into the securing posts.

He wanted to get a look at the contraptions, out of simple curiosity and a desire to be distracted, but every time his eye wavered from the specter of Matron Mother Zhindia Melarn, who was sitting on a wide-backed chair with its metal twisted and etched to resemble a spider's web with a thousand arachnids scrambling about, the priestess behind him whipped him with her scourge.

Braelin had not been very familiar with the Melarni in his days in Menzoberranzan. Like every male in the city who was not of House Melarn, he wanted nothing to do with the Lolth zealots. They were a particularly cruel lot, even by the standards of Menzoberranzan.

And they loved their driders, and had warped more drow into the eight-legged abominations than any other House in the city—than any ten Houses combined.

Braelin winced.

"If you will have me, I will willingly serve House Melarn," Braelin replied. "I am glad to be back in Menzoberran . . ."

He gasped and groaned as the priestess behind him struck him brutally. The snake heads of her whip bit and tore long lines into his flesh, their poison igniting new fires so painful Braelin hardly registered the repeated jolts of lightning searing the flesh of his wrists.

"At least try to be clever," Zhindia Melarn remarked. "Do you think I accept your loyalty? Do you think me fool enough to ever allow one of Jarlaxle's lackeys in my ranks? And a heretic lackey at that?"

"I am no heretic," Braelin managed to spit out before he got struck again—and again and again and again.

Nearly unconscious, his sense of time and place stolen by the blistering, tearing, and searing agony, Braelin was surprised to find Matron Mother Zhindia standing right in front of him, yanking his head up so that she could look him squarely in the eye.

"And a mere male at that?" she added with an evil laugh.

She spat in his face and whirled away. "Turn him into a soldier for the army of Lady Lolth," she instructed, and Braelin knew he was doomed.

◆　◆　◆

"I DO NOT understand," Matron Mother Quenthel said when Minolin Fey guided her and Mistress Sos'Umptu to one of Yvonnel's antechambers. At Quenthel's instruction, the illithid Methil followed.

A new construction lined the left-hand wall, a series of ten separate cubbies, each with a single seat large enough for one person to sit. They were designed so that someone sitting within could see out into the room, but could not view anything in any of the other compartments.

All of them now had easels, facing out and each holding a painting of a different drow woman, naked except for a belt of pearls and a gemstone-studded tassel, and in exactly the same pose.

"These were all painted at the same time," Minolin Fey explained. "And by ten of Menzoberranzan's most renowned artists."

"Interpretive," Sos'Umptu remarked.

"But not so!" Minolin Fey explained. "They were instructed by the subject to paint her exact likeness, and warned not to stray."

Quenthel wore a curious expression. She looked from the paintings to the empty divan, imagining Yvonnel sitting there in the pose depicted, then turned back again to the paintings. Several of them were quite similar, but none exact, and often with differences too distinct to be an accident. Yvonnel's hair was white in a few, pink in another, blue in a pair—nor was the cut ever exactly the same, and in the most disparate instances, not even close.

The same was even true of the hair on her loins!

"Matron Mother Byrtyn did an eleventh painting, with the same subject and the same instructions," Minolin Fey explained.

"Then of course they are interpretive," said Sos'Umptu, but Quenthel cut her short.

"Did the artists regard the work of the others as they painted?" the matron mother asked.

"No."

"Then when they finished? Did they compare?"

"No, Minolin Fey answered. "They finished and they left."

"And each was, in turn, congratulated by Yvonnel, and each believed his or her likeness perfect," Quenthel reasoned, nodding with every word as she began to catch on.

"As did my mother," said Minolin Fey. "A perfect representation of the subject."

"Whose painting of Yvonnel was also as she sees the young . . . woman."

Sos'Umptu looked at Quenthel, seeming at a loss.

"Which do you think most resembles Yvonnel?" Quenthel asked her.

The Mistress of Arach-Tinilith studied each briefly, then pointed to the third from the far end.

Quenthel looked to Minolin Fey, who answered by pointing to the painting nearest them, which drew a curious look from Sos'Umptu.

"We are not seeing the same person when we look upon Yvonnel," the matron mother explained.

"We each see our own version of her," Minolin Fey followed, nodding at her revelation.

"And is she not among the most beautiful, most alluring women you have ever witnessed?" asked Quenthel.

"The most disarming," Minolin Fey remarked.

"Her very being is enchanted," Sos'Umptu said. "She is cloaked in deception."

"In illusion," Minolin Fey added.

"Everything about her," said the matron mother, her tone more of admiration than anything else. She gave a little laugh. "She lets each of us paint our own image of perfection upon her, and gains advantage in that. Are not the most beautiful prisoners the most difficult to torture? Do we not listen more attentively to people we consider attractive? Do we not hope for beauty to succeed?"

"Unless we know better concerning the motivations and intentions of the beauty in question," replied Sos'Umptu, whose tone was much less admiring.

"What does she really look like, I wonder?" asked Minolin Fey.

"It does not matter," said Quenthel. "She is no doubt beautiful, and adds the deception to elicit appropriate and helpful reactions from those who look upon her. Perception is everything in this matter. When we look upon another, I might see innocent beauty, where another would see sensuality and the promise of carnal pleasure, where another might see plainness. With our dear Yvonnel, though, it seems we see her as *she* chooses."

"And where is she?" asked Sos'Umptu. "And what do you suppose she might do to you if she learns that you brought us to see this?"

"I did so at her bidding, Priestess," Minolin Fey replied.

Sos'Umptu's eyes widened, but Quenthel began to laugh.

"Because she does not care that we know," the matron mother explained. "Yvonnel is secure now that she is in control. She is pleased to let us view this great achievement—and can we deny that it is exactly that? What power must it take to maintain such a distinctive illusion? Perhaps she shows us this to learn if we, knowing now the truth, can see through her facades." She gave a helpless little laugh. "Though I am confident that we will not, and so is our dear Yvonnel, no doubt."

It was obvious to the other two that Sos'Umptu wasn't very happy with that answer, but she said nothing to deny it. She stood there shaking her head, again studying the paintings as if looking for clues. Finally she simply shrugged and sighed and let it go.

What could be said, after all?

◆ ◆ ◆

MATRON MOTHER ZHINDIA'S audience chamber was right next to the chapel, close enough for her, First Priestess Kyrnill Melarn, and their guest to hear the screams from Braelin as his long and excruciating transformation began.

"You are interested in the ceremony?" Zhindia asked her guest, seeing the priestess staring at the wall with clear intrigue.

"I have only witnessed it once," Kiriy Xorlarrin replied, "when I was much younger. I have heard that it is quite satisfying."

"Immensely," Zhindia confirmed.

"But it would not do," said Kiriy. "We cannot have Braelin seeing me here with you now."

"There is no danger," Kyrnill explained. "When Braelin walks as a drider, he will remember nothing but the agony of this day. And for the rest of his miserable days, if any thoughts against Lolth or the matron mother he serves enter his head, he will revisit that agony. He could never find the strength to betray your secret."

"Do they suspect House Melarn?" Zhindia asked.

"House Do'Urden is full of clever nobles now," Kiriy replied. "I have led them astray, as we agreed, into thinking that Bregan D'aerthe likely ambushed their patrol, but that theory will not hold long, particularly if the wizard Jaemas is somehow in league with Jarlaxle, as we believe."

"We should move quickly then," said Kyrnill.

"We must move quickly, particularly if these other whispers from the tunnels prove true," said Zhindia.

Kiriy looked at her curiously.

"A sickness of the mind," Matron Mother Zhindia explained. "Some say it is the thinning of the Faerzress. Others pose that the presence of the demon lords in the Underdark is the cause of the madness. But we know better. It is House Do'Urden, its mere existence, that so offends Lady Lolth. It will not stand." She looked directly at the First Priestess of House Xorlarrin and qualified the remark, "Not in its present form."

Kiriy nodded. They were going to tear down the hierarchy of House Do'Urden, murder that abomination Matron Mother Baenre had placed on the throne, and replace it with a House to the liking of the Spider Queen. It would be a House devout, in Melarn's own image, a House that would correct both the abomination of Matron Mother Baenre and the wayward path Matron Mother Zeerith had steered for House Xorlarrin at the same time. And it would be a House with males put in their proper place in accordance with the edicts of Lolth, at long last.

If the fall of the abominable House Do'Urden also led to the fall of House Baenre, might the new Xorlarrin quickly ascend the city's ranks? The thought teased Kiriy, particularly if they could wrangle an alliance with their once arch-rival, House Barrison Del'Armgo.

The promise of glory for the Xorlarrins remained, if the family had the foresight and the courage.

The promise of a new House devout, in Lolth's favor, and in alliance with the new powers of Menzoberranzan: House Melarn and House Barrison Del'Armgo.

House Xorlarrin, led by Matron Mother Kiriy.

◆ ◆ ◆

"WHAT ELSE DID you give to the child beyond the memories of Yvonnel the Eternal?" Quenthel asked Methil later on when they were alone.

"I did as I was instructed," the illithid answered in his gurgling voice. "Much as I did for you."

"Much, but not all," Quenthel accused. "There is more than simple illusion at play with that one. But it is not magical illusion at all, is it?"

"I am quite sure that it is," Methil answered. "Your mother had some understanding of the old illusionary magic, and I know that this child was quite attentive when those memories were imparted."

"More than that!" a frustrated Quenthel retorted. "A simple illusion would alter Yvonnel's appearance somewhat. Even I can do that, and I cared little for that part of your . . . instruction. It's not difficult for one skilled in the Art to simply alter her appearance, but what Yvonnel is doing is beyond that. She is not merely altering her appearance, but subtly managing the expectations and desires of each individual who looks upon her, even multiple individuals in the same room with her at the same time. And she's doing it in a way that will gain her the greatest individual advantage over each observer."

"Indeed, and she is doing it continually."

"How?"

"I do not know," the illithid replied. "Her sensitivity to the perceptions of others is instinctual."

"No, she took this from you," Quenthel said. "When your tentacles were in Minolin Fey's womb, this baby, this creature, took more than you were offering. She borders on the mind magic of the illithids, if she is not fully there."

"You would be better served in directing this to Lady Lolth," Methil replied. "I do not doubt the power of Yvonnel. She is as strong as the Eternal."

"*I* am as strong as the Eternal!" Quenthel snapped back.

Methil didn't answer, and the matron mother understood that as a clear repudiation of her claim—and she knew, to her ultimate frustration, that Methil was correct in his assessment.

"The powers come so easily to her," Quenthel lamented, more to herself than to the mind flayer. "To maintain such a ruse . . ."

Chapter 9 ◈

The Cycle of Life

E WAS A LITTLE OLDER, A LITTLE THICKER, HIS HEAD A BIT SHINIER, but Catti-brie recognized Niraj's brilliant and inviting smile. She flew above the Desai encampment, just a short distance south of the mountainous area where the floating city of Shade Enclave had tumbled from the sky to crash and break apart in the foothills. He tended some sheep, filling a water trough and taking the time to speak to and pat each and every one.

The giant crow remained up high and circling. Catti-brie allowed herself a few moments to remember the earliest days of her second life. She had slept so peacefully in the arms of Kavita, and had enjoyed, with the perspective of an adult, the unconditional love and fatherly protection of Niraj as he fawned over her.

She would have her own children this time around, she told herself, and her crow head nodded. In that first life, there had been so many pressing needs—one adventure after another. Catti-brie didn't regret any bit of that existence, didn't lament her lack of progeny, but this time, it felt right to her. She was determined that she would share with Drizzt the warmth of familial love she had shared with these two.

But she had a terrible feeling that it wouldn't come to pass, that Drizzt wouldn't return to her this time. Had she waited too long already?

She shook aside her doubts and circled lower. When she was halfway to the ground, Niraj looked up at her. His eyes went wide and he stumbled back a step—this crow descending upon him and the tribe's sheep was as large as he!

"Ah, back!" he stammered, and he backstepped and tried to shoo the sheep behind him.

Catti-brie swerved to the far end of the field and set down, transforming back into her human form. She approached an apprehensive Niraj, her face brightly smiling, her arms out to her sides.

For a moment, he seemed confused, but the word "Zibrija" slipped from his mouth.

Zibrija, the desert flower, the nickname Niraj had placed on his beloved daughter two decades ago.

Catti-brie held her arms out wider and shrugged, the sleeves of her magical garment dropping loosely above her elbow, revealing her spellscars. He sprinted at Catti-brie and crushed her in such a hug it lifted her from the ground and sent them both a few steps back the way Catti-brie had come.

"Zibrija, my child!" he said, his voice thick with emotion, his cherubic brown cheeks already wet with tears. "Zibrija!"

"Father," she replied, and she hugged him back just as tightly. She loved this man, her father, with all her heart.

"Oh, the tales I have to tell you," she whispered in his ear. She could tell he wanted to respond, but didn't dare try to talk for fear that his voice would issue only a happy wail. He hugged her all the closer.

"Tell me that my mother is well," Catti-brie whispered, and Niraj squeezed tighter and nodded emphatically.

Finally the brown-skinned man took a deep breath and steadied himself, and managed to push Catti-brie back to arms' length.

"My Ruqiah," he whispered, using the name she had been given at her second birth. "We never surrendered hope that we would see you again, but still . . . I cannot tell you how my heart wants to push right out of my chest!"

"You need not tell me," Catti-brie replied. "I know."

Niraj pulled her in close for another lengthy, tight hug.

"My mother," Catti-brie whispered after a few moments, and the man nodded again and moved back, turning to the side and never letting go of her hand as he led her away.

Many eyes turned upon them as they entered the tent encampment of the Desai tribe, and many whispers erupted in their wake. Catti-brie resisted the temptation to cast a spell to heighten her hearing. She heard her name, Ruqiah, several times. The tribe remembered her.

"Whatever happened to that boy?" she asked Niraj. "The one who threw me into the mud?"

"Tahnood," Niraj said solemnly, his tone alerting her. He turned to meet her concerned stare as he finished, "He did not survive the war."

Catti-brie's regret washed away almost immediately on deeper concerns as she registered the last word.

"The war?" she echoed.

"The Netherese," Niraj explained. "The plains were afire with battle for many months. The crows of our lands are fatter now."

He turned to her and gave a sly wink. "Not as thick as the crow who spied upon me at the sheep pen, though."

Catti-brie managed a smile, but her heart was heavy. "Did you fight?"

"We all fought."

The woman didn't know what to say, and settled on, "I am sorry, Father. I should have returned to you."

"My greatest joy in that dark time is that you were not here. Would that Kavi, too, had found another home for those dark years."

"Not with me," Catti-brie remarked. "I assure you my own road was no brighter." She stopped the march and tugged Niraj's hand to force him to stop, too, and to look at her. "I have so much to tell you. I don't know if you'll enjoy my tale or not, but it is one I must share honestly."

"You are alive and seem well."

She smiled and nodded.

"Then no tale you tell me can wound me, my little Zubrija."

When they entered the family tent, Catti-brie had to leap across the floor to catch Kavita, who gasped and collapsed in joy at the sight of her.

Catti-brie gladly buried her face in Kavita's thick black hair, and she drank in the smell of the woman, the smell of her childhood.

"You haven't aged," Catti-brie whispered in the woman's ear.

Kavita kissed her on the cheek.

"Nayan keeps her young," Niraj said, and when Catti-brie looked back at him, he nodded his chin toward the far end of the room.

Catti-brie's gaze locked on the small bed, and her jaw drooped open.

"Nayan?" she whispered, pulling back from Kavita. She looked to her mother, who smiled and nodded then motioned for her to go and see.

Catti-brie quietly moved across the room. She saw a bit of movement first, under some blankets, and she paused, overwhelmed by the thought that she had a brother—overwhelmed and not sure how to even consider this child. Was he really her brother? Similarly, were Niraj and Kavita actually her parents? She had come back to the world fully conscious of her previous life, a life where she had been born to other parents, though she had barely known, and remembered nothing of, her father, and had known her mother not at all.

Still, where did she fit here with this Desai family? She did not even consider herself Desai! Was Kavita no more than a carrier for the will of Mielikki?

These questions had followed Catti-brie since her earliest days in this strange second life.

The blankets moved and the little boy, Nayan, rolled over into sight, his head covered in thick black hair like Kavita, his mouth and jowls wide and expressive like Niraj.

And Catti-brie had her answer, to all of it. The explosion in her heart offered no room for doubt.

This was her baby brother. And these were her parents, her mother and her father, and that it was her second life mattered not at all.

She was home. This was her family, as much as Mithral Hall had been her home and Bruenor was forever her Da.

Whether she was Desai or not mattered not at all, no more than the fact that she wasn't a dwarf—nay less, she decided, because she was human, just like this family, just like this tribe. The rest of it—skin color, hair color, homeland—was nonsense, fabricated by people who needed to pretend that they were somehow superior for such superficial reasons.

None of it mattered. This was her family, and she could only love them as such.

Nayan opened his dark eyes then. He looked right at her and his whole face smiled, his mouth all crooked and wide and with just a couple of tiny teeth showing.

Catti-brie, charmed, turned back to her parents, who stood together now, leaning on each other.

"May I?"

Kavita laughed. "I will be angry with you if you do not!"

Catti-brie scooped Nayan up in her arms, lifted him up in front of her eyes, and made giggling, nonsensical noises. She had no idea why she might be doing that, but she surely was, and as Nayan thoroughly enjoyed it and laughed aloud, she didn't stop for a long while, until her arms got tired and she brought the young mister in close on her hip.

"He's beautiful," she said, turning back to Niraj and Kavita. "He has just enough of both of you, the best features of both."

"We are just glad he got Kavita's hair," the bald-headed Niraj laughed and winked.

"Tell me you are returned to us," Kavita bade her. "The threat of Shade Enclave is no more. We are safe now, and so much happier will we be with our Ruqiah with us."

The smile disappeared from Catti-brie's face and she gave a resigned sigh. "Mother, Father . . ." she began, shaking her head. "I have so much to tell you, so much I can tell you now. I left you confused."

"Speaking of the goddess Mielikki and spouting prophecy about the return of Anauroch," said Niraj.

"You are a chosen, so you claimed," Kavita added.

"You remember."

"Remember?" Kavita echoed incredulously, and she rushed across the floor. "Every heartbeat, I remember," she said, and she seemed as if she was about to wail. "It was the day I lost my baby girl." Her voice began to crack. "It has haunted my dreams for twenty years."

"We always hoped you would come back to us," Niraj added, moving beside Kavita and taking her arm.

"Let us sit," Catti-brie bade them. "And I will tell you everything. All of it. And you must believe me, and you must understand that none of it changes the way I feel about you, the love I know here from you. That love sustains me. I need you now, both of you."

On her hip, Nayan gurgled a spit-filled response.

"And you, too!" Catti-brie said with a laugh. She jostled Nayan, and that was all it took to get him laughing yet again.

"All of it," she said more seriously to Niraj and Kavita, "the truth of the past, the truth of my arrival into your home, and the promise of the future."

She motioned to the small table and chairs in the tent and the three sat down, Catti-brie placing Nayan on a rug right beside her chair, Kavita tossing her a bunch of plains-grass dolls Niraj had made for the child, to toy with or chew on as he chose.

And so Catti-brie somberly told her parents the truth—everything, from the details of her previous life to the journey that had led her from Mithral Hall to the divine forest of Iruladoon to Kavita's womb. These two were not simple nomads; both were trained in the Art, and though Catti-brie noted the doubts expressed initially on their faces—surely they thought their daughter had lost her mind—she could see that she was clearly breaking down the barriers of denial. She watched as Kavita's hand crept nearer and nearer to Niraj's, finally clasping his hand tightly and squeezing as if to save her very sanity.

And he was no less glad of the grasp.

Catti-brie told them of her departure from the Desai, trapped and dragged to her time in Shade Enclave with Lady Avelyere and the Coven. She told them of Longsaddle and her journey to fulfill her promise to Mielikki and go to Drizzt, her drow husband—which raised a few eyebrows—on Kelvin's Cairn. She told them of the war in the west, the Silver Marches.

She told them of Gauntlgrym, of her other father who was now king, of her current quest to rebuild the Hosttower of the Arcane, and the mission that had brought her back to their side.

She finished and leaned forward, placing a hand on the knee of each. "Every word I told you was the truth. You deserve that much at least from me."

Kavita nodded, but Niraj just sat there staring blankly, trying to digest the amazing story.

For a long while, they sat in silence, other than when Nayan found something particularly amusing or tasty.

"The Netherese remain in the hills below where Shade Enclave once floated," Niraj confirmed for her, finally.

"You cannot go to them," said Kavita, shaking her head. "The war is over, but they are no friend to Desai. They will throw you in shackles and use you—"

"I go with the imprimatur of a very powerful friend, who is allied with Lord Parise Ulfbinder," Catti-brie replied. "An urgent request the Netherese lord will not ignore, and so he will not dare threaten me in any way."

"You cannot know!" Kavita retorted, but Niraj put his hand on her leg and nodded comfortingly to the rightly-worried mother.

"Perhaps our little Ruqiah has earned our trust," he said.

Kavita looked into Catti-brie's eyes. "Our little Ruqiah," she echoed in a whisper. "Can we even call you that?"

"Of course you can," said Catti-brie, grinning happily, but that smile did not charm Kavita.

"A mother wishes to pass on wisdom to her child," she said. "A mother hopes to give to her child all she will need to be happy in life. How can I call you my Ruqiah? You needed nothing from me other than nourishment in your earliest years. You needed none of my wisdom or experience. It seems that your life—*both* your lives—were more filled with experience than my own."

Catti-brie shook her head through every word.

"I wish you were my Ruqiah," Kavita finished. She lowered her head and Niraj grabbed her close.

"You are wrong," Catti-brie flatly declared. "I thought the same thing, even when I was leaving you. I was grateful—how could I not be?—but I, too, saw this life here with you as a stopover, and feared in my own heart that you, that you both, were no more than innkeepers along the road of my journey."

She could see from Niraj's shocked expression and from Kavita's bobbing shoulders that her honesty stung them, but she pressed on.

"But now I know I was wrong," she said. "I knew it from the moment I returned to this land on a separate matter, not so long ago, and now again that I have come back. I knew it without doubt when I looked upon Niraj, my father, and upon you, my mother, and upon my baby brother."

Kavita looked up and stared into her eyes.

"There was little you could teach me about being an adult, true," Catti-brie went on, and she gave a little laugh. "Even then as your infant, I was older than you by two decades! But being a parent, being a family, is much more than simple education. What you gave to me was your love. Even when I put you in danger, were your thoughts anywhere but upon my safety?"

The two Desai looked at each other, then back to Catti-brie.

"I carried that with me, that knowledge that somewhere out there were two people who would forgive me, no matter my actions, who would love me, who would do anything for me. That was my crutch and my armor. Those feelings, so deep and so true, helped me more than you can imagine on those dark and difficult stretches of my journey.

"And now my joy at the victories my friends and I have achieved is tenfold because I have shared it with you. And now my quest, as difficult as anything I have ever tried to do in my life—in both of my lives!—is easier. Because I know that even if I fail, you will be here for me, loving me. Not judging, but helping. I cannot tell you how important that is to me. My steps are so much lighter . . . I go to Shade Enclave unafraid.

I return to the Hosttower's ruins confident. I am not afraid of failure because I know you are here."

The tears flowed freely, from all three, and the hugs lasted a long, long while.

Then it was Kavita and Niraj's turn to tell Catti-brie about the war on the plains of Netheril, of how they fought side by side, adding their sorcery to the sheer grit and muscle of the proud and fierce Desai.

Catti-brie was horrified to learn that the two had battled the same Lady Avelyere in a contest of fireballs and lightning bolts. Avelyere was much more accomplished in the ways of the Weave, Catti-brie was certain, but Avelyere's principal studies were on the arts of deception and clever diplomacy.

The auburn-haired woman found herself breathing an audible sigh of relief to learn that Avelyere, too, had left that field very much alive—and Catti-brie hoped that was still true.

Her reaction caught her parents off guard.

"She was kind to me," Catti-brie explained. "And she did not kill you when I fled her coven, though under Netherese law, she could have. Perhaps there is some good in our enemies—in some at least."

"I don't know if she lives or if she perished in the war," Niraj said.

"That battle was early on, in the first attack by the Netherese," said Kavita. "Long before Shade Enclave fell from the sky."

"I hope she is alive and well," Catti-brie admitted. "And I hope that my hope is not troubling to you."

"The war is over," said Kavita. "Neither side is unburned in a simmering pot."

The sheer generosity of that remark had Catti-brie smiling yet again.

"So be it, but I fear you going there," said Niraj.

Catti-brie nodded, understanding his sincere concern. "I am a capable priestess and sorcerer," she said with a wry grin. "And I've been trained to fight by the most capable warriors in the land. You should witness the spectacle of my drow husband wielding his twin scimitars!

"But I'll need none of that. I come with a message from—"

"Yes, yes," Niraj interrupted.

"A drow husband . . ." Kavita whispered, and shook her head.

"He is as fine a man as I have ever . . ." Catti-brie started, but Kavita stopped her with an upraised hand.

"If he makes you happy, then he makes me happy," she said. "But it is beyond my understanding!"

"You will meet him and your understanding will change," Catti-brie assured her. "And your expectations, too, I expect."

"This does not change the fears I hold for you going back to the Netherese," Niraj said.

"Find the finest warrior in the tribe and send him to me, and I will leave him sprawling in the mud," Catti-brie replied.

Kavita laughed and said, "I have seen that before, my Ruqiah!"

"Yes, yes, you already explained. We could not stop you from going on your journey when you were but a child, so we know that we cannot stop you from your chosen course now. Please come back to us when you are done with the Netherese, and before you travel to the west, that we know you are safe."

"I promise."

◆ ◆ ◆

GIANT BROKEN STONES and crumbled castle walls formed a natural maze in the foothills of a small mountain cluster on the Netheril Plain, the detritus of the fallen city. Shade Enclave had towered over the plain from on high, a testament to magical power and architectural grandiosity.

And now it was a ruin, fallen from the sky, shattered, its broken bones scattered all around the foothills.

Catti-brie rode into the pile of mountains, stone, and masonry on Andahar. She had thought to summon a simple and more typical spectral horse, that she would not broadcast her allegiance to a goddess the Netherese would not favor, after all, but in the end, she had settled again on Andahar. She came as a representative of Jarlaxle and Bregan D'aerthe. She need not fear.

What seemed chaos showed more order than she had anticipated as she approached the piles of rubble. Among those broken stones, the Netherese had fashioned walkways, chambers, and parapets, and, finally, a very heavy iron door.

Faced by a line of grim-faced guards glaring down at her, all armed with long spears and crossbows, Catti-brie dismounted and dismissed her summoned unicorn.

"Your name?" one of the guards demanded.

"I am Catti-brie of Icewind Dale," she said, and she wished that she had considered her identity more carefully before saying that. Would that name mean anything to the people of this new Shade Enclave? Would Parise Ulfbinder know it? Jarlaxle had hinted to her that the Netherese lord wasn't completely ignorant of the goings-on that had brought her here, or even of the godly intervention that had brought her back to Faerûn from the afterlife.

"I beg entrance," she said.

"On what grounds?"

"I once lived here," she replied, and she turned her face skyward. "Up there. I had friends—"

"That was a long time ago."

"Not so long."

"I was there," said the guard.

"We all were," said another. "I know not your face or your name."

Catti-brie held up her hands. She wasn't sure how far she could go. When she had run out on the Coven, Lady Avelyere's school of magic, she had faked her own death. She had no way of knowing how far that news had spread, and no way of knowing if others of Avelyere's students had left Shade Enclave.

She simply didn't have enough reference points to properly bluff, so she decided upon the barest truth.

"I trained with Lady Avelyere," she said. "Circumstance removed me from Shade Enclave, and only upon returning to the plain was I aware that the floating city was no more."

"Avelyere?" the first guard asked, and before Catti-brie even nodded he turned to the woman standing beside him and whispered something she could not hear, That woman ran off.

Catti-brie held her breath. She wasn't very good at this game. Had she erred in the admission? Was Avelyere alive, perhaps? Or another of the Coven who could identify her?

She started to speak again, but was silenced immediately by the guard, and when she moved to argue, he pointed at her threateningly.

She fell quiet and stood there for a long, long while—so long that she moved to some shade and sat down upon a flat stone. Finally she noted a commotion up above, with several of the guards moving back out of sight and returning to stare down at her once more. The war was over, so said Niraj and Kavita, but there was nothing welcoming about this place.

Strangely, the approach to this city among the ruins made her think of Citadel Adbar. She kept that in mind, and reminded herself that the dwarves of that citadel were not an unreasonable lot, even though they were no more welcoming than this group. She thought of Mirabar, too, with its imposing wall and grim-faced guards. She couldn't really blame the Netherese, surrounded by enemies, surrounded by tribes that held long and justified grievances for decades of oppression.

The great door creaked as it swung open and a host of soldiers rode out astride large, black-furred mounts with curving ram horns. Darkness seemed to follow their every stride, for they exuded the stuff of shadow. Unsure what to make of the greeting, Catti-brie quietly prepared a spell as they neared. With a word, she would exact a blinding holy light to steal the shadows, and before her foes recovered, she hoped, the large raven would fly away.

The riders, five in all, flanked her to either side, with one stopping right in front of her.

"Lady Avelyere, you said," prompted the apparent leader of the group. She was a thick and clearly strong woman, wearing black plate armor, and with a huge sword strapped to the side of her heavy saddle.

Catti-brie nodded.

"And your name was Catti-brie, so you said."

"Yes."

"Stay close and run. We will move quickly."

"I can summon a mount . . ." Catti-brie tried to say, but she was moving, having no choice in the matter, as the riders closed in around her and trotted off for the town.

The great gates were closing even as Catti-brie crossed into the settlement, and it felt to her as if they had closed the very sunlight, as well. The place had the smell and taste and images of the Plane of Shadows, a gray and muted place indeed.

The architecture was undeniably beautiful, though. The Netherese had carved out a functioning enclave within the rubble of a mountain and city that had fallen from the sky and shattered. In the chaos of the debris, they had found some measure of order, with Houses carved into great rock walls, a marketplace created from a boulder tumble, and neat roads of black stone cutting smartly through it all.

The pace of the escort remained furious, with common folk dodging aside all the way through the town. They rushed down to a small valley between two rocky mountain spurs. Within the arms of the mountain, a circle of boulders had fallen, or more likely, given the exact spacing of the ten great stones, had been placed. Each was hollowed in some form or another, and with black metal stairwells, railings and balconies set about—it seemed to Catti-brie like some squat version of the drow stalagmite mounds of Menzoberranzan.

The riders dismounted around her, and the commander took Catti-brie by the arm and roughly tugged her along. They went between the nearest two stones, revealing to Catti-brie, in the middle of the circle, a small square structure, open on one side and with a descending stairway.

"She is already announced," came a voice from those stairs and a woman climbed into view. She was young, younger than Catti-brie even, and dressed in a loose blouse and gray pants, a uniform Catti-brie knew well.

"You may go back to your duties," the young sorceress told the guard.

"She is a known threat," the soldier protested, and that caught Catti-brie by surprise for both claims—that she was "known" and a "threat."

"Lady Avelyere is touched by your concern," the young student of the Coven, clearly coached, replied. "She is also disappointed in your lack of faith in her ability to control this situation."

The female guard leader held up her hand in acquiescence and turned around, waving for her minions to go off with her.

On the stairs, the young woman motioned for Catti-brie to join her.

They descended several levels, through a maze of corridors and rooms all splendidly decorated and meticulously cleaned. This was Avelyere's home, Catti-brie realized, and like the Coven in the floating Shade Enclave, the lady kept true to appearances.

They came to a door hung with curtains. Catti-brie saw Lady Avelyere through the glass, and a mix of emotions swirled. Avelyere had been Catti-brie's captor, though she had been allowed many privileges. But Avelyere had been as a mentor to her as well, and sometimes a caring one at that. There were occasions where Avelyere, under the terms of the capture, could have punished Catti-brie—indeed, Lady Avelyere could have simply executed Catti-brie at any time, and no one who cared would have ever known.

Inside the room, the lady motioned, and Catti-brie's escort opened the door and stepped aside, then closed the door behind her, leaving Catti-brie alone in the room with the middle-aged woman.

"Ah, Catti-brie," Lady Avelyere greeted. She motioned to a chair set across a small table from where she was a seated, and where a glass of white wine was set. "Or should I call you Ruqiah?"

Catti-brie took a deep breath to compose herself, and to remind herself that she was not the little-skilled child who had been in Lady Avelyere's care. She was Chosen of Mielikki, and a powerful wizard trained by the Harpells. She had faced down Archmage Gromph Baenre, who could likely reduce this woman sitting in front of her to ashes with a snap of his dark fingers.

"I prefer Catti-brie," she replied.

"Even then, no doubt, when you lied to me under my own roof."

"When I was a prisoner, you mean, stolen from my family."

Avelyere started to respond, but just tipped her wine glass.

"I did not kill the body I put in the House to disguise my escape," Catti-brie told her—for some reason she didn't yet understand, she wanted Lady Avelyere to know that truth.

"I know."

"What else do you know?" Catti-brie asked. She picked up the wine and started to bring it to her lips, then paused and looked at it suspiciously.

Then she looked at Avelyere and nodded, and took a sip.

"You fear it poisoned?"

"Lady Avelyere is far too clever and charming for such things. Besides, why would you be angry with me?"

"You left without my permission, and in complete deception."

"And I return without your permission, and indeed, not even to see you. I came to speak with Lord Parise Ulfbinder, as I was bidden by a mutual friend. I accommodate you by visiting now, but if you wish, I will be on my way to Lord Parise."

"And if I tried to stop you?"

"I would burn your house down."

Lady Avelyere stared at her hard and long. "You believe you can do exactly that, don't you?"

"I believe my road has been difficult enough without your judgment."

Lady Avelyere continued to stare for only a short while, then smiled and held up her hands. "I am glad that you accepted my invitation, Ruqi—Catti-brie," she said.

"Then I am, too," Catti-brie replied. "There are too many questions along too many hallways. But I know in my heart that I bear you no ill will. Believe it or not, good Lady Avelyere, but I am truly glad that you are alive, that you survived the catastrophe that befell Shade Enclave."

"I believe you, Ruqiah," the older woman, who was not really older, replied. "And forgive me, but that name still brings joy to me. We watched you, you know."

"When I was here?" a confused Catti-brie asked.

"When you left. We found you in Longsaddle, or rather, when you were leaving Longsaddle. I watched you climb the lone mountain in Icewind Dale, and reunite with Drizzt Do'Urden. Our lives became complicated, and war came to our door, but still I found time to look in on you from afar during your struggles in the Silver Marches."

"We saw your victory over the drow and the orcs," said another voice, a man's voice. A well-groomed, smartly-dressed man with a beautifully-kempt gray beard and piercing eyes entered the room.

"This is the man you came to speak with," Lady Avelyere explained.

"Through a scrying mirror, we watched the light emanate from Drizzt Do'Urden, destroying the roiling blackness the drow had placed over the Silver Marches," Lord Parise Ulfbinder explained. "We witnessed the victory of Mielikki over Lolth, and it was a grand display indeed."

"Should I feel violated?" Catti-brie asked as she rose and offered the lord her hand. He took it gently and kissed it.

"Lovely lady, we watched only from afar. How could we not, knowing that two goddesses were waging a proxy war through you?"

Catti-brie stepped back and took her seat, lifting the wine for another sip as she tried to figure out what was going on here.

"Did you witness my fight with the woman named Dahlia?" she asked at length.

The two looked at each other, then back at her, and she knew they had not.

"That, I expect, was the truest battle, waged between myself and the troubled elf named Dahlia, with me serving as proxy for Mielikki,

163

and Dahlia championing Lolth, though I doubt the poor woman even understood her role."

"Will you tell us?" Lord Parise asked, his eagerness not hard to discern.

"An entertaining tale," Catti-brie promised. "Unless, of course, Lady Avelyere has poisoned my wine here and I will fall dead before I can complete it."

"Oh, do not be foolish," Avelyere protested with a sarcastic sigh.

She looked Avelyere right in the eye and remarked, "You never brought pain to my parents."

"There was a war," Parise said from the side, where he gathered up a chair and a glass of wine for himself. At the table, Lady Avelyere didn't let go of Catti-brie's stare.

"I do not take pleasure in inflicting pain," Avelyere replied.

"I know, and that is why I was indeed very glad to learn that you had survived the troubles that happened here, in this fallen city, and in the war. I am not your enemy, nor have I ever been."

"And I did not poison the wine."

With that, Catti-brie lifted her glass in toast, and Lady Avelyere tapped it with her own.

"It is so good to be among people who understand that life is more complex than darkness and light," Lord Parise remarked.

In both her lives combined, few words had Catti-brie ever heard that brought a truer sense of comfort. Lord Parise had spoken a simple truth, and a sad one.

Would that more people understood.

Again Catti-brie told her tale of the fight in Gauntlgrym, and the return to Gauntlgrym, where Bruenor was now king. She used that last battle to segue into the issues at hand, the rebuilding of the Hosttower of the Arcane, and at that point, she handed the Jarlaxle's missive to Lord Parise.

"Wonderful," he remarked repeatedly as he read the parchment, and when he finished and handed it to Lady Avelyere, he added, "What an amazing opportunity!"

"You will join our efforts, then?"

"I would be forever angry if you did not allow me to do so!" Lord Parise said. He glanced at Avelyere. "Perhaps in this, Ruqiah can be the teacher."

"The invitation is for you," Avelyere replied.

"It is a request, not an invitation," said Catti-brie. "I do not know the level of magic that will be needed on every piece of the Hosttower as we reconstruct it, but we are not afforded the luxury of turning away powerful spellcasters." She paused and reached across the table to squeeze Avelyere's hand. "Particularly if they are trustworthy."

"I would like to join in this quest, then," Avelyere said. "And I have a few students who might prove useful."

"This could take years," Lord Parise warned.

"Perhaps decades," said Catti-brie. "The work on the Hosttower might continue long after we are all dead."

"Still, it is the journey of life that matters, and not the goal," said Lord Parise. "And this journey will prove exhilarating, I expect. To converse with the Archmage of Menzoberranzan! And dragons! Jarlaxle's missive speaks of dragons!"

"Tazmikella and Ilnezhara," Catti-brie explained. "Copper dragons, and sisters, and both very powerful in the ways of the Art. A very unusual duo."

"Splendid!" Lord Parise said, and clapped his hands together. "What wondrous things we might learn."

Lady Avelyere nodded, but then put on a curious expression as she regarded Catti-brie. "What of your Desai parents?"

Catti-brie wasn't sure how to take that.

"You do not know? They are capable wizards, both."

"There are many capable wizards," Catti-brie replied. "They have a child, a young child."

"You do not wish them in the midst of a city controlled by the drow," Lord Parise suggested.

"Reconsider, then," said Lady Avelyere. "The practices of the Desai spellcasters, who spent decades hiding their talents, are a bit different from those I taught at the Coven, as, I'm sure you discovered, mine are different from those of the Harpells of Longsaddle, and those are different from those of this Archmage Gromph."

"To truly recognize the old and lost magic that originally built the Hosttower, we may have to look at it from many different perspectives, and so from people skilled in the Art who have trained and honed their skills differently," Lord Parise added. "This is why Jarlaxle has brought in Archmage Gromph and the dragons, and why he sent you to fetch me. Do not discount the potential contributions of the tribal casters, who employ different vocalizations and movements, even different spell components, in enacting their magical spells than wizards of other areas and schools."

"I will consider it," she replied, in a tone that ended that line of discussion. "Time is short."

"And Jarlaxle is waiting," said Lord Parise.

"No," Catti-brie said, and the other two looked at her curiously. "Jarlaxle is away on a most important mission."

"Another tale!" Lord Parise said happily. He finished his glass and turned back to the bottle.

But that, too, Catti-brie denied. "We must be on the road, immediately."

"I will find someone to teleport us."

"There is a place I must go first," Catti-brie said. "A place not far."

They left the Netherese enclave soon after, Catti-brie astride Andahar, and her companions upon magically summoned mounts. They rode hard to the south and soon came in sight of the Desai tents.

"Better that we wait here," Lord Parise said, tipping his chin to Lady Avelyere.

"The war is over," Catti-brie reminded him.

"I know that, but do they?"

Catti-brie started to reply, but held back as she considered the tribe beyond the tent of Niraj and Kavita. The Desai were ferocious warriors, many of whom had no doubt suffered great losses at the hands of the Netherese. She could not argue with confidence that her companions would be safe among those tents.

She rode in alone to the Desai encampment to bid farewell to her second family, while Lord Parise, Lady Avelyere, and a few others of Avelyere's Coven, who had caught up with them, waited for her on the Netheril plain.

When the troupe turned to the west, for Luskan, Niraj and Kavita were not among their ranks.

CHAPTER 10 ◈

Confusion

NYONE WATCHING FROM THE SIDE WOULD HAVE THOUGHT THEM a single being, a marilith, perhaps, with six arms, all holding deadly weapons of extraordinary craftsmanship and imbued with powerful magic. Even those who knew these three warriors well—Drizzt, Entreri, and Jarlaxle—would have simply sat back and gasped.

Their coordination was marvelous. Their intertwining dance—rolling over each other's thrusts, following a sweeping blade to cross to the other side of their battle line, ducking beneath the sidelong swipe of an ally's weapon, even leaping at the last possible instant as a long sword or scimitar cut beneath—mesmerizing in its perfection and timing.

The demons in front of them, including balgura and manes, melted away, cut a dozen times, stabbed in the eye, the heart, the groin, and the line of three warriors steadily advanced, stepping over the smoking, dissipating husks of the fallen.

When the corridor widened, so, too, did their line. Whichever two were on the ends moved out wide, which only made the rolling dance a more athletic endeavor. Simple turns became dramatic leaps, and simple steps become quick jaunts. Having more enemies clustering in front of them only gave them more things to hit. The demons couldn't keep up with the trio, and never seemed close to getting a weapon or a clawed hand anywhere near an intended target.

The power . . . Jarlaxle heard in his head, and it seemed more an expression of ecstasy than anything else.

The mercenary concentrated on the fight at hand, stabbing Khazid'hea forward, then twisting to parry the swing of a balgura's heavy hammer.

In the simple parry, meant to deflect and not to block, the demon's weapon fell apart, the shaft sliced cleanly and even the heavy stone head falling to the stone floor in two pieces, cut diagonally. Jarlaxle, intent on finishing the brute, which he did with a second thrust, only barely registered the destroyed hammer, but that image stayed with him as he moved forward.

He knew Khazid'hea, Cutter, was a powerful blade—a sword of sharpness—but the thought that such a simple twist could cut a heavy warhammer so easily and cleanly seemed purely ridiculous!

The power . . . he heard again in his head, and this time he knew it was the blade telepathically communicating.

Jarlaxle dismissed the noise in his thoughts and focused more fully on the battle at hand, reminding himself that working with such allies as Drizzt and Entreri could get one as readily killed by a friendly sword as an enemy blade if one was imperfect in the dance.

But that was exactly what seemed to be happening around him.

Drizzt leaped forward and fell into line, right beside a balgura. The demon hesitated only for the blink of an eye before biting at the drow dinner that had just served itself.

Jarlaxle's fine sword intervened, cutting the balgura in the side of its face. But then Drizzt's blade parried Jarlaxle's, and a riposte sent Jarlaxle sliding backward.

"Foul tricksters!" Drizzt yelled. "Be warned, we are deceived!"

Entreri leaped past Jarlaxle then, going at Drizzt—clearly to kill the drow rather than support him!

Jarlaxle didn't know what to do, so he reacted with the wand that had served him so well all these years. He hit the pair with a summoned gob of goo.

"You are both deceived!" he shouted as they tumbled away, and Jarlaxle filled the void immediately to stab hard at the balgura, forcing it back. To the side, Drizzt and Entreri were already both extricating themselves from the goo. Jarlaxle had only scored a glancing hit.

Jarlaxle threw down the feather from his magical hat, bringing forth the giant diatryma bird, and bade it drive back the balgura and the few remaining minor demons behind it. From a ring, he launched a blade barrier, a whirlwind of summoned swords, into the back of the demon pack, chewing at them and slicing them apart. From a necklace, he detached a small ruby and threw it to the far side of the enemy forces, melting a bunch of manes with a fireball.

Jarlaxle hated wasting his precious contingency spells and items—he could not summon the diatryma for another day, could not use the spell from his ring until he managed to get it recharged by a powerful priest, and it would take him many coins to replace the ruby on his necklace of fireballs. But there were other concerns.

He looked to his companions, shouting at them to stop. They were nearly free then, and already trying to swing at each other.

"By the gods, you idiots," Jarlaxle screamed, "the fight is ended!"

The volume of his scream and the atypical behavior from Jarlaxle finally seemed to get through to them. Drizzt tore free of the remaining goo and stumbled backward, scimitars still in hand as he eyed Entreri suspiciously.

"Show your true form, d-demon," Entreri ordered, but he stuttered at the end and blinked repeatedly, then stood up straight and glanced at Jarlaxle, clearly confused.

"It would seem that our demon enemies have some tricks of their own to play," said Drizzt, who also sheathed his weapons then.

But Jarlaxle was only half-listening, if that.

Do you feel it? Khazid'hea asked in his head. *The magic of life, the music of chaos . . .*

Jarlaxle wasn't sure what to make of it, but then it occurred to him that this part of their journey had taken them very near the Faerzress. Khazid'hea was a drow blade, and so the magic of that mystical radiation had been instrumental in giving the sword sentience and its magically enhanced keen edge.

You have been here before, many times, Jarlaxle reminded the blade. He was confident that the sword had traversed these tunnels in the past. *Yet I sense your surprise.*

Never like this, he felt from his excited sword.

Jarlaxle wasn't sure what to make of it, but he slid the sword away for safekeeping and focused again on his companions. Both were shaken and scrutinized each other as if they both expected a demon to take shape from within the other's drow form.

"The mask," Drizzt said, confirming Jarlaxle's fears. "How do we know it is truly Artemis Entreri beneath Agatha's Mask?"

"Because I gave it to him and watched him put it on," Jarlaxle replied in a deadpan, incredulous tone.

"A major demon would be clever enough to continue Entreri's exact ruse if it got its claws on that magic mask," reasoned Drizzt.

Entreri pulled off the mask and reverted to his normal form immediately. "And a major demon would be clever enough to deflect attention in such a manner as you just did," he said, aiming the remark at Drizzt, who seemed very much his adversary at that point.

"I have magical truesight," Jarlaxle interrupted and when both turned to regard him, he tapped his heavily enchanted eye patch. "Though Agatha's Mask could fool me. Its magic is ancient and powerful, no polymorph enchantment a demon might wage would deceive me. Even one cast by a major demon."

"And a demon lord?" asked Drizzt, who seemed unable to let this go.

"Aye," the equally suspicious Entreri echoed.

Jarlaxle stared at Drizzt and held up his arms as if in surrender. "It is Artemis Entreri," he said to the ranger. He turned to the assassin. "Put the mask back on, and leave it on. And it is Drizzt Do'Urden before you and no demon imposter. What foolishness has possessed you? Both of you?"

"We are dealing with powerful denizens of the lower planes," Entreri said, and he became a drow once more. "What you call foolishness, I deem caution."

"And if you had killed each other? What then?"

"Then it would all be, perhaps, as it was ever supposed to be," Entreri said with deadly seriousness. He looked at Drizzt as he issued the threat.

"If the last thing I do before I cease to draw breath in this life is to end the life of Artemis Entreri, then I know I will leave this world a better place than I found it," Drizzt returned.

Jarlaxle kept his hands out to the side, too flustered to even realize his arms were out there. This seemed to him a throwback to days long past—hadn't Drizzt and Entreri gone far beyond this foolishness? They had traveled together for many years, indeed had done incredible things together, in Port Llast, particularly.

Now, for no reason Jarlaxle could discern, they were ready, eager even, to kill each other.

"Demogorgon," Jarlaxle whispered under his breath. Wasn't one of the greatest weapons of the Prince of Demons his ability to drive men mad? That unsettling thought nagged at Jarlaxle and had him looking over his shoulder more than once, as if expecting the gargantuan Demogorgon to come crashing through the hall at any moment.

The way was clear—both ways now that the remaining pack of demons had been properly dispatched. To the side, the great flightless bird pecked at the smoking corpse of the balgura.

Jarlaxle wearily rubbed his face and considered the warnings Faelas had given him regarding Menzoberranzan. None of this was going as he had expected. Every step seemed to bring new challenges—would he even be able to take his rest this day with the possibility that he would awaken to the sounds of Drizzt and Entreri engaged in mortal combat?

"I know not what has brought to you both these . . . suspicions," he said. "Is there so little trust to be had between we three?"

Drizzt and Entreri scowled at each other.

"Then we should turn back for Gauntlgrym," said Jarlaxle.

"Aye, and be rid of this one," Entreri said with a nod at Drizzt. "We shouldn't have brought him in the first place."

Jarlaxle sighed and held his thoughts silent. If Drizzt had not agreed to come along, he wouldn't have made this journey. He didn't care enough about the elf Dahlia to risk so much. And though he, or at least Bregan D'aerthe, was indebted to Artemis Entreri for his loss of another lover, another woman, a half-elf named Calihye, Jarlaxle had no intention of risking his life repaying that debt.

What Jarlaxle couldn't tell Entreri was that this journey really wasn't about Dahlia. He meant to rescue her, and hoped Kimmuriel would find some way to unwind the writhing snakes in her mind. That would aid Jarlaxle in his greater aims, and indeed, had served him as a catalyst for convincing Drizzt to come in the first place. But Dahlia's fate was not paramount.

Jarlaxle was bringing Drizzt to Menzoberranzan to exploit a growing rift among his people, a rising scream of protest from the males of Menzoberranzan that they would not forever be held as vassals to the matriarchs. For more than a century, Jarlaxle and so many others had looked to Drizzt as the one who found freedom, the one who denied the ways of Lolth and escaped, and indeed thrived. Even Gromph couldn't help but nod approvingly—if secretly—when he thought of Drizzt Do'Urden. That was why Gromph had chosen to clandestinely use Drizzt's body as the conduit for his great dispelling magic to boil away the Darkening that Tsabrak Xorlarrin, acting on the will of Lolth, had created above the Silver Marches.

Drizzt was Jarlaxle's chance to exploit the rift in Menzoberranzan, and Matron Mother Zeerith Xorlarrin's chance to regain her stature in the city.

The arrival of Drizzt—to pull Dahlia from the ridiculous reincarnation of House Do'Urden, to poke his finger in the eye of Matron Mother Quenthel Baenre, to send great waves through the city—was

Jarlaxle's countering wave against the rising tide of zealotry growing in Menzoberranzan. Unyielding fealty to the strictest edicts of Lady Lolth would push all the males of Menzoberranzan far back down the ladder of ascension, and would indeed threaten even Bregan D'aerthe. Jarlaxle had worked too hard and too long to let that happen.

But ah, what now? he wondered, looking at his companions. Their mission suddenly seemed ill-fated. He had gone into it unsure, and indeed with some of his advisers and even Gromph warning him that there was too little certainty and too much to lose. And now, in the few days since they had marched from Luskan's Undercity, they had learned that their destination had been virtually shut down, even to magical intrusions. They had found corridors full of demons, and now this, some strangeness that had infected his companions in a most dangerous way.

"We will return Drizzt to King Bruenor's court, and then we will return to, and remain in, Luskan," Jarlaxle said.

Entreri's face contorted with a clear undercurrent of growing rage. "You promised me this," he said in a quiet and deadly voice. "You owe me this."

"We cannot do this without Drizzt," Jarlaxle said, and convincingly despite the secretive other half of the equation,. He, Drizzt, and Entreri were gaining something special here, and they all knew it. Their work together in fending off the demon hordes was no minor matter—he and Entreri simply couldn't replace Drizzt with someone else and go their merry way.

"I give not a damn about Drizzt," Entreri growled back at him.

"Then you give not a damn about Dahlia," Jarlaxle said. "Without him, we cannot get near to her."

"I don't believe you."

"Then we return the way we came."

"No!"

The two stared at each other, Entreri hatefully, Jarlaxle curiously.

"We go on," said Drizzt, and both turned to him. He looked Jarlaxle in the eye. "Or I do, alone. Dahlia is down there. She was my companion, my friend. I cannot abandon her in her time of desperation."

"Will you take a second wife, then?" Entreri asked.

"She would be better off as my slave than as consort to the demon masked in the body of Artemis Entreri," Drizzt snapped back, and both drew their blades once more.

"One strike!" Jarlaxle warned, stepping between them. "One blade against blade, one wound from either of you upon the other, even in the midst of battle, even by accident, and our quest is ended." He looked to each, staring sternly until the blades went down then went away.

"When Dahlia is returned to the World Above, I give you leave to murder each other, if that is your choice."

◆ ◆ ◆

SHE HEARD THE whistle, a strange sound indeed, that reverberated like the beacon of a lighthouse in K'yorl's mind, and so, too, in Yvonnel's.

What was this sensation?

And then Yvonnel's heart leaped. They had done it! K'yorl had sent her thoughts out from the stoup and across the planes to contact Kimmuriel. And there, in the hive-mind of the illithids, she had found her son.

That elation turned to doubt, though, when Kimmuriel recoiled in anger.

Kimmuriel chastised his mother for causing him to deliver to Gromph Baenre the fabric of the spell the deceived archmage had used to bring Demogorgon to the Underdark, and in doing so, thinning the boundary of the Faerzress itself.

Yvonnel couldn't sort it out for a long while, but as K'yorl responded to Kimmuriel, it became clear: Lolth had done this. In the Abyss, in a balor's lair, the Spider Queen in K'yorl's form had used Kimmuriel to deceive Gromph. And now Kimmuriel was in hiding from the dangerous Gromph. Yvonnel could feel Kimmuriel's hatred and could sense his desire for vengeance against his mother. And even K'yorl's doubts and confusion would have no sway here in convincing Kimmuriel that she had not done this to him.

Yvonnel felt the battered woman's deep regret. The former Matron Mother of House Oblodra desperately wanted to set things straight with her son—not out of any love for Kimmuriel, of course, but simply out of worry over her own legacy. What a curse her name would become, perhaps even centuries after her demise, when all the drow believed it was she who broke the boundary of the Faerzress and loosed the demon lords upon the Underdark. And there was nothing K'yorl could do about it.

Kimmuriel shut them out then, so suddenly and forcefully that Yvonnel was thrust from the melding, and her eyes blinked open back in the

Room of Divination. She suppressed her panic, and her instinct to slap K'yorl, too, out of her trance. Instead she focused on the image in the scrying bowl, nodding as she realized that K'yorl was no longer in the hive-mind, that her consciousness was flying fast along the corridors of the Underdark—backtracking the call of the whistle, perhaps.

The image flickered and formed, then went away again, repeating the process several times.

And the last image caught Yvonnel's attention and took her breath away.

But the stoup waters cleared, and K'yorl groaned and opened her eyes, the connection broken.

"Where are they?" Yvonnel Baenre demanded, the bared power of her voice forcing K'yorl from her thoughts and into the present. K'yorl stared at her adversary, and even sneered.

"Where are they?" Yvonnel repeated. "Tell me or I will fetch the illithid Methil and bid him wrest the information from your thoughts. In that event, he will leave some foul presents behind, I promise."

K'yorl tried to maintain her glare, but Yvonnel's expression made it clear that she was not bluffing. The illithid Methil El Viddenvelp would implant deep suggestions, even memories, to terrorize K'yorl, leaving her helpless to distinguish reality from nightmare.

"Kimmuriel is not certain . . ."

"Of their exact location," Yvonnel finished for her. "Where are they? And who are they? Jarlaxle, I know, but the others . . ."

"Drizzt Do'Urden," K'yorl blurted and Yvonnel's breath left her once more.

"Where?" she demanded with what little voice she could muster.

"You ask . . ."

"Last opportunity," Yvonnel said with a low and threatening growl.

K'yorl stuttered no more. "Jarlaxle and his companions are in the Underdark, a few days out from Menzoberranzan."

Yvonnel pulled her hand from the magical stoup, but commanded the enchanted Baenre tool to hold K'yorl in place. Glowering all the way, the young and dangerous Baenre walked up to stare K'yorl in the face, her eyes barely an inch away.

"You do not need to make me your enemy," she said with surprising tenderness. "I understand that you hate me—no, more than that, I understand that you hate House Baenre above all others. That is well and good and likely deserved. And I do not care."

She paused and cupped K'yorl's chin in her hand. "Why are they coming?"

K'yorl's responding expression was one of pure incredulity. "For House Do'Urden," Yvonnel said. "To rescue the elf called Dahlia."

K'yorl managed a small nod of affirmation.

"This is marvelous, do you not see?" Yvonnel asked, and she spun away, laughing. She stopped quickly and spun back on K'yorl. "Jarlaxle is hiding Gromph from Matron Mother Quenthel?"

K'yorl nodded, her expression showing her belief she was surely doomed now.

"Bold!" said Yvonnel. "And brave—Jarlaxle comes personally to see to this. Marvelous!"

K'yorl stared at her incredulously, having no way to sort out the glee, unexpected for such a dangerous situation.

"And we have a better way to spy!" Yvonnel said.

K'yorl's jaw drooped open and she shook her head, clearly at a loss.

Yvonnel understood that dumbfounded look. To K'yorl Odran, this Yvonnel Baenre standing in front of her was a reflection of, perhaps a reincarnation of, or indeed perhaps even one and the same with, the Yvonnel Baenre she had known before.

She did not understand that this mere child before her was so much more.

"Splendid!" Yvonnel cried out, rushing back around the stoup and sinking her hands once more into the rim, to again contact the hands of K'yorl Odran.

"Go, now," Yvonnel instructed, and when K'yorl did not immediately respond, she added, "To Jarlaxle! At once!"

She paused a moment, then reconsidered. "No, to Kimmuriel," she instructed. "To him, but do not contact him."

"The illithids . . ." K'yorl meekly protested.

"Go!"

In moments, they were across the planes once more, though as soon as they neared the spot where Kimmuriel stood, his delicate hands massaging the brain of the great hive-mind, Yvonnel telepathically instructed K'yorl away. *Follow the path again to Jarlaxle.*

Perhaps they could have gotten out there straightaway from the Room of Divination, but Yvonnel had wanted something else, ever so briefly. She had felt the power surrounding Kimmuriel on their initial pass, emanating at the edges of her consciousness. The hive-mind.

Glorious power!

Oh, but she would experience that someday, she promised herself as her thoughts and K'yorl's wound back to Toril, and back to along the winding corridors of the Underdark. In a heartbeat, though Yvonnel was not even aware of her own heartbeat at that amazing moment, she found herself looking at the mercenary leader, Jarlaxle.

Her uncle.

The purple eyes of one of his companions caught her and held her. From the memories of the Eternal, this new Yvonnel knew this was Drizzt Do'Urden, the ultimate heretic, and also, in the greatest of ironies, the beloved tool of Lolth. And they were heading, blindly, to Menzoberranzan.

Yvonnel could hardly contain her joy.

She telepathically bade K'yorl to flicker through Drizzt's thoughts, then to the third, unknown companion.

There, she got an amazing surprise, to learn that this was no drow but a human in perfect drow disguise. A human . . . weak-minded, susceptible.

Yvonnel sensed Jarlaxle's unease—the wary mercenary suspected that something was amiss.

At her bidding, K'yorl went back into the thoughts of the disguised human, and there they stayed, hidden from Jarlaxle and Drizzt, and even from the unwitting human host. As they had done with Minolin Fey in the corridor in an earlier session, they now looked out through the eyes of Artemis Entreri.

A short while later, Yvonnel emerged alone from the Room of Divination. Minolin Fey waited outside. The priestess glanced past her into the room, looking curiously at the unmoving K'yorl, who remained at the stoup, her hands melded with the stone.

"She is held, mind and body," Yvonnel explained. "You will go to her often and magically sustain her."

"Mistress?"

"It could be days, tendays even. I'll not have her die of thirst."

Minolin Fey seemed not to understand.

"If K'yorl Odran perishes, or becomes too weak to continue her task, I will return you to Errtu in the Abyss in her stead."

Minolin Fey's widening eyes told Yvonnel that she had heard that command clearly.

"And inform Matron Mother Quenthel and all the others that no one is to enter this room," Yvonnel added. "Any who disobey will face my wrath, and it will not be a pleasant thing."

"Yes, Mistress."

Yvonnel swung around and walked away to the echoes of her favorite words. She wasn't quite sure what she had done, or how. Through some combination of her own divine magic and the powers of the scrying room, she had magically held K'yorl. That alone was nothing special of course, but in this case, it had accomplished much more. K'yorl was locked in place, in body and in thought. She saw the world through the eyes of Artemis Entreri, though neither of them knew it.

And Yvonnel, too, could access that vision simply by looking into the waters of the stoup. She had magically created the perfect spy in the adventuring trio's midst: one of their own. And in the process, she had turned K'yorl Odran into what amounted to a living crystal ball.

What a fabulous day it had been! They were coming. Drizzt Do'Urden was delivering himself to her in Menzoberranzan.

◆　◆　◆

"I KNOW NOT what to make of it!" Jarlaxle said to Matron Mother Zeerith the next morning, when he had slipped away from the other two to meet the woman in an appointed place, less than a day's march from the gates of Menzoberranzan.

"Have you called to Kimmuriel?"

"Finally, he answered," Jarlaxle said, holding up the small silver whistle he kept on a chain, one Kimmuriel had psionically attuned to his thoughts so he could hear it across miles, even across the planes of existence. "I had thought him lost to me."

"He is in the hive-mind of an illithid colony," Zeerith reminded him.

"He will be of little help on our mission," Jarlaxle explained. "None, actually, until we are back in Luskan, where he will try to unravel Dahlia's insanity. He will not venture into the Underdark."

"Gromph is about," Zeerith reasoned.

"It is more than that," Jarlaxle explained, and he reflexively glanced back in the direction of his companions, who had been acting so curiously. "There is something about the thinning of the Faerzress . . . a mind sickness."

"The chaos of the Abyss seeps through?" Zeerith wondered aloud.

"The illithids are very sensitive to such things, and terrified of them, of course," Jarlaxle explained. "Kimmuriel will not come here."

"Do you still wish to follow through with your plans?" Zeerith asked, after a long pause to digest the information.

"I want to get Dahlia out of there, yes. It will wound Matron Mother Baenre, but not mortally, and will force her hand in allowing the Xorlarrin family to assume complete control over House Do'Urden."

"Or she will disband House Do'Urden all together."

"She'll not do that," Jarlaxle said with some confidence. "She has pressed the other Houses into a tight corner—even her allies have come to fear her as much as they fear their rivals. She has shown them that she considers herself far above them, above their counsel even. The matron mother's one play to assure no movement against her is to bring House Xorlarrin back, and to do so in a way that offers them, you, the same independence as every other House. Are your children up to that task?"

Zeerith gave a little noncommittal laugh. She wasn't going back to Menzoberranzan, they both had decided. Jarlaxle's play to weaken the matriarchy had Matron Mother Zeerith's fingerprints all over it. Those other matron mothers who decided to wage war to keep their power unchallenged would surely conspire to murder Matron Mother Zeerith first, if they could find her.

"You will need Kimmuriel before this is through," she said, and Jarlaxle didn't argue the point.

"I might need him simply to deal with my companions," he replied, glancing back the way he had come, to the chambers that held Drizzt and Entreri.

"Our people are running patrols in the outer corridors," Zeerith explained. "I can lead you there and give you my imprimatur. That should get you into the city, though from there, there is little I can offer."

"Who among your children know I'm coming for Dahlia?"

"None."

"Thank you," Jarlaxle said with a bow. He didn't trust Zeerith's flock, of course. There was simply too much opportunity for personal gain for any of them. In truth, Jarlaxle was shocked that he trusted Zeerith—might she not regain favor with Quenthel by double-crossing him?

It was a calculated risk. Zeerith might come to consider that Jarlaxle's odds of succeeding were so tiny and, given that, any gains she might make with him would not outweigh the possibilities for her to find favor with the Ruling Council once more.

But no, he decided, Zeerith's best play was with him. Her relationship with the men of her House was no ploy. She hadn't elevated the Xorlarrin males in any twisted plot to give her an edge on the other Houses—far from it! House Xorlarrin's climb was in spite of Zeerith's unusual feelings toward the weaker gender, and not because of them. But she had held her ground through the decades because there was honest conviction behind her decision. To Zeerith's belief, subjugating the males of Menzoberranzan meant that the drow could only achieve half of their potential.

"This journey has left me uncertain," he admitted. "Nothing is as it should be, or as I anticipated."

"Demon lords walk the Underdark. Are you surprised by the chaos?"

Jarlaxle thought of the fit of—of what? Delusion? Insanity?—that had come over Drizzt and Entreri in the earlier fight. Might that increase? He was tempted to take off his eye patch, that he might experience whatever had gripped the two, if indeed it was some outside influence, but he quickly dismissed that notion.

"Concerned, more than surprised," he replied. "Let me go to them and offer the choice. I will return to you this way momentarily, and if with them, then know we will press on. I would like to be in the city this very tenday."

"They are not to know of my involvement, on pain of their deaths," Matron Mother Zeerith reminded him.

"You don't trust me?" Jarlaxle asked, feigning dismay.

"I do not trust them," she corrected, and Jarlaxle grinned and spun away.

◆ ◆ ◆

HE WAS BACK with Entreri and Drizzt a short while later, the two settled very near to where he had left them. Entreri guarded the north corridor, a winding and climbing trail, absently spinning his jeweled dagger on its point against the tip of his extended index finger.

Drizzt sat across the way, on a ledge of rock in front of the corridor that had brought them to this crossroads.

"The way is clear, for a bit at least," Jarlaxle announced.

Entreri nodded, but Drizzt didn't lift his face, apparently distracted.

Jarlaxle didn't much like the look of that, but he pressed on. "Now I must tell you that at every turn, my expectations have been altered. You know of the unexpected challenges Faelas Xorlarrin explained, and there are more, I fear. Something—I cannot quite discern the source—but something is amiss down here in these deep tunnels. We will likely get into the city, but from there, I cannot predict our fate."

"Are you saying that we should turn back?" Entreri asked, and every word was accompanied by a profound scowl.

"I am only offering the truth."

"You promised me that we would do this. You owe this to me!"

Jarlaxle held his hand up in the air to calm the man, and was afraid that Entreri might leap at him with deadly intent. "What say you, Drizzt?" he asked.

The ranger didn't seem to hear.

"Say it!" Entreri demanded, apparently taking the silence as an admission that they should indeed turn back. For a moment, Jarlaxle expected another skirmish.

But Drizzt looked up finally and said, "We came for Dahlia. She is still in the city?"

"Of course," Entreri snapped, at the same time as Jarlaxle replied, "That is my belief."

"Then let us be done with this," said Drizzt. "We came for Dahlia, and so we shall find her and deliver her from Menzoberranzan."

Jarlaxle was glad to hear it, though he certainly had expected nothing less. But his smile wouldn't hold. Something in the way Drizzt rose, something etched on his face that Jarlaxle couldn't quite place, spoke of a profound unease. With every step Drizzt took it seemed as if he wanted to wince—not from physical pain, but from something within him that was surely less than comfortable.

Jarlaxle led the way quickly, determined to get into the city as soon as possible. He knew that Zeerith was watching, and that she was ahead of him. He found her signal scratches here and there, guiding him along his path.

Matron Mother Zeerith was doing her job, and Jarlaxle was confident that she had set up the means to get them into the city with a patrol.

But Entreri simmered on the edge of explosive outrage and Drizzt wore an expression that seemed utterly defeated, forlorn beyond anything Jarlaxle could imagine from Drizzt, or anything he had ever seen from the ranger before.

Jarlaxle only liked riddles when he knew the answer.

Chapter 11 ◈

Eclectic Allies

THEY SAT ABOUT A CIRCULAR TABLE, AGREED UPON BECAUSE NONE would therefore be at the head, but Catti-brie and everyone else in attendance understood who was driving this meeting and its agenda.

They were in Illusk, the ancient Undercity of Luskan, and down here, the drow ruled. Down here, dark elves patrolled the corridors, hand crossbows at the ready, speaking to other patrol groups with flashing fingers. Down here, Gromph Baenre was in control.

Athrogate and Ambergris flanked Catti-brie, and she looked to them now for their opinions. Unsurprisingly, both shook their heads at her solemnly and determinedly, clearly in no mood for another of Archmage Gromph's lectures.

When Catti-brie looked at the others around the table, she noted mostly hesitation and discomfort, except from Lord Parise Ulfbinder, tap-tapping his fingers together in front of him, seeming eager and smiling widely. That one was only interested in knowledge, Catti-brie reminded herself. He had about him a demeanor of distance, as if he was unaffected by the events that unfolded even right in his face. Catti-brie didn't know the Netherese lord well, of course, but from her time with him, and from what Jarlaxle had told her of him, she had already come to understand that Parise Ulfbinder was an explorer and student, more concerned with attaining knowledge than with his own power or safety.

He was not her enemy, nor was Lady Avelyere, who sat beside him.

"Pray tell us, Archmage, why you have assembled us," Lord Parise asked. "If you are interested in reviewing the information we have brought to this city, then I am sure I will need more time to unpack my belongings and catalogue my scripts."

Catti-brie stared at Gromph as Parise rambled on, noting that the drow didn't blink, and that the scowl did not diminish upon his handsome, but surely dangerous face. She wondered if Gromph would silence the Netherese lord. Was this meeting to become Gromph's attempt to dominate this entire mission?

"I brought you here that you might hear my news," Gromph said, a perturbed element clearly evident in his melodic voice. "If I wished to know what you had brought, I would have asked."

"Well, that one's in a bit of a fit, sister," said Ilnezhara.

"He's the frost of a white dragon biting his bum, I expect," Tazmikella replied.

Catti-brie's eyes went wide and she held her breath, expecting catastrophe at the not-subtle reminder of the dragon fight in the Silver Marches, where Tazmikella and Ilnezhara had killed the son of Arauthator, the great White Death, and had chased the mighty white dragon off, as well. More than a few rumors hinted that Gromph had played a role in luring Arauthator to that battlefield, and his expression twisted as confirmation to that very notion.

Beside Catti-brie, the dwarves both giggled, and Gromph's face screwed up even tighter. How dare anyone speak to the Archmage of Menzoberranzan, to the great Gromph Baenre, in such a manner!

But these were dragons, Catti-brie reminded herself. As mighty as Gromph might be, was he truly in the mood for a fight with a pair of clever dragons?

"We have among us a sage," Gromph said, and he relaxed a bit, purposely it seemed to Catti-brie, to show that he was not insulted. He motioned to Parise Ulfbinder, who nodded humbly at the compliment.

"A sorcerer," he said, and Lady Avelyere bowed her chin.

"Some . . . wizards." Penelope Harpell seemed less than amused by his rather insulting pause.

"And a Chosen," Gromph said with a derisive snicker aimed at Catti-brie, "though she cannot seem to decide if she is wizard or priestess."

"She might be better at both than any o' either ye'd find," Athrogate interrupted.

"Dwarf fodder running about the stone, the greatest of the drow, Netherese lord and lady, a pair of dragons, and . . ."—again with that clearly insulting pause—"humans.

"We hold among us the knowledge of many races, the understanding of wizardry from three different eras and from many different styles," Gromph continued. "We access the Weave, but from perspectives and training of great variance. That is our strength in seeking the secrets of the Hosttower of the Arcane."

The archmage paused and stood up, pacing imperiously.

"Wizardry and spells divine," he muttered, and nodded toward Catti-brie and Ambergris with faked deference. "But there, too, are other powers."

"Necromancy," said Lord Parise.

"It is mere wizardry, distorted," Kipper Harpell argued.

"A separate art!" Lord Parise insisted.

"That, too, will be properly in place. Jarlaxle has sent to us a necromancer named Effron, who carries an artifact of great power, taken from a skull lord," Gromph explained.

Lord Parise held his breath at that, quite aware of the necromancer named Effron, and his unsavory relationship with Parise's closest friend and secret ally in this endeavor, Lord Draygo Quick.

Catti-brie, too, perked up at the mention of Dahlia's son. She looked to Ambergris, who had been a traveling companion of Effron's in the last days of the Spellplague, to find the dwarf beaming with excitement at the news.

"But no," Gromph continued, "I speak of an entirely different power, one equal to those divine and arcane."

One of the mind, they all heard in their heads, though it took some of them a while to understand that it had been a telepathic impartation.

"You see, Chosen of Mielikki, you are not the only one here who brings magic from two different sources," Gromph explained.

"Well, this is news," Tazmikella said. "The Archmage of Menzoberranzan is a psionicist, is he?"

"Gromph Odran?" Ilnezhara teased.

Gromph sneered a bit at the mention of the cursed House, and the reminder that Kimmuriel was still out there beyond his grasp.

"I am only beginning to explore this strange art," Gromph admitted, "but I have witnessed enough to understand that it is a beautiful thing, and one that can be entwined with the Weave."

"With Mystra's Weave?" Catti-brie asked, though of course she knew of what he was speaking. Given Lolth's failure to take the Weave into her domain, Catti-brie thought a reminder of which goddess held the Weave might be appropriate, and perhaps a bit humbling to the haughty drow wizard.

In response, Gromph offered a bored, somewhat scowling look.

"I have arranged for a representative of the hive-mind to come among us," he explained. "The illithids are quite interested in this most unusual and powerful endeavor."

"Oh grand!" Parise Ulfbinder said without a hint of sarcasm, and clapped his hands.

Catti-brie sighed, not surprised at that reaction.

"You are bringing a mind flayer into Luskan?" Ilnezhara asked, seeming much less enthusiastic than the Netherese lord.

"A stinkin' squid head?" Athrogate demanded. "By the hairy bum o' Moradin, ye've lost yer sense, drow!"

Gromph's stare alone seemed as if it might prove enough to explode Athrogate's head—so much so that Catti-brie actually feared the Archmage was launching a psionic attack upon the black-bearded dwarf. But Athrogate remained unbothered and unshaken, and didn't shrink back a bit from the glare. In fact, he returned it with a grin that seemed to welcome any challenge.

Catti-brie reminded herself that there were two undeniable truths in the Realms: It was very easy to overestimate a drow and even easier to underestimate a dwarf.

And both races could, and usually did, use that mistake to their respective advantage.

The notion followed to a deeper level with Catti-brie, a poignant reminder to her that the physical trappings of an individual—race, gender, attractiveness, size—played such an important role in perception of everything else related to that individual, indeed could sometimes outweigh the quality of action or words.

It was such an absurd notion, when she stripped it down to that level, and so, in this tense moment, with so many powerful beings sitting about, the woman couldn't help herself and began to laugh. And not just a titter, but an actual laugh, a belly laugh, a reaction to absurdity that had everyone in the room staring at her as if she had lost her mind.

Gromph turned his glare upon her. The dragon sisters seemed perplexed for a moment, then they, too, began to laugh.

"What're ye doin', lass?" Athrogate said with obvious concern.

It took Catti-brie another few moments to comport herself. When she did, she planted her hands firmly on the round table and stood up, commanding attention.

"We are here under dangerous circumstance for common gain, personal insight, and to be a part of something grander than our individual lives," she said. She took a moment to look around at all gathered, letting her gaze settle on each for some time to acknowledge them individually.

"We all have different reasons for being here, and will find different gains both for ourselves and, for some, for those we have come to represent," she continued. "There are possibly competing interests here, but they are within a common goal. And each of these competing interests, as much as they might diminish another's, are muted and countered by third interests and fourth. I can see in looking around that there is to be no supremacy here, as much as any of us might desire it." She paused and offered a sidelong look to Archmage Gromph. "And so I insist that any additions to the collection be agreed upon by all at the table. There will be no shifting of the balance."

"The illithids are coming," Gromph stated.

"Surely they are aware of our efforts here," Lord Parise added. "There is little of any importance that escapes their view. And do not doubt that their contribution will be great—perhaps as great as any here assembled."

"But they are ugly things, aren't they?" Ilnezhara asked.

"Squid heads," Athrogate grumbled.

"I doubt you not, Lord Parise," said Catti-brie. "The larger question I have, the larger concern I have, is whether or not their presence will give advantage to any personal agendas above the common goal." Again she ended with a glance at Gromph, who stared at her now with open contempt.

"Doubtful," said Tazmikella. "They are illithids, mind flayers. None here can discern their desires, let alone trust any alliance with them. They are as foreign to us, even to my sister and me, as we are to the houseflies we might swat. In all the millennia, none have quite sorted the true intentions and motivations of the mind flayers." She, too, turned an eye to Gromph, and finished pointedly, "Not even the Archmage of Menzoberranzan, who, after a recent disaster, should be most concerned among us regarding the intentions, motivations, and methods of those psionic beasts."

"Then do we allow them audience with our efforts?" Penelope Harpell asked.

"They already are aware of what is happening here," said Catti-brie. "So the audience is a foregone conclusion, whether we allow them into our circle or not. Is there anything we could truly hide from an illithid hive-mind?"

"Particularly since one sitting here seems to think 'em friends?" Athrogate added and gave Gromph a sidelong glance.

"At this point, that would hardly matter," said Tazmikella.

"They will greatly enhance our efforts," Lord Parise put in. "The knowledge of the race is extensive, perhaps beyond the knowledge of any other race of beings. Their libraries are alive within their own thoughts, forefront in their everyday existence. They need not dust off ancient tomes to try to recover what their ancestors might have gleaned. It remains within their collective thought, ever and always."

"You seem to know much of them," said Catti-brie.

"I do, and with extensive experience."

"Then we are agreed?" Catti-brie asked.

"Squid heads . . ." Athrogate muttered.

"Best cooked with wedges o' lemon, and fried deep," Ambergris added.

Catti-brie couldn't suppress a bit of a laugh at the dwarven banter around her, but she maintained a modicum of seriousness and looked all around, eliciting agreeing nods from each of the other delegations.

"Then we are agreed, Archmage Gromph," she said at length. "Your illithid emissary, or delegation, is welcomed here."

"No delegation," said Ilnezhara. "Just one."

"And we will watch him carefully," added Tazmikella.

"Aye, not to doubt that," said Athrogate, who wasn't joking at all at that moment.

After that bit of important business, the meeting turned to the progress each member was making in his or her assigned tasks. Almost all the recounting involved research and the names of various tomes being studied, with only three exceptions.

The dwarves detailed the rebuilding of the root of the tower, informing the group that they had recovered enough large pieces to fairly reconstruct it—as soon as the durned wizards figured out how to magically join the stuff back together. As they finished, Ambergris turned the floor over to Lady Avelyere, who was leading the way in locating the pieces of the tower, which had been blasted all around the island, into the water, and back into Luskan, and some of which, apparently, had been stolen by the greedy citizens of Luskan as mementoes, perhaps, or for their own use in the construction of ships or homes.

"I have honed my spells of seeking to catch the emanations of the strange ancient magic still imbued upon the tower shards," the woman explained. "With permission, I would like to bring in some members of my Coven, to expand our vision many-fold."

The others all nodded, except that Gromph also waved absently, clearly to signal that he was not intimidated by whatever army of sorcerers the likes of Avelyere could summon.

When she finished, the floor at last came to the dragon sisters.

Ilnezhara rose and spoke first, explaining the insights she had garnered from an ancient silver dragon who resided in the area and had often viewed the Hosttower of the Arcane from high above. She added a delightful anecdote the silver had recounted, for Catti-brie's benefit no doubt, of a dwarf flying about in a flaming chariot.

Then came Tazmikella, who wore a sly smile. "We have found another ally in this," she announced, and she sat down and seemed as if she would say no more.

"Would you care to elaborate?" an annoyed Gromph asked at length.

"Not really," said the dragon.

"We would not wish to miss your reactions when our dear friend arrives," Ilnezhara added.

"This is unacceptable," said Gromph, and all the others bristled, too, except for Catti-brie, who looked at Tazmikella and got a wink in reply.

"Acceptable or not, it is our choice," Tazmikella replied.

"You will know later this day, Archmage Gromph," said Ilnezhara. "When our friend arrives, we can send her on her way, if that is the decision of this table."

"Oh, it won't be," Tazmikella answered her sister, and both laughed.

Catti-brie kept her gaze on Gromph through it all, judging the simmer in his amber eyes. She recognized the explosive rage there. This one wasn't used to being trapped into a role where he was not supreme—not by any other than the most powerful matron mothers of Menzoberranzan, at least. And he clearly didn't much like it.

But he had erred, badly, back in the Underdark. He had cost himself dearly by bringing Demogorgon to Menzoberranzan, and thus, he was not in a position of power here.

And it was driving him quite mad.

Catti-brie lingered as the others departed so that she would be the last in the room with Gromph. He noted her intent long before the rest had gone, and sat staring at her from behind his tapping fingers. He had a way of flaring his eyes to make it seem as if some great catastrophe was about to befall all within his line of sight—and no doubt that look often preceded exactly that.

Catti-brie was neither impressed nor concerned.

"A grand speech you gave," Gromph said when at last they were alone. "Lined with laughter to profess confidence. An amazing act, after all."

"No act," the woman replied.

"Then foolish confidence."

"Simple truth of the matter before us."

"You mistake your position here," said Gromph. "I did not destroy you in the primordial chamber of Gauntlgrym, out of deference to those around me because I expected you might be of use to me going forward. Now, in this, you are of use to me—perhaps—but do not make the mistake of believing that the annoyance and insubordination you offer will not ever outweigh the perspective gain."

"Insubordination? So we are still there? Perhaps it remains you who misunderstands the situation at hand and the hierarchy in place here at the Hosttower."

A snarl escaped his lips.

"I do not claim rank above you, but neither do I concede the same," Catti-brie said.

"Shall I show you the bared power of the archmage?"

"A threat?"

Gromph lifted his hand and slowly began to turn it in the air, palm rotating to face up. He looked as if he was gathering magical energy, and Catti-brie could feel that he was doing just that.

"Hold!" she demanded.

"Wise choice."

"Oh, if ye insist on continuing, then know ye'll be findin' a willing opponent," Catti-brie clarified, her reversion to Dwarvish brogue a clear sign, even to her, that Gromph was indeed getting her hackles up. "But know that ye're thinkin' to wage a fight ye canno' win."

"You have no idea, young human."

"Not so young," the woman replied. "And sure but I'm old enough to understand the jar o' worms ye'd be opening. If ye beat me—"

"No doubt," Gromph said evenly.

"Then Drizzt would kill you," Catti-brie replied with equal enunciation and tone.

Gromph snorted as if that notion was even more preposterous—and Catti-brie knew it probably was. Could Drizzt, could any warrior, ever even get close to this mighty spellcaster?

But she didn't back down. "And King Bruenor would send every dwarf in Faerûn to hunt ye and kill ye. Every one. Not to doubt, and oh, but they'd come for ye by the thousand."

Gromph seemed to be paying more attention then.

"And Jarlaxle, such a dear friend of me husband, would reveal ye to the Matron Mother o' Menzoberranzan," she stated. "Oh, but he would. So for just yer stubborn pride, ye'd throw all the best chances away, would ye now?"

She paused and rose, and brushed some hair from the front of her magical blouse, and in doing so, brushed away, too, her Dwarvish edge.

"I am not your enemy, Archmage Gromph," she said in proper Common. "We are allied in this endeavor, and when the Hosttower is rebuilt, I have no interest in the structure or its hierarchy, other than continuing the flow of its magic to hold the primordial in check. And I have learned enough of the ancient magic here, of how it was constructed and the safeguards that were placed upon it and still remain in the residue of the tower, to understand that the magical flow to Gauntlgrym is something that no one will be able to do anything about once we are finished with our work. Not even you, should you claim the title as Archmage of the Hosttower of the Arcane, as I expect is both your and Jarlaxle's plan. And so, you see, dear Archmage Gromph, that I simply do not care about your personal designs regarding the lordship of the Hosttower beyond our alliance here, no more than I care that Jarlaxle rules Luskan from the shadows. It is not my affair, and so I am not your enemy. We would both be better served to keep it that way."

Gromph kept tap-tapping his fingers together, staring at the woman for a long, long time.

Catti-brie recognized that to be as solid an answer as she was going to get from the angry wizard, so she smiled again shook her head, and walked past Gromph to the doorway beyond.

For all her confidence, she was indeed quite relieved when she reached the hall and closed the door behind her.

◆ ◆ ◆

THE WIND BLEW cold off the dark waters of Luskan Harbor, carrying drizzle with the smell of brine.

Catti-brie was so engaged she hardly noticed the chill or the wetness as she stood with her shawl tightly wrapped around her. To her right stood Ilnezhara and Tazmikella. On the other side, Lord Parise Ulfbinder and Lady Avelyere whispered quietly with Penelope, Kipper, and the other Harpells. Back behind them all, Archmage Gromph sat on a grand chair he had summoned from nowhere, one finger casually rubbing across the lips of his handsome face. Catti-brie understood that there was something dangerous in that look from Gromph. Likely, he spent as much time considering the weaknesses and vulnerabilities of his allies as he did in focusing on the monumental task at hand.

Catti-brie purposefully and repeatedly reminded herself of that truth. Her personal experiences with drow on the surface of Faerûn, with her husband of course, but even with Jarlaxle and his associates, were not indicative of the methods and ethos of the sinister culture of Menzoberranzan.

She could not tell herself that truth too often.

Archmage Gromph was tied to Jarlaxle now not out of temperament, but out of necessity. He was a product of Menzoberranzan, who had thrived in those shadows and by all accounts instigated more than a little of the calamity around him.

This was not Jarlaxle. This was Gromph Baenre. This drow was dangerous.

The woman silently nodded as she played through the reminder, telling herself to be ever vigilant.

But then she imagined Gromph towering over her, in a very different light. His amber eyes bored into her, devouring her every inch of flesh. She saw his lips. She both heard and felt his breath. In her mind's eye, he raised his hand and freed some mysterious magic, and goose bumps grew upon Catti-brie's arms.

A confused Catti-brie dismissed the thought forcefully, rejected it and silently berated herself.

She meant to turn and scowl at Gromph then, just to reassure herself, but was distracted when, all around the principal wizards, a thousand dwarves halted their work, the whole area going suddenly quiet. Catti-brie looked on curiously, her gaze going from one group of dwarves to the next, when she realized that they were all looking in the same direction: out to sea, to the southwest.

The woman turned back slowly, noting the other wizards and sages around her, jaws inevitably dropping open, and the dragon sisters smiling.

She was not surprised, then, but surely amazed, when she again gazed out to sea, then high above the surface to the gray and black outlines of the heavy cloud cover, and to one cloud in particular that she soon realized was much more than a cloud.

Its bulging front took firmer shape: the curving wall of a huge tower.

It seemed of like substance to the other clouds—perhaps it was—but it revealed more definite shape than its fellows as it drifted out of the bank: towering, running walls of gray, the rest of the giant floating castle.

As if that wasn't enough to transfix the gathering and all of those looking on from the mainland of Luskan as well, a sudden noise to the side startled most, including Catti-brie.

Gasps of surprise turned to coos of appreciation of the image in front of them as a pair of copper-colored dragons flew up for the immense castle of clouds floating in the air. That giant structure settled into place just offshore, and the dragon sisters flew up over the wall and disappeared from view for few moments. They reappeared, coming back for the gathering, bearing between them a giant litter, a giant throne, with a huge, blue-skinned woman seated upon it. She held a bejeweled scepter across her bosom and a crown of glittering gold and rubies was set upon her head, pinning back her thick and flowing white mane.

The dragons set her down in front of the gathering. The wizards held their ground, but many of the dwarves fell back into more defensible positions.

The cloud giant rose and slowly advanced, Ilnezhara and Tazmikella becoming human women once more and flanking her advance. She moved directly up to Catti-brie and gave a respectful bow—one which, even if she had bent fully perpendicular at the waist would have still left her head high above the human. Though she was similarly proportioned, the giant queen stood thrice Catti-brie's height, at least.

"I am Caecilia," she said in a loud voice, but with a quality that still gave it some delicacy. "My friends Ilnezhara and Tazmikella here thought that I might be of service to you, and in an endeavor that they knew I would find most wondrous."

"We welcome any who would aid in our most important quest," Catti-brie said, trying to sound calm, but surely overwhelmed. She remembered then to reciprocate the bow, albeit she did so with far less grace than Caecilia had managed.

"With your blessing then," Caecilia replied. She turned back to the distant castle, lifted her hand, and shot forth a bolt of brilliant white light.

"I will require a large tent and a large bed, of course," she said. "I trust that you will see to my proper accommodations."

"Of course, Lady," Catti-brie replied, and that last word left her mouth awkwardly. Was she to call this giant "Lady," after all? What rules of etiquette might apply to a giantess?

Up above the bay, the giant castle began to recede, floating back into the thick overcast to blend to practical invisibility. Many lifted faces continued to stare up that way, unsure if the massive structure was gone or simply hiding in the clouds.

Only gradually did the dwarves and others go back to their work, with Caecilia going off with the dragon sisters to be brought up to date on the efforts. Catti-brie took a deep and steadying breath, reminding herself that these amazing sights and guests were all for the good. Her focus had to be on the Hosttower. If it could not be rebuilt, then Gauntlgrym would fall to utter ruin.

She turned away from the cloud bank, shaking her head, steeling her resolve.

And then she saw Gromph, sitting on his throne, staring at her, amused, or perhaps bemused.

The fantasy of the archmage bent over her, kissing her, touching her, returned suddenly—so quickly, unexpectedly, and powerfully that Catti-brie staggered for a step and nearly stumbled.

Gromph was smiling.

CHAPTER 12 ◈

The Great Pillar Cavern

ARLAXLE EXAMINED ENTRERI, THEN NODDED APPROVINGLY AT the disguise. "If you slip into the common tongue of the surface, do not grow anxious," he instructed both his companions. "You are of Bregan D'aerthe. As far as any we will see knows, it has been years since you have been down here in Araunilcaurak."

"What?" Entreri asked.

"Araunilcaurak," Drizzt answered before Jarlaxle could. "The Great Pillar Cavern that Houses Menzoberranzan." Jarlaxle and Entreri continued talking, but Drizzt receded as soon as the words had left his mouth. That word, *Araunilcaurak*, echoed in his thoughts. It was a word he hadn't heard since childhood.

He thought back to the day he'd cast Menzoberranzan behind him, Guenhwyvar beside him, to venture into the wilds of the Underdark. It occurred to him at that moment, for the first time in more than a century, the first time since he'd ventured to the surface, that perhaps his decision on that long-ago day had not been so wise. He could have remained in the city, could have lived as Zaknafein had lived. Perhaps his family would still be alive in that event, instead of this abomination that had been created of House Do'Urden for no better reason than to smear his name.

Perhaps his father would not have been killed.

And his poor sister, Vierna, too kind for the title of priestess of Lolth. Would she have been spared? Drizzt himself had killed her, after all.

Even his friends on the World Above would have been better off, he realized to his horror. He had known this before, after the drow had come to Mithral Hall, after Wulfgar had fallen into the grasp of a yochlol. On that occasion, Drizzt had returned to Menzoberranzan, to surrender himself rather than place his friends in worse jeopardy.

Catti-brie had come for him, and their subsequent escape—Artemis Entreri beside them—had shown Drizzt the error of his ways.

But he now realized his love for Catti-brie, his gratitude to her, had blinded him to the truth of it all.

"What is it?" he heard Jarlaxle ask, drawing him from his thoughts. He looked at his companion, and at Entreri, too, who was staring at him.

"For all these years, I have thought myself brave," Drizzt admitted. "Now I see that I am a coward, after all."

Jarlaxle and Entreri exchanged glances, curious and concerned, at that strange remark.

"He's not looking forward to walking into Menzoberranzan any more than I am," Entreri decided.

When Jarlaxle nodded and turned a sympathetic eye, Drizzt let it go. Let them believe what they needed to believe, but it was not as they had assumed. He was not afraid to enter the city of his birth. He was ashamed that he had deserted it in the first place.

"So let us be done with it, and quickly," Entreri remarked.

Jarlaxle held up his hand, and fiddled with his pouch, producing a small gemstone ring. He tossed it back and reached in, bringing forth another ring. When this one, too, seemed wrong, he tossed it back and shoved his arm into the pouch up to his elbow—even though the pouch seemed far too small to hold even his hand.

This time he brought his hand forth with a pile of rings in his palm, and he sorted through them for a moment, then slid a gold band set with some light stone, perhaps a diamond, onto his finger. He paused a moment, placed his finger against his temple, and issued a command word.

His great hat shifted, then seemed to rise a bit of its own accord. Jarlaxle solved the mystery for the other two by reaching up and pulling off the hat, letting a mop of white hair fall down over his shoulders. Thick and styled, one side was cut in layers, the other hanging over the shaved side of Jarlaxle's head.

Jarlaxle slapped his hat against his thigh and the magical thing seemed to fold in upon itself, becoming small enough for Jarlaxle to easily slide it into his pocket.

"I'm sure we're better off in disguise," the mercenary explained with a wink—or maybe it was a blink. His eye patch remained in place. He dropped the ring back into his pouch, replaced it with some other magical ring, and motioned for the others to follow.

The trio met up with an agent of Matron Mother Zeerith's in the next chamber, a broken cavern of slanted walls and natural chimneys.

Nowhere was the ground even, a situation made worse by the blood and goo that covered the stones.

"You should have arrived sooner," remarked Palaenmas, a young warrior of House Xorlarrin. "We could have used the extra swords."

"I am surprised to find you by the Wanderways," Jarlaxle replied, referring to a group of tunnels leading off of the most remote eastern reaches of Menzoberranzan.

"The Masterways are closed, both magically and physically," Palaenmas explained, the Masterways being the main routes in and out of Menzoberranzan. "Only a fool would test the glyphs and wards the priestesses and wizards have placed in those corridors."

"And no doubt they are tested daily," said Jarlaxle.

"Constantly," Palaenmas replied. "The corridors are filled with the stench of demon corpses. War parties venture forth every hour to place new wards. But the foolish beasts keep coming, and so they die before they get near to Menzoberranzan." He looked around at the trio. "It is a testament to your skill and cunning that you even made it to this point. You will find your path easier now."

Somehow the three travelers doubted that.

Palaenmas nodded for them to follow and led them back to the main patrol group, explaining them as refugees from a separate failed patrol.

Their timing had been perfect. The group was already on the way back to the city, and was only a few turns and chambers from the straight, well-defended passageway leading into Araunilcaurak.

The troupe went through the checkpoints and newly constructed gates without incident and was dismissed as soon as they entered the great cavern. They began dispersing just inside to the various ways of Menzoberranzan.

Jarlaxle paused there, holding his two companions back, and so Drizzt took a moment to reorient himself to the city. To the left of them, the rothé cattle lowed and grazed on the small island in the midst of the lake named Donigarten. Mushroom groves and fungi farms filled the area in front of them, with small cottages and large storehouses built low on the stones. The nearest of the houses of the city proper began several hundred feet down to the right, in the Braeryn, the slum region known as the Stenchstreets. Farther along the cavern wall loomed the Clawrift,

Drizzt recalled, and beyond that the Masterways and then Tier Breche, the raised antechamber that held the drow Academy.

He looked directly across from the entryway, to the southwest and the structures of the greatest noble Houses on the higher plateau known as the Qu'ellarz'orl. The lights of the city captured his vision, the perpetual blue and purple and green faerie fire that artistically highlighted every stalactite and stalagmite, the beautiful decorations that made Menzoberranzan so much more than Araunilcaurak.

He continued his scan, his eye roving to the north, caught and held by the glow of Narbondel, the great pillar that gave this cavern its name. By the height of the glow of that gigantic pillar, Drizzt had once set the regimen of his days.

Narbondel was discipline within chaos, was the constant within the swirl, was the symbol of the hour, the day, the eternity of the drow.

"We'll go to the Stenchstreets," Jarlaxle said when the three were isolated enough just inside the city gates. "I'll find my information there . . ." He paused, his voice trailing off as he noted Drizzt.

The ranger stood there, transfixed, staring at the great column.

But Drizzt's thoughts, revealed in his wistful and unresponsive gaze, were far, far away.

◆ ◆ ◆

BRAELIN HAD NEVER imagined the possibility of such pain, the burn unrelenting and so much worse than anything he had known from the scourge of his matron mother or the hateful magic of some high priestess.

He could not believe this. It would not relent. He was certain he would soon be driven completely insane by the sheer, brutal agony of it all. He watched helplessly, shackled and held above the floor by his bloody wrists, as his right leg bloated and swelled. Braelin could not imagine greater pain, but that didn't matter as the bones in his leg split in half, skin and muscles tearing.

They would split again, so promised the chants of the Melarni priestesses dancing around him, their vile magic coagulating in Braelin's tormented form. One leg would become four, then the other would complete his arachnid lower torso.

He should have passed out long before, but that, too, was part of the magic of the demon priestesses, keeping him alert to witness his brutal and agonizing transformation.

Braelin screamed—oh, how he screamed! He screamed until he could not draw enough breath to make any more noise. His head lolled from side to side, his arms twitched, but had little strength remaining to cause more than a ripple of movement from his trembling body.

"It doesn't get better," one of them or all of them said—Braelin was too far removed from reality to know which. In any case, the words reverberated in his thoughts, ominous portents as the pain continued on and on.

"You will feel this for a century," another voice told him.

"Unrelenting."

"The curse of the drider."

Even in the midst of mind-swirling agony, Braelin understood that the vicious priestesses were enjoying this torture.

But then it stopped, though it took Braelin a long, long while to understand that it had. The sound of metal he heard above him was the key sliding into the shackles.

He dropped hard to the floor, his leg exploding in a wave of new agony as it touched ground.

"Heal him," Braelin heard, distantly, and somehow he recognized that particular voice, the sharp intonations of Matron Mother Zhindia Melarn.

Soon after, the first wave of warm healing washed over him, and Braelin fell into a deep slumber.

◆ ◆ ◆

"You are certain of this?" Matron Mother Zhindia asked Kiriy Xorlarrin. "Jarlaxle, here in the city?"

"It was confirmed by my envoy," Kiriy assured her, "a Xorlarrin who escorted Jarlaxle and two others in through the eastern gate, as Matron Mother Zeerith had instructed."

"To Baenre's call?"

"No," Kiriy replied with confidence. "The matron mother does not know of Jarlaxle's arrival—he is not here at her command. This is his own mission, to his own ends."

"And those are?"

"I do not know. But it is surely of importance for Jarlaxle to venture here at this time, through tunnels filled with demons."

"Matron Mother Darthiir," Zhindia said, nodding.

"Matron Mother Zeerith does wish to make a play for House Do'Urden," said Kiriy. "If Jarlaxle seeks the *iblith* Dahlia, then Matron Mother Zeerith would certainly welcome and facilitate the move. It would leave a void, one to be filled by a Xorlarrin, no doubt."

"By High Priestess Kiriy Xorlarrin, who has not forgotten the ways of the Lady of Chaos."

Kiriy smiled.

"I do not think Matron Mother Zeerith will be happy with the fruition of her plans," the Matron Mother of House Melarn remarked. "She does not understand her eldest daughter."

"She will not come near to Menzoberranzan to discover the truth."

Matron Mother Zhindia shook her head at that. "Once House Do'Urden is secure, Matron Mother Zeerith cannot be allowed to live. She will not accept the truth of House Do'Urden when you reveal the new ways of Xorlarrin. She will connive with the matron mother to be rid of you."

"Jarlaxle will lead us back to her, perhaps."

"Jarlaxle will be dead," Matron Mother Zhindia assured her. "But there are others of Bregan D'aerthe who will be useful to us. But first, we have much to do. This is too much supposition. We do not truly know Jarlaxle's plans here in the city."

"I will see what I can learn."

Matron Mother Zhindia shook her head. "Just lead me to him. I have a way."

Kiriy looked to the door to her right in the small chamber, the antechamber to the torture room where Braelin Janquay recovered from the brutality of his trials.

"We stopped it in time to use him," Matron Mother Zhindia assured her.

"Jarlaxle's players are fiercely loyal," Kiriy warned her.

"There is no loyalty in the face of the punishment the rogue Braelin knows will be returned upon him if he disappoints me."

"That punishment will be returned upon him even if he does not."

"Of course, but he does not know that, and with the memories of the transformation so fresh in his thoughts, he will not allow himself to believe that."

◆ ◆ ◆

THE DEMON SHOWED him Catti-brie, his wife, and let him live with their children, and all was well, and all was grand.

And the beast Errtu ate them, chewed them, tore them apart, before Wulfgar's eyes, shattering his mind . . .

The brutal conjuring of that image jolted Drizzt from his slumber at the table in the nondescript common room in the ramshackle building in the Stenchstreets. He opened his eyes to find Jarlaxle and Entreri staring at him incredulously.

"We are at the most dangerous point of our journey and you think it time for a nap?" Entreri asked angrily.

Jarlaxle tried to calm Entreri with a patting hand, while he looked at Drizzt carefully. "Are you all right, my friend?" he asked.

"Is anything all right?" Drizzt replied. "Ever?"

Jarlaxle and Entreri exchanged yet another concerned glance. "He sounds like me," Entreri snorted. "And he considers me the dour one!"

Jarlaxle shook his head, dismissing the superfluous conversation. "Drizzt," he said earnestly, "we are almost there. Our goal is in sight on the western wall."

Drizzt stared at him and couldn't be bothered with even a nod of agreement. He understood his role here, and though he now doubted the value of it, he would gladly fight—more gladly than ever—against anyone who got in his way.

Simply because he wanted to kill something.

"For Dahlia," Jarlaxle said, and Drizzt wondered if it really even was Dahlia seated as Matron Mother of House Do'Urden. How deep, how complete, might the deception go?

"There's your friend," Entreri interrupted and he led Jarlaxle's gaze to the entry area of the common room, and to Braelin Janquay who came limping toward them, heavily favoring his right leg.

He glanced around as he neared the table, then sat opposite Drizzt, to Jarlaxle's left. He stared at Jarlaxle only briefly, then leaned to the edge of the table, his hands beneath. He started signing, but stopped and cautiously glanced around once more.

Then his fingers began their dance, the chatter of the drow, and the words he formed told Jarlaxle that all was well and that the way was clear to House Do'Urden. He explained that Dahlia was seated as expected, paralyzed by her jumbled thoughts in the audience chamber. No one knew of Jarlaxle's entrance into the city, so said Braelin's waggling fingers, and no other House was moving against Do'Urden. All was as it should be, as they had hoped it would be, and this was the perfect time to execute their devious plan.

Braelin glanced around again and struggled to stand. All three noted it and glanced at his leg.

"Injured in a patrol," Braelin replied to Jarlaxle's concerned look. "It is well on the mend."

When he was gone, Jarlaxle looked to the others and nodded.

◆ ◆ ◆

AT THE SAME moment, in House Baenre's Room of Divination, the daughter of Gromph Baenre considered the image in the stoup water and laughed heartily. She grasped K'yorl's hands tightly and forced herself more deeply into the powerful psionicist's mind. This cistern was serving her well.

◆ ◆ ◆

AT THE SAME moment, Matron Mother Zhindia Melarn told Kiriy Xorlarrin, "Prepare now for the defense of House Do'Urden,"

"You will help?"

"They are only three," Zhindia replied, but with a sly tone that didn't offer any definitive answer to the question.

"Then let us kill them where they sit and be done with it," Kiriy replied.

"Catching Jarlaxle of Bregan D'aerthe as he tries to rescue the damned Matron Mother Darthiir will greatly shake dear Quenthel's confidence and position," Matron Mother Zhindia said.

"And so, too, will this moment of Jarlaxle's treachery offer us the opportunity to be done with House Do'Urden," Zhindia went on. "The news of Bregan D'aerthe conspiring overtly against House Baenre will embolden Matron Mother Mez'Barris Armgo to take the steps at long last to put House Baenre back into its proper place and destroy the tyrannical and wrongheaded rule of Matron Mother Quenthel."

She cast a knowing glance at Iltztrav, the Melarni House Wizard who had facilitated the clairvoyance and clairaudience spells so they could witness Braelin's deception. Then she added, "Particularly so when Jarlaxle's companion is revealed."

She turned back to Kiriy, who was staring at her with confusion and intrigue.

"You did not notice?" Zhindia asked.

Kiriy shook her head ever so slightly.

"The one across from Braelin," Zhindia explained. "The one with the purple eyes."

Kiriy Xorlarrin lost her breath and rocked as she stood there. "Drizzt Do'Urden," she mouthed.

"In Menzoberranzan," a grinning Zhindia replied, "on his way to House Do'Urden, where we will indeed send assistance to you to ensure his capture."

Kiriy's heart was beating so furiously she feared she might faint and fall to the floor.

"Of course we will help—oh, more than help!" Matron Mother Zhindia said. She turned to her wizard. "Alert Shakti Hunzrin. Tell her that the time is upon us." Then to her daughter, "First Priestess Kyrnill, prepare the war room."

"So quickly," an overwhelmed Kiriy remarked.

"We are prepared," Zhindia replied. Her smile was awful at that moment, but she added a bit of warmth to it as she promised the future Matron Mother of House Do'Urden, "I will arrange for you to be at Council when I present Drizzt Do'Urden to the ruling matron mothers. You will be there when I throw him at the feet of Matron Mother Quenthel and name him as the murderer of Matron Mother Darthiir. When I declare that the great Lady Lolth used this traitor Drizzt to her own advantage as assassin of the abomination Quenthel foolishly seated on the Ruling Council.

"Then, my dear High Priestess Kiriy, Menzoberranzan will know true chaos and upheaval, as is demanded," the zealous Matron Mother Zhindia Melarn explained, savoring every last word.

"And House Do'Urden will be mine, and a new alliance will bring Baenre to its knees," Kiriy finished.

PART 3

Ghosts

I HAVE HEARD POWERFUL MEN WITH IMPERIAL DESIGNS CLAIM THAT reality is what they choose it to be. That they make their own reality, and so decide the reality for those in their way, and while others are trying to decipher what is truth, they move on to the next conquest, the next creation, the next deception of malleable reality.

That is all I could call it—a grand illusion, a lie wrapped as truth, and so declared as truth by the controlling puppet masters of the powerful.

I rejected—and still do, to great extent—the notion. If there is no truth, then it seems to me that there is no basis of reality itself. If perception is reality, then reality is a warped and malleable thing, and to what point, I must ask?

Are we all gods within our own minds?

To entertain the notion is to invite the purest chaos, I fear—but then, is it not to also offer the purest harmony?

I choose to be happy, and happiness is indeed a choice. Every day I can rise from my Reverie and gnash my teeth at what I do not have. Or I can smile contentedly in appreciation of what I do possess. To this level, then, I must agree with the hubristic conqueror. In this emotional level, perception can indeed be the reality of one's feelings, and properly corralling that perception might well be the key to happiness and contentment. I know many poor men who are happy, and many rich men full of discontent. The failings of the heart—pride, envy, greed, and even lust, if such will result in pain for another—are choices as well, to be accepted or denied. Acceptance will lead to discontent, and so these are, in the words of many texts of many cultures and races, considered among the deadliest of sins.

But aside from the false justifications of the conqueror and the choices of honest perception, is there another level of contortion where perception and reality cross? Where perception, perhaps, is so powerful and so distorted that it masks reality itself, that it replaces reality itself? And in such a state, is there a puppet master who can shatter perception as easily as a powerful smith might punch his sledge through thin glass?

This is my fear, my terror. My nightmare!

All the world beneath my feet shifts as the sands of a desert, and what those sands might conceal . . .

Were it not for Wulfgar, I would not now recognize what has been cast upon me. When he fell those many years ago in Mithral Hall, beneath a cave collapse in the tentacle arms of a yochlol, Wulfgar was taken to the Abyss, and there enslaved by the demon named Errtu.

Wulfgar told me of his trials, and of the worst of the tortures— the very worst, torment beyond any possible physical pain. With his demonic magic, Errtu gave to the battered and beaten-down Wulfgar a new reality, a grand illusion that he was free, that he was married to Catti-brie, that together they had produced fine children.

And then Errtu ate those children in front of Wulfgar's eyes, and murdered Catti-brie. This is the very essence of diabolical torture, the very epitome of evil. The demon created reality within a beautiful deception, and destroyed that reality right in front of the helpless victim.

All Wulfgar could do was scream and tear at his own ears and eyes as the sights and sounds ripped open his heart.

It broke him. When rescue finally came, when Wulfgar once more walked in the shared reality of Faerûn among his friends, those dreams did come. The deception of Errtu remained, and waited for him in every unguarded moment and drove him to the bottle and to the edge of absolute despair.

I know of this from Wulfgar, and so I am better prepared. Now I recognize the awful truth of my life.

I do not know how far back this grand diabolical game began upon my own sensibilities, but to that dark night at the top of Kelvin's Cairn, at least.

Perhaps I died there.

Perhaps there Lolth found me and took me.

And so the deception, and when I step back from it, I am amazed at how blind and foolish I could have been! I am stunned at how easily what I so desperately wanted to be true was made true in my mind! I am humbled at how easily I was fooled!

A century has passed. I saw the deaths of Catti-brie and Regis in Mithral Hall. I know that Wulfgar grew old and died in Icewind Dale. I held a dying Bruenor in my own arms in Gauntlgrym.

"I found it, elf," the dwarf said to me, and so Bruenor Battlehammer died content, his life fulfilled, his seat at Moradin's table assured.

They were all gone. I saw it. I lived it. I grieved it.

But no, they are all here! Miraculously so!

And Artemis Entreri, too, walked through the century. A human of middle age when the Spellplague began, and yet here he is a century removed, a human of middle age once more, or still—I cannot be certain and it does not matter.

Because it isn't real.

Too many!

I am told that the Companions of the Hall returned because of the blessing of Mielikki, and that Entreri survived because of a curse and a sword, and oh, how I wanted and want to believe those coincidences and miraculous circumstances! And so my desire is my undoing. It tore the shield from in front of my heart. This is not the blessing of Mielikki.

This is the curse of Lolth.

The grand deception!

She has made my reality to lighten my heart, so that she can shatter my reality, and in so doing, shatter, too, the heart of Drizzt Do'Urden.

I see it now—how could I have been such a fool?—but seeing it will not protect me. Expecting it will not shield my heart. Not yet.

I must act quickly, else Lolth will break me this time, I know. When all of this is shown to be the conjured dream of a scheming demon goddess, Drizzt Do'Urden will die of heartbreak.

Unless I can rebuild that shield, strip by hardened strip. I must accept again the death of my friends, of my beloved Catti-brie. I must return my heart to that calloused place, accept that pain and the grief and the emptiness.

Alas, but even should I succeed, to what end, I must ask? When this grand illusion is destroyed, with what am I left?

And knowing now that perception and reality are so intimately twined, then I ask again, to what end?

—Drizzt Do'Urden

Chapter 13 ◈

Stone Heads and
Agile Fingers

TONE HEADS!" RAVEL CRIED. HE HELD UP HIS HANDS, AT A COMplete loss. Those were Hunzrin soldiers Kiriy had set into position along the House Do'Urden perimeter, and House Hunzrin was no ally of House Xorlarrin. Their rivalry had grown particularly cold since Matron Mother Zeerith had established Q'Xorlarrin, a city set to facilitate trade with the surface and thus rob Matron Mother Shakti Hunzrin of her most important resource, her House's great commerce.

"Just soldiers," First Priestess Kiriy Xorlarrin calmly corrected her younger brother. "House Do'Urden is in need of soldiers, and so I have collected some."

"Without asking," Saribel said, but a threatening look from Kiriy quieted her.

"Should I beg permission from mad Matron Mother Darthiir, who doesn't even know her own name?" Kiriy spat in retort.

Off to the side, Tiago started to chuckle, but he held his hands up, desiring no fight, when both Kiriy and Saribel cast him threatening sidelong glares.

The arrogant Baenre brat was rather enjoying this sibling spat. And she expected that he'd soon enjoy it much, much more—right up until he was killed.

"You are not alone here," Ravel dared say to the First Priestess of House Xorlarrin. "And not without allies who know better the lay of Menzoberranzan and of House Do'Urden at this time . . ."

"Silence, male!" Kiriy snapped at him, reaching for her whip. Ravel was so shocked his eyes seemed as if they would simply roll out of his face. Jaemas and Saribel, too, gasped. That was not a common phrase, tone, or attitude in the House of Matron Mother Zeerith Xorlarrin. The ever-angry Berellip had used that tone often, and Berellip was dead.

"Yes," Kiriy said to the dumbfounded stares coming back at her. "The times have changed. Lady Lolth demands it of us."

"Matron Mother Zeerith . . ." Saribel started to say.

"Is not here," Kiriy finished for her. "But I am. Kiriy, High Priestess, First Priestess, Eldest Daughter of Xorlarrin."

"Yes, and your elder, the male Tsabrak, is Archmage of Menzoberranzan," Tiago Baenre put in then, a not subtle reminder that Matron Mother Baenre had installed the Xorlarrin wizard into that post, and by extension, a not subtle reminder that Matron Mother Baenre had created House Do'Urden, as well.

"House Hunzrin is no friend of the Baenres," Ravel dared to add.

"And allied with Matron Mother Mez'Barris Armgo and the Second House, by all accounts," Tiago added.

Kiriy started to respond, but bit it back and just chuckled instead.

"Send them away," Ravel demanded. "The mere presence of the stupid stone heads will anger Matron Mother Baenre."

Kiriy continued to chuckle. "And worse," she admitted, "there are rumors that House Hunzrin has allied with House Melarn."

The other three Xorlarrins and Tiago all glanced at each other, taken aback by those words, given that Kiriy had let soldiers of House Hunzrin right into their compound. Had she brought in these soldiers as a ruse, then, to steal some of Shakti's soldiers so that they could be sacrificed by House Do'Urden? Was it something else, some underlying pact that none of them knew about?

"Rumors," Kiriy said with a laugh. She reached into a pouch and pulled forth a trio of small spiders, or so they seemed. She dropped them to the ground, the others staring in confusion, their eyes gradually widening as they realized that these were not spiders.

"Rumors," Kiriy said again, and she turned and swept out of the room. At that same moment, even as all four in the room began to protest, the arachnid creatures grew, blossoming to full size.

The four drow remaining in the Do'Urden audience chamber found themselves engaged with Melarni driders.

◆ ◆ ◆

"BE WARY, AND with your hands near your weapons," Jarlaxle told his companions. He rose from the table and moved quickly to the bar, arriving there at almost the same time as Braelin exited the common room.

"Did you catch the conversation?" Entreri asked Drizzt, referring to the hand exchange Jarlaxle and Braelin had shared under the table.

Drizzt shook his head. "It's been a long time since I've conversed at any length in that manner."

"Something about the way to House Do'Urden being open," Entreri said, leaning in close. "But if that is the case, then why the warning?"

Entreri's nod signaled to Drizzt that the mercenary was returning.

"I have secured us a room," Jarlaxle announced. "Come, we must rest quickly and make our plans."

The other two exchanged curious looks. Their plan, after all, was to come into the city and go straight to House Do'Urden, the reasoning being that the less time they spent in this land of drow, the better. Certainly if any of them were recognized, their mission would become much more difficult.

Drizzt started to ask a question, but Jarlaxle gave him a curt little head shake as he swung around and started for the staircase, the other two in tow. There weren't many rooms upstairs. Indeed, the place hardly seemed to be an inn, and when Jarlaxle pushed through the door, they came into a comfortably furnished room with a pair of decorative swords hanging above a stocked hearth, cushy chairs set in front of it.

Jarlaxle swung back and pulled the hesitating Drizzt into the room before he quickly shut and bolted the door. The lower class of inns as one might find on the Stenchstreets didn't typically have doors that could be locked from the inside.

"What is this place?" Drizzt asked.

"It doesn't matter," Jarlaxle replied, starting across the room.

Drizzt moved to respond, but Entreri intervened, grabbing Jarlaxle by the arm.

"Enough," he said. "We follow you willingly, but enough of the secrets."

"There is no time," Jarlaxle said, and he tried to pull away.

"You waste more time by arguing," Entreri replied, and did not let go.

"This is the tavern owner's personal quarters, and I paid him handsomely to allow us a short respite, and only that. We are not staying," Jarlaxle explained. He moved to the back wall. He ran his hands along the planks of mushroom stalk, tapping and listening carefully.

"Then why?" Entreri asked, or started to. Jarlaxle held up his hand to quiet the man.

The mercenary leader produced his great hat from his tiny belt pouch, slapped it open against his leg, then reached inside and pulled forth a black disc of some satiny material. He spun it on his finger a couple of times, elongating it, then tossed it against the base of the wall, opening a portable hole in the structure, and revealing a secret tunnel beyond.

"Quickly," he instructed motioning into the tunnel. "This will afford us the time we need."

Drizzt went in, followed by Entreri. Jarlaxle came through last, removing the portable hole as he entered, and the wall was just a wall once more.

The corridor stretched down a ramp, padded to silence footfalls, doubled back on itself, and continued to descend. They moved below the floor level, and lower still, beneath the tavern's wine cellar and into the sewers of the city.

When they all dropped down into that smelly corridor, Entreri once more grabbed Jarlaxle and held him back.

"Now explain."

"There is no way out of that room save through magic—and any use of teleportation magic within the city would be detected. There are wards set everywhere," the mercenary replied. "If enemies come against us, they will not know how we managed to leave that room—and the tavernkeeper will honestly tell them that he set us up for capture."

"What enemies?" Entreri asked.

"Who knows we are here?" Drizzt added.

"I will explain in time, but on the move," said Jarlaxle. "We have an opportunity here, but only if we are clever and only if we are quick!"

He rushed off, the others keeping pace. Despite the maze of sewers, Jarlaxle seemed quite confident in their course. Drizzt wasn't surprised. There was little Jarlaxle didn't know, after all, like the secret passageway in this particular building beyond the owner's room. Drizzt had no doubt that if enemies did come looking for the trio, the most surprised person upon discovering that they weren't in the room would be the tavernkeeper himself.

They emerged aboveground far from the tavern, indeed far from the Stenchstreets, and much farther along the West Wall district of the city, where sat House Do'Urden.

There it was, the high balcony entrance off to their left, and Drizzt could only take a deep breath to steady himself at the sight of his former home. So many memories came rushing back to him then, of Vierna and Briza, of Matron Mother Malice.

Of Zaknafein.

Given what he knew now, given the grand deception awaiting his return to the surface, what did it matter, after all?

What did anything matter?

The truth he now knew mocked his precious morals and principles.

He looked around at his companions and felt a keen urge to draw his blades and slay Entreri then and there. Be done with him.

Damn him!

Entreri was part of the lie that Drizzt had lived, and a focal point of the foolish optimism that had carried Drizzt through his days. Why did he ever think he could redeem this murderer? This petty assassin? This wretched and heartless beast?

Drizzt caught himself, shook the thought away, and only then realized that he had drawn Icingdeath halfway from its sheath.

And Jarlaxle was speaking, to both Drizzt and Entreri.

"Braelin told you the way to House Do'Urden was clear," Entreri replied to whatever it was Jarlaxle had said.

"No," said Jarlaxle, and he started away toward the West Wall, but to the right and not in the direction of House Do'Urden.

"I saw it with my own eyes," Entreri protested, hustling to keep up.

"Where are we going?" Drizzt asked.

"Be wary of pursuit," Jarlaxle warned. "House Hunzrin's war party was trying to intercept us, and so steal the glory."

"Steal the glory?" Entreri asked. "The glory of catching us?"

"From whom?" Drizzt asked, finally catching up.

And when he did, rounding a corner to come face up with the cavern's wall, Drizzt's breath caught in his throat. There in front of him stood one of the most distinct and strangely beautiful structures in Menzoberranzan, indeed, as beautiful as any building Drizzt had ever seen. Graceful and intricate webbing climbed up the wall, with great bridges of spiderwebs flying back and forth around it. Faerie fire was marvelously placed among those shining strands to accent the grace and feeling of movement the wall of webbing evinced.

"To steal the glory from their allies," Jarlaxle explained, "House Melarn."

Drizzt noted Entreri's curious and unsettled expression.

"To any outside observer, my dear and trusted Braelin told us the clear way to our goal," Jarlaxle explained. "And he also told me that House Hunzrin had refused to ally with House Melarn against the matron mother, and so House Melarn had forsaken any immediate plans to deal with Dahlia and the abomination of House Do'Urden. He also told me that the arrival of First Priestess Kiriy Xorlarrin had shaken the resolve of any waiting enemies. Her loyalty to Matron Mother Zeerith and Zeerith's loyalty to Matron Mother Baenre has made both Baenre and Do'Urden untouchable."

Now Drizzt's expression was no less unsettled than Entreri's, and Entreri echoed Drizzt's thoughts perfectly when he asked, "Then why are we here, instead of House Do'Urden?"

"Because Braelin prefaced his report with this," Jarlaxle explained, and he held up his left hand and scraped his thumb over the back of his index finger. "Which means that everything he subsequently told me was exactly opposite of the truth. And he picked his words most carefully."

The other two digested that for a moment in light of Jarlaxle's report. Hunzrin and Melarn had joined in common cause and were going after House Do'Urden and Dahlia—and right now. And they knew of the trio's arrival in the city.

"But then why are we here?" Drizzt asked.

"Because their eyes are elsewhere."

Jarlaxle turned to Entreri. He took a mirror out of his bottomless pouch and held it up in front of the assassin.

"Matron Mother Shakti Hunzrin," he explained, and Entreri's drow reflection shifted to become the image of the Matron Mother of House Hunzrin. "Use the mask to replicate this visage. The deception will be unsolvable, for the magic of Agatha's Mask cannot be detected."

"You want me to—"

"Turn yourself into Shakti Hunzrin, and be quick about it," Jarlaxle ordered. "We have an audience with Matron Mother Zhindia Melarn."

◆ ◆ ◆

"I NEED YOU to be better," Yvonnel told K'yorl, sitting across the stoup from the psionicist, their hands joined in the magical meld. "Stronger."

She felt K'yorl fall deeper into the magic of the holy water, felt her and followed her as the woman let go of her thoughts and sent them into and through the basin. They spun and twined and were one again when they escaped the room, Yvonnel and K'yorl sharing the vision of their disembodied consciousness.

Now Yvonnel reached deeper, and instead of focusing her thoughts on the external images flying about them, on a sudden impulse, she turned inward, into K'yorl. At first, there was only darkness, and she could feel her partner resisting.

She prodded with thoughts and promises of peace and comfort, of pleasure and not pain. So long had this woman been battered and tortured, so brutal had been her fall.

K'yorl wanted to resist, but Yvonnel wouldn't let go—and she even let K'yorl into her own thoughts to witness, naked, her sincerity. Yvonnel had no desire or reason to torture K'yorl. It would offer her no benefit and give her no pleasure.

Her offer, her promise, was real, and K'yorl came to believe that, Yvonnel knew, when those barriers began to thin and wash away.

And a grand revelation followed when Yvonnel began to understand this strange magic of the mind so much better. She didn't expect that she would learn psionics in this way, but the beauty of this melding was that Yvonnel realized she didn't have to.

She had a weapon. K'yorl was her weapon, and she could use the woman as readily as she might trigger a wand or fire a bow.

She scoured the woman's thoughts, asking questions and finding answers. What powers might be available to her? What strange spells could she cast through the melding, through the instrument that was K'yorl?

She eased her thoughts back to their surroundings. Their blended consciousness had escaped the Room of Divination once more, now moving about the corridors surrounding the room, which were mostly empty, as Yvonnel had demanded.

They witnessed Minolin Fey in a side chamber, lighting the many candles on a crystal candelabra, performing a common ceremony of meditation.

Yvonnel telepathically whispered to K'yorl Odran, setting her mental fingers to the bowstring.

K'yorl hesitated only briefly, only until Yvonnel assured her that her future was not back in the pit of the balor Errtu.

The joined women loosed the psionic arrow.

Minolin Fey's thoughts scrambled under the invisible barrage. Her words slurred and became nonsensical. Her hands fumbled, the candle falling to the floor at her feet.

The poor woman muttered, stammered, stuttered, garbled gibberish spilling forth.

The flames caught the bottom of her robe.

She didn't even notice.

Yvonnel gasped with delight.

"Stop!" Yvonnel at last instructed K'yorl, and the two let go their mental clamp.

Minolin Fey nearly pitched over headlong, gasping back to her sensibilities. Still, it took her a few heartbeats to realize that she was on fire, and then she screamed, batting at her robes.

Yvonnel reached into her own magic, casting a simple spell to create water, thinking to douse her mother.

But no, she found. She couldn't do that. She couldn't find any avenue to use her magic through the scrying stoup. Perhaps she would need to invite other Baenre priestesses to join her in ritual, as gatherings of priestesses did when waging war on another House, as the Melarni were likely soon doing, or perhaps even then doing, to House Do'Urden.

She focused outward again. Minolin Fey had shed the gown and stumbled away. She leaned heavily against the wall, trembling hands reaching for the burns on one shin. Yvonnel appreciated her mother's calm as Minolin Fey cast anew, a healing spell to repair the burns.

As soon as that was completed, the priestess glanced around the side chamber, out of embarrassment or confusion, or perhaps fear. There was a wariness in her darting eyes, Yvonnel noted, as if she sensed something.

So, we are not fully invisible, Yvonnel thought, and she felt K'yorl agree. *Still, what a wonderful weapon!*

Yvonnel guided the blended consciousness back to the Room of Divination, then pulled her hands from the stoup and clapped them excitedly.

"Oh, you are wonderful!" she told K'yorl when the woman blinked open her eyes. "The power of your mind is glorious! That you are able to extend it out through the divination, to so fully disembody our thoughts from our bodies . . . Glorious."

"I . . . I . . ." K'yorl stammered, not seeming to quite have a handle on all of this.

"There are powerful crystal balls that offer telepathy through their scrying," Yvonnel explained. "They are very rare—many think them rumor and false legend. But we have done that, here, together. We can channel our power through the magic of the scrying waters."

She was careful to say "our" instead of "your," and took great pains to concentrate and make sure that K'yorl was no longer in her thoughts. The last thing Yvonnel wanted was for this prisoner to come to the realization that she had some measure of control—what a monster K'yorl Odran might become within this Room of Divination. Could she sit there and attack her enemies from afar, secure in the midst of House Baenre?

That was Yvonnel's fear, and her hope—as long as she could keep K'yorl under her guidance and her control.

Yvonnel realized then that she could no longer ever allow K'yorl to remain active with the scrying waters without her hands on top of the prisoner's hands and her thoughts on top of the prisoner's thoughts.

She sank her fingers back into the stone rim, felt again the soft hands of K'yorl within the magical device.

"Come," Yvonnel bade K'yorl. "Back out, quickly. Let us find Jarlaxle and his companions and see again through the eyes of the human, Entreri."

◆ ◆ ◆

KIRIY GIGGLED AS she exited the room, even before the cries of surprise and alarm erupted behind her.

Matron Mother Zhindia and her cabal of priestesses were watching her, she knew, and so she was not surprised when the Melarni gathering reached out magically to slam the Do'Urden audience chamber doors behind her.

"What?" cried out one of the guards in surprise.

"Priestess Kiriy?" asked the other. But the woman was already several steps beyond them.

Kiriy swung about, eyes flashing. "You are Bregan D'aerthe," she said to one of the men. "And you are Baenre!" she called to the other, in clearly accusatory tones.

The two young warriors looked at each other, then back at her, confused. "Do'Urden," one replied, but too late. Balls of fire appeared in the air above each of the two, and lines of searing flames shot down over them, immolating them where they stood.

Kiriy laughed again. Matron Mother Zhindia was with her! It had been so many years since she had been involved in an inter-House war. So many boring years! These wars showcased the epitome of drow battle prowess and glory, where priestesses hurled their magic across the city, through scrying portals enacted by infiltrating agents like Kiriy.

These were the fights, priestess against priestess, where Lady Lolth could fully determine the outcome. And now, with the guards writhing and dying on the floor, Kiriy knew with all her heart that Lady Lolth was with her cause.

Priestess Kiriy would depose Dahlia and Matron Mother Zeerith at long last. Lolth was with her, and would see a new House Xorlarrin arise from the ashes of House Do'Urden and from the corpses of those Xorlarrins who chose to side with Zeerith.

She looked again to the audience chamber guards, writhing on the floor pathetically, melting under the wrath of Lolth. She heard the fighting in the audience chamber now—even if her siblings and their allies won out in there, they would be too late to stop the coup.

She pictured the spider-shaped table in House Melarn, brilliantly ornate and as fabulous as the one in the Ruling Council, by all accounts—though Kiriy had never actually seen the one in the chambers of the Ruling Council. Why didn't the other great Houses of Menzoberranzan have tables, gathering places for priestesses, as beautiful as the one in House Melarn? Why wasn't a tribute like that commonplace? Surely House Xorlarrin never had such a beautiful tribute to Lady Lolth in all their vast compound.

But House Do'Urden, soon enough to be the new House Xorlarrin, would, Kiriy vowed. She pictured the Melarni war room, the magnificent spider table set between the prized bronze doors, Matron Mother Zhindia in her black gown, her war gown, seated at its head.

And they were with her now. Lolth was with her now.

"Quickly!" Kiriy heard in the air around her, and she smiled. It was Matron Mother Zhindia reminding her, magically whispering to her: "Darthiir is the key! You must be rid of her."

Kiriy was already moving in that direction, though she didn't agree with that estimation, and certainly not with the urgency in Zhindia's voice.

"She is a babbling idiot," Kiriy whispered, knowing the Melarni priestesses could hear her. "She is no threat."

"She is Baenre's puppet," Matron Mother Zhindia's voice sounded in the empty air beside her. "Kill her quickly. Sever the tie."

Kiriy moved more deliberately. She dismissed her curiosity about her siblings and the others in the audience chamber. She would sort out the remains of that battle later.

She heard other fighting then, echoing along the corridors. A young priestess rushed toward her from the side.

"High Priestess!" the younger woman cried. "They have made the balcony!"

"They?"

"Hunzrin!" the young woman explained. "Those guards who arrived have turned on us and have helped reinforcements to our balconies! Our enemies are in the House!"

The frantic young woman turned to sprint away, but Kiriy called to her, "Who are you, young priestess?"

The woman turned and looked at her curiously, clearly perplexed by such a question at that critical time.

"It is all right," Kiriy assured her. "We will defeat the stone heads. Who are you?"

"Ba'sula," she replied.

Kiriy studied her more closely, trying to remember this one. "Who is your mentor?" she asked. "Who sent you to House Do'Urden?"

"I serve High Priestess Sos'Umptu in the Fane of the Goddess," Ba'sula replied.

"Ah, you are Baenre," Kiriy said, nodding in recognition, and smiling— and if Ba'sula had been more perceptive, she would have known it to be the grin of a hunter.

"What are we to do? Where would you have me go?"

"Go?" Kiriy asked incredulously.

"We are under assau—"

Her voice stopped as she froze in place, caught by a spell of holding cast by the Melarni priestesses. Kiriy felt that magic flowing through her, and felt privileged indeed to be used as a conduit for the glory of the Spider Queen.

She walked by the magically frozen Ba'sula, lifting a hand to gently stroke the young priestess's smooth neck. She could see the terror in

Ba'sula's eyes, could feel the woman trembling slightly, but only slightly. The spell would allow nothing more. Kiriy thought for a moment that she should keep this one, a plaything for after victory was won.

But no, she was Baenre, Kiriy reminded herself. Keeping her alive, if she was discovered, would give the matron mother all the excuse she needed to throw all her considerable weight at House Do'Urden.

The same hand that so gently stroked Ba'sula's throat now waved in the air, fingers casting a spell as Kiriy passed.

It was a simple poisoning dweomer, one that would normally kill a victim with little outward sign. But Kiriy had cleverly altered this one, as much for the viewing pleasure of the Melarni priestesses as because she wanted this priestess, this Baenre, to know the full horror of approaching death.

Images of large spiders, a large as Kiriy's open palm, appeared in the air all around the trapped priestess, floating on strands of glistening webs. They scrambled hungrily, the strands swaying. They leaped to the priestess's face and shoulders. She saw them—and they bit her. It didn't matter that they were magical illusions designed to simply add terror to the pain of the poisoning spell. They bit her and she saw them biting, and she felt them biting. They bit her eyes. They crawled into her mouth and they bit her tongue. One skittered down her throat and bit her all the way to her belly.

Kiriy walked away, confident that her display would please Matron Mother Zhindia. She got confirmation of exactly that a dozen steps later, when the Melarni priestesses dispelled their holding spell, freeing Ba'sula Baenre.

And the dying woman screamed, and gurgled, and choked on the sensation of spiders crawling down her throat.

Sweet music to Kiriy Xorlarrin's ears.

◆ ◆ ◆

ENTRERI TURNED A doubtful look to Drizzt, who could only shrug, equally at a loss. "Matron Mother Shakti?" he asked doubtfully. "A woman?"

Jarlaxle motioned to the mirror, which now showed the image of Shakti Hunzrin superimposed over his own reflection.

"You are insane."

"Let your thoughts align the images," Jarlaxle explained.

Entreri looked to Drizzt.

"Dawdle and we will be caught, and your dear Dahlia will be quite dead, I assure you!" Jarlaxle cried.

Entreri looked more deeply into the looking glass and offered a profound and resigned sigh. Agatha's Mask turned back to a simple white stage mask for just a moment. Then it began to shift, and so, too, did Entreri's face and body, the illusion of Shakti Hunzrin coming to life before Drizzt's astonished eyes.

"Now what?" Entreri asked when the transformation was complete—and even his voice had changed.

Jarlaxle pulled forth a wand, held its tip up to his temple, spoke a command word, and he, too, became a woman, a priestess of Lolth. He looked at Drizzt and reminded him, "You are a mere male and these are fanatical Melarni. Two steps back and head bowed." Then he led the way to the webbed front of the Melarn compound.

As they neared, Jarlaxle stepped behind Entreri—let all the detection magic focus on the Matron Mother of House Hunzrin, and so fail against the powerful magic of Agatha's Mask.

"Just glare at them," he whispered to Entreri as the trio neared the House guards.

Entreri did—and few in the world could freeze a target with a look as fully as Artemis Entreri.

In any form.

◆ ◆ ◆

"Oh, brilliant!" Yvonnel exclaimed as she and K'yorl watched Jarlaxle's group outside of House Melarn. "He sorted through the webbing and strikes from behind."

"It pleases you when one House attacks another?" K'yorl said, the interruption shocking Yvonnel so profoundly she nearly pulled her hands from the stoup. K'yorl rarely spoke, other than to answer direct questions, and never before had she found the courage to interrupt Yvonnel, particularly not when they were in this melded state, their joined consciousness far from the room that held their corporeal forms.

"Jarlaxle is of no House. Nor are his companions."

"But there is a war. You approve."

Yvonnel opened her eyes, and looked again back in the Room of Divination, staring across the water that showed Jarlaxle and his friends in their disguises nearing House Melarn.

She stared at K'yorl for a moment, then glanced into the stoup to regard the scene. On a sudden impulse and a sudden fear, she closed her eyes, and then breathed a sigh of relief to find herself looking through the eyes of Artemis Entreri. So she was in two places at once, she thought, but then corrected herself. She could be in either of the places, here in her corporeal form, or out there with the disembodied consciousness, but not in both. She opened her eyes again to regard K'yorl, who grinned.

That grin came as a warning to Yvonnel, for while she could be in one place or the other, she only then realized that her prisoner was truly in both, simultaneously.

I approve that the aggressor House Melarn will not ruin my plans, she telepathically told K'yorl, and Yvonnel went back to the distant place, inside the eyes of Artemis Entreri.

"They are fanatical disciples of the Spider Queen," she both heard and felt K'yorl reply.

So Yvonnel tried the same. She forced her mouth to speak her response, but kept her eyes and sensibilities out there, approaching House Melarn. "As are we all," she said and thought, and she heard her voice in the background, and she sensed that her sudden mastery of this dual-experience had caught K'yorl off her guard. "Yet some will win, and some will lose. Too often do we attribute such outcomes to the favor of Lady Lolth."

"You do not believe in such a thing?"

"I believe that Lady Lolth favors those who are most expedient and clever among us. You should hope for that truth, K'yorl Odran. In it, you might find your salvation."

Whatever threat she had sensed from K'yorl was gone then, vanished in the possibility of redemption, of salvation.

She put her focus back to the situation at House Melarn, where Jarlaxle, Drizzt, and Entreri were approaching some wary House guards.

Using K'yorl's powers, her psionic bow, Yvonnel imparted suggestions of uneasiness and fear into those guards, who were clearly already intimidated—and why not, with Matron Mother Shakti fast approaching?

◆ ◆ ◆

"To MATRON MOTHER Zhindia, at once!" Jarlaxle ordered the intimidated Melarni guards.

"We will announce . . ." one soldier started to reply, but Jarlaxle was ready for that, and even as the warrior started talking, Jarlaxle started casting through a ring he wore on his left hand. He gestured and the guard melted into a slug on the ground at the base of the webbing.

"To Matron Mother Zhindia!" Jarlaxle told the remaining soldier, and the mercenary squashed the slug with a grinding heel.

Drizzt tried not to wince. He understood the stakes, of course, but the sheer brutality of Menzoberranzan had caught him off guard.

And the deaths were only just beginning.

Drizzt scrambled to keep up, the surviving guard leading them quickly along the swinging web bridges. As they went, Jarlaxle emphatically and repeatedly signed to him, and to Entreri: *Do not hesitate!*

Near the top of the webbed front, high from the cavern floor, the group went into the complex, which was organized much like a conch shell, with circling corridors winding tighter to the center, surrounded by small chambers all the way.

Many dark elves noted their passage, with several dropping into polite bows at the sight of the Matron Mother of House Hunzrin.

Jarlaxle had guessed right, Drizzt realized. Shakti had been here before, likely recently, and much was afoot now regarding the joint attack on House Do'Urden—how else to explain the deference being shown here, and the hustle to the audience chamber of the Melarn compound?

At last, down one last side passage, they came to a pair of large bronze doors, decorated with jewels and detailed sculptures of Lolth and driders and spiderwebs.

"It is heavily warded," the leading Melarni guard explained, pausing, but Jarlaxle had an orb in hand—whence it came, Drizzt did not know—and pushed right past the guard. He hurled the orb into the door, where it exploded into a puff of spinning, shining bits of some silvery material, all of which seemed attracted to the door. It settled there and began to pop with tiny explosions.

And Jarlaxle, still appearing as a Hunzrin priestess, just stormed ahead, and pushed right through the doors.

Entreri, as Matron Mother Shakti, went with him. The guard started to protest, but only started. Drizzt took him down by slamming Twinkle's pommel into the back of the man's neck, dropping him to the floor.

Beyond the doors, the room's curving walls formed an oval, longer than it was wide. A second identical set of doors stood closed directly across from them. Torches burned along the curving side walls, the flickering lights dancing across tapestries depicting the many glories of the Spider Queen.

A circular table supported by eight external spider-like legs stood in the middle of the floor, a priestess standing in each gap between the appendages. A large decorated golden bowl was set in the middle of the table, still water reflecting the torchlight.

A scrying bowl, Drizzt realized, and in the instant he considered it, he could guess easily enough that these priestesses were looking at House Do'Urden.

It didn't, couldn't, hold his attention for more than that instant, however. As he crossed the threshold into the room, Jarlaxle raised his clenched fist and enacted some magic, and the doors swung shut behind Drizzt with a resounding slam.

At that same moment, the priestess farthest from them, on the far side of the table, screamed in protest. "Matron Mother Shakti, you dare disturb us!"

But Entreri didn't hesitate to answer the woman, who was obviously Matron Mother Zhindia. He drew his blades and leaped ahead—Jarlaxle had told them not to hesitate!—and the nearest Melarni priestess fell dead before she even realized she was being attacked.

A twist of Drizzt's wrist on his belt buckle brought Taulmaril to his hand, an arrow going to it and flying away, and the priestess next to Entreri's victim gasped and folded over the table, neither her wards nor her enchanted robes sufficient to defeat the power of Drizzt's lightning missile.

"Down!" Jarlaxle yelled, and Entreri dived to the side and Drizzt went to one knee, setting another arrow.

Jarlaxle reached inside the front of his blousy white shirt and brought forth a large red gem, which he hurled into the midst of the gathering of priestesses, bouncing it right under the table, where it exploded into a devastating fireball.

In the flames, Drizzt could still pick out a second target. Away went his next arrow, and another priestess tumbled.

As the flames abated, Entreri went forward—and it was Entreri now. He tore the mask from his face, reverting to his human form. He leaped into the midst of a pair of priestesses, standing along the right hand side of the table, both of them with wisps of smoke rising from their gowns, both of them clearly shaken, but also beginning their spellcasting.

Charon's Claw and that deadly jeweled dagger went to work, though, and the two Melarni priestesses became too concerned with diving away to continue their spells.

A third arrow led Drizzt's way to the table, but his intended target, the matron mother directly across the way, already had a powerful ward in place. The arrow exploded in a firework burst of multicolored lights before it could reach its mark. Drizzt hardly noticed. He dropped his bow and drew out his blades, leaping over to the table's left hand side.

But the moment of surprise was over. If these had been common drow, all eight in the room would have been slain in short order, dead before they could begin to react. But these were priestesses of the Spider Queen, zealots all, including the Matron Mother of House Melarn and the first priestess of the powerful House.

Three were down, one by Entreri's blades, two by Drizzt's arrows. A fourth had been wounded in Entreri's charge, but still fought, and a fifth was on the floor, having dived from the assassin's charge, and there she knelt, fingers gesturing.

Behind them, the doors exploded open once more, compelled by a countering spell from Matron Mother Zhindia, and Drizzt heard the charge of Melarni reinforcements.

And he and his companions had nowhere to run.

CHAPTER 14 ◈

Pale Yellow Orbs That Rule the Night

AM SO PLEASED THAT YOU EXTENDED THE INVITATION TO INCLUDE the wizards of Longsaddle," Penelope Harpell said to Catti-brie. The two worked in an open tent near the reconstruction of the trunk of the Hosttower of the Arcane. Dwarves bustled all around, bringing in chunks of the fallen tower, cataloguing them and bringing them to another huge tent where the puzzle was being placed back together. Fortunately, thus far at least, it seemed as if the parts nearer the place of destruction were the lower pieces of the tower.

"Your input here, as in Gauntlgrym, has helped so much and given me strength," Catti-brie replied. She paused then and looked out at the hustle off to the side, where some dwarves were arguing, hands on hips, with Lady Avelyere. Yes, Catti-brie thought, Penelope's presence did lend her strength, as did the person of Lady Avelyere. Despite their unorthodox, unbalanced relationship, Catti-brie couldn't deny her affection for the sorcerer.

Avelyere looked truly flustered as the dwarves bounced and waved and pointed all around her. She glanced at Catti-brie and Penelope, who was now also watching, and gave a helpless sigh and shrug.

The two women shared a laugh at that.

"Her work has been tremendous," Penelope remarked, turning back to the maps of the North, Luskan to Neverwinter, they had spread upon the table. They had drawn the location of Gauntlgrym on one copy, and Catti-brie had traced in lines to represent the tendrils of the Hosttower that carried the water and the elemental power to the primordial pit.

"Your insight seems plausible," Penelope admitted, nodding. Catti-brie had raised the possibility that they could detect those underground tendrils by following the lines of forest between the two locations. "Particularly the willows! Is there anything in all the world that chases water more determinedly than a willow?"

"As determinedly as a dragon chases gold," Catti-brie replied.

"Or a dwarf chases ale," Penelope added with a smile.

"Or Penelope chases men," Catti-brie remarked, stealing the mirth, for a moment at least, as Penelope looked up at her curiously.

"I mean no offense."

"You have found a unique manner of proving that."

"Am I wrong about you and Wulfgar?"

"Does it bother you?" Penelope asked.

"No," Catti-brie replied. "Truly, no. I apologize. Let us pretend that I never made the remark. Like an elf chases stars, I should have said."

"Why?"

Catti-brie looked at her closely.

"Why, then?" Penelope reiterated. "I do believe that you meant no offense, and so I take none, but your words were no slip of the tongue. They came from somewhere, yes?"

"Curiosity," Catti-brie admitted.

"You already know of the tryst between me and Wulfgar."

"And he wasn't the first."

"The first?" Penelope laughed. "Oh, by the gods no!"

"Even though you are married."

"Oh," Penelope said, catching on. "Yes, well, my marriage is a different arrangement than you have perhaps encountered before. There is nothing deceptive about my . . . adventures, however I choose to find and enjoy them."

"And Dowell?" Catti-brie asked, referring to her husband, a most gracious man and friend to Catti-brie in the years she had spent at the Ivy Mansion.

"His life is exciting, too, I assure you."

"Then what about love?"

Catti-brie appreciated the sincerity in the sympathetic, but surely not superior look Penelope offered.

"I choose to separate the adventure of new relationships and the deep and abiding love I share with Dowell," the Harpell explained. "I will live once. My healthy years of adulthood will span perhaps fifty, perhaps longer if I am careful, or if an enemy does not kill me, or if I can find some magic to extend my time."

"There is such magic. Would you use it?"

"Of course!"

"Many would not," Catti-brie said, and it was certainly true enough. Potions of longevity and the like were not nearly as commonplace as Penelope's attitude would indicate, nor were spells of resurrection.

"Many expect a better existence beyond this life we know."

"There is," Catti-brie replied with some certainty.

"And I do not diminish or doubt your beliefs," said Penelope. "For me, this is what I know, and I choose to enjoy it—in every way I can. I find joy in meeting new people, and in exploring more deeply with those I meet and come to like."

"With the men, you mean."

Penelope shrugged and grinned, letting Catti-brie know that perhaps that didn't matter quite as much as she supposed.

"For carnal pleasures," Catti-brie clarified.

Penelope shrugged. "Sometimes."

"As with Wulfgar."

"They are called pleasures for a reason, my friend."

Catti-brie started to respond, but Penelope cut her short with an upraised hand. "Perhaps now I should be taking offense?" she asked. "Or is your obvious frustration with me now an honest inquisition or, as it seems, a judgment?"

"No," Catti-brie stammered, at a loss. She had lived into her forties in her previous life, and now again for more than two decades. She had faced mighty enemies—dragons and demons, even—and had fought as a proxy for Mielikki in a great struggle with the goddess Lolth. She had passed through death. She had been afforded the insights of divine beings.

How could this uneasiness that had come over her be placing in her into such a spot of judgment and emotional distress?

"I do not try to judge," she explained after taking a deep breath to center herself. "I am simply trying to unders . . ."

She paused as movement to the side caught her attention and drew her eye to Archmage Gromph, who was crossing by Lady Avelyere and the dwarves. She couldn't help but note the haughty dark elf, seeming so far above their petty quibbling. Or at least, her initial reaction began that way, though it soon shifted to her insight that yes, indeed, Gromph did appear so far above that pettiness, seeming so much above those other mere mortals.

Seeming to her almost godlike.

Many heartbeats passed by unnoticed to Catti-brie. Gromph turned and flashed her a smile and his amber eyes would not let her go.

"He is attractive, isn't he?" Penelope asked, the woman's voice jarring her from her near-trance. "And powerful." There was no denying the admiration in Penelope's tone, and for a moment, it occurred to Catti-brie that Penelope might wish to lie with Gromph. And for a moment, Catti-brie wanted to slap her.

"So amazingly proficient with the Art," Penelope continued. "It is hard not to be taken with him."

It took a few moments for that last remark to truly sink in, but when it did, it shook Catti-brie and she snapped her head around to view Penelope. Penelope wasn't looking at Gromph, as she had expected, but at Catti-brie, and with a knowing grin.

"He was the Archmage of Menzoberranzan," Catti-brie blurted, "serving Lolth and the vile matron mothers."

"Yes, dangerous," Penelope said, never blinking, and Catti-brie got the distinct feeling that the woman was mocking her.

Despite that, Catti-brie found herself staring at Gromph once more, and in her thoughts, she imagined herself amorously entwined with the archmage. She tried to shake that vision away, but it held on stubbornly, and when she managed to turn her eyes outward, there was Gromph, smiling at her from afar.

"It is hard not to be taken with him," Penelope Harpell said again.

"I am not!" Catti-brie protested, never turning around. "He is evil. Who knows how many innocents have fallen to his evocations?"

"Are you telling me, or yourself?" Penelope asked.

Now Catti-brie did spin back again on Penelope, though in no small part because Gromph turned away and walked farther from her, his eyes going to something else. She stared hard at the Harpell woman, trying to find some stinging retort. She wanted to lash out, but as she realized that truth, she turned it inward.

Penelope's words had struck her because she was having a hard time denying them.

"There is nothing wrong with wondering," the woman told her.

"Or with acting out on that wonder, if I were like you," Catti-brie replied, and she wanted to retract the words as soon as she uttered them.

Penelope shrugged—if she took offense, she didn't show it. "If that is your way," she answered. With a smile and a wink, Penelope shifted her gaze past Catti-brie and over to the distant Gromph. "I would spend a long tenday with him," she said, "as long as we had enough food."

Catti-brie felt herself blushing.

"Life is an adventure," Penelope said. "A beautiful adventure."

◆ ◆ ◆

GROMPH WATCHED THE two women retreat from the open tent, the Harpell wizard moving to join Lady Avelyere, and Catti-brie heading for the bridge to Closeguard Isle. She'd cross, almost certainly, and then on to the mainland, to replace her maps and search for others in the repository Bregan D'aerthe had set up to hold the scrolls and tomes found in Illusk and elsewhere.

Gromph's stare followed the intriguing woman across that first bridge, and all the way past the tower of High Captain Kurth, who, coincidentally, was even then approaching Gromph from the other direction.

"Well met, Archmage," Beniago said, still in his respectful bow when Gromph turned to regard him.

"You look ridiculous," Gromph replied, shaking his head in open disgust at the Baenre drow's human facade, with that flaming red hair.

"It is a useful tool, nothing more."

"You are a Baenre," Gromph scolded. "At what point does the embarrassment of your disguise outweigh the small utility it provides?"

"When Jarlaxle tells me so, I expect."

The reminder of Beniago's true allegiance drew a slight grimace from Gromph, but the point was well made.

"What use is it at this point, in any case?" Gromph asked. "Most of the city knows the truth of House Kurth, and knows that the drow are in control. There is nothing they can do about it, and likely nothing they would want to do about it. We are as much their armor as their potential enemies."

Beniago shrugged, somewhat dismissively. "Perhaps the deception is to deter eyes outside the City of Sails. Waterdhavian lords, drow matron mothers . . ."

"Tiago knew the truth of you, as did the Xorlarrins," Gromph said. "And so, too, Matron Mother Baenre. Who, then, are you deceiving, other than yourself?"

"You would have to ask Jarlaxle," said Beniago.

"Your loyalty is commendable, I suppose."

"It was earned, many times over, and all in Bregan D'aerthe would agree, Archmage. Jarlaxle need not rule with threats, but merely by asking. All in Bregan D'aerthe would fight for him and die for him."

Gromph looked very carefully at the drow in human disguise, recognizing that there was a message there beyond the words, a not-so-subtle warning, perhaps.

"She is beautiful, is she not?" Beniago asked unexpectedly, gesturing with his chin in the direction of Closeguard Isle. "For a human woman, I mean."

Gromph glanced back, then back at Beniago, his expression caught halfway between confusion and an incredulous grin.

"The wife of Drizzt," Beniago clarified, his reference to the rogue Do'Urden making much more than the woman's identity clear in Gromph's mind.

"And Jarlaxle would not take kindly were I to bed her, is that your point?" Gromph asked bluntly.

Beniago put on an innocent aspect, even held up his hands as if at a loss.

But Gromph knew better, and he laughed aloud then, amused that he was being threatened by such a creature as this pitiful red-haired human imposter standing in front of him.

"Jarlaxle will take as I demand, whatever I may give to him," Gromph replied, too calmly. "Ah, yes, the wife of Drizzt. I hadn't thought of pretty Catti-brie in those terms before—but bedding an *iblith*? Absurd! That is the stuff of Jarlaxle, whose tastes allow for. . ." He paused and laughed again, gesturing to indicate Beniago, and more pointedly Beniago's disguise, as he finished with a derisive snort, "This."

"There is much to Jarlaxle's world that you do not understand," Beniago warned. "And since this is now your world as well, perhaps you should."

"And perhaps you would be wise to beware your indiscipline."

Beniago bowed again. "I only wish to inform, Archmage."

"Yes, of course," said Gromph, and he looked back to Closeguard Isle and beyond, and began stroking his chin and making small humming sounds, as if considering something.

"Catti-brie," he said. "Pretty Catti-brie." He turned back to Beniago, his face now bright. "I had not thought of her in those terms, High

Captain. But now perhaps I shall. Perhaps it will be worth my time to bed her, just to witness Jarlaxle's reaction."

"And Drizzt's?" Beniago managed to say, and his wince gave Gromph great pleasure, confirming that he had put the fool on his heels.

"Who?" Gromph said with a snicker, and walked away.

◆　◆　◆

"I WAS TEASING you, and I should not have," Penelope Harpell said to Catti-brie later that night, the two alone sitting on the edge of the bed in Catti-brie's tent, with Penelope brushing Catti-brie's thick auburn hair. "Your emotions were honest, and in sharing them, you trusted me with something beyond such childish—"

"I gave you reason," Catti-brie interrupted. "I should not have judged you. I simply do not understand."

"Perhaps you place a higher value on such acts than I," said Penelope.

Catti-brie grabbed the brush so she wouldn't get scratched by it as she turned to stare earnestly at the woman. "You diminish yourself?" she asked.

"Oh, no," Penelope clarified. "It is not a contest. I place no value on placing such a value, if you get my meaning."

"So you mock me my morals?"

"Of course not!"

"You claim that I place great value upon it, and then dismiss that value as useless."

"I do not!" Penelope declared in no uncertain terms. "It is your way, and I respect that."

"How can you, if to you the act of lovemaking is so trite?"

"I never said that."

"It is surely implied!"

Penelope sat back and nodded, staring openly at Catti-brie all the while as if she was honestly trying to understand, or perhaps to explain herself better. "Is it the act itself on which you place the value?"

"I value it."

"If you were not with Drizzt, would you be celibate?"

Catti-brie started to respond, but cut herself short and sat back, her expression perplexed. Penelope had caught her off guard.

"If I were not in love . . ." she said tentatively.

229

"But you could be in love with another?"

"I cannot imagine that."

"Did you not once love Wulfgar?"

Catti-brie sucked in her breath—Penelope had hit a nerve. Once she had thought herself in love with Wulfgar indeed, and he was the only other man she had ever lain with in both her lives.

"I thought I was . . ." she started to say, but Penelope held up her hand to stop her from elaborating.

"Wulfgar was in love with you," Penelope said. "Of that I have no doubt. Do you regret . . . ?"

"Yes!" Catti-brie blurted, then "No!" followed by a helpless shrug.

"It is not the act itself for you, I think," Penelope said. "Nor for many, I am sure. It is, rather, the honesty and the integrity. There is no deeper secret a person might hold than those moments, and so perhaps it should only be given, by man or by woman, in great trust."

"And how many do you trust?" Catti-brie asked, rather sharply.

"If I place less value on the act of love than you do, it is not out of a lack of self-respect, my friend," Penelope answered, trying hard, and mostly successfully, to keep her own budding anger out of the response. "Nay, value is the wrong word, I fear. I should not have brought that word into this conversation."

She could see that she had Catti-brie's attention then, the woman's guard still up, obviously. But in Catti-brie's eyes, Penelope saw curiosity—and Penelope got the feeling that this entire conversation was striking at Catti-brie's sensibilities more than it should. Something, the Harpell woman thought, was not quite as it should be.

"Not value," Penelope said. "Perhaps you tie the physical act more tightly to your ethical being than do I."

"Spiritual being," Catti-brie offered in correction, but Penelope would hear none of that.

"Not so," she said. "No, I do not divorce the physical from the spiritual. There is a not-subtle difference between being adventurous and being wanton."

"Or is the difference merely a matter of how you wish others to perceive you?"

Catti-brie hadn't spoken the words sharply, but she might as well have followed her question with a slap across Penelope's face, as far as Penelope was concerned.

"Are you trying to save me?" Penelope shot back. "I told you once that my attitude on this subject was in no way a reflection of my own self-worth. I need no saving."

Catti-brie started to reply, but Penelope cut her short.

"And I'll hear none," she said. "We are friends, and I wish to keep it that way."

Catti-brie looked away. Penelope noted moisture rimming the bottom of her large eyes.

"I do not judge you," Penelope said softly. "As with whatever god we might choose, this is a personal choice, and if you're not harming anyone, then there is no right or wrong . . ."

"No!" Catti-brie said, spinning back. "I cannot accept that. Not with Drizzt . . ." She sucked in her breath and turned away again.

"Not with Drizzt?" Penelope said, and a thought hit her hard then. "Not with Drizzt going off to rescue Dahlia?"

"She was his lover," Catti-brie mumbled.

"After you had been dead for more than half a century!" Penelope retorted before she took a moment to consider her response. Was Catti-brie jealous? It made no sense to her. She had known Catti-brie as a sister those days in the Ivy Mansion—there was no basis for this, nor was it in any way in character for the strong, self-reliant, and purposeful woman.

"I do not need you to remind me of my history," Catti-brie said, seeming totally flustered and out of sorts.

Penelope couldn't begin to sort it out.

But then, Penelope was not in the mind of Catti-brie, where once more images of lovemaking with Gromph Baenre teased her and tempted her, and that in turn assaulted her every denial, and chewed at the edges of her understanding of the very essence of her relationship with Drizzt.

◆ ◆ ◆

"You look troubled, my dear," old Kipper Harpell said to Penelope when she returned to the main tent in the Harpell complex, which had been set up just over the bridge on Closeguard Isle.

The woman walked over and slumped into the chair next to her uncle, and Kipper moved a hand across to massage her shoulder.

"Something is not quite right, and I cannot yet distill it," Penelope admitted. "Catti-brie is quite in distress, I fear."

"About the Hosttower?" Kipper asked. "I believe the construction is going splendidly! We are far ahead of where I thought—"

"No," Penelope said. "This is on a more personal level. Perhaps she fears for Drizzt."

"He is going to Menzoberranzan, so say the whispers," said Kipper. "I fear for Drizzt!"

Penelope looked over at him with all seriousness. "Or perhaps she fears because of the elf woman Drizzt is going to rescue."

Kipper looked at her curiously for just a moment, before putting on a perfectly perplexed expression. "Drizzt?" he asked incredulously. "Is there a truer heart in all Faerûn?"

"As I said, something is not quite right." Now it was her turn to put an honest and sober look over Kipper. "And I fear it has more than a little to do with our host here in Luskan."

"Jarlaxle? Beniago?"

"Our real host."

"Oh, that one," Kipper said, assuming the exasperated expression that he always wore when Gromph Baenre was in the room or in the conversation. "Well then, I fear that your concern is well placed."

◆ ◆ ◆

SHE AWAKENED DRENCHED in sweat, her breath coming is short gasps. She didn't know whether to be terrified or wonderfully contented, and the wild disparity of the two offered no resolution.

And she saw them still, the pale yellow eyes, just a hint of pink around the amber iris, like a simmering demonic presence hidden beneath the startling beauty of the mighty dark elf.

Catti-brie tried to calm herself, whispered reassurances, and even placed a hand over her fast-beating heart.

A dream?

Was she alone?

Had she been alone?

She forced herself to take a deep breath. It was too dark in her tent on this moonless night—she couldn't tell dreams from present reality.

She reached her hand out tentatively across the bed, fearful that she might find someone sleeping there. When that dark thought proved unfounded, she moved her hand out to the small night table, thinking to reach the small lamp.

Before she got her fingers to it, though, she found another item, one more comforting.

"Guenhwyvar, oh I need you," she whispered, bringing the onyx figurine in close to her chest.

A few heartbeats later, she felt the panther climb up beside her, then flop down with her back against Catti-brie's leg, as if reading the woman's mind.

The bed groaned under the weight of the great cat, but Catti-brie didn't care. Even if it broke, she would lie there on the fallen mattress, safe with Guen so close. She reached down to ruffle the panther's fur, and the cat looked up to regard her. Even in the dim light, those feline eyes shined.

And Catti-brie took great comfort—for a moment.

Then the image in her mind changed, the panther's eyes transforming into those pale yellow orbs that ruled Catti-brie's fevered night.

CHAPTER 15 ◈

The Power of Insanity

ARLAXLE WAS NEAREST TO THE OPENED DOUBLE DOORS. HE SPUN to meet that threat, Khazid'hea in one hand, a wand in the other. A mob of Melarni guards rushed to the defense of their matron mother—then stumbled as one when a blob of syrupy goo slammed into the leading pair, stopping them cold. A second heavy glob flew in to further bind and entangle the group.

For a moment, Jarlaxle thought he had the situation in hand, but above that second magical glob came a huge spear—and the mercenary realized that one of the famed and deadly Melarni driders had come.

"Do not hesitate!" Jarlaxle warned his capable companions once again, a command doubly critical now that he had to abandon the fight with the priestesses and retreat to the doors, to get them closed and secured before all hope was lost.

◆ ◆ ◆

"THE BALCONY," MATRON Mother Zhindia said from beside Kiriy.

Kiriy had reached the main corridor to the room where Matron Mother Darthiir Do'Urden was, her goal nearly in sight. But at the intersection was also the corridor leading to the forward guard chambers, with the balcony entrance to House Do'Urden just beyond those.

Kiriy's instincts told her to go straight to dispose of the wretched surface elf abomination, and so she didn't welcome the order to defend the balcony instead. She understood Zhindia's insistence, though, from a practical standpoint. The war was clearly on now, given the sounds echoing about. The Hunzrin soldiers were advancing. This fight had to be about more than Dahlia

She started to respond, but felt a jolt. Though it was a sensation Kiriy had never before experienced, she somehow understood that the connection to the Melarni war room had been severed. Instinctively, she glanced back the way she had come, expecting the troublesome and impudent Ravel and his loyal wizards to come rushing down against her.

But no, the path behind her was clear, and she had left the audience chamber and her siblings far, far behind.

"Are you there?" she whispered.

No answer.

She was torn. She glanced again along the corridor that would wind around the House chapel and take her to Darthiir's room, but she knew in her heart that she couldn't go that way. Not yet. She had to obey Matron Mother Zhindia. House Melarn would be all-important to her ascent and restructuring of House Xorlarrin. She picked up her pace and was soon sprinting along the corridor. She burst into the first guard station to find a handful of House Do'Urden soldiers milling about anxiously, weapons drawn.

For a moment, Kiriy expected they would turn and attack her, but she quickly remembered that they thought her on their side.

But she surely wasn't an ally. They were Baenre and Bregan D'aerthe soldiers.

"What is happening?" she asked sharply.

"First Priestess, they are battling on the balcony," one answered.

"It is House Hunzrin," said another. "The stone heads!"

"And you are *here*?" Kiriy asked with as much incredulity as she could manage.

"We will use the choke point of the door to hold them, First Priestess," answered the first of the previous speakers, who seemed to be the leader.

"Fools!" Kiriy scolded. "House Baenre is watching and will see our troubles, surely—indeed, they already have, of course!" She wasn't sure if she was correct or not, but likely it was true that the battle had been noted beyond the balcony of House Do'Urden. Kiriy left out the part where House Baenre would do nothing to help the doomed House Do'Urden, caught as they were in the tangled web Archmage Gromph had made.

"To the balconies with you!" she cried. "At once. Put on a grand display. Fight for your House and your honor until the Baenre garrison arrives, and let all the Hunzrin fodder die out there on the balcony."

The guards looked at each other doubtfully, and Kiriy hid her smile at the confirmation that the Hunzrin forces had come in great numbers.

"Go!" she shouted. "Let our enemies know complete defeat before they have ever entered our house! Go, I say, or feel the wrath of Lady Lolth, who will brook no cowardice!"

The five scrambled out, and Kiriy followed, waving for the guards in the next room to join in with the first group. From that second doorway, the first priestess got a glance at the balconies, where Hunzrin soldiers swarmed and Do'Urden guards died.

"For the glory of Lolth," she whispered, hoping against hope that Matron Mother Zhindia could hear her and had seen the beautiful battle through her eyes.

Kiriy ran back through the rooms and along the corridor, smiling, giggling even, at the thought of murdering the abominable Matron Mother Darthiir. She considered the spells she would use to incapacitate the fool, and decided that the final blow would come from her hands—physically. She would feel Dahlia's blood. She would hear the last gasping breath of this abomination whose very existence mocked the glory of the Spider Queen.

◆ ◆ ◆

THE PRIESTESS STANDING in front of him sneered when Artemis Entreri came out of his disguise, revealing himself as a mere human. That would be to his advantage, Entreri knew. The dark elves would not understand the weight of the threat he posed in this "inferior" skin.

The whip cracked above his head, and he ducked and reflexively threw Charon's Claw up horizontally to keep the stinging weapon high. But in came the skilled priestess, low and fast with her mace, the weapon sparkling with magical energy, and it took all of Entreri's balance to allow him to backtrack enough to avoid a brutal strike.

And so the assassin reminded himself not to fall victim to the same thing, not to underestimate these opponents. These were dark elves, supremely trained, marvelously agile, and worse, these were drow women, whose training typically exceeded that of the males.

He came back to an upright and balanced position and began a countering routine, trying to find some fast way inside the reach of that vicious whip.

It cracked again, just to his left, too far to pose a threat, and so he thought he had his chance.

But before he could even take the first step forward, something magically appeared in the air to his right, and he understood a moment before the summoned magical hammer struck him that the priestess in front of him had snapped her whip merely as a distraction for her sister, who remained on the floor to the side.

Entreri took the hit, turning and bending at the last instant to accept it on the shoulder instead of the side of his face. He continued turning, and threw himself to his left in a spinning dive, which froze the priestess in front of him in surprise and afforded Entreri the moment he needed.

As he turned in that spin, he noted the kneeling priestess, once more spellcasting, and his left arm flicked beneath his downward-facing chest in a sudden backhand.

The kneeling priestess had magical wards engaged, of course, but magical, too, was Entreri's jeweled dagger. It hit the protective shield and drove through, diving into the priestess's wide eye.

She wailed and fell away, mortally wounded. Her trembling hands reached for the killing blade, but she could not find the courage to touch the quivering dagger.

Entreri crashed down to the ground and bounced himself to his knees, then threw himself to his feet with great speed and agility.

Not fast enough, though, to avoid the snap of his other foe's whip, lashing against his leg, thigh to shin across the side of his knee.

He grimaced and spun to square off, and found the priestess already there, right in front of him, her mace whipping for his face.

A sudden parry with his sword intercepted the heavy weapon, but the force of the blow knocked his blade back and he only barely managed to avoid being clipped by the deadly red blade of Charon's Claw.

Horrible death loomed less than a finger's breadth from his cheek.

He fell back, trying to regain an even footing with his foe, but the priestess pressed on relentlessly, working her weapons brilliantly.

◆ ◆ ◆

DRIZZT KNEW THE priestess at the end was Matron Mother Zhindia, and knew that he had to get to her as quickly as possible. But there remained two others between him and Zhindia Melarn on this side of the table.

Soon to be one, he believed as he came in hard. The apparently surprised priestess hadn't even drawn her weapons. He stabbed with Icingdeath, certain he had a kill.

But the priestess spoke a word, just a single word, and she was gone, simply vanished, and Drizzt's thrusting blade hit nothing but air.

He didn't immediately understand the move, though he was familiar with such spells as Word of Recall, but he was wise enough not to even try to understand it then, and instead pressed forward for the next priestess in line.

And he was in darkness, complete and impenetrable, which was not unexpected when dealing with powerful dark elves. So he charged on, focusing on the mental image, sword leading, to try to get to the woman before she could turn out of the way.

He felt the tingle of magic, and deep in his thoughts realized that he had stepped upon a magical glyph just an instant before the jarring blast of lightning crackled up his leg and launched him sidelong into the air. He kept his wits enough to twist and roll about, fighting past the spasms evoked by the lightning to get his legs out just before he collided into the left-hand wall of the oval room.

He crashed down hard to the floor, focusing on simply not dropping his weapons. His hands shook wildly, his forearms flexing and jolting so forcefully that his elbows hurt. He wasn't in the globe of darkness any longer, which left him exposed and disoriented. He recognized his vulnerability and stubbornly demanded his center and his balance as he forced himself to his feet.

The priestess was out of her conjured darkness, too, moving back from the table nearer the room's far doors. She was casting again, but that was the least of Drizzt's troubles. Matron Mother Zhindia, who stood directly in front of the second set of bronze doors, was casting, too.

Before he could make his move, a line of fire shot down from above, brilliant and intense, covering him, engulfing him, melting the stone of the floor at his feet.

Within the crackling flames, Drizzt heard the laughter of the confident priestesses.

◆　◆　◆

YVONNEL'S THOUGHTS SCREAMED in protest when she saw the immolating fires sweep down over Drizzt.

"To him! Protect him!" she screamed, both telepathically to her entwined out-of-body companion and audibly back in the Room of Divination in House Baenre.

Even as she cried out, though, Yvonnel saw the truth, and her admiration and curiosity soared.

The jolting experience as they flew out of Entreri's eyes sent the world spinning.

◆ ◆ ◆

IF THE ROOM behind him was full of confusion—priestesses tumbling, magic exploding, darkness stealing half the table—then the corridor just beyond the room had devolved into absolute chaos.

Just the way Jarlaxle wanted it to be.

His magical globs had caught the leading warriors, reducing their charge to a stumbling obstruction for those scrambling to get past them and into the fray. Jarlaxle stood at the entryway to the room, putting his magical bracer to good use. His arm pumped repeatedly, and with every retraction, the bracer slipped another summoned dagger into his grasp. A line of the deadly missiles flew down the corridor, past the jumbled lead warriors. Like a swarm of angry bees, they stung at the next dark elves in line, forcing them to dodge and to duck and to dive aside, and all that while trying to navigate around the six-legged gooey tangle.

Whenever one of the group managed to get past that trio, Jarlaxle focused his fire, a stream of death soaring out to pummel the would-be attacker before he could begin to gain any momentum.

But this was a losing proposition. Behind him, his friends were engaged and outnumbered by high priestesses of the Spider Queen.

And it only got worse, even as Jarlaxle tried to sort out a solution. The corridor behind the tangled group seemed to calm for just a moment, before the three caught in the syrupy globs went flying to one side of the passageway, slamming into, and sticking to, the wall to Jarlaxle's left.

Around them came a monstrous beast, its eight-legged charge led by a huge spear, flying fast for the mercenary's head.

Even as he ducked, Jarlaxle kept up his flow of flying daggers, but he knew that these missiles would not stop the drider. He thought of his wand. A glob of goo might entangle a leg or two.

The drider had many to spare.

So, purely on instinct, the mercenary backed quickly into the room but continued to let fly the daggers. In the midst of that assault, he brought his right arm down low on one roll and halted the magic of the bracer just long enough to launch a different missile. He didn't aim at the drider, but rather at the floor just inside the threshold.

He was right back to launching his stream of daggers at the beast as that thin black missile spun and elongated and came to rest in front of the threshold.

The drider, axes now in both hands, batted aside most of the daggers, taking a few minor hits. It shoved through the tangled blockade and charged into the room, clearly oblivious to Jarlaxle's subtle trap. It only realized its mistake, its face twisting with rage and denial, when its leading legs stamped down upon empty air and the beast tumbled face down into the mercenary's portable hole.

Jarlaxle flipped his hat onto his head and sent another couple of daggers flying down the hall as he scrambled ahead. He leaped the ten-foot expanse of his own trap, pulling his wand as he went and launched a glob of goo down at the drider, just to keep it busy and disoriented.

He winced, though, as he landed, hoping he had been counting his shots correctly.

He skidded over to one of the large bronze doors and swung it closed, then rushed to the next.

The Melarni dark elves came from the hallway—an arrow nearly put an end to Jarlaxle, and ended up sticking in his wide-brimmed hat. He made a mental note to find that archer and punish him severely for making a hole in his fine hat.

But first the doors.

He banged the second one shut then shot a glob into them at the base, sealing them. Another flew from his wand, up at the top of the jamb for good measure. With that, the wand became no more functional than a simple stick, its charges expended.

I have to replace that one! Jarlaxle thought, and he cursed aloud as he drew forth yet another wand.

Still muttering curses to himself as he turned back to the room, the mercenary also uttered a command word and dropped a fireball into the portable pit as he leaped it again.

The drider's shriek helped to compensate for the loss of his wand.

He landed easily, reaching into his pouch and pulling forth a long bar of silvery metal, a special metal indeed that ignited easily and burned white-hot. Into the pit it went, followed closely by a second fireball, and while the magical flames would burn and bite at the drider, wounding it, perhaps even mortally, the metallic bar took all doubt from that outcome. A brilliant white glow emanated from the pit, like the blinding ignition of a new sun. The drider's screams became something more profound than mere agony, higher-pitched and full of terror.

And full of the frantic realization that death had come.

◆ ◆ ◆

HE FELT A bit off balance, with just his sword in hand, but it wasn't simply a sword, of course, but Charon's Claw. He stayed one-handed with the blade, even though the hilt was long enough for him to take it up with both hands.

The priestess was too quick for a two-handed style, though, her mace and whip working with seeming independence, as was so typical of the truly ambidextrous dark elves.

So Entreri kept his left hand free for balance, and kept his left shoulder back, fighting more like a fencer than a brawling warrior.

He measured the strikes of his opponent.

Down he cut to intercept a low sweep of the mace, and the whip cracked near his left ear. He almost reached for it with his open hand—if he could move inside as the priestess struck, he might grab the length of the whip.

She came on again, mace coming across, then again on the backhand, and as she opened up with her arm swinging back wide, the whip snapped again.

Entreri was down low, though, beneath it, and he almost made the grab.

Not yet, he told himself, even though he knew that he hadn't much time here, that they needed to be done with the room and out of House Melarn. But he couldn't make his play until he knew it was there for him to take, or the priestess would recognize the danger and so would protect against it.

He had to goad her, had to let her grow confident—no difficult plan, given his diminished stature as a mere human, and a human male at that.

She came on more boldly, mace sweeping, whip cracking, and Entreri expected to find his opportunity soon.

But a wave of dizziness assaulted him and he stumbled. His leg went numb.

The priestess laughed at him and pressed on.

The whip—the infernal whip carried poison!

Now he took up Charon's Claw in both hands, needing to drive the aggressive priestess back. The red blade swept in front of him, hooking and batting the whip before it could snap. Entreri would have used that moment to try to tug the weapon from the priestess's hand, but in came the mace, hard at his left side, and he had to bring Charon's Claw across to block.

The mace crackled with unexpected power, lightning energy arcing across its head, and even with that block, the off-balance assassin was driven hard to the side. He stumbled, throwing himself into a roll that got him away from the priestess, and one that brought him near the other, with Entreri's dagger buried into her eye.

He needed that dagger back now, to fall into his more normal battle routines, but he got a surprise as he reached for the weapon. The drow priestess mewled softly—she wasn't dead.

Entreri grabbed the jeweled hilt, but didn't tear the dagger free. He called upon it and let it drink the wounded priestess's remaining life energy, drawing it into himself, feasting as a vampire might.

His energy returned slowly, the injection of life energy battling the poison.

The other priestess was over him now, attacking with her weapons, but Entreri held on a bit longer, Charon's Claw working furiously to block the mace and keep the cracking whip out wide.

Just a bit more, he knew.

The numbness left Entreri's leg. Even the cut healed.

He tore out the dagger, the priestess falling over sideways to the floor, and he put his legs under him.

At that moment, Entreri saw Drizzt engulfed in fire, and thought he had lost one of his allies.

No time, he realized.

Across went Charon's Claw, and Entreri enacted a different bit of its magic, the blade trailing an opaque magical ash that hung in the air like a curtain between him and his foe.

He flipped the dagger into the air and dived out to the right, through the curtain.

He came up to see the gaze of the oblivious priestess rising up with the spinning missile, the jewels catching the torchlight.

She turned finally, as if only then realizing that Entreri had gone through the strange floating ash, and her expression shifted from confusion to a mask of fear. For now Entreri was too close, and he held that mighty sword in both hands out wide to his right, and when that blade came across so expertly no magical armor would stop it.

Artemis Entreri cut the priestess in half at the waist.

◆ ◆ ◆

DRIZZT KNEW THIS was no simple flame strike. He had witnessed more than a few of those in his life, including many from Catti-brie. This one came from a matron mother of a ruling House, and the fires roared and stung and bit.

But Drizzt emerged, uncomfortable but unharmed, much to the surprise and dismay of the two priestesses, including Zhindia, who were focused on him at that time.

"How?" he heard the nearby priestess whisper as he descended upon her, his blades working in a blur, defeating her magical armor and tearing at her skin. Her puzzlement didn't surprise Drizzt. She couldn't know of the frostbrand named Icingdeath, which provided him protection from even powerful magical fires. The discomfort had been all too real for Drizzt, the matron mother's magic nearly overwhelming the defenses of the blade. For a fleeting instant, Drizzt wished he hadn't given the protective ring to Catti-brie. But in the end, in the mere eye-blink it took Drizzt to react, the defensive powers of the scimitar proved sufficient, kept him alive and kept him free of serious harm.

The priestess went down, gasping and reaching at her torn throat. Drizzt turned his attention to the far doors, to the matron mother standing in front of them, already casting once more.

She would be wise enough to avoid fire.

The ranger felt the waves of gripping magic, a spell of holding. He was already on the move, diving back the way he had come, but he crashed hard to the floor under the disorienting blast. He was trying to sheathe his blades as he went, a maneuver he had practiced and used for decades to great effect, but that spell from Matron Mother Zhindia assaulted him, and Twinkle went skidding aside even as Icingdeath slid into its sheath.

Drizzt ignored it and turned the fall into an awkward roll, scooping up Taulmaril as he went.

He came back to his feet wobbly, his brain numbed by the magical assault. He kept enough of his wits about him to control his movements and focus. He had the first arrow away before Zhindia could finish her next spell.

The shot seemed true, but at the last moment a blade, spinning and dancing in the air, clipped the arrow and turned it aside.

She had set up a blade barrier, Drizzt realized.

Another arrow suffered the same fate. A third got through, but exploded into fireworks as it hit Zhindia's personal defensive magic shield.

In the flash of those multicolored fireworks, Drizzt got a good look at the spinning blades in front of Matron Mother Zhindia. The ranger dived and rolled, back and forth, and sent a stream of arrows at the woman. He recognized that he wouldn't get through those magical defenses, that he wouldn't kill Matron Mother Zhindia with his bow from afar.

But that was no longer his purpose.

He was gaining a measure of the blade barrier, watching its patterns, witnessing the speed of the blades and the areas they patrolled.

A magical hammer appeared in the air in front of him, crackling with black arcs of some lightning-like energy—surely garnered from the lower planes.

Drizzt dodged. He threw Taulmaril out to block and his hands tingled from the impact, black tendrils reaching out from the hammer along the bow's shaft and biting him.

A step back and a leap to the side bought him enough room to let fly another arrow, but so engrossed was Matron Mother Zhindia that she didn't even blink as this one came in and burst into fireworks right before her eyes.

She reached up into the air in front of her and began to draw with her finger, the digit leaving a line of sparkling light where it passed.

She sketched a symbol, a rune of power, hanging in the air. Drizzt fell back and clutched at his chest, which burned suddenly with intense pain.

Across the table, a priestess fell hard, cut in half. But even as she fell, her killer, Entreri, stumbled and gasped at the flowing agony of Matron Mother Zhindia's symbol.

The magical hammer swept in at Drizzt from the side, and he knew it had him.

But a blade intervened—a diving Jarlaxle stabbed Khazid'hea forward.

A reprieve, one reprieve, and no more, Drizzt realized. Jarlaxle, too, felt the pain of that symbol, and his dive left him on the floor, cringing in agony.

Zhindia drew a second magical symbol in the air, and Drizzt knew he and his friends couldn't win, that they were overmatched and surely doomed. He wanted to throw down his bow and surrender, and beg for a quick death.

"Drizzt!" Jarlaxle called from the floor. "Deception! A rune of despair!"

Jarlaxle started to rise, but the hammer swept in again and struck him hard, dropping him to the floor.

A missile flew out from Drizzt's right, a jeweled dagger spinning for Matron Mother Zhindia. A magical blade from the defensive barrier clipped it, but did not defeat the throw. The dagger turned through the barrier, past that wall of dancing blades, but could not get through Matron Mother Zhindia's wards, and another multicolored explosion flashed in the room.

And Drizzt knew that they were doomed.

Entreri cried out and fell to one knee, clutching at his chest.

Drizzt's heart fell, for they were beaten.

Jarlaxle would die here, and Dahlia was doomed.

Why had they come to this place? They couldn't win. Catti-brie would not bear his children, and it wasn't even Catti-brie anyway—just a horrible deception, wrapping misery into more misery. And so his life would go full circle, with him dying in this, the place of his birth.

The hammer clipped him and sent him tumbling. The waves of pain and despair from the floating, glowing runes chased him to the floor and assailed him.

But Drizzt laughed. What did it matter, after all? It was all a ruse, all an illusion, all the great deception of some demon goddess who was toying with him as Errtu had toyed with the heart and soul of Wulfgar those years before.

It didn't matter.

Drizzt leaped to his feet and stared at the Matron Mother of House Melarn, supreme zealot among the fanatical priestesses of Lolth.

Catti-brie was long dead, Regis crossing into the nether realm beside her. Wulfgar had died in Icewind Dale, and Bruenor's last words echoed in his thoughts. They were all dead anyway. It was all a sick joke, and so nothing really mattered.

And he laughed.

Because it was all a horrible game, and in that unreality, what power might a Symbol of Hopelessness hold over him? And in that special insight, even the agony of the Symbol of Pain couldn't lay him low. He refused to accept it, and refused to consider that any physical pain could possibly be worse than the grand deception that had made him believe that his friends were alive.

The hammer came at him and he threw Taulmaril into it, turning it aside.

He drew out Icingdeath and he charged.

His eyes remained on Zhindia—he let her become the focal point of all the pain and all the rage. He understood the rhythm of the blade barrier—he knew the dance of those magical swords, like sentries patrolling a wall.

He saw the priestess's eyes widen with surprise, and widen more with fear. Behind her, the doors opened and she turned and scampered, the doors ponderously closing behind her.

"No!" Drizzt roared. He leaped, not for all his life, but simply because this kill would serve him. This kill would deny the deception, would hurt Lolth as she had ruined him.

He went horizontal in the air, throwing his feet out to the side, and he tucked and contorted and twisted and flew through.

Several blades clipped him and cracked against him, but he felt no pain. He landed on his feet, stumbling forward into the doors, unsure of why the blade barrier hadn't torn him to shreds. He crashed into the doors and felt a burst of energy flow from him, throwing the doors wide, and if he had paused long enough to notice, he would have seen that his shove had caused great gashes into the thick bronze, slicing part of the metal into ragged shards.

But he didn't notice, bursting through in a run. Matron Mother Zhindia was just ahead. As Drizzt crossed the threshold, he crossed, too, a second glyph of warding, and he was flying again, jolted by a mighty blast of lightning.

He held his scimitar with all his might, determined that he would not drop it with his twitching muscles. He held it and he put all his focus on it, and used that to ride through the jolting blast, coming down from his impact against the wall once more in a run. He saw the matron mother down the corridor, turning into a side room.

He knew that his companions were behind him, that they likely needed him.

Or were they even his companions?

Was it Jarlaxle and Entreri, or two lesser demons, serving Lolth in her grand deception to utterly break Drizzt Do'Urden?

They were hurt behind him, but Drizzt didn't care. Not then, not with Matron Mother Zhindia Melarn in his sights.

◆　◆　◆

Yvonnel, in spirit and in body, could hardly contain her glee. Truly, she wanted to leap up from the stoup and run around it to wrap the glorious Matron Mother K'yorl in a loving hug.

She had felt the infusion of kinetic protection into the heretic Drizzt, but still had winced when he foolishly tried to leap through Matron Mother Zhindia's defensive wall of spinning blades.

And Yvonnel felt the exultation, the ecstasy, the brilliant release of tremendous power when Drizzt had shouldered the doors, inadvertently, unwittingly, unknowingly releasing the powerful energy the spinning blades had exacted upon his torso to be gobbled up and held by K'yorl's brilliant ploy.

It wasn't over yet, she reminded herself, and focused once more on Drizzt. He ran, he turned, he burst through the door in close pursuit of Zhindia.

Another glyph exploded, sending him sidelong, burning him. K'yorl's shield was no more.

And there was Zhindia in a small side passage, barely more than a deep alcove, her fingers moving, her lips curled deliciously as she completed a spell, one that would surely end this battle.

Yvonnel screamed into K'yorl's thoughts. Desperately, she imparted an image of Minolin Fey, babbling and bumbling about with the candles.

And K'yorl understood and complied, a blast of psionic energy rolling forth, leading the way for Drizzt.

It caught Matron Mother Zhindia by surprise. She stuttered. Her spell fell away, her defenses lapsed.

Shock and confusion filled her red eyes.

And fear. So much fear.

◆　◆　◆

DRIZZT STUMBLED FORWARD with every bit of life he could muster, stabbing his blade at the personification of all that pained him. The tip struck some magical shield and was deflected, but only barely. With a roar of protest, Drizzt brought the scimitar back to bear, and both he and his opponent understood that her ward had been defeated.

He was inside her defenses, then, both magical and martial, and she could not stop his thrust, and could not turn aside. He had her helpless and soon-to-be-dead.

She stared at him, her faced locked in an expression of utter despair.

And it was not Matron Mother Zhindia he saw . . .

But Catti-brie.

Chapter 16 ◈

Upon the Unwilling

REQUEST ENTRY, ARCHMAGE GROMPH."

The voice caught Gromph by surprise. The night was late, well past midnight, and the moon had set. Darkness had fallen deeply over Luskan.

Gromph slipped a robe over his slender shoulders and moved to the tent flap, pulling it aside just enough to view the woman standing a little ways back from his heavily warded entryway.

It was Catti-brie, dressed in a simple shift, and with her black lace cape pulled around her shoulders.

Gromph licked his thin lips. He knew his psionic intrusions were assailing her and confusing her, and possibly even tempting her.

But this?

"What do you want?"

"You know what I want," she answered, and the archmage swallowed hard.

"Then enter," he said, stepping back and pulling the flap wider. "I command the glyphs and wards to allow you."

Catti-brie came forward on bare feet, looking more nervous with each step, as if she expected some burst of magical energy, lightning or fire or freezing cold, to assault her as she entered the wizard's private tent.

By the time she arrived inside, Gromph had already conjured a magical light, one tinted blue, quietly glowing. In that glow, Gromph could even better appreciate the sheer beauty of this woman, her beautiful skin, so smooth and clear, and those huge blue eyes. And that hair! Auburn locks thick enough to get lost in. Her shift clung teasingly to her frame, solid and strong, but so promisingly supple. She was not drow, but Gromph could not deny her beauty.

"Well met," he said with a smile. "This is a night I have long awaited."

"No more than I," said Catti-brie, and her black lace cloak fell to the floor behind her.

◆ ◆ ◆

KIRIY STOOD ALONE in the hallway, the sounds of battle all around her, and waited.

"Matron Mother Zhindia?" Kiriy called again, and again she waited. Every glance about grew a bit more nervous. Had her siblings escaped the driders? And what of the dangerous Tiago?

And where were the Melarni priestesses? Kiriy had come into House Do'Urden as their conduit. Their ritual allowed them to follow her every movement, allowed them to intrude upon her enemies with mighty spells hurled from afar. But where had they gone?

Kiriy knew Zhindia would not answer, that the matron mother could not hear her. Her efforts to reach the matron mother were desperation and fear, not certainty of success.

It occurred to her that perhaps she had been set up by the Melarni. Perhaps the invasion of House Do'Urden would fail—maybe with House Baenre coming again to its aid—and in that event, would Kiriy be named as the perpetrator?

"No," she said resolutely. "The Spider Queen is with me—is with *us!*"

She nodded, knowing what she must do. Even without the Melarni, even without knowing why the magical connection had been severed, Kiriy understood her mission. It was, in fact, as clear to her as the door just down this curving corridor, the door of the private quarters of Matron Mother Darthiir Do'Urden.

Nodding, the first priestess moved to the door. She cast several protection spells upon herself, then disenchanted the door. With a deep breath, for she could not truly know the extent of explosive magical warding placed upon this door, she pushed through into the anteroom.

The door to her right was closed, the one to her left ajar, enough for her to see the abominable surface elf seated in a curled position on the bed, hugging her bare knees and rocking in a stupor.

Kiriy closed the door and cast a spell of holding upon it, then moved for her prey.

"Do you know me, *iblith?*" she asked, entering.

Dahlia glanced up, but her stare remained blank.

"Do you know why I've come?" Kiriy asked.

No response at all, and Kiriy sighed. She had hoped it would be more fun than this. She started around the bottom of the bed, grinning as she

250

turned her glance sidelong at Dahlia. She noticed then that the woman was holding something, some metal bar, beneath the bend in her legs. Kiriy took a cautious step away and began quietly casting, deliberately going through the words and movements of a spell of holding.

She wanted to take her time here, to make this abomination feel every moment of terror and agony, but she reminded herself that time was not on her side. Above all else, she had to make sure that Dahlia was dead—and consecrated in such an unholy manner that she could not, could never, be resurrected.

Her spell was complete and Dahlia started, as if in shock, then froze in place.

Kiriy Xorlarrin laughed at her. "Now you will be set free, *iblith*," she whispered. She drew out a ceremonial dagger. She wanted to feel her blood, and wanted to be close enough to see the pain in the woman's eyes.

She knew just when to free Dahlia from the spell of holding, too, just enough to hear that last wail before death.

◆ ◆ ◆

"I ALWAYS WONDERED how some of my kind could find a human attractive," Gromph said. He let his robe slip to the floor and sat naked on the edge of his bed, patting the spot next to him. "Now I see you and I understand. I will show you pleasures you cannot begin to imagine."

Catti-brie wore nothing but her smile and that simple nightgown, almost sheer, and hanging only to mid-thigh.

She didn't feel naked, though. Her grin was full of knowledge, and her knowledge was as protective as the finest suit of mithral armor.

"As pleasurable as you expect I found those mind-magic intrusions you have been injecting into my thoughts?" she asked.

That got Gromph's attention, and he looked at her curiously for a moment, then painted on an incredulous, surely feigned expression.

"That is quite a game that you designed and delivered," Catti-brie went on. "I suppose I should be impressed—"

"You should be thankful," Gromph interrupted. He sat back easily, turning up his hips to more fully expose himself, letting her know that he understood the game to be up, and more importantly, that he didn't care.

251

"That I, the Archmage of Menzoberranzan, would take the time and effort to so pleasure you from afar."

"But I find myself truly disappointed," Catti-brie resolutely pressed on. "To think that one as accomplished as you, one whose reputation rivals the legends of Khelben, or even Elminster, would unlock such new and great mysteries of this other magic for use in such a petty manner."

Gromph laughed at her and patted the bed again.

"Though I suppose that after so stupidly summoning Demogorgon to Menzoberranzan, you find it refreshingly small to attack a person in such a manner from afar," Catti-brie finished, and Gromph's demeanor turned ugly for a brief and telling instant. Catti-brie knew she had hurt him with that remark.

She wanted to hurt him a lot more than that.

"Attack?" he echoed, his expression reverting to confidence and ease. "I merely offered to you a vision. You let me in. Willingly. And in your accusation you referred to 'those mind-magic intrusions,' inferring more than one instance. Yet only once did I offer you a telepathic hint of the pleasures we two might enjoy together."

His laughter cut into her heart. She didn't want to believe him, and logically did not believe him, but the doubt . . .

"The rest—and were there many?—came wholly from your own imagination," he said slyly. He beckoned to her with one hand and touched himself with the other. "Come," he said, patting the bed insistently. "Do tell me of these fantasies. Let us see what pleasure they might inspire."

And Gromph found that he was not alone on the bed—an unexpected guest was now sitting beside him, hot breath on his neck.

"Have you met Guenhwyvar?" Catti-brie asked.

Gromph snickered, but glanced warily at the huge black panther out of the corner of his eye. "Do you mean to kill me then?"

"Would I not be justified?"

"You would not be able to, but that is beside the point. Are you angry with me, or at yourself for your own weakness and infidelity, because you know in your heart that you liked what you imagined?"

"It was an attack," Catti-brie insisted. "Without consent!"

"So you must tell yourself."

"That is the only way you could ever have me, Gromph Baenre. Without my willingness, and thus, you will never have my heart or my soul."

"I have already proven that thinking errant, woman!" the archmage replied. He sat up straight, and as Guenhwyvar beside him growled, he snapped his fingers in the air and the panther exploded into a cloud of gray mist, swirling and dissipating back to her Astral home.

"I have been in your mind," he went on. "And I see now that you have witnessed our lovemaking as surely as any physical lover you might ever have known."

"Without consent!"

"Does it matter?"

"You'll not get back into my thoughts, Archmage. I see you now. I know you now."

"And I know you, in the most intimate of ways."

"You know nothing," Catti-brie retorted. "You are a rapist and nothing more."

"You hide behind a label and false claim," he replied through a wide smile. "What you felt, you felt alone—oh, would that it were different!" His laughter mocked her outrage. "So deny me now, and go and hide from me. But can you hide from yourself?"

"You have no power over my free will, and that is the measure of intimacy," Catti-brie pressed on against his sheer awfulness. "You'll not get back into my thoughts, nor will you ever get beneath my robes."

"Truly?" Gromph asked slyly. "Dear human, you will be amazed by the things I can accomplish, particularly when a woman tells me that I cannot."

"And you will be amazed at what I might do. Do you actually believe that you needed to invite me in so that I would not be destroyed by your glyphs and wards? Then what of Guenhwyvar, who crawled in under the back flap of your tent without a magical whistle of warning? Oh yes, mighty Gromph, I dispelled your defenses long before you knew I was near to your abode."

Gromph held up his hands and sighed, as if in some sort of perverse salute. "You are impressive, I must say, and in so many ways," he admitted. "I find it truly lamentable that you are wound up in your nonsensical notions of fidelity, and to a pathetic warrior no less! And I am disappointed that one of your accomplishments—a chosen priestess, I am told, and a wizard of no small measure—clings to some ridiculous peasant superstition of entwining honor and sex."

"I don't even bother to pity you," Catti-brie replied, coolly and confidently. "You are merely revolting."

Gromph shrugged as if it did not matter, then waved his hand and magically sent his robes up and over his shoulders, dressing fully though he didn't even sit up, as if it, too, no longer mattered.

"I will let you be gone from this place," he said, and he sighed once more and looked over his shoulder plaintively at his bed. "Ah, pretty Catti-brie," he said, and turned back.

But the woman was already long out of there, had simply vanished.

Gromph spent a long while sitting in that place, replaying that unexpected and, he had to admit, troubling encounter. This woman was clever, and very powerful. She had unwound his psionic intrusions, though there was little chance that she had ever trained in, or even experienced, such things as that before. And surely, given the strength and intensity of his suggestions, her mind had ruled above her flesh—no small feat for anyone.

And on a more pragmatic level, she had almost won out fully—Gromph knew that he must not ever allow that to happen again. If he had not, coincidentally and for another purpose, memorized a spell for dispelling magic that night, the sensations upon his delicate flesh would have been delivered not by Catti-brie, but by the claws and teeth of that terrible panther.

She had dispelled his wards. Few matron mothers could do such a thing.

Catti-brie was, he feared, more powerful than she knew.

That was often a dangerous thing.

◆ ◆ ◆

SHE ROCKED BACK and forth, lost in the roiling current of half-finished thoughts that dived over bottomless waterfalls and hurled her into unrelated internal conversations. This was the essence of Dahlia's life, with lucid moments being the rarest event of all.

She clutched Kozah's Needle between her knees, her hands holding the four bars tightly together. The feel of that powerful magical weapon sometimes gave Dahlia a focus to break free of the wildly running rivers of her thoughts. Her most lucid moments in her time in Menzoberranzan had been in battle, when the demons had come. The intensity of those moments, the rush of excitement, the surrender to instinct, all of it, forced clarity and focus.

But not now. Not sitting on her bed in her empty room, in her empty life. In these moments, as her mind wandered in and out, she often took up Kozah's Needle, hoping against hope that she might find a lifeline to clarity.

She was just rocking now, thoughts careening and meandering, with no rationality or reason or purpose.

The river of her thoughts slowed then, as if a mental dam was being constructed right in front of them. Fluid notions coalesced and circled, suddenly stagnant and rolling back in on themselves. Even in her ongoing bewilderment, Dahlia sensed the change, and from somewhere in the far recesses of her mind, from some memory of a similar mental weight, she understood it to be an attack.

Only then did she realize that there was another person in the room—she could smell the perfume. A priestess, no doubt, and so she knew the dam being constructed in her mind was a magical spell of holding, to freeze her and render her helpless.

She felt Kozah's Needle. Tangible. Focal.

She heard a whisper, but the words would not yet register fully.

She felt a blade against her right side, just under her armpit. The tip bit into her, the poison burned.

Back rolled Dahlia, her right arm snapping out from under her bent legs, wrist twisting to crack the flail out hard, striking the priestess against the shoulder. The drow woman spun away, her dagger flying from her grasp.

Dahlia leaped up to stand on her bed and put her twin weapons into a gracefully spinning routine, the muscle memory forcing her focus, the imminent danger and incoming battle bringing her fully into the present moment.

She saw the priestess—she did not recognize this one—fall back farther and regain her balance, her other arm, and one of those terrible snake-headed whips, coming up in front of her. And she began to cast another spell.

Dahlia leaped from the bed, flipping a somersault sidelong, and not at the priestess. Not yet. It would bring her too close to those biting serpents, and she wanted nothing to do with them. The ribs on her right side burned and she felt the dullness of the drow sleeping poison.

She slapped her flails together repeatedly, sparks flying with each metallic clang. Both arms rolled out wide, then came crashing back together, inner palm to inner palm, the collision resealing the ends of the flail together, combining the two weapons into one.

Dahlia leaped again, diving off to the side and only narrowly avoiding a magical hammer that appeared in the air and struck at her.

The priestess was casting again, and coming forward, the four snakes of her whip writhing and hissing, eager to bite.

Kozah's Needle, now in its staff form again, kept the snakes and the priestess at bay, but, to Dahlia's dismay, this one, like all the drow, was quite skilled at martial combat. She couldn't get close enough to score a solid hit.

And the spell seemed nearly complete.

Dahlia didn't want to do it. She knew the charge in her weapon wasn't strong enough, but she had to interrupt that spell, so she stamped Kozah's needle on the floor, releasing the lightning energy.

The priestess lifted off the floor and flew backward, her white hair dancing wildly, her spell scrambled and lost. But she wasn't hurt, not badly at least, and she was right back to her feet, in a defensive crouch, and with another spell on her lips.

With a growl, fighting the interminable confusion, Dahlia came on. She found, though, that the turmoil in her mind was not her only unseen enemy. The wound in her side burned, slowing her.

Desperately, she thrust her staff ahead. She got inside the priestess's reach, prodding the woman hard. But she was bitten on her forearm by two different snakes. She recoiled, gasping in pain, and overwhelmed with poison.

Dahlia stumbled across the room and fell back onto her bed. She tried to stand again, but her legs gave out beneath her and she crumpled to the floor.

◆ ◆ ◆

KIRIY XORLARRIN GATHERED up her dagger, determined to kill this one slowly. She barely had the weapon in her hand, though, when the door burst open and her brother Ravel and that wretched Tiago Baenre charged in.

They surveyed the scene quickly, and Tiago's face was a mask of outrage.

"You," he said, shaking his head and coming forward. Behind him, an equally angry Ravel was casting a spell, and behind him, in the hall,

Kiriy noted Saribel—no doubt the priestess these two males wanted to put on the throne of House Do'Urden.

Kiriy's plan unwound right there, right then.

"Drizzt Do'Urden is in the city!" she cried the moment before Tiago leaped at her with that terrible sword of his.

◆ ◆ ◆

CATTI-BRIE SAT ON her bed, heavier robes tight around her, and wrapped in her blankets as well, as if that extra fabric was somehow shielding her from the memory of her encounter with the insufferable Gromph.

She watched as the gray mist formed around her, as Guenhwyvar became substantial once more, returning at her call.

How glad she was when the panther appeared, unhurt, and hopped up on the bed beside her.

"Oh, Guen," Catti-brie said, burying her face in the soft black fur. She wrapped her arms around the giant cat's muscled shoulders and pressed her face in tighter, and her shoulders began to bob.

She had to give herself this moment, had to allow herself to break down and just melt.

But only for a moment, and then she sat back up and forced a wide smile on her face as she considered this wonderful feline friend.

"He'll not ever be forgettin' that meetin'," she whispered, letting the dwarven brogue come back to her, using it to bring the strength and resolve of Clan Battlehammer. "We surprised him, we two, aye, and he's knowing that his little tricks won't be workin'."

Guenhwyvar yawned hugely, those great teeth shining in the candle-light of Catti-brie's tent, then slid down on the bed.

Catti-brie bent over the panther and nuzzled her, drawing strength from her, confident then that she had done the right thing, and that her confrontation with Archmage Gromph had put them back on proper footing. In the solidity of the black panther, so too did Catti-brie find solidity under her feet once more.

"Aye," she said again to the cat, and to herself, and she closed her eyes and let herself fall into a restful and much-needed sleep.

Chapter 17 ◈

The Blasphemy

THE DEADLY BLADE, PERFECTLY AIMED FOR A QUICK KILL, STOPPED short. There the scimitar held, and the wielder quivered.

His mind screamed at him that it was a trick, but his thoughts could not overrule his heart, and his heart showed him something he could not strike.

Because Drizzt could not strike Catti-brie.

He heard Jarlaxle and Entreri approaching from behind, and glanced to regard them. When he turned back, as they rushed up to join him, Matron Mother Zhindia was gone.

"Where is she?" Jarlaxle asked frantically.

"Did you wound her?" Entreri demanded.

Drizzt blinked and shook his head, though obviously not in response.

Jarlaxle pushed past him into the deep alcove, throwing glittering dust out in front of him, an enchanted spray that would reveal all the alcove's secrets to him. He noted no traps, no more glyphs, but at the far end, the lines of a secret door were clear to see.

"Go!" Entreri bade him, but Jarlaxle shook his head and spun back.

"To Do'Urden," he said, and tossed Twinkle, which he had recovered in the war room, back to Drizzt. "House Melarn is out of the war at least. Her priestesses are slain and Zhindia cannot replace them quickly enough to resume the fight."

"She will likely resurrect them!" Entreri argued.

"And we will be long gone from this city by then," Jarlaxle countered, pushing past and starting back the way they had come. He paused, though, and closed his eyes, considering the layout of the strange house and the forces they had left behind, trapped behind the magically stuck bronze doors.

He started off the other way, along the curving corridor.

Entreri snarled and spat, not thrilled with leaving a nearly-defeated Matron Mother Melarn behind, but he moved to follow. Then he paused long enough to grab Drizzt, who seemed almost incoherent in that strange moment, and drag him along.

◆ ◆ ◆

MATRON MOTHER ZHINDIA stumbled into her private chambers. Her sparkling red eyes aptly reflected the red wall of anger that coursed through her. "Sornafein!" she called, seeking her patron, her plaything, a handsome musician who would often help her sort through her volatile, careening thoughts and find a proper course.

And Matron Mother Zhindia had a lot to think about at that moment. Six of her priestesses were dead, and only she and Kyrnill had escaped. She flinched as she considered the image of Kyrnill so quickly departing the battle, then grimaced more as her memory took her to the other side of the table, where that human intruder had jammed a dagger into the eye of priestess Yazhin Melarn, Zhindia's only daughter, whom Zhindia had recalled from her studies at Arach-Tinilith simply so that she could witness the glory of an inter-House war.

Zhindia had been trying to groom Yazhin to succeed her, perhaps even above Kyrnill, and certainly if Zhindia outlived the former Matron Mother of House Kenafin. She resolved to ask Lolth's blessing in resurrecting Yazhin. She did not wish to begin anew her efforts.

"Sornafein!" she called again, growing angrier by the moment. What was taking him so long?

The handsome patron stumbled out of the side room then, and fell to his knees. He stayed there gasping, eyes far too wide, hands slapping at his throat as if he could not draw enough breath.

Zhindia started for him, but fell back when a young woman strode out of the side room to stand beside the kneeling Sornafein. This creature—Zhindia did not know her—held a rope in her hand, and tugged it casually. Another woman, this one old and emaciated, a battered thing indeed, came crawling out to kneel on the other side of the young one, who dropped a hand and gently stroked the hair of the withered old thing as one might do to a pet dog.

Up came Zhindia's hands, in the beginnings of a spell.

"Halt!" the young woman demanded, and the weight of the command slapped Zhindia across the face as surely as a heavy punch, and sent her staggering backward several steps.

"I am not your enemy, Matron Mother Zhindia," the young woman said. "Though you would be wise to never consider me a friend."

The proud and volatile Zhindia growled and began casting once more, and again, the young woman yelled "Halt!" and magically slapped her across the face.

Again Zhindia staggered under the weight of the magical blow, but this time, she came up in a charge, her snake-headed scourge in hand.

The young woman, so incredibly beautiful, merely smiled.

That alerted Zhindia and she led her charge with another spell, one that wasn't interrupted, one that would dispel any defenses this impudent young creature had enacted.

Or it should have, at least. Zhindia realized it hadn't when she was flying backward, thrown by the power of a repulsion spell.

She hit the far wall hard, shocked by the bared might, that she, a matron mother, had been so casually thrown aside by this intruder drow priestess who could not have yet lived a quarter of a century.

Common sense told Matron Mother Zhindia to opt for discussion then, but her outrage would not allow it. She still leaned heavily on the wall, but turned to glare at the intruder and stubbornly returned the wicked grin. She realized that her spell, though unsuccessful, had not been interrupted.

"You have exhausted your commands, I see," she said, and she launched into another spell.

"Halt!' the young woman cried, and Zhindia felt that stinging slap across her face.

"Halt!" she said again, and again, and again, and each time brought a painful stinging slap, sending Zhindia into a turn one way and then the other.

It went on for many heartbeats, many incantations, many slaps, and when it ended, it took Zhindia a long while to even realize that she wasn't being magically slapped any longer.

"I am the favored of Lolth!" she growled, and she clawed at the wall to regain her footing, stubbornly turning to face her adversary squarely—and noted then that the young woman was quietly spellcasting.

Matron Mother Zhindia howled and leaped forward, but too late. The young priestess finished her incantation, throwing one hand out to Zhindia, the other reaching for the kneeling Sornafein.

Zhindia saw her patron go flying aside, his skin erupting in brutal wounds as he bounced to the floor and lay face down, blood pooling around him. Then she too felt the stab of the powerful spell. It slammed her back against the wall, and opened a deep gash from her shoulder, down across her chest to her opposite hip.

She gasped and crumpled to her knees, staring in disbelief.

"I am in the favor of Lolth," she said, blood dripping with every word.

"Apparently, so am I," the young woman replied.

"Who are you?"

"Someone you will come to know, I assure you," the woman replied. "Unless of course, your stubbornness forces me to utterly destroy you here and now. I expect that Kyrnill will not be displeased, at least."

Zhindia fell to all fours and spat blood onto the floor.

"You are out of the fight with House Do'Urden," the young woman stated, "by order of Matron Mother Baenre, by order of Lady Lolth."

There it was, a name to enrage Zhindia once again. Fire burned in her eyes as she snapped her head up to glare at the intruder, but her outrage became confusion as she noted a third drow enter, a naked woman, who smiled at her and addressed her with great familiarity.

"Enough, Zhindia," she said in a watery voice, one that triggered Zhindia's recollection. "There is more afoot than you can know."

"Yiccardaria?" Zhindia whispered.

She saw Yiccardaria turn her attention to the young priestess, who shrugged. The handmaiden scowled and motioned for the priestess to proceed.

With a resigned sigh, she did so, and Zhindia felt waves of healing magic flooding through her. Glorious magic that sealed her wounds, and those of Sornafein, she could tell from the man's relieved groans.

"Her attitude annoys me," the young priestess said to Yiccardaria.

"Enough, Yvonnel," the handmaiden replied, and Matron Mother Zhindia's eyes widened at the mention of that name. "You are done here."

"She is out of the fight," Yvonnel said, pointing to the vanquished Matron Mother of House Melarn.

"She is out of the fight," the handmaiden agreed. "She will turn her attention to the fallen priestesses in her war room." She stared directly at Zhindia. "Perhaps Lady Lolth will see fit to grant you some powers of resurrection."

"Perhaps not," Yvonnel added with a laugh, and she and the handmaiden retreated into the side room, the withered old woman crawling
behind them.

The finality of the slamming door was not lost on the shaken Matron
Mother Zhindia.

◆ ◆ ◆

THEIR MOVEMENTS WERE too swift and too coordinated as they careened
along the curving corridors of House Melarn. Most of the remaining
priestesses had run for the war room, trying to save those not yet quite
dead, or were even then banging on the door of Matron Mother Zhindia's
private quarters.

House Melarn was not strong with wizards, and most, like House
Wizard Iltztrav, were too concerned with simply maintaining the sup-
porting web structure to focus on the battles Zhindia chose to fight. And
all of them, especially Iltztrav, had been wary of going against House
Do'Urden from the beginning. It was no secret that the Xorlarrins were
infiltrating and dominating the fledgling House, and Tsabrak Xorlarrin
had just been named as Archmage of Menzoberranzan.

So that left the warriors, and those drow who encountered Drizzt and his
two companions were sent fleeing almost immediately, overwhelmed. Many
of the famed Melarni driders were off to House Do'Urden. Many, but not
all, and not the newest of them. It was the newest drider, Braelin, who at
last stood between Jarlaxle and the others and the exit from House Melarn.

Drizzt and Entreri broke left and right, Drizzt rolling to his feet with
Taulmaril in hand, but Jarlaxle, in the middle, was first to act. "Hold
your shot!" he ordered Drizzt, and Drizzt nearly paid with his life for
complying as the drider heaved a javelin at his head.

A second roll got him clear.

"Braelin!" Jarlaxle yelled. "Oh, Braelin!"

To the left, Entreri sucked in his breath, recognizing the Bregan
D'aerthe warrior.

The bigger question loomed, however: Did Braelin recognize himself?

It didn't seem that way when he charged forward, a heavier spear in
hand. He thrust the weapon at Jarlaxle, and the mercenary had to retreat
fast, calling to him plaintively all the while.

"He cannot understand you," Entreri said, moving around to the drider's right flank, Drizzt coming to Braelin's left. "It is not Braelin! No more!"

"Take him!" said Drizzt.

"You will be doing him a favor," Entreri added.

Jarlaxle cast a plaintive stare over his former scout, his former friend. He could not dispel this kind of magic and he could never reach the drow known as Braelin trapped inside the horrible form. To do so would ensure a most terrible death for Braelin. The new identity of a drider was the only defense from memories too awful to be survived.

"Ah, Braelin, my friend," he said quietly, dodging back as the drider came on fearlessly. "I fear this will prove my greatest gift to you of all."

And with that, Jarlaxle nodded.

Charon's Claw took a drider leg, and before Braelin even tipped that way, a lightning arrow hit him in the back of the neck. He stumbled and swerved, seven legs skittering wildly to keep him upright, his head lolling from side to side.

A second arrow plunged into his back. Entreri got underneath enough to prod Charon's Claw into the drider's spidery belly, spilling ichor.

Braelin tumbled against the wall and folded over, struggling mightily, but futilely.

Drizzt put the bow up and Entreri backed away, both allowing Jarlaxle to move in for the final blow.

"Ah, Braelin," the mercenary said, kicking aside the spear and moving in close to regard his old companion.

The drider grabbed at him, even got his hands around Jarlaxle's throat.

But only until Jarlaxle's fine-edged sword sliced into Braelin's heart.

Jarlaxle stood up and gave a sigh.

Noise down the corridor behind revealed pursuit, and so the three ran off, out the door and onto the web bridges that fronted House Melarn.

They didn't descend, and if they had, they would have found an organized ambush awaiting them.

"Use the emblems," Jarlaxle instructed.

When the three were able to levitate, the mercenary led them off along the western wall of the great cavern, toward the sound of fighting on the balconies of House Do'Urden.

◆ ◆ ◆

BACK BY THE doorway on the bridge of webs, the drider heaving his dying breaths behind them, Yvonnel and Yiccardaria watched the three depart. Behind them, studying the dying abomination, K'yorl seemed quite amused.

"The champion battle should be singular," the handmaiden instructed, and Yvonnel nodded.

"That human has been in the city before," said Yiccardaria.

"I know, from the memories of the Eternal. He is Artemis Entreri."

"It is a small world after all," said Yiccardaria. "And one rich with the simple beauty of coincidence."

Yvonnel looked at her curiously.

"Artemis Entreri," the handmaiden prompted. "There is history with House Horlbar."

Yvonnel got the reference then, and chuckled.

"So you have not forgotten."

Yvonnel laughed louder. "Beautiful indeed!" she replied. In his escape from Menzoberranzan those many years ago—thirteen decades and more—Artemis Entreri had encountered one of the two Matron Mothers of House Horlbar, a woman named Jerlys, and had promptly and efficiently dispatched her.

Jerlys Horlbar was Matron Mother Zhindia Melarn's mother.

"Matron Mother Zhindia's daughter, the young priestess Yazhin, was in the bloodied war room," Yiccardaria explained. "And she, too, fell to Artemis Entreri."

"And Lolth will not allow her resurrection?"

"Lolth cannot."

That brought a surprised look from Yvonnel.

"The human carries a most awful and effective dagger," Yiccardaria explained. "Matron Mother Zhindia will learn that there is nothing left of Yazhin, no soul, to resurrect."

Yvonnel nodded and looked at the now-distant departing trio. "And Kyrnill will be in the room before Zhindia, no doubt," she said. "Perhaps Zhindia will blame her rival for her inability to bring back her dead daughter."

"Chaos is a beautiful thing," said the handmaiden. "Full of excitement, the very edge of existence."

Yvonnel looked back, and stuttered. Yiccardaria had become again a yochlol in form, ugly and without symmetry, tentacles waving and dripping ooze.

"We will be watching with great amusement," Yiccardaria promised in her bubbly, watery, mud-filled voice, and with that, she melted away.

Yvonnel light-stepped past the puddle of Abyssal mud left in the departing yochlol's wake, back into the corridor.

"Come, my pet," she told K'yorl. "I will give you the image of House Do'Urden and show you where to bring us."

As K'yorl began to fall within herself, within her psionic powers, a death rattle issued from crumpled Braelin.

"Wait!" ordered Yvonnel. She moved fast to the drider and began casting, and in moments, Braelin's breath came easier, as Yvonnel healed his mortal wounds.

And then Yvonnel did something else, something she wasn't supposed to do, something she wasn't supposed to be able to do, and K'yorl gasped in recognition and in horror.

Even she understood the blasphemy.

And the sheer power.

CHAPTER 18 ◈

Fevered Dreams

A TRIO OF WARRIORS DROPPED UPON THE BATTLE RAGING ON THE balcony of House Do'Urden.

They had been up on the wall, levitating and pulling themselves along until they were above the balcony. And there they had waited, sorting out the combatants, determining Do'Urden defenders from the invading Hunzrin warriors. Hands flashed the silent drow code, the three coming to agreement and tactics.

Down they went, landing in the midst of the Hunzrin line, exploding into coordinated motion before the enemy drow even realized they were there. A blurring dance of four masterful swords, a jeweled dagger, and a stream of magical daggers fed into Jarlaxle's free hand by his enchanted bracer soon broke the center of that Hunzrin line so brutally, so efficiently, that the remaining invaders wanted no part of this whirling cyclone of death.

More went over the balcony railing than continued to fight, and with the Do'Urden garrison pressing from the room beyond, Jarlaxle and his companions soon confronted the House defenders, a group that clearly didn't know what to make of them.

"Step aside, you fools!" Jarlaxle insisted, and he dropped his magical disguise and revealed himself. "Your salvation has arrived!"

Gasps and cheers followed the trio through the anteroom, and many of the garrison moved to follow.

"This is your post," Entreri said, turning back on them and pointing to the balcony. "The enemy will likely return! Do not let them through this door!"

They ran through the second anteroom, and into the winding corridor within the house proper, and there the trio almost crashed into Faelas Xorlarrin.

"The Xorlarrins and Tiago should be soon to this place," Faelas warned the Bregan D'aerthe leader. "I received a magical whisper from Jaemas that they had just dispatched Melarni driders." He pointed down to the right and motioned for them to be away quickly.

Jarlaxle nodded and patted the wizard on the shoulder, starting away, Entreri close behind.

"Tiago?" Drizzt asked, his lips curling into a snarl.

"Pray go," Faelas said, shaking his head. "And be quick!"

But Drizzt didn't move, and his hands tightened on the handles of his bloody scimitars.

"Not now!" Jarlaxle scolded, moving back a step.

Entreri took it even farther, leaping back to grab Drizzt by the arm. "Dahlia!" he said, and he pulled Drizzt along.

Drizzt went, but kept glancing back, hoping they would be too slow and Tiago Baenre would catch up to them.

They found few guards and no enemies along the crisscrossing corridors, and through many chambers.

"We can wind about the chapel and approach from the rear of the compound," Jarlaxle explained.

"This way," corrected Drizzt, and he kicked through a side door opposite of Jarlaxle's instruction. He moved with purpose and with confidence. It was all coming back to him, and he felt as if he had never left this place, his first home.

He could almost hear his sister Vierna's voice as he stormed through the familiar rooms, and down a secret passageway that even Jarlaxle had not yet discovered. The passageway was small and tight, one that child Drizzt had often run along to frustrate his violent sisters.

Vierna thought it an amusing game.

Briza would beat him for it.

At one point, Drizzt almost broke off along a side passage, one that would put them farther from their goal. It led to a training room where the ghosts of the past haunted Drizzt still.

"Why have you stopped?" Entreri demanded. "Are you lost?"

"Double-cross down," Drizzt whispered, though it didn't seem as if he had heard Entreri at all.

With a sigh, Drizzt pressed on.

They came into a larger room, the war room of House Do'Urden, the room in which a lavender-eyed child had been born to Matron Mother Malice . . .

The sound of battle from somewhere beyond the walls kept Drizzt focused then. Across the way, separated by small partitions, loomed three doorways. But which led to the battle, they could not immediately determine. Drizzt broke off to the door on the far right of the opposite wall, Entreri to the left, and Jarlaxle to the center, and while the latter two pressed their ears to their respective doors, Drizzt didn't even wait, and simply kicked his open, eager for a fight.

His next step failed him, though. There in front of him stood a most beautiful drow, a woman whose beauty gave him pause.

He couldn't tell dream from reality then. The woman became Catti-brie—she was Catti-brie!

"My love, they have captured me," she said. "Help me . . ." She reached out.

Before he could even register the strangeness of the moment, the entranced Drizzt slid Icingdeath away and reached for his beloved with his empty hand.

But the woman laughed at him, and became a drow again—the most beautiful drow he could imagine—and the hand he reached to take became a serpent, floating in the air.

Floating and biting, so fast!

A shock, like lightning, cascaded through Drizzt's body. He tightened his other hand upon Twinkle, trying to use that tangible item to keep him from melting to the floor. He stumbled backward, beyond the partition, but he wasn't even aware of his surroundings at that moment.

Except for the drow woman. That one he saw clearly, smiling, beckoning, inviting him to a journey he wanted to take. She stepped backward down the corridor beyond the opened door and her form wavered. As it did, Drizzt saw past her.

He saw Vierna. She knelt and sobbed, clutching at her chest, at a bloody wound.

"Drizzt?" Jarlaxle called, but Drizzt did not hear. He sheathed his other blade and leaped forward through the door, running for Vierna, rushing to his sobbing sister, whom he had slain.

◆ ◆ ◆

"By the gods," Entreri growled when he noted Drizzt's charge. He started that way, joining Jarlaxle's pursuit of their confused companion, but both stopped, both lifted an arm to bar the other, and both fell back suddenly when a strange wave of energy rocked the war room and a violet glow, a great ray that went from the opened doorway to the opposite wall, appeared in front of them.

"What?" Entreri demanded, and tentatively started forward.

"Do not!' Jarlaxle warned. "Prismatic!"

"What?" Entreri asked again, turning to face the mercenary.

Jarlaxle shook his head, his face a mask of fear—and that alone kept Entreri back. The mercenary rushed to grab one of the room's chairs, then sent it skidding into the purple glow.

The chair's form waved, as if a ripple of water were suddenly above it, and then it vanished, and was simply gone.

"Prismatic magic," Jarlaxle said, barely able to get the words out. "Purple . . . a plane shift."

"Drizzt has traveled to another plane?"

"Demons," Jarlaxle reminded him, and both of them could only assume that their friend had been lost to the Abyss.

"Come and be quick," Jarlaxle said. "To Dahlia . . . then we must be out of this place."

"Drizzt!" Entreri growled, motioning to the glow.

"We cannot help him. Not here. Not now."

Jarlaxle steadied himself and led the way out the central door.

Entreri followed, but more hesitantly, glancing back with every step. "Drizzt?" he whispered, and the word pained him more than he would have ever believed, or admitted.

◆　◆　◆

DRIZZT HADN'T FELT the purple ray. He was beyond it, into the corridor, before Yvonnel enacted the magic.

Drizzt didn't know of it, and didn't look back. He was with Vierna then, his sister kneeling and crying. She reached up a bloody hand and grasped his arm.

"Dinin, the drider," she whispered, and Drizzt flinched at the reminder of his doomed brother.

"How are you here?" he asked.

She seemed not to hear him.

"Atone!" she warned. "We are given a chance, all of us! Our fates are not sealed. The river of time moves all around, and flows back upon itself."

"This is madness!"

"Madness? Or a dream? Your dream, your perception, your creation. You destroyed us, my young brother. Oh, worthless honor! And you would kill me. And I loved you."

"No," Drizzt cried, falling to his knees in front of her and holding her closer—and trying to stem the flowing blood with his hands. "No!"

"You cannot save me with your hands," she whispered. "Swim upstream, brother. Unwind your heresy. Accept your fate . . ."

And she slumped to the floor, face down in front of him, and he knew she was dead before he looked into her lifeless eyes.

But was she? Was anyone truly dead?

"I died on Kelvin's Cairn," he whispered, certain that this, all of this, was a grand deception. Still, there had to be a strand of truth somewhere in the midst of these illusions and warped designs.

Was it Vierna?

Was this all, after all, a backflow of the river of time itself?

That was not more irrational than the appearance of his dead friends, after all.

"Have I chosen wrong?"

Drizzt rose to his feet and stumbled along the corridor, muttering to himself, trying to make sense of the nonsense, trying to see truth when all around him was surely a lie. He thought of Wulfgar, and replayed the lesson.

"Errtu ate those children in front of Wulfgar, and murdered Cattibrie . . . the demon created reality within a beautiful deception, then destroyed that desired reality right in front of the helpless victim," Drizzt whispered. "It broke him, and so it breaks me."

He stumbled against the wall and needed it for support, else he would have surely crumbled to the ground and lay helpless.

". . . every unguarded moment . . . the awful truth of my life. Dead on Kelvin's Cairn. Lolth found me and took me."

He stumbled along again, kicked through another door. "A century—I saw them die! I am a fool!" He imitated Bruenor's voice, "I found it, elf!"

Then he growled and drew his blades and went into a dance, swinging with ferocious control, striking at imaginary foes.

"No miracle, nay! A deception! Not the blessing of Mielikki, nay! This is the curse of Lolth, the grand deception!"

"What is deception?" a sharp female voice intoned. "Idiot child."

Drizzt swung around, scimitars at the ready, and there he froze in place, held by overwhelming and debilitating shock.

There stood Matron Mother Malice Do'Urden, his mother, the woman who had used the moment of his birth to send powerful magical energy into her war on a rival House. The woman, his mother, who should have loved him, but had never shown him any interest at all except what he might do to improve the status and situation of herself and her House.

She stood there, staring down at him imperiously, and Drizzt felt small indeed.

"What is not?" he answered, trying to summon enough anger so that he could turn away from her penetrating and judging stare.

"Perhaps nothing," she said. "You call it deception, but is it not merely altered reality?"

"What do you know of it? Of anything?"

"I know what you ruined, and in pursuit of futility!" Malice answered. "And to what end, my idiot child? What have you gained that puts you here in this place, in this time, in utter despair? Do you claim victory between your tears?"

"No!" His cry was one of denial, a rejection of her and of this place, of his life, of his unavoidable fate. In truth, though, and Drizzt knew it, that denial was also a correct answer to her last question.

There was no victory here, just a cruel joke, the deception of a demon.

"You'll not shatter my heart," he said to her. "I accept the death of my friends. I will find instead the Hunter. I deny you and deny your pain!"

He pointed a scimitar at her, his face a mask of outrage, summoning the courage to charge at this demon figure and put an end to her.

"My friend will be silence," he said, striding at her. "I will be left with nothing, but that will be enough!"

"Only because you are too stupid to see the opportunity presented before you," Malice replied, and Drizzt stopped his approach and looked at her warily.

"To what end?" Malice asked.

Drizzt blinked, not quite catching on. It was his own private question, reflected back at him.

"Knowing now that perception and reality are so intimately twined, so I ask you again, to what end?" Malice asked, only slightly altering the question that had been burning in Drizzt's own thoughts—as if she had read his mind.

"You ruined me," Malice went on. "Your brother was twisted to abomination, your sister murdered by your own hand, your House thrown to ruin. All that I built—"

"It was you!" Drizzt accused, pointing at her with his blade.

"You can unwind it," said Malice. "The river flows backward. This is your moment and your choice."

"I made my choice! To the Abyss with . . ."

"Zaknafein?" Malice asked, and the word nearly knocked Drizzt from his feet. "That is the moment before you, my idiot son. Come and witness my dagger sliding into his chest . . ."

Drizzt cried out, an indecipherable roar of outrage, and leaped forward, Icingdeath coming across viciously to cut Matron Mother Malice apart. But the blade went right through her less than corporeal form, and Drizzt nearly fell, overbalanced by the swing that caught only empty air.

Malice's laughter echoed down the hall, mocking his worthless passion. He saw her image departing then, sliding through the right-hand wall farther along.

◆ ◆ ◆

"You have broken him," K'yorl Odran said with a giggle, watching Drizzt dancing about, swinging wildly and screaming at himself in the corridor in front of her.

"He is sick with the Abyssal emanations of the Faerzress," Yvonnel answered, seeming quite intrigued by it all. "He has lost the firmament of truth, of reality. He walks in dreams and nightmares."

Yvonnel's expression turned curious then, partly amused and partly pitying this lost heretic.

"Lost," she whispered.

"And so open to suggestion?" K'yorl asked.

"The chapel," Yvonnel whispered, and K'yorl reflected that thought in the mind of the distant Drizzt Do'Urden.

"Now, follow," Yvonnel instructed her slave. "We must be quick."

272

◆ ◆ ◆

"DRIZZT HAS ENTERED the city and is coming for her," Kiriy said, pointing frantically at Dahlia, who lay unconscious on the bed.

"And so you threw driders into our midst?" Ravel questioned with a disbelieving, even derisive, snort.

"I needed to keep you away."

"So that you could kill her and claim the throne of House Do'Urden," Saribel said accusingly.

"Yes!" Kiriy retorted. "Yes, as Matron Mother Zeerith determined. By word of Matron Mother Baenre," she added quickly, seeing Tiago's sudden scowl.

"This abominable *darthiir* you mean to murder is the matron mother's creation," Tiago said.

"And she has outlived her usefulness to House Baenre," Kiriy replied, too smoothly for the others to determine whether or not she was improvising. "House Xorlarrin returns, and we are many times more valuable to the matron mother than this . . . this creature. Or this mock House that invites the scorn of all other Houses in Menzoberranzan."

"And so you mean to correct that," Ravel asked skeptically, "in the midst of a war?"

"It will settle the war!" Kiriy insisted. "When Dahlia . . . Darthiir, is dead, the Melarni will no longer ally with House Hunzrin. They care not for Hunzrin trade. The abomination sitting upon the Ruling Council is their only reason for waging war on House Do'Urden, as they view Matron Mother Darthiir as an insult to Lady Lolth herself. When she is no more, the Melarni will be appeased, and without them, the stone heads will flee. They alone are no match for the garrison of this House. The House will be ours, as will the seat on the Ruling Council."

"Those things are ours now," a doubtful Ravel reminded her. "They will be *yours*, you mean."

"Do'Urden, not Xorlarrin! And they have come for her!" Kiriy said. "She must die, either way."

Tiago drew Vidrinath.

"No!" Saribel insisted. "If Darthiir is slain, Kiriy becomes matron mother!"

"Kiriy, who just attacked us," Ravel added.

"Matron Mother Baenre demands it," Kiriy declared, aiming her words at Tiago, relying on his allegiance to Baenre. "Darthiir must not be taken by the heretic Drizzt."

Tiago glanced back and forth from Kiriy to the others, his hand wringing the pommel of Vidrinath, the glassteel blade's tiny stars sparkling in the low candlelight of the room.

"Your story is babble!" Saribel accused.

"How dare you speak to me in that manner?" Kiriy retorted.

"Because your tale is nonsense," Ravel shot back. "If Matron Mother Baenre so desired what you claim, she would have sent the Baenre legions and chased off the Hunzrin and Melarni."

"She does not wish to expose herself. There is no need. We know not the disposition of House Barrison Del'Armgo in this matter."

"None of us wish to see this abomination remain alive," Tiago put in, and he moved for Dahlia.

"She is your bait for Drizzt," Jaemas remarked, freezing the young Baenre in his tracks. "If what First Priestess Kiriy says is truth."

"It is not!" Ravel insisted.

"Not all, perhaps," Jaemas agreed. "But a lie is all the stronger with truth embedded, is it not?"

"You dare call me a liar?" Kiriy said, and her wizard cousin bowed and respectfully shrank back. But he added, "If you kill her, the heretic Drizzt will leave." He knew who traveled with Drizzt, of course, and understood Jarlaxle's intent. "And the head of Drizzt Do'Urden is a prize that will announce the glory of the rebirth of House Xorlarrin like no other, while the head of Darthiir Do'Urden is nothing more than another *iblith* trophy, whose name will be forgotten before the turn of the approaching century."

Close enough to strike Dahlia dead, Tiago locked stares with Jaemas.

"Kill her," Kiriy insisted. "Or we will all be dead before Drizzt Do'Urden even arrives."

"Do not," said a newcomer, striding in confidently through the door. The others all turned to regard the young drow woman.

"How dare you?" Kiriy retorted, eyes wide with outrage and snake-headed scourge in hand.

"Melarni?" Saribel added with a snarl.

"I should kill you for even suggesting such a thing," the woman answered. Kiriy started to scold again, but the newcomer cut her short.

"I am Baenre," Yvonnel said. "New to the First House, and yet I have lived there all my life."

"A commoner servant newly inducted . . . ?" Saribel started to ask, but Kiriy's gasp cut her short, and indeed, was so desperate that all turned to regard her.

She stood staring at the intruder, eyes wide, and it seemed as if she kept forgetting to draw breath. Matron Mother Zeerith had warned her about this one, this daughter of Gromph and Minolin Fey, who should be a toddler.

"Your mother told you," Yvonnel said. "Good."

"I have lived in House Baenre my entire life," Tiago argued. "I would know . . ."

"If the daughter of Gromph had grown up?" Yvonnel teased, and he too fell back a step.

As did all the others when another drow woman, this one naked, entered the room holding a leash that produced a moment later yet another. This drow woman looked ancient and haggard, crawling at the end of the leash. The naked woman transformed suddenly—though fortunately briefly—revealing her true tentacled form as a handmaiden of Lolth.

"I am Baenre, the Eternal Baenre," Yvonnel announced, and with K'yorl's help, she telepathically imparted to both Saribel and Kiriy, *You wish to lead this House. I can make that happen, or I can prevent it.*

"The war is already over," she announced aloud. "In outcome, at least. There are more to die, and mostly Hunzrin fools. Matron Mother Melarn has abandoned their cause. The driders are already in flight from this compound. House Hunzrin is the snake's body, but the serpent has no head."

She let her grin fall over each of them in turn. "Unless some in this room see through the snake's eyes," she said slyly.

Ravel, Saribel, and Tiago all glanced Kiriy's way, as did Jaemas, though he did well to keep from swallowing hard.

"Never were we allied with House Melarn," Ravel insisted. "We are Do'Urden, defending from an unprovoked—"

"Indeed," Yvonnel said, in a tone that didn't display confidence in that claim. "Then go defend your House, Do'Urden nobles. Go!" She waved Ravel and Jaemas out. "You, wizards, clear and secure the balconies."

The two looked at each other helplessly, unsure of what they should do, even with a handmaiden in the room—if it was a handmaiden.

"Lolth is watching," Yiccardaria said in that unmistakable gurgling voice.

Jaemas nodded and led the way, respectfully bowing as he passed the trio of newcomers.

"Go and direct the battle, young priestess," Yvonnel instructed Saribel. "Prove that you are worthy, and with confidence of your just reward."

Saribel paused just long enough to glare at her sister, then glance at Tiago and, finally, at the unconscious Dahlia.

Tiago started after her.

"Not you, Tiago Baenre," Yiccardaria told him. "Priestess Kiriy spoke truly. Drizzt Do'Urden is here in House Do'Urden. Long has the Spider Queen waited for this moment. Are you ready to champion Lady Lolth?"

"For the glory of Lolth," Tiago replied.

"And of Tiago?" Yvonnel asked, and Tiago nodded, not catching the sly undertones of her mockery.

"And you remain here, with this one, and woe to you if any harm comes to her," Yvonnel told Kiriy. "I name you as Darthiir's guardian."

"Guardian?" Kiriy stuttered, hardly able to form the word. "She is abomination!"

"You presume so very much," Yiccardaria the yochlol answered before Yvonnel could reply. "How will your pride carry you, I wonder, when you are kneeling before the Spider Queen, stammering to explain your insubordination?"

◆　◆　◆

His thoughts were a jumble of his fevered imagination intermingled with the ghostly resonance of this place, House Do'Urden. His home.

That was the magic of Yvonnel's poisonous snake, casting Drizzt into a trance that transcended the barrier of death and of time itself. And so he walked among the dead who had made this place, and now, in the chapel, saw the moment of his ultimate horror as it had occurred.

There lay Zaknafein, his father, tightly bound upon the spider-shaped altar, stripped of his shirt.

There stood Vierna, staring down at Zak, trying to hide her sympathy.

And there stood Maya, the youngest of the Do'Urden daughters. Maya! Drizzt had rarely thought of her through the passing decades. Ever had she seemed to him to be at a crossroads, her ambition assailing her compassion, and always winning that struggle. She seemed cruelly content now.

Drizzt glided across the floor. He called to Zak, to Vierna, too, but they seemed not to hear him.

As he neared the altar, though, he heard them.

"A pity," Vierna said, and the sound of her voice brought him back more fully to this place. So many times had he taken comfort in that voice, recognizing always the truth in Vierna's heart even against the lies she was forced to speak.

"House Do'Urden must give much to repay Drizzt's foolish deed."

With those words from Vierna, Drizzt's thoughts careened to another time and another place, but only briefly, only enough to see the scared eyes of an elf child peeking out at him from under the body of her dead mother.

Drizzt crossed his arms over his chest and rubbed at the coldness that had come over him.

"You ruined me," he heard Malice scold again. "Your brother was twisted to abomination, your sister murdered by your own hand, your House thrown to ruin."

And then Drizzt understood, all of it. On a surface raid, he had saved an elf child from the drow murderers. That was the action Malice said he could unwind.

The cruel irony of it all struck him and he rubbed his forearms more forcefully, but the cold would not relent. He had killed that elf child, decades later, in self-defense. She had lost her reason to bitterness and had made Drizzt the focal point of her unyielding rage at the murder of her people, of her mother, lying atop her.

Had he struck her down on that starlit field . . .

"Cry not," he heard Zaknafein say, drawing him back to the scene playing out in front of him, and thinking, hoping, that his father was speaking to him.

But no, he saw, his father looked to Vierna, and added, "My daughter."

Drizzt could hardly find his breath. He knew, of course, that Vierna was fully his sister, the only one of his siblings who shared his father. He had said as much to her in their last, desperate fight, when Drizzt had killed her.

When he had slain his sister.

He felt the tears coming from his eyes.

He saw Matron Mother Malice again, then, now in her ceremonial robes. And Briza, evil Briza, walking beside her, chanting.

That dagger in Malice's hands, shaped like a spider, with small side blades, spider eyes on the hilt—how often had the child Drizzt polished that ceremonial, sacrificial dagger?

Drizzt rushed at her, wanted to chase her away, wanting to deny the coming sacrifice, the murder of his beloved father. But he was the ghost here, it seemed, more than they. He could make no tangible contact, and his screams of denial were not heard.

Or were they, he wondered when he stumbled to the side, to see Malice's dagger hand hovering so near to Zaknafein's exposed flesh. And Zaknafein turned his head, and seemed to be looking at Drizzt, and whispered something Drizzt could not hear.

The dagger stabbed at Zaknafein's heart.

The dagger stabbed at Drizzt's heart.

CHAPTER 19 ◈

Lolth's Champion

A NOTHER UNINVITED GUEST," KIRIY MUTTERED TO THE STILL-unconscious Dahlia when she heard approaching footsteps in the hallway outside the door. She wasn't worried, and even hoped that it might be this Drizzt Do'Urden creature. She was confident in the glyphs she had placed upon the entryway.

"Come, dear," she said, slapping Dahlia's cheek. "Come awake now and greet our visitors."

Dahlia did groan a bit, the first signs that the sleeping poison was finally beginning to wear away—though Kiriy figured it would be several hours yet before she awakened.

Kiriy slapped her again, harder, just to hear her groan, and the sound brought a smile to the eldest daughter of Matron Mother Zeerith Xorlarrin.

The smile went away instantly, though, when the door burst in, and no glyphs exploded, and two drow males crashed into the room.

"How dare you!" Kiriy shouted, leaping up and drawing her whip.

"My dear Kiriy, High Priestess, do you not recognize me?" Jarlaxle asked, and he tapped his finger to his temple and dispelled the illusion and became again the mercenary leader.

The priestess gasped. "What are you doing here?" Kiriy drew a dagger and placed it against the back of Dahlia's neck, and the elf groaned.

Jarlaxle held his hands out wide, innocently. "I serve House Do'Urden," he replied. "And so, apparently, I serve you."

"Then be out on the balcony and repel the stone heads, and be quick!" Kiriy ordered, or started to order, for Jarlaxle's companion took a different tack than the mercenary leader.

Entreri pulled off his mask, becoming a human once more, and threw it aside.

"Iblith!" the priestess gasped, her dagger arm coming out for Entreri.

And he exploded into motion, charging ahead, his sword arcing out in front of him and creating a wall of floating black ash.

Kiriy thrust her scourge forward, the snake heads hungrily striking through the ash wall as she began to cast a spell. Confident the immediate way was clear, and that her spell was ready, she burst through the opaque barrier, ready to destroy the foolish human.

But Entreri wasn't there.

"She is Xorlarrin!" she heard Jarlaxle cry, aiming it past her, and only then did the priestess begin to understand the truth of Artemis Entreri, a recognition that lasted only the eye-blink it took Charon's Claw to slash against her back.

Kiriy was fully armored, both with exquisite drow mail woven into her robes and with her own considerable defensive magic. No normal sword could have gotten through that wall.

But Charon's Claw was no normal sword.

No enchanted blade could have delivered a serious blow.

But Charon's Claw was no mere enchanted blade.

Kiriy Xorlarrin staggered forward under the weight of the strike. She rolled, grimacing in pain, but ready to battle.

And there was Entreri, in her face, sword spinning and weaving, and his other hand, gripping a dagger, flashing all around.

Kiriy had raised her scourge and commanded the snakes to strike, twice, before she realized that not a serpent head remained.

She cried out and fell back, moving the dagger to defend.

But in came the red blade, striking all around, always just ahead of her defensive turns or blocks, always finding a strong angle. Just when she at last thought she had caught up to the human, he rolled behind her block and she felt the bite of a dagger in her ribs.

"Oh, not that!" she heard Jarlaxle say, and to her relief, briefly, she thought she had found reprieve.

But then the red blade came across, brutally, perfectly, and Kiriy's head flipped up into the air.

"You didn't have to do that," Jarlaxle said from the bed, where he was examining Dahlia and had taken her staff in hand.

"I have had enough of drow priestesses," Entreri replied.

"She is the eldest daughter of Matron Mother Zeerith."

"Was," Entreri corrected.

"Why must you make my life so difficult?"

"To have me walking beside you is a privilege," Entreri replied, wiping his sword on Kiriy's headless body. "I want you to earn every step."

Jarlaxle surrendered with a sigh, his gaze going to Kiriy's head, which had landed upright, her eyes still open. "I should craft a human disguise," the mercenary mused. "They always underestimate you."

"So you do."

Jarlaxle began to reply, stopped and blinked, then started again, and stopped again when Dahlia stirred beside him. She met his disarming smile with a left hook, screamed, and leaped upon him.

Artemis Entreri was there in a heartbeat, before his dropped weapons even hit the floor. He grabbed at Dahlia as Jarlaxle fell away from her, finally tackling her to the bed. She kept up the struggle, punching and clawing, and even tried to bite Entreri.

Entreri sat up and pulled her up to her knees. He lined up her face in front of his own, gripping her arms tightly, pinning them down and holding her back.

"Dahlia!" he said.

She smashed her forehead into his face.

Entreri pushed her back a bit more and spat blood. "Dahlia! Dahlia, do you not know me?"

The elf stared at him, wide-eyed, her face contorting into a mask of the sheerest confusion.

"Dahlia!"

She seemed about to say something, but seemed confused too, and shook her head in denial.

"Dahlia," Entreri said softly, and he felt all the strength go out of the elf. She simply collapsed, falling forward into his waiting hug, and there he held her tightly, whispering to her, promising her that he would get her out of this place.

"No, truly," Jarlaxle said from over the headless body of Kiriy Xorlarrin. "You really didn't have to do that."

"I didn't have to, but it felt good," Entreri said, holding Dahlia close.

Jarlaxle started to reply, but shrugged instead. He took up Dahlia's wondrous staff, quickly examined it, then broke it down and tucked it into his pouch.

"We must be away," Jarlaxle said, and Entreri wasn't about to argue.

"Indeed," a woman's voice replied, and there stood Matron Mother Quenthel Baenre, where a wall had been just a moment before. The disfigured illithid stood beside her, the pair flanked by Sos'Umptu and

Minolin Fey. A cadre of the Baenre garrison hovered about, close behind, protecting the matron mother and the Archmage of Menzoberranzan, Tsabrak Xorlarrin, who maintained the passwall. Before Jarlaxle or Entreri could react, the room's door banged open, and another battle group appeared, this one led by Weapons Master Andzrel Baenre.

Jarlaxle glanced at Entreri and shook his head.

The Baenres had come prepared.

"We saved Matron Mother Darthiir, your voice on the council," Jarlaxle said when he noted Quenthel Baenre's disgusted expression as she looked upon the headless corpse at her feet.

"For just that reason, I am sure," the matron mother sarcastically replied.

◆　◆　◆

ON THE BALCONY of the House chapel, Yvonnel, K'yorl, Yiccardaria, and Tiago looked down upon Drizzt Do'Urden.

He didn't know they were there. His vision and thoughts were caught in the web of a clairvoyance enchantment that had sent him back through the decades. Drizzt gasped and stumbled to the altar, trembling, his knees giving out beneath him, but he crawled on, reaching desperately.

"He is a confused and tormented soul," Yvonnel explained. "He witnesses now a moment that brings him great pain, and great doubt. He has no footing now, no confidence in his principles or his code of honor. He is a pitiable thing."

"He is a heretic," Tiago corrected, sword in hand and buckler unwinding into a larger shield. "An abomination, and soon to be a gift to Lady Lolth."

"When you are told," Yiccardaria said in no uncertain terms, and even stubborn Tiago had to back off a bit at the command of a yochlol.

"Your bravery is commendable, if your temerity is not. Do you underestimate this warrior, Tiago? Do you place no value on the brilliance he has attained?"

"I have battled him before," the young upstart weapons master replied.

And so Drizzt knows what to expect from you and your unusual weapons, Yvonnel thought, but did not say. She did smile, though, and offered a rather evil chuckle that should have warned Tiago somewhat—if he wasn't so cocksure of his own expertise.

"He does seem a pitiful thing," Yvonnel said instead, nodding down at the seemingly broken drow, who knelt by the empty altar and held onto it for support. "There will be little glory in killing him when his eyes and his thoughts are caught in the past. The headsman is not regarded as a hero for his actions on the gallows."

Tiago stared at her, clearly confused, trying to form some rebuttal and looking very much as if he suddenly believed that his trophy had been stolen from his grasp yet again.

"But that will not be the case," said Yvonnel. "The enchantment upon Drizzt is mine own. I can dismiss it easily. Do not doubt that he will find focus when you go down there against him."

Tiago visibly relaxed.

"Do you deny any aid when you are in combat with Drizzt?" Yiccardaria asked.

"I do not understand."

"Shall I incapacitate Drizzt Do'Urden if you are losing?" Yvonnel explained. "Or heal your wounds if he scores first blood?"

The young weapons master seemed unsure, eyes darting from Yvonnel to Yiccardaria.

Yvonnel took great pleasure in his obvious unease, and nearly laughed aloud when he licked his lips. He was measuring his own confidence against his desired glory. If he agreed to the help, his glory would be diminished.

If he did not, he might well end up dead.

"No," he said at last. "I ask for this kill, by my sword alone."

Yiccardaria nodded and seemed contented, while Yvonnel was delighted. She wouldn't have helped him anyway.

"He will die," Tiago promised.

Yiccardaria motioned to the tight circular staircase off to the side of the balcony, but Tiago took his own route, lifting a leg over the balcony railing and simply dropping over, tapping his House emblem to enact a levitation enchantment so he could touch down easily onto the floor some twenty feet below.

Even as he landed, Yvonnel dismissed the enchantment over Drizzt.

"They both champion Lolth," Yiccardaria remarked. "But only one knows it."

◆ ◆ ◆

DRIZZT REACHED FOR Zaknafein, his father, as the great warrior lay bleeding, dying upon the altar.

But Drizzt's hand passed right through the image and scraped the top of the altar-stone as he pulled back, and the images around him of his family, of his gasping father and his murderous mother, of his three priestess sisters in their Lolth-worshiping raiment—of Vierna in particular, and Drizzt thought he spied a tear there as she watched her father die—cast him back across the decades and shed a dark light upon his choices.

But Vierna was a ghost. They were all ghosts. And then they were gone.

Leaving Drizzt kneeling beside the altar, staring at the hand he had put through the image of Zaknafein, seeing blood on that hand.

Drizzt understood it now. Yes, his hands were soaked in blood. He had caused the downfall of House Do'Urden, the sacrifice of Zaknafein, who had lain upon that altar willingly in his stead.

And for what?

He had saved an elf child. His principles, his conscience, had demanded it, but he had killed her anyway, later. She had come for him and he had killed her anyway.

What did it matter? What did any of it matter? Of what value were his principles when he continually cast them against the incoming tide itself?

How much of a fool was he, standing alone, and so desperately clinging to images of his reborn friends that he now knew to be mirages, illusions, deceptions?

There was no solid ground beneath his feet. He felt as if his entire life had been a lie, or a quest to tilt his lance at statues of dragons that would only be rebuilt if he somehow managed to topple them.

He could not win.

What, then, the point of fighting?

He took a deep breath. He sensed something, someone, behind him and glanced over his shoulder to see a drow warrior, Tiago Baenre, floating down from above, landing lightly on the floor some steps away, his sword and shield at the ready.

"Why are you here?" Drizzt asked him. "Why now?"

"To kill you, of course. To finish what should have been done in the tunnels of Q'Xorlarrin."

Drizzt looked down again at his hand and gave a soft chuckle. The blood was still there—the blood would always be there.

"Q'Xorlarrin," he whispered. "Gauntlgrym."

Or was it? Did it matter?

"Am I to lie upon the altar, then, and accept your blade?" Drizzt said, twisting to face Tiago as he rose to his feet.

"The result would be the same," Tiago replied. "Though I prefer to again defeat you."

Drizzt's thoughts went back to that room in Gauntlgrym, where he and Tiago had fought, and where he was certain he had Tiago beaten and dead, until Doum'wielle intervened with the same mighty sword Jarlaxle now carried.

"I am happy to kill you again in combat," Tiago teased, "for the glory of Lolth."

Drizzt simply shrugged and let Tiago have his delusions.

He drew his scimitars, and as they slid free of their sheaths, Drizzt planted in his mind the image of Zaknafein, upon this very altar, in this very place, being sacrificed to the goddess Tiago now championed.

Drizzt looked at Icingdeath and Twinkle as he rolled them over in his hands. So many memories.

He smiled as he thought of the dragon that gave his right-hand scimitar its name, as he recalled Wulfgar's implausible throw to drop the giant icicle spear upon the unwitting wyrm.

But he forced fully back into his thoughts the image of Zaknafein, dying in his stead. Dying . . . Zaknafein murdered . . . because of Drizzt . . . because of cruel Lolth . . .

Tiago, self-professed champion of Lolth, leaped and came on.

The Hunter waited.

Tiago opened with a bull rush, shield leading, seeking to drive Drizzt back over the altar.

Drizzt, outwardly seeming hardly ready, was quicker, though, and he flashed out to the left, forcing Tiago to skid to a stop and swing about, launching his sword in a wide sweep to keep the dodging ranger at bay.

A moment of darkness crossed Tiago's face as he squared up to his foe. There stood Drizzt, scimitars up and ready, diagonally out from either hip, head bowed but coming up. When Tiago glanced upon that face, into those lavender orbs, at that sly smile, he saw the truth.

Drizzt didn't care.

Tiago went in carefully, Vidrinath stabbing ahead.

Drizzt, in no hurry, tapped the blade aside, left and right, and measured his ripostes, more to see how Tiago would react than with any hope of scoring an early hit. And so they felt each other out for a few turns and routines, mostly blade tapping blade, and only once with Drizzt putting Icingdeath out far enough and fast enough for Tiago to block with his shield.

But shield and scimitar barely connected, and Drizzt had the blade away before the webbing magic of Orbbcress could be activated. Drizzt covered that retraction with a secondary spin and strike, desiring that Tiago not know what he remembered from the last encounter.

Drizzt understood the properties of that shield, and believed he knew how Tiago would try to use it.

Tiago's fine sword averted the second strike, and the deft drow quickly forged ahead, stabbing repeatedly from around the edge of his shield, forcing Drizzt into a retreat.

Drizzt focused his counters on that sword, parrying and rolling, seeking some way to twist it from Tiago's hand. But whenever he got any leverage on the starlit glassteel blade, Tiago was fast to turn, bringing his shield into play and forcing Drizzt to surrender the twist or be caught.

This young warrior was very skilled. Drizzt reminded himself of that with every parry and every counter.

He was also very confident, seizing the initiative and pressing his attacks.

Drizzt let him, and continued his measured retreat, swinging to the far end of the room from the balcony where Tiago had leaped, and then coming back around to the right, gradually putting the balcony behind him and backstepping to the altar.

Tiago's cadence, strike and step, was almost hypnotic, the flecks caught within Vidrinath sparkling like the stars seen atop Kelvin's Cairn. Drizzt could almost feel the chill breeze on his face again, and how he wanted to be there . . .

Tiago huffed and puffed as he scrambled to keep pace and keep the offensive press, but Drizzt easily turned the stabbing blade.

Tiago dropped his right shoulder back and leaped ahead with unexpected ferocity, shield leading. But only for a moment. As Drizzt reacted, so, too, did Tiago, anticipating Drizzt's reactions perfectly.

Drizzt went right and Tiago turned right, Vidrinath coming forward.

Tiago had first blood, and Drizzt's hip burned from the poisonous strike.

Drizzt reset his position and his pace, accepting the gash and confident that he could defeat the drow sleeping poison.

The sight of the blood spurred Tiago, it seemed, and he came on as before, only much quicker now, Vidrinath leading and stabbing, changing angles with each strike, short stabs and sweeping reversals.

Twinkle and Icingdeath met the barrage, the three blades ringing together and scraping apart, and always that shield finishing the exchange, cutting off Drizzt's attack.

The altar was near, and the young Baenre came on with a shield rush again, angling to Drizzt's right. And as with the initial attack, he forced Drizzt out to the left—but this time, with Vidrinath ready.

But Drizzt knew that, and so didn't go left. Icingdeath came down hard on the shield, a stunning blow that interrupted the bull rush.

Tiago cried in glee, thinking he had him, and enacted the web properties of his shield to grasp Icingdeath fast against it.

But then Drizzt, his feet on the top edge of the altar for leverage, was against that shield, too, pressing forward from above, driving Tiago back and down and twisting, and leaving the surprised warrior at a sudden and likely fatal disadvantage.

Tiago had no choice. He had to force Orbbcress to release its hold, or he would have been driven to the ground awkwardly, and thus exposed to Drizzt's free scimitar. He spun desperately out to his right as he released Orbbcress's grip, and so did Drizzt, diving down the other way from the altar, landing in a headlong roll that brought him right back to his feet, where he spun about in time to engage the angry Tiago's renewed charge.

"You fight with tricks of your fine armaments," Drizzt accused him, spinning and parrying, his feet moving too fast for Tiago to properly pursue in time so that he wasn't simply blocked yet again. "Where are you, Tiago Baenre, without those gifts your heritage provides?"

"Do you claim no baubles?" an increasingly-agitated Tiago countered.

"Won in fair combat," taunted Drizzt. "Can you say the same?"

On came Tiago with a wild sweep of his sword, and Drizzt sucked in his belly and leaped back out of range.

But in came the growling Baenre, throwing himself into Drizzt, shield leading. Drizzt struck down hard with both his blades to break the rush and keep the fierce warrior at bay.

And Orbbcress caught both of Drizzt's scimitars, hilt to tip.

Drizzt couldn't press forward this time. He had no altar behind him to bring him up high and grant him overpowering leverage. He tugged back, but futilely.

Tiago had his feet under him, and had both of those blades captured. He rolled his chest down and to his right, turning his shield, driving Drizzt over, and flipped a reverse grip on Vidrinath as he went.

If Drizzt let go of his caught blades and tried to grapple, Tiago would simply continue the turn and put a backhanded strike through the fool's chest.

But Drizzt didn't let go and was pulled with him.

Tiago stepped forward with his left foot and jerked back strongly to the right, eyes sparkling as both blades were pulled from Drizzt's grasp.

He must have seen Drizzt's feet beneath his moving shield, the unarmed heretic trying to get away—but even with his magical enhancements, Drizzt could not get out of range.

◆ ◆ ◆

THE MOMENT OF glory was upon him. With his legs properly placed under him, with all of his core strength driving up against the overbalanced drow, Drizzt had to stumble backward as Tiago whipped his shield back around to the left, arm going out wide while he flipped Vidrinath in his right hand for a brutal slash.

Tiago opened his shoulders—his entire body moved in perfect balance and perfect harmony, the power of the mighty swing coming from the strength of his legs, from the turning of his hips.

Undeniable.

Deadly.

◆ ◆ ◆

"BRILLIANT!" YVONNEL GASPED as she saw Tiago executing that turn and swing, as she noted Drizzt without his scimitars, fighting for balance.

"A champion is crowned," said Yiccardaria.

CHAPTER 20 ◈

Baubles

A THROGATE STOOD BY THE STEM OF THE NEW HOSTTOWER OF the Arcane, hands on hips and a continual sigh blowing from his mouth.

Ambergris was there with him, moving about the recently constructed trunk of the planned tower, examining the joints between the fitted pieces, casting a spell here or there, but ultimately shaking her head.

"It ain't workin'," Athrogate explained to Catti-brie, when she and the other magic-using architects of the project arrived to his summons. A swarm of dwarves was gathering as well.

"The progress seems remarkable," Lord Parise Ulfbinder replied, nodding as he worked, his eyes up the ten-foot-tall trunk of the structure. "Better than I would have ever imagined!"

Athrogate snorted derisively.

"Can you not find enough pieces?" Ilnezhara put in, and she looked from Athrogate to Lady Avelyere, who was leading the search for shards from the original Hosttower.

"We'll never find them all," Lady Avelyere replied, "but surely a substantial portion will be recovered."

"Won't matter," Athrogate told them. "Ain't workin'!" He moved over to the structure and Ambergris, and motioned for Skullbreaker, her two-handed mace. He spit into his hands, hoisted the weapon, and to the shock of all watching, slammed it against the side of the tower.

The stone disintegrated beneath the weight of the blow, and large cracks ran out from the spot of impact.

"Wouldn't hold a twig for long, ne'er mind a branch big enough to hold rooms and such," the dwarf explained.

"If we thicken the walls, we might be goin' up higher," Ambergris agreed. "But we'll not e'er replicate them tree branches that made for the first tower."

"We'll need to find different spells to strengthen the bends and joints," Catti-brie suggested.

"Or better builders," Gromph remarked.

"No designs to support a one-armed arch, ye durned elf," Athrogate argued, and others, wizard and dwarf alike, took up the debate.

"Or our puzzle approach is errant," one giant voice yelled above them, drawing the attention of all.

"This was my fear," the cloud giant, Caecilia went on. "We have approached the reconstruction as a matter of collecting the old pieces and then weaving dwarven masonry and magical spells to put the puzzle back together. I was doubtful from the start."

"Ye got a better idea?" Athrogate asked skeptically, hands on hips and a scowl on his face. "We got no design prints."

"We're not even for knowin' what them pieces are made of," Ambergris added. "Seem to be crystal, mostly, aye, but there's more."

"The lack of a design rendering is damaging," Caecilia admitted.

"Because it was constructed wholly of magic," Gromph argued.

"Puzzling, as well," said Lord Parise. "Surely they worked with a plan."

"Surely they did not," argued Gromph. "The Hosttower was a magical artwork, not a dwarven construct."

"We're knowing that dwarfs were a part of it," Athrogate protested.

"So were mules, likely," Gromph retorted.

"Bah, as ye wish," said Athrogate, "and ye're knowin' the spells that might paint her anew, are ye?"

Gromph scowled at the sarcasm.

"We've no hint of any such thing," Tazmikella put in. "Whatever magic that might have built the Hosttower is not revealed among the ancient knowledge of dragonkind."

"Or you simply haven't found it yet," Lord Parise replied, and both Tazmikella and Ilnezhara looked at each other and shrugged.

"Then might we all go back to our libraries, or repositories, our most learned scholars, and delve deeper into the magic," Caecilia said, and others nodded.

Gromph stared hard at the two dwarves standing by the trunk, as if judging them for this failure.

Many whispered conversations erupted all around the field on Cutlass Island, not in disagreement with Caecilia's last advice, but neither in support. They reflected the pall that Athrogate's undeniable observations had so abruptly thrown over the progress they had been making these tendays.

Indeed, the whole field around the structure became a cacophony of groans and muttering.

Gromph Baenre wasn't listening, though, nor was he including his own voice in the arguments. He noted that Catti-brie, too, had tuned all of it out. She walked slowly to the pile of shards that lay to the side of the tower, picked up a small one in one hand, then conjured a ball of flame in her other hand.

She examined the shard, then put it, her hand, and that curious ruby ring she wore into the summoned flame. Then, to Gromph's surprise, stuck her face into the flame as well.

And there she remained, and many began to take note, and so the murmurs quieted, until the only sound on the field was the hissing burn of Catti-brie's summoned flame, a hiss that grew louder as the flames intensified, shifting to a more furious orange, then to a bluish white, and finally just a pure white. Those nearest the woman had to step back from the intense radiation of heat.

But Catti-brie kept her hand and face in the fire.

◆　◆　◆

WITH HIS SHIELD arm swinging out wide to the left, Tiago could feel the two scimitars trapped, and no more in the grasp of Drizzt Do'Urden. That arm led the turn, the rising twist lifting up from his feet, his legs, his hips, his chest, his entire spine rotating in a beautiful and deadly dance.

The proud young Baenre roared in anticipation of his ultimate victory as his head came around, leading the way for his swinging sword arm.

And that roar became something very different when Tiago saw his target clearly, standing exactly where he had expected, easily in range.

But hardly unarmed.

The astonished Tiago stared at the sharp end of an arrow, and Drizzt held a bow—from where it had come, Tiago could not begin to guess in that flash of recognition, that singular terrifying instant before Taulmaril was released and a bright flash of burning whiteness consumed the Baenre warrior's thoughts.

Tiago Baenre's head simply exploded.

"Baubles," Drizzt said dryly, and flashed his left arm across to use the bow to block the swinging sword, though Vidrinath came across with no strength behind the swing. "Fairly earned and wisely mastered."

◆ ◆ ◆

CATTI-BRIE WAS LAUGHING and shaking her head at the simplicity of it all when she pulled her face out of the white-hot flame. With a puff of breath and a word, she blew out the flame, extinguishing her spell.

"What'd'ye know, girl?" Athrogate asked.

"Limestone," she said, holding up the shard.

"Too hard," Athrogate replied. "Marble, then, but aye, too brittle!"

"Crystalline," Ambergris added.

"What do you know?" Gromph demanded.

"No wizard built this tower," she said to the great drow. "And no priest, and no dwarf, and no dragon, and no giant," she added, looking in turn at Ambergris, Athrogate, the dragon sisters, and Caecilia. "Though all helped, do not doubt."

"Now you speak in riddles?" an agitated Gromph remarked.

"Though all helped, and all were surely needed," Catti-brie said. "To contain the magic."

"Say it plainly, woman," an obviously intrigued Lord Parise begged. The scholar Shadovar leaned forward, pulled toward Catti-brie.

"The Hosttower of the Arcane was built by the primordial beast that resides in Gauntlgrym," she answered with all confidence. She had seen. In the intense heat, the shard had revealed itself, and through the intense fire and through her Ring of Elemental Command, Catti-brie had peered into the realm of fire once more, and had heard the echo of the primordial's memory.

A hundred confused, mostly disapproving scowls came back at her.

"The roots were first, bit by bit, the tree grown later," the woman explained, to even more confused stares.

"Grown?" Lord Parise and Caecilia asked in unison, and Catti-brie nodded.

"As if t'were alive?" Ambergris asked, and Catti-brie nodded.

"Then we canno' rebuild it and Gauntlgrym's doomed," Athrogate said logically.

"Yes, we can," said the smiling Catti-brie, looking right at Gromph. "Yes, we can."

◆ ◆ ◆

BY THE TIME Tiago's sword hit the floor, Drizzt already had his second arrow away, this one shooting up at the trio on the balcony.

The woman in the middle of the group smiled even as the enchanted missile sped for her face. Her wards caused it to explode into a shower of harmless, multi-colored sparks long before it got near enough to hit her.

So Drizzt would send a steady stream, he decided, but before he had the next arrow on the bowstring, he was in utter blackness.

Instinctively, and quite used to such an occurrence, he dived into a roll. So experienced was he with the drow darkness that he knew precisely how many rolls he would need to get out the side of it, figuring it had been centered on him.

And so he came around to his knees ready to shoot.

But was still in total darkness.

He fired anyway, knowing the general direction, but only one shot. He had to be moving quickly.

And so he was rolling again, over and over, and each one seemed slower to him, and he couldn't understand that. The floor felt less solid—it was as if he rolled in bubbling tar, as though he were sinking into it. It caught him and held him and tried to flow up over him.

It was just darkness then, and Drizzt wasn't even rolling, just flopping slightly, his shoulder coming off the floor but sagging back down, broken and caught.

Chapter 21 ◈

Secular Hubris

Gromph Baenre was in a foul mood—more foul than usual, even. The witch had taken the lead from him with her knowledge of fire and of the primordial.

He sat in his grand chair, behind his grand desk, staring at the tent flap through which Caecilia had just departed.

Even she had fallen for Catti-brie's lies.

And the Shadovar Lord Parise, too, with whom Gromph had spoken right before Caecilia had come to call. It made no sense to him. How could anyone believe Catti-brie's lies? How could any of these learned scholars for a moment think it a good idea to let a primordial of fire free of its cage, even a bit?

And worse, the former archmage mused, why would anyone believe a simple human above the words of Gromph?

He tapped the tips of his fingers together, as he did when deep in thought, and tried to organize a new strategy regarding the dragon sisters. They might be his last hope to stop Catti-brie. The foolish Harpells would blindly follow her, and if the dwarves were to be persuaded, it wouldn't be from anything he might say.

Into Gromph's thoughts, then, came a plea, and it took the archmage a while to sort it out.

I wish to speak with you directly, Archmage.

When he at last identified the source of the communication Gromph's eyes went wide, and his lips curled down in a most wicked scowl.

"Come in!" he said and telepathically imparted at the same time. "Oh do!"

"Know that I come at the behest of the hive-mind," a voice replied, both in Gromph's head, and in his room, and he watched as Kimmuriel appeared in view, stepping through the distance-bending magic of psionics.

"I am connected to them even now, Archmage, and they will look unfavorably upon you should you try to foolishly take out your vengeance

294

upon me," Kimmuriel warned. "They are quite involved now in the wake of the summoning of Demogorgon and the breaking of the boundaries of the Faerzress."

How Gromph wanted to lash out and obliterate this impudent fool. Ever since he had completed the incantation, to find the Prince of Demons materializing in his chamber in Sorcere, Gromph had known that Kimmuriel had waged the ultimate deception upon him, and had ruined his name and reputation. And now here Kimmuriel stood, in Gromph's own room, vulnerable.

Or perhaps not.

Gromph bit back the invective bubbling in his throat and the spell he wanted to utter to obliterate Kimmuriel. He had no desire to anger the illithid hive-mind. There wasn't much in the multiverse that frightened Archmage Gromph Baenre, but angering a hive-mind wasn't something he ever wanted to experience.

"How dare you come to this place?" he said.

"You requested an emissary from the hive-mind to aid in the work on the Hosttower."

"But *you?*" an incredulous Gromph cried.

Kimmuriel shrugged. "The choice is theirs, not mine. I am bid to be here, by your side, and so I am."

"Perhaps the illithids wished to see you destroyed, then."

Kimmuriel sighed. "I was equally deceived, Archmage," he said with a respectful bow.

"Were you now?" Gromph answered, full of doubt.

"Yes, and by Lady Lolth herself. It was she who deigned to weaken the Faerzress, so that she could expel the demon lords from the Abyss and gain control of the plane."

Gromph cocked an eyebrow at that, his expression both incredulous, and despite his best intentions and great discipline, intrigued.

"Yvonnel has risen," Kimmuriel said, and Gromph's expression shifted more to confusion.

"Your daughter," the psionicist clarified. "She has taken control of the levers of power of Menzoberranzan."

"She is a baby!"

"No more," Kimmuriel replied. "Never in her mind, with the memories of Yvonnel the Eternal, and now, through wizardry, neither in body."

"Quenthel is no more the matron mother?"

"In name only. Yvonnel has cowed the Melarni and crowned the Champion of Lolth—a most unlikely champion—to prepare for the destruction of the beast you summoned to the Underdark."

"You babble!"

"She knows where you are, Archmage," Kimmuriel warned. "Yvonnel is well aware of your location, and the circumstances around it. Even now, she speaks with Jarlaxle in the dungeons of House Baenre."

Gromph started to argue, but that last bit of information stole his breath.

"She may call upon you, and in that event, you would be wise to heed that summons," Kimmuriel said. "But for now . . ." He held out his hand to Gromph, and the archmage stared at him incredulously.

"Come," said Kimmuriel.

"To where?" Gromph demanded. "To Yvonnel?"

"To the hive-mind," Kimmuriel explained. "At their invitation, and this is no small honor. Witness this and you will understand your daughter, and that is knowledge I believe will serve you well in the coming days of chaos and conflict."

"Then why would Kimmuriel offer it to me?"

"In exchange that my debt to you be repaid," said Kimmuriel. "I wish to return to Bregan D'aerthe, and to serve as the emissary of the illithids, and here, you, too, will remain. I would not spend my days expecting retribution."

"Retribution you earned."

Kimmuriel shrugged. "These are strange times of unexpected occurrence, Archmage. I did not know that the invocation I helped you to sort out through the combination of magic arcane and psionic would bring Demogorgon to the Underdark, or that it would so damage the Faerzress as to give other mighty demons access to the corridors of Faerûn's underworld.

"Had I known that, surely I would have helped you to avoid that . . . trouble." He shrugged again. "Come, Archmage. You will find the journey enlightening in ways you could not ever before imagine."

Gromph tapped his fingers together again, staring at this confusing drow. The hive-mind!

From everything Gromph had ever learned regarding the mind flayers—and thanks to Methil El Viddenvelp, his knowledge of the subject was extensive—the illithid hive-mind was perhaps the greatest repository of knowledge and understanding of the multiverse in existence.

He took Kimmuriel's hand.

◆ ◆ ◆

THE FLOOR STILL had him. Even though Drizzt had come to believe once more that he still had a corporeal body, that he wasn't dead, he couldn't feel anything, even pain. Nor could he see. The blackness remained.

Then he heard a woman's cry and he knew the voice.

Dahlia.

Drizzt struggled against the magical bonds that had entrapped him. With great effort, he forced his eyes open. The blackness began to lighten, ever so gradually.

He heard another cry of terror from Dahlia, then his own grunt as he tried futilely to stand. He surrendered and exhaled, only to have his chin drop to his chest, and then he realized he was standing,. He was chained to a pole with his arms outstretched to either side, held by strong cords.

Many more sounds came into focus: movement all around him; Dahlia softly weeping; another voice, Entreri's voice, calming her.

"Iblith," another woman said with utter contempt.

"Whenever her mind allows her some clarity, she realizes the truth of her desperate situation," another said, speaking in the tongue of the drow, and the rhythm of the words, abrupt and harsh halts breaking up flowing lines of melody, all too clearly reminded Drizzt of the paradox of his people.

At once, the drow were beautiful and flowing, yet hard and sharp as Underdark stone. Melodic and discordant. Alluring and vile.

The blackness had become a lighter gray now as he floated back into consciousness, and now and again he noted the ghostly silhouette of a form moving past him.

"Ah, Jarlaxle, whatever am I to do with you?" one asked.

"Let us go, of course. We are of more use to you back where we belong than in the dungeons of House Baenre."

The dungeons of House Baenre.

Those five words assaulted Drizzt's sensibilities. He had been in this most awful place before.

His eyes focused at last, and he blinked against the sting of the torch-light. He had no idea how he had come to this terrible dungeon—he tried to remember the culmination of the fight in the Do'Urden chapel. He saw again Tiago's head explode under the power of his enchanted arrow. He considered the trio on the balcony, three drow women, two in fine robes and one standing naked.

He blinked open his eyes again, to find one of that same group standing right in front of him, smiling disarmingly. Despite the horrors of his surroundings, despite his very real fears, Drizzt was surprised to see that he could not deny the beauty of this very young drow. Her long hair, so lustrous that it sparkled in reflections of the torchlight, shined mostly white, but all the colors of the rainbow seemed captured within that, revealing hints of those colors with the slightest turn of the head. Her eyes were a startling amber, but not uniformly. Like her hair, they teased with color—the softest pink, a hint of blue.

"I am glad you returned to us, Drizzt Do'Urden," she said, moving closer and running her hand lightly over Drizzt's naked chest.

There was some magic in her fingers. The sensation seemed to pull his senses nearer to his own skin somehow.

"I—I did not wish to . . . fight him," Drizzt stammered, not even knowing what he could say. He was in the dungeon of House Baenre, after all, and he had just splattered the head of a Baenre noble.

"You seemed willing enough," the woman answered.

Drizzt didn't want to take his eyes off the young woman, but he couldn't help but notice a second drow, one more his own age, wearing the robes of the matron mother. She stood to the side and scowled at him fiercely, appearing very much as if she wanted to torture him to death then and there.

Drizzt steeled his own gaze and locked stares with her. He didn't care. He truly didn't care, and that indifference revealed that he would not be intimidated.

The woman in front of him turned and glanced at the matron mother, nodding and obviously noting the glowering exchange.

"Leave us," she instructed the matron mother.

When that older drow woman turned about and swept out of the dungeon chamber, Drizzt looked back at the young creature in front of him, his expression betraying his incredulity.

"Petty creatures, these matron mothers," the woman said. "Do you not agree?"

"Who are you?"

"I am young and I am old," she teased. "I am new to the City of Spiders, yet I know its memory more fully and clearly than the oldest of the old dark elves. I am bound to lead here, to rule as Matron Mother Baenre, and yet I find myself intrigued by . . ." She grinned and ran her finger over Drizzt's lips. "By you. Why is that, do you suppose, Drizzt Do'Urden?"

"I am sure that I do not know." Drizzt steadied himself with a deep breath and pulled his gaze from the young woman, staring past her defiantly.

"Are you so removed?" she asked. "Are you so above all that you have left behind?"

"Do you always speak in riddles?"

The woman laughed and snapped her fingers, and Drizzt, without any movement of his own, turned right around, though he had no sensation of movement. He was suddenly just facing the other way.

He tried to sort through that disorienting shift, but lost those questions as soon as he registered the image in front of him. There sat Entreri, who was once again in his normal, human form, along with Jarlaxle and Dahlia, the three locked in a prison of bars that crackled and sparked and was made of streaks of lightning.

"Still uninterested?" the woman teased from behind Drizzt.

Jarlaxle stood up and shrugged, as if apologetic for his failure. "Almost," he said, motioning to Dahlia.

"Only because I allowed it," the woman replied rather sharply.

Jarlaxle shrugged again.

The young drow stepped by Drizzt and waved her hand. "Be gone," she said, and the glowing cage turned black and disappeared from Drizzt's sight. No longer did he hear Dahlia's sobs or the crackle of lightning sparks, or any other noises coming from the magical cage.

"What am I to do with them?" the woman asked with exaggerated exasperation. She turned back to Drizzt, smiling again. "I cannot make a drider of Artemis Entreri, but I am certain I can find other ways to torment him."

"Do you think to impress me, or disgust me?"

"Do I disgust you, Drizzt Do'Urden?" she asked in a very innocent voice, and she moved up right in front of him again and ran her hands lightly about his face and chest. "Is that what you feel, truly?"

"What do you want? And who are you?" he demanded.

She slapped him across the face, and he could hardly believe the strength behind the blow. He felt his legs go weak beneath him and knew that the only thing keeping him upright were the ties that bound him.

"Whatever I want from you, I will take," she warned. "And who am I? I am Yvonnel the Eternal. Do you not understand? I am Matron Mother Baenre, whenever I choose to be. This is my city, and these my subjects. My city, Menzoberranzan, which you have betrayed."

"Never."

"Never? Shall I recount the many treacheries of Drizzt Do'Urden? Shall I speak of the dwarf you befriended who split my head in half?"

That remark hit Drizzt as hard as the previous slap, and he looked upon this young drow woman with deep confusion. Was he lost in time and space, meandering through his life rewound as if in a dream, again?

"I raised no army against Menzoberranzan," Drizzt answered, little strength in his voice or in his heart, so overwhelmed and confused was he at that dark moment.

"Neither did you help our cause. Indeed, you fought against your own people."

"Bruenor is my friend. The dwarves were my own people—by choice, and not by blood."

"And so you admit your treachery."

"I admit my free will. Nothing more."

She laughed. "Ah yes, your choice, your free will, that led to the chop of a dwarf king's axe."

"Upon the head of your namesake," Drizzt said, trying to make sense of it all.

Yvonnel laughed again. "Oh, much more than that!"

Drizzt could only look at her with confusion.

"Enough of this," Yvonnel said with a dismissive wave, her voice calm once more. "What is past is past. Now tell me, what am I to do with your friends?"

"Whatever you please."

"You don't believe that. You cannot believe that. I asked you a question."

Drizzt looked away.

"If you do not care, I will bring them in here, lay them before you, and cut them up into little pieces," Yvonnel said. "Is that what you want?"

Drizzt refused to look at her, refused to give her the satisfaction of an answer.

"Or I could let them go."

"You will never do that," Drizzt replied, still not looking at her.

But then she moved up to him again, grabbed him by the chin, and forced his head around. Her stare held him as surely as had her hand, and she ran her fingers over his flesh, igniting little fires in their wake. She was so close, her breath sweet on his face, her eyes stealing his soul, it seemed, and holding his stare.

"Love me," she whispered.

Drizzt sucked in his breath and fought to turn his gaze away.

"Love me and I will let them go."

"You won't."

"I shall! They are nothing. You are the prize."

"No," Drizzt said, and closed his eyes.

She grabbed him and kissed him hard, forcing her tongue into his mouth. He felt such a sensation of power and intensity he couldn't even gasp.

She stepped back and laughed—and slapped him again, nearly knocking him unconscious.

"Love me and I will let your companions live!"

"No . . . I cannot."

"You can."

"I cannot!"

"Then show me fealty."

"I cannot."

"Even for the sake of the three you claim to love?" Yvonnel asked. "You would let them die?"

"You offer me no choice, because what you ask is not a choice."

"I am the Chosen of Lolth and you are the Champion of Lolth."

"No, never!"

"Yes, Drizzt Do'Urden. There is no choice in that matter for you. Love me! Show me fealty."

"I cannot," Drizzt replied, but his tone was broken, less defiant. He sighed and moaned and fell limp against his bonds.

Again Yvonnel grabbed him by the chin and made him look her in the eye, but it was a gentle touch now. "Who is your god?" she asked quietly, and he felt her sympathy and believed it sincere.

"What would you have me say?"

"Just the truth."

"Mielikki was the closest I found."

"You name Mielikki as your goddess?"

Drizzt found himself sinking into emotional quicksand. It wasn't even as if he was speaking to this strange drow woman at that point, but more that he was being forced to admit the truth to himself, honestly, emotionally stripped.

"She was the closest, a name that I put upon what was within my heart. But even of that I have become unsure. So, no, I do not."

"You claim no god?"

Drizzt shrugged.

"You will not even say it, will you? Do you claim that you are your own god then, miserable mortal?"

Drizzt steadied himself and found some solid ground then. "I claim that what is right is in my heart," he answered. "That I do not need to be told right from wrong, and if I am weak, and when I am weak, then I know that I have chosen wrongly. And that error is my failing, and not that of any external god."

The woman's demeanor shifted visibly then, and her smile returned.

"Then be weak," she said, moving forward to kiss him.

He turned away.

But she grabbed him again. He could not resist that strength, and she kissed him again. With her lips and with her tongue came that intensity, a hot fire all around his body, to the very edge of pain, promising excruciating agony and unbearable ecstasy all at once.

But it never quite got there.

"You wish your friends to live," Yvonnel said, pulling back. "In truth, I would take little pleasure in killing them. They showed great courage in coming here for Dahlia, and I must admit that I admire such daring, even if I believe it stupid."

"Not stupid," Drizzt said through gritted teeth.

"Truly?"

"No, it cannot be, else what is the point?"

"What point?"

"Of anything. Of life itself. What is the point of anything without honor and loyalty and friendship and love?"

He knew her smile to be sincere then, and she nodded slightly, as if digesting and considering his words. That surprised him.

"Perhaps there is something to your claim," she admitted. "But I cannot simply allow your friends to leave, of course. Nor you, though murdering you would be much like throwing blood on the most beautiful of paintings."

"You would prove a most fitting matron mother to do exactly that," Drizzt replied.

Yvonnel slapped her hand over her mouth to catch her own laughter. "Oh, the spirit!" she said. "You beautiful, stupid drow."

Drizzt stared at her hard.

"I offer you a deal."

"I cannot show you fealty."

She held up her hand to stop him short so she could clarify. "A great prince of demons has been loosed upon the Underdark. The beast loiters in the tunnels nearby, and will soon enough return to Menzoberranzan. You will serve as my champion and as my instrument."

"Instrument?"

"Defeat Demogorgon and I will let your friends leave, without injury, without pursuit, without any future retribution. I will even return to them all of their belongings, and that is no small hoard of treasure, you well know from your time with Jarlaxle. All of it, including the rescued Dahlia, without future retribution. Free and successful in their mission."

"I am to believe . . ."

"Upon my word," she said, moving very near and staring him in the eye. Drizzt tried, but could not disbelieve her in that moment.

He settled back and tried to digest it all. His thoughts swirled about that name, Demogorgon. He had heard of the prince of demons, of course, but he knew so little about any of demonkind, other than the balor Errtu.

But still he replied, "I cannot champion you."

"Because this place is so repellent to you?"

Drizzt had no answer.

"Is everything here evil, then, Drizzt Do'Urden?" Yvonnel asked. "Simply, irredeemably evil? Demogorgon will run mad across the city if he is not stopped. How many young Drizzts will he kill, I wonder? How many Zaknafeins?"

The mention of his father, the image of Zaknafein's sacrifice still fresh in his thoughts, tugged at Drizzt's sensibilities.

"Who would your morals favor in such a fight, the demon prince or the drow?"

Drizzt licked his lips.

"It is a simple question."

"I do not wish destruction upon this place," Drizzt admitted. "I came here only for Dahlia."

"But now it is much more complicated, is it not?" she asked. "And perhaps you will find what you sought after all. But only if you serve as I demand. Prove to me that you are no threat to Menzoberranzan. Prove to me that in your heart, you would defend this place, your people, my people, against the ultimate evil that is Demogorgon. Is that too much to ask of Drizzt Do'Urden? Are you to be a hero only for the dwarves, then, or the humans, and not for your own race?"

She stepped back and waved her hand, and the lightning bars of the cage reappeared, Drizzt's three companions still inside. Jarlaxle and Entreri stared at him, their expressions giving him the distinct impression that they were well aware of his conversation.

"If you cannot be a hero merely for Menzoberranzan," Yvonnel said, "then, as you planned, be one for Dahlia, and for Artemis Entreri and Jarlaxle. Serve as my champion. Help me to defeat this demon prince, and I will let them leave, unharmed and with no future recourse against them. Upon my word."

"For them," Drizzt said, but Yvonnel turned on him sharply.

"And for Menzoberranzan," she demanded. "And I will let your friends leave, alive and unharmed."

"And with our possessions . . ." Jarlaxle started to say, but Yvonnel fixed him with such a glare that he bit back the thought.

Drizzt didn't hear any of it. If the ground beneath his feet before this moment had been as quicksand, now it was water, ready to swallow him and drown him in confusion and despair. He tried to tell himself again that none of it mattered anyway, that everything was, after all, merely a grand illusion.

Catti-brie was long dead and buried, he reminded himself, as were Regis and Wulfgar, and he had witnessed Bruenor's last breaths. Perception was not reality.

And perception could not be reality, else what purpose was left?

No matter how hard he tried to convince himself, however, a nagging doubt lingered and nibbled at his resolve. In the end it left him hanging there, overwhelmed.

CHAPTER 22 ◈

Of Every Arrow and Every Spell

THE FORMER ARCHMAGE OF MENZOBERRANZAN WAS NOT USED TO feeling vulnerable, and it took him a long while to admit that there was nothing, no magic, no willpower, he could rely upon to protect himself should his mind flayer hosts decide to destroy him.

"Lower your defenses," Kimmuriel urged him, audibly and in his mind. "The illithids have no reason to show you enmity. It was they who bid me to bring you."

Gromph looked at Kimmuriel with great suspicion, and thought for a moment that he had foolishly accepted the invitation, and that this, after all, might be no more than a ploy to eliminate a threat to Kimmuriel, who had long been favored by the squid-headed beasts.

But Kimmuriel shook his head.

"They would take no sides in our dispute, even if I so wished," he said. "They would know with confidence that whichever of us proved the stronger would willingly work beside them, to learn from them as they learned from me, or you.

"Lower your defenses, I beg," he went on. "They cannot serve you here in any case, and hiding behind walls of useless wariness will only prevent you from experiencing the power of this place of ultimate knowledge."

It made sense to Gromph, but still it took a while for him to lower his guard enough to truly experience the energy around him. He found himself sliding into telepathic debates and images he could only barely comprehend, and at one point nearly lost himself to the fallacy that there was, in the end, no material reality, that it was all a conjuration, a great shared thought experiment.

He followed Kimmuriel down a maze of ringed balconies and spiraling stairways. At the bottom of the long descent, Gromph found himself speechless, a stuttering fool in the face of a gigantic pulsing lump of flesh fully twenty feet in diameter.

Welcome, he felt in his thoughts, throughout his entire being, and as he thought to answer, he found himself mentally within that giant brain, the hive-mind, the repository of illithid knowledge, the mental eye of this thought collective.

If before the archmage was interested in psionics, now he found himself desperate for the art. Within this hive-mind lay all the components of all magic. Anything he might know, anything he might deign to know, would be in there, the secret of life itself.

"Perhaps," Kimmuriel said, breaking him from his trance. He turned and stared at the drow, who merely shrugged.

"Come," Kimmuriel bade him, moving to another stairway.

It was hard for Gromph to leave this place, even when Kimmuriel telepathically assured him that they would return soon enough.

Up the stairs and through a door, and the pair seemed to be walking through an invisible corridor, as if they were floating among the stars, all the colors of the universe splayed out around them, the shining lights unblocked by the ceilings of the Underdark and unblemished by the clouds of Toril.

Gromph had traveled to the Astral Plane before, but never like this, never secured in one place and untethered all at the same time. He felt as if he could simply leap from whatever platform might be beneath his feet and become one with the glory around him. And he was truly sorry when Kimmuriel led him through another substantial door, and into a solid room.

A group of illithids milled about in there, none taking note of the new arrivals. Centering the room was a large pedestal, and upon it was set a crystal ball the size of a mountain giant's head. Illithids moved to it and placed their hands upon it, tentacles waggling, and then they would move away, those strange appendages tapping those of another mind flayer as they shared thoughts on what they had seen.

After a few heartbeats, Kimmuriel nodded and led Gromph to the crystal ball. Following Kimmuriel's lead, the archmage placed his hands gently on the hard surface and closed his eyes, and let come what may.

"K'yorl," he whispered a moment later. Then he gasped, "Yvonnel?"

He understood that this was his daughter, and he found himself in the exchange between Yvonnel and Kimmuriel, a line of communication facilitated by K'yorl.

Lolth's champion is chosen and the prince of demons approaches, Yvonnel told Kimmuriel. *I will call upon you and you will give to me what I asked.*

I cannot speak for the hive-mind, Kimmuriel replied, and Gromph knew it wasn't the first time he had made that disclaimer. The fear in his thoughts were evident, the stakes apparently ultimate.

You will, Yvonnel told him.

Gromph could not sort it out fully, but it seemed to him that there was a great battle about to ensue, another proxy fight for Lady Lolth.

If Demogorgon is defeated, your crime will be pushed aside, Yvonnel went on, and it took Gromph a long breath to realize that she was communicating to him then, and not to Kimmuriel. Indeed, he was somehow certain that Kimmuriel hadn't even heard that telepathic impartation.

We will speak in the future, Yvonnel promised, and the communication was cut off. Gromph fell back from the crystal ball, staring at Kimmuriel, blinking at him, trying futilely to hide his awe.

"Your matron mother?" he asked of the son of House Oblodra.

"Through her, your daughter found me. And now she demands of me."

Gromph let that notion settle for a bit, then merely shrugged, painted on a rather smug expression, and replied, "She is Baenre, after all."

"And now she demands of us," Kimmuriel clarified, and Gromph winced, just a bit.

◆　◆　◆

Drizzt walked along the corridors of the Masterways, silently and in darkness. He had all his gear with him, along with a brooch the strange young woman named Yvonnel had pinned upon him—one that would offer him some protection, so she said, and also that would allow her to observe his progress.

He had spent much of his time out of Menzoberranzan that day considering Yvonnel. He still couldn't sort it out—was she yet another person reborn in the time of the Sundering? Or was he lost wandering the looping corridors of time, living in existence past and present, and so she was truly Yvonnel the Eternal?

Or perhaps she was just another Baenre named Yvonnel.

Or perhaps he had gone truly insane, or the world around him ever had been and only now was he coming to understand the awful truth that nothing really mattered at all.

It had taken the ranger many twists and turns in the corridor to dismiss those questions and doubts, and to focus on the task at hand, repeatedly reminding himself that he had to take each moment at face value and appropriately respond, at least until he had come to some measure of certainty regarding all of this.

Right now, that meant finding this creature, Demogorgon, so that his companions could be freed. Whether they were actually his companions was a question for another, less urgent, moment.

A new pouch hung on Drizzt's belt, another gift from the young Baenre, though he knew not what it contained. She had specifically instructed him not to even look into it unless and until he desperately needed it. Similarly, his scimitars remained in their sheaths. He carried a Y-shaped wand, a divination device attuned to the most powerful of demonkind.

Strangely, and ominously, Drizzt had encountered no minor demons as of yet, though the corridors had been thick with them not long ago, by all reports. He continued at a swift pace, putting Menzoberranzan far behind—so far that he wondered if he could simply throw aside the brooch and keep on walking right out of the Underdark.

But no. He had given his word, and the three in the cell in the dungeon of House Baenre needed him.

Down one long and narrow corridor, the divining wand tingled in his hand. Drizzt paused and sniffed the air, and from the slight air currents, he sensed that the corridor would widen not too far ahead.

Drizzt fell into himself, finding his center, finding that ultimately calm being, that pure warrior he had so often summoned in his days wandering these same tunnels.

Your foe is ahead . . . in a great cavern, he heard in his thoughts, and recognized it to be Yvonnel.

The Hunter grabbed the brooch and thought to throw it aside.

But no, he decided, though he steeled his thoughts, wishing no more intrusions.

He crept ahead in the near-total darkness, the illuminating lichen barely casting his shadow as he passed. He quick-stepped to the edge of the cavern, and there paused. It was brighter inside, the perimeter of the place lined with glowing lichen, and with glow worms crawling about the walls and ceiling, their blue light appearing almost like the night sky atop Kelvin's Cairn.

The Hunter remembered that place, faintly, but did not let his thoughts slide back across time and space. He reached for his own belt pouch, then grimaced as he realized that Guenhwyvar was not with him, that he had left his faithful feline companion with Catti-brie in Luskan.

Except that it really wasn't Catti-brie . . .

Drizzt dismissed that thought. He had no time for that now, no time for any doubts or distractions. He considered the large cavern and its far wall and high ceiling, sorting the pattern of the many stalagmite mounds and stalactites hanging from on high.

The Hunter entered, rushing to a nearby mound, slipping around it to sprint to the base of another.

He heard the beast before he saw it, a great scraping sound of claws on stone, followed by a snuffling and grunting chorus.

"Smells!" screeched a voice, like the shriek of a giant ape.

"Hunger!" another, deeper voice answered.

And then the Hunter saw it, and for all his discipline, for all his experience, for all the many battles he had waged, his knees went weak beneath him. Looking upon this monster, this prince of demons, could drive even a great drow mad.

But Drizzt was not alone. Yvonnel was there in his spinning thoughts, fighting the urges, driving them aside, and so he found the pure concentration of the Hunter again, and so he looked upon the beast as it scraped its way across the cavern, giant raptor claws digging trenches in the stone floor, serpent-like tentacle arms waving from its shoulders, rolling and occasionally snapping about a stalagmite mound.

The beast stood five times his height and more. Its two heads seemed that of a great, gigantic ape, with frightening orange fur shining even in the meager light, and large black eyes that looked down from on high with a lamplight gaze that mocked the Hunter's attempt to hide.

He drew his scimitars and stepped out.

He looked at the weapons, then back at the beast, and shook his head in disbelief.

He heard Yvonnel in his thoughts but shut her out, dismissively thinking her an idiot, and himself worse. Why was he out here, and what in all the world was he supposed to do against this . . . walking catastrophe?

He looked at Twinkle and Icingdeath again, the two blades that had served him so well for more than a century.

He slid them away.

A flip of his hand across his belt buckle brought him Taulmaril—the Hunter had no intention of getting anywhere near this prince of demons.

And so he was off, running and diving, sliding to his knees and letting fly, the silver trails of his magical arrows so dense the cavern looked like it held a thunderstorm. He knew his line of arrows were scoring hit after hit— how could he miss something the sheer size of this beast, after all?—but if they were doing anything at all to Demogorgon, the demon didn't show it.

Or at least, they weren't doing any visible harm to the beast. They certainly seemed to be angering it.

The ape-heads screeched and shrieked and the beast rushed for him, those long, snake-like arms whipping and chipping stone with their godly strength.

All the Hunter had was his speed and his diminutive stature, and so he sped across the mounds, diving, rolling, shooting, desperate to stay ahead. To get clipped even once by this nightmarish behemoth was to be utterly destroyed.

He looked for wounds on the pursuing beast and noted none. He listened for some hint that he was wounding the monster, but there was only screeching rage and hunger in Demogorgon's pursuing cries. How many shots would it take to harm the beast? How many to kill it? A thousand? Ten thousand?

He would need a thousand thousand, and more!

He wanted to scream at Yvonnel. He wanted to grab her and yell in her face at the sheer stupidity of this quest. But he couldn't.

He could only run.

On one dive and roll, Drizzt skimmed the side of a large mound just as Demogorgon's snapping tentacle skipped across it, shattering stone and jolting the whole cavern with a thunderous tremor.

Drizzt scrambled to back away and fell, and grimaced against the sting as he felt Yvonnel's pouch against his hip.

He rolled to his back, his legs pumping to slide him across the floor. He lost his breath when he saw Demogorgon's two heads staring down at him from over the stalagmite, saw the other tentacle rolling up over the gigantic shoulder to snap down upon him.

With every ounce of training and strength and agility he could find, Drizzt twisted his weight back the other way, every muscle in his back and legs straining to pull him up to his feet, to stand and to pitch forward at the creature even as the mighty tentacle smashed against the floor and cracked the stone right behind him.

His magical anklets propelled him into a dead run. He dived as he passed the stalagmite mound, only so that he could shoot an arrow straight up between Demogorgon's heads. The Hunter rolled right back to his feet, never slowing, and as those two ape heads turned to face each other and the line of silver lightning that shot up between them, he went right between the beast's massive legs.

He dodged past the tail, which, too, could swing as a devastating, stone-crushing whip and which chased him and cracked against another mound as he passed.

He heard the creature turn in pursuit. He heard a stalagmite explode under the weight of a monstrous kick, and those shrieks reverberated so profoundly that the Hunter was certain he would get shaken to the ground.

Somehow he got around the next mound, darted past another after that, and then found his way blocked, as all the floor in front of him simply turned to lava.

Drizzt turned and looked to either side, but no, that, too, was cut off, the stone melting in front of his eyes, becoming angry red and flowing all around. Demogorgon closed, the ape heads screeching and laughing.

At the last moment, he realized he wasn't feeling any sensation of warmth at all, though lava was all around him. He looked at Icingdeath, considering its fire shield, but no, this was too complete.

"Clever," the Hunter whispered, and he turned and sprinted through the illusionary molten stone.

Demogorgon's cries turned angrier, turned into hoots and howls that nearly deafened the fleeing ranger. Even with his magical anklets, he couldn't outrun the beast, so he moved in a zigzagging pattern, using every stalagmite mound he could find as a barrier against those deadly tentacles.

He thought he had gained some distance, but he came around one large mound and Demogorgon was simply there, bending low to the ground, toothy maws ready to suck him in and chew him to bits.

Had the creature teleported to this spot?

Had Drizzt's concentration not been perfect, had this been any other than the Hunter, the battle would have come to a sudden end. But even in that moment of desperate shock, the Hunter reacted, bringing up Taulmaril and sending off two arrows, perfectly aimed, one for each ape face.

Even mighty Demogorgon had to react to that, and as the creature jolted upright, Drizzt dived again between its legs. Now only his great agility and those magical anklets saved him, allowing him to skip and slide out to the side as the clever monster simply dropped to its butt, trying to crush him beneath.

On the Hunter ran, gaining some distance, but turning every blind corner warily, expecting that the monster might lay in wait. He heard the mounds exploding behind him again as the prince of demons crashed through them, and he feared that soon enough this cavern would be devoid of the barriers he needed.

Now, out of options, the desperate drow dropped his hand into the pouch Yvonnel had given him and pulled out several small spider statues.

"You could have told me what to do with these," he muttered as he ran desperately, and with no choice, he simply spun and threw them back behind him, in the path of the pursuing demon prince.

The Hunter had run many steps before he even realized that the sudden tumult behind him spoke of more than just Demogorgon. Still, expecting to be crushed at any moment, he dived around another mound of stone before daring to glance back.

A handful of gigantic jade spiders crawled about the mounds in front of the demon, which shrieked and cracked at them with its tentacles.

Drizzt's hope couldn't hold, though. The spiders seemed more like statues, simply standing there as one tentacle strike after another cracked upon them.

"Fight it!" Drizzt yelled in frustration, and to his surprise, he found that the animated spiders heeded his call, all scrabbling for the demon prince. And so began the most titanic battle Drizzt had ever witnessed, as five jade spiders scrambled about the stalagmite mounds and the great Demogorgon, their massive mandibles snapping tirelessly.

Webbing flew at the demon prince. One spider shot a strand up to a stalactite and lifted itself right off the ground, climbing the web to the tapering stone and there grabbing on to bite at Demogorgon's face.

Nodding as one spider construct after another leaped upon the ugly beast, Drizzt put up Taulmaril, seeking the best targets, perhaps the eyes. For a heartbeat, he thought he had turned the tide and would prevail.

He didn't truly understand his enemy.

With a sudden and powerful shrug that sent the whole of the cavern into an earthquake roll, Demogorgon threw off the constructs.

When he recovered his balance, Drizzt couldn't even find the strength to lift his bow, could only watch in awe and humility as Demogorgon's tentacles each snapped up to enwrap a huge stalactite.

The beast pulled them free and swung them as immense clubs, batting the jade spiders aside.

Down came one stone club, right atop a spider, and the arachnid construct shattered into a million bits, the shrapnel blasting past Drizzt and forcing him over in a desperate crouch. He staggered back to his feet with a dozen cuts and a dozen more bruises, and he could not see out of one eye.

Another spider exploded. A third went flying across the cavern.

Drizzt looked at Taulmaril, and a great despair washed over him that he could not turn the bow upon himself.

He noted that he was near where he had entered the cavern then, and only that insight saved him. He put his magical anklets to good use.

And fled.

He ran down the long corridor and into another, hoping that the small size would block pursuit and having no will to ever confront that monster again, whatever the cost or gain.

He heard the continuing roar of battle behind him, the shrieks of the spiders failing with each ground-shaking explosion.

And then the corridor began to tremble with such violence that Drizzt could barely hold his balance, and the howls of pursuit deafened him once more.

Demogorgon was coming, tearing through the stone walls and ceiling as easily as if it was a shark swimming through water.

And Drizzt ran, his heart thumping in his chest. He had never really been afraid of death, but he was terrified now.

Did he even know the way?

Did he even know where he meant to go?

He came to a fork in the corridor, slowing, unsure, but one of the two passageways in front of him lit up suddenly, magically, and he chose that one. At every intersection now, a path lit in front of him, showing him the way, and he came to trust in those lights—surely the work of Yvonnel or her minions—when he recognized some of the passages and knew that he was well on his way back to Menzoberranzan.

He was leading Demogorgon back to the drow city!

Drizzt shook his head. He couldn't do that. For all his desperation, for all the certainty of his own death, for all his anger toward his people and that place, he simply could not inflict such a catastrophe upon the dark elves of Menzoberranzan.

At the next intersection, he chose the darker path.

No, you fool! Yvonnel screamed in his head, and he skidded to a halt.

You beautiful fool! he heard in his thoughts. Yvonnel had come to realize his plan, his sacrifice for the good of the drow, and she approved.

Take Demogorgon here, Champion of Lolth, to Menzoberranzan. Her people are ready!

Drizzt didn't know what to think or believe at that moment. He sensed no anger from the voice in his head, though, and surely Yvonnel knew that her enchanted spiders had been obliterated.

He sped down the lighted tunnel instead, and noted as he turned into it that the priestess or her cohorts who were lighting the way for him were not shutting down those beacons in front of Demogorgon.

Perhaps they were ready.

He turned the last corner and saw the massive gates the drow had erected to fortify their defenses at the entrance from the Masterways. Those gates sat closed, but a small door at the bottom, large enough for Drizzt to slip through, did open at his approach.

Any hesitation Drizzt might have held blew away when he heard Demogorgon close behind him again.

He saw no other drow as he sprinted along the narrow tunnel through the thick gates, but that changed when Drizzt Do'Urden ran again into Menzoberranzan.

The whole of the city was there, it seemed, fanned out in a wide semicircle around and upon every building and every mound. House banners flew all around, propelled into wild and boastful flapping by magical spells.

Overwhelmed by the sight, Drizzt couldn't help but slow, scanning for House Baenre, which was easy to find, and for Yvonnel, who was not to be found.

The gates behind him exploded then, great stones flying all around, sure to bury Drizzt where he stood.

But a hand reached out to him and grabbed him by the front of his armored tunic, and he was yanked into the air so forcefully he almost left one boot behind.

Space distorted around him, elongating in his mind-warping flight. He landed in a skid, barely stopping at the feet of Yvonnel and the matron mother, and came up to his knees to find himself face-to-face with the broken old hag that Yvonnel dragged around like a pet dog. They were at the center of the drow semicircle, atop a tall, flat-topped stalagmite mound.

Already the explosions of battle began behind him, and Drizzt glanced back to see a blinding display of magical power, lightning bolts and fireballs fully obscuring the form of the great prince of demons, as if every wizard and priestess in Menzoberranzan was hurling every bit of destructive magic at the fiend all at once.

"Constructs!" the matron mother cried, her voice magically amplified to echo all around the great cavern.

"Get up," Yvonnel said to Drizzt, and he did. He glanced back to see a swarm of jade spiders rushing for the gates, and other unthinking instruments of war—iron golems, stone golems, animated gargoyles—charging right behind them.

"You fled," Yvonnel accused.

"I . . . you said . . ."

She held up a sword in front of him, its glassteel blade slightly curving, and holding a universe of twinkling stars within.

He stood up and took Vidrinath.

Yvonnel's pet also stood and clasped her hand over Drizzt's. He looked at the old and clearly battered drow with confusion, then back to Yvonnel.

◆　◆　◆

Gromph heard Yvonnel's call at the same moment as Kimmuriel. And like Kimmuriel, the archmage understood that here lay his forgiveness, in this one great task. He looked at Kimmuriel, who nodded and led the way down the stairs swiftly to the hive-mind, where a host of illithids had gathered.

Gromph followed him to the fleshy brain, and, following the other's lead, Gromph bent in and gently placed his hand on the communal brain of the illithid community.

So many illithids followed suit, and Gromph felt himself drawn into their collective thoughts, swirling about and becoming so powerfully one, singular in purpose.

And he giggled—he could not help it—as he felt the power coursing through him, through his mind, and he tried to help and strengthen it, though he understood that he was a miniscule psionicist next to these practiced giants.

He thought of Yvonnel's promise of forgiveness, and knew that he hardly cared.

He needed no coaxing.

Not for this.

◆ ◆ ◆

"Your glorious moment," Yvonnel whispered to the woman. The young drow raised her hand, holding now a jewel-encrusted orb, and smashed it between the feet of the couple holding Vidrinath up high.

A great wind sent them flying, floating out from Yvonnel and the matron mother.

Drizzt could see them standing there, staring back, but only for a moment.

Only until every priest, every wizard, every archer in the city of Menzoberranzan let loose their most powerfully destructive spells and bolts at him and this aged and battered woman.

◆ ◆ ◆

"No," Dahlia gasped in a rare moment of perfect clarity. She came forward in the magical cage, which Yvonnel had placed on a rooftop not so far away so that the three prisoners could witness the spectacle.

"After all that trouble, they simply use him to lure in the beast and then sacrifice him to gain favor with their wretched demon goddess," Entreri spat with disgust.

But Jarlaxle shook his head, grinning. He knew better. He had seen this trick before, only on a scale miniscule compared to this grand display.

"Do you remember, long ago, before the Spellplague even, your last true fight against Drizzt, in the tower I constructed for just that occasion?" Jarlaxle asked.

Entreri looked at him curiously, then turned his eyes again to the conflagration and explosions filling the air in front of the entry from the Masterways, fully obscuring Drizzt in fire and lightning and swarms of missiles.

316

He winced as a great spinning web of lightning flew forth and fell over that spot, and exploded in brilliance that stole his vision.

"It cannot be," he breathed.

"I have come to doubt nothing anymore," Jarlaxle said.

◆ ◆ ◆

DRIZZT HELD ONTO Vidrinath for all his life, that focal point was the only thing that lay between him and utter insanity as a thousand spells exploded around him. He didn't know what to think or why he was alive or how he could be anything more than splattered dead across the floor. Lightning bolts rained upon him. Fireballs roiled over one another or filled the air, flame strikes slashing down amid them, spinning their flames into somersaulting dances in front of his eyes. A meteor swarm pounded around him, compliments of the new Archmage of Menzoberranzan. A thousand arrows struck him, and bounced off of him.

But their killing energy did not bounce away. It spread about the drow, caught by the great kinetic barrier an illithid hive-mind had raised around him.

He trembled under the press of power, under the containment of more energy, more destruction than he had ever before witnessed, all at once. The bared power of Menzoberranzan, the thousands of dark elves, the minions of Lolth, acting in unison, sending all their hate and power at him.

And then it was over and Drizzt was back on the roof, and the old drow woman holding his hand smiled at him, her eyes wide and wild. She let go, and shrieked and gasped and simply exploded, but so fully that she became nothingness, her final expression a bright burst of ultimate ecstasy.

She was gone, and Drizzt stood there, holding Vidrinath, trembling under the power, increasingly uncomfortable as it demanded release.

Across from him stood Yvonnel. To the side, and not so far away, the matron mother scowled both at Drizzt and at the other woman.

And behind them, Demogorgon approached.

"Now is your moment, Drizzt Do'Urden," Yvonnel said. "Now you prove yourself. There is the Matron Mother of Menzoberranzan, Quenthel Baenre." She pointed at Quenthel, whose eyes went wide indeed.

"You feel your power," Yvonnel said. "One strike and she will be obliterated, and you will have dealt a great blow against Lolth and against this city."

She paused and bowed. "Now is your moment."

Drizzt stared at the matron mother, stupefied, and trembling so hard he could barely stand. He could feel the power—of every spell and every arrow—beginning to eat through the strange shield that held it at bay.

Heartbeats, no longer than mere heartbeats, and he would be obliterated, like the woman who had served as a conduit, who had let go of his hand.

He saw the fear in the matron mother's eyes. She knew she was doomed.

And he didn't know . . . anything.

He looked down and drew out Icingdeath with his free hand. He fell within himself and became, again, the Hunter.

This was his moment.

He heard the approach behind him—how could he not?

Slowly, Drizzt's eyes scanned upward. He saw the robes of the unusual young drow. He followed up her shapely body to that pretty neck and rainbow hair, to that beautiful face, staring back at him and smiling knowingly.

So close, but not afraid.

Because she knew.

This was his moment.

Drizzt roared and spun, his blades going high. And he ran—how he ran!—and he leaped with all his strength and all his might, falling, flying from on high at the approaching prince of demons.

And Demogorgon screamed, and all the city screamed, and Drizzt plummeted between the biting ape-heads, too close for the winding tentacles to deflect him, and he drove his blades down together in a singular, magnificent strike, plunging them into the massive chest of the gigantic demon beast.

And the destructive power of every arrow and every spell coursed through him in that strike, and he felt the monster melting beneath him. He continued to fall, right through the giant body of the beast, never slowing until he plunged into the stone floor.

Tons of blood and guts and shattered bone and two giant, orange-haired ape heads, tumbled atop him.

Epilogue

ROMPH AND KIMMURIEL WALKED SIDE-BY-SIDE THROUGH THE passageways of Gauntlgrym, a host of dwarf guards directing them. King Bruenor hadn't been pleased to see them, but at least they had come to see him properly, in accordance with Catti-brie's wishes.

Gromph hadn't much noticed or cared. He had only come to this place now because of Kimmuriel's insistence. Since he had accepted Kimmuriel as the official ambassador of the illithid hive-mind in the rebuilding of the tower, Kimmuriel's wishes were no small thing.

"It is an amazing insight, perhaps," Kimmuriel offered as the party descended the long circular stair to the main chamber of the lower levels.

"It is idiocy," Gromph replied with calm confidence. The only thing preventing him from a complete explosion of outrage here were his most recent memories. Never had he felt such power flowing through him as when the illithid collective had sent the kinetic barrier to the waiting K'yorl. That had felt to Gromph to be the purest and most intense expression of intangible power he had ever experienced. In those moments of flowing perfection, he believed that he had come to know what it was like to be a god.

But now this.

In the few short days Gromph had been away, the infernal human woman had strengthened her hold on the others—and they had wasted not a moment in coming to this place to meet with King Bruenor.

And now the work had apparently already begun.

"One thing I have learned in my years with the illithids, Archmage, is to never underestimate the power of viewing the world through a glass bowed. The truths we know are solid paradigms only in our wider expression of the world as a whole."

Gromph looked at him curiously for a moment, but then grumbled, "Her glass isn't bowed. It is painted with pretty flowers." He stopped as the pair neared the Forge Room, noting some dwarves moving along a corridor off the side, towing carts loaded with stone.

Gromph shook his head and turned to face Kimmuriel directly.

"Only those flowers are dragons, and they will melt us all," he said.

They went into the Forge Room then, to the incredulous and suspicious stares of the dwarf craftsmen. Over on the far wall were large tables covered with parchments. The dragon sisters were there, along with Caecilia, Lord Parise, and Penelope Harpell, all discussing some image splayed in front of them and pointing and nodding.

Kimmuriel started that way, but paused when he realized that Gromph wasn't following him.

"You go," the archmage said. "I've another I wish to speak with, and I know where to find her."

He swept across the room then, veering left and never even looking back where the other architects of the new Hosttower had gathered.

A pair of dwarves stood blocking the door in front of him.

"Get out of my way," he told them.

"He the one?" one asked the other.

"Aye, the stubborn one," said the other, and they parted.

At the other end of the tunnel loomed the primordial chamber, and there, as expected, Gromph found Catti-brie. She stood at the edge of the pit, staring across at the area that held, beneath the cooled magma, the antechamber and the key lever.

Beside the woman lay several metal beams and cut stones, the ingredients for constructing a new bridge to the antechamber.

"You have wasted no time," Gromph said.

"We have little to waste." She didn't seem surprised by his entrance, nor did she bother looking over at him as he approached.

"It seems that you have convinced the others."

"They have decided nothing."

"Good, then I will . . ."

Now Catti-brie did turn on him, her eyes narrowed, her face a mask of determination. "I will do this with or without them, and with or without you."

"Indeed?"

"Yes, indeed."

◆　◆　◆

ONCE AGAIN, DRIZZT awakened deep within himself, settled deeply into darkness. He wasn't standing this time, he realized when the pain in his stretched joints began to register.

"At last," he heard, the voice of a drow woman.

"You should have just left him for dead," said another, whom he recognized as Matron Mother Quenthel.

"Oh shut up," said the first, Yvonnel.

Drizzt felt something upon his belly then, square and solid. It was jostled about and he felt the bottom pulled out, then small feet and tiny claws moving back and forth excitedly. He opened his eyes, blinking repeatedly as he adjusted to the dim light of the room—of the dungeon, yet again, in House Baenre.

He groaned, in pain. While he wasn't standing, neither was he actually lying down. He was on a rack, suspended by his ankles and wrists. He worked his shoulders, trying vainly to relieve some of the tension on his elbows, but the ties were simply too tight and his efforts only brought him more pain.

He did manage to lift his head a bit to see Yvonnel, Quenthel standing behind her, and to see the small box Yvonnel had placed upon his naked belly.

The bottomless one that held a rat.

"Ah, good, you have returned to us at last," Yvonnel said to him and she moved up and leaned on the crank, and the rack pulled a tiny bit more.

Drizzt grimaced against the pain.

"I have your friends here," she said happily. "Would you like to see?"

Drizzt closed his eyes and tried to send his thoughts far away.

"This is so much like the wheel of history returning to the same place anew, don't you think?" Yvonnel said, and Drizzt was sure that he had no idea what she was babbling about. "As your actions doomed your father before, so now, one of your friends."

Drizzt's eyes popped open wide and he glared at her.

"But I will let you pick," she said. "Which of your friends will satisfy my sacrifice? The human? He is an angry one, always so full of scowls. You'd be doing him a favor."

"Damn you."

"Of course," she said. "Or the elf. She is quite crazy. She probably won't even understand. Or shall I kill Jarlaxle? You would at least be repaying me, I expect, since that one is drow, and valuable to me. Do you have that in you, heretic, to turn my request against me?"

"You gave me your word," Drizzt gasped, and his words came out unevenly—Yvonnel played with the wheel throughout his sentence.

"And so two will leave, and the third . . . I will make it an easy death. A simple beheading."

"Damn you," Drizzt said again, and he settled back and closed his eyes.

"Choose," Yvonnel instructed.

He didn't answer.

But then she was there, right above him, one knee up on his chest and pressing down, increasing his pain. He opened his eyes to find her face very near his own, and with one hand raised.

"I admire your bravery," she said, and snapped her fingers. In her palm a small ball of fire flared to life.

Yvonnel kept her smile very close as she reached her hand down lower, and lit the rat box.

"You will choose," she whispered.

Drizzt felt the creature scrambling within the box, the front claws digging against his flesh.

"Choose!" Yvonnel demanded.

"Take me!" Entreri shouted. "Let him go and take me, you witch."

Drizzt opened his eyes and strained to see in the direction of the voice, and there was the cage of lightning, Entreri up near the bars, Jarlaxle beside him with a hand on his shoulder.

Yvonnel had turned away to regard them, too, and she began to laugh. "Shut up!" she commanded. When Entreri began to yell at her, she waved her hand and the cage faded away, and so, too, did his protests.

Yvonnel was back at Drizzt's face, so close. "Choose," she whispered.

He shook his head, growling and grinding his teeth against the pain of the rack and the claws of the terrified rat.

"It is all a lie anyway, Drizzt Do'Urden, as you know," she said. "So why does it matter?" She leaned on his chest and his elbows and knees felt as if they would simply explode. "Why does anything matter more than stopping the pain? Pick a friend."

"No!"

"Pick a friend!" she said more insistently.

The rat bit him hard and began to burrow.

"No!"

"Why? It is all a lie."

"No."

"It is! So choose."

"No!"

"Then tell me, Drizzt Do'Urden," she said, her voice going softer. "Before you die, tell me why. It is all a lie, so why will you not choose?"

Drizzt opened his eyes and looked into Yvonnel's colorful amber orbs, fighting to maintain control as the rat burrowed.

"Because I am not a lie," he insisted through gritted teeth.

Yvonnel fell back from him, the pressure of the rack easing, at least. She stared at him for a long heartbeat, her expression one of confusion, perhaps, or of disbelief.

"Get those three out of here," she turned and told Quenthel, then spun back to stare at Drizzt, shaking her head with a crooked smile, as if she had just learned something.

She slapped the burning box and the rat off of him and cast a spell with a wave of her hand that pulled the locking pin from the rack crank. Drizzt fell heavily to his back, where he lay gasping, too broken to even pull his arms down.

Yvonnel fell over him once again, her face close.

"They are free, all three," she whispered. She kissed him, and in that kiss was a spell of healing and of slumber. "Sleep well, hero," she added as Drizzt faded back into welcomed blackness.

◆ ◆ ◆

"Do what?" Gromph demanded. "Do you mean to clear that chamber and free the primordial?"

Catti-brie didn't blink.

"You have forgotten Neverwinter?"

Again, no answer.

"You do not understand the power of this creature."

"But I do."

"Yet you mean to free it!"

"In a controlled—"

"You cannot control such a beast as this, fool!"

Catti-brie grinned. "Come," she bade him.

He looked at her curiously, puzzled.

"I will allow you into my thoughts," she explained, "where once you were comfortable. I will show you."

Gromph made no move for a long while, then narrowed his amber eyes and projected his thoughts into the waiting mind of Catti-brie.

And from there, she took him through her ring, to converse with the primordial, to see what she had seen from ancient times, when the volcano had roared through the tendrils and through the stone of Cutlass Island, melting the crystal of the limestone into something stronger, something magical, and pressing it out of the ground to grow. Squeezing it, hollowing it, pushing it farther, more and more crystal. Bubbles became holes became branches, flowing and growing.

A long while later, she cut off the communication and images, then abruptly dismissed Gromph from her thoughts and opened her eyes to stare at him once more.

The archmage licked his lips. He tried to appear nonchalant, but, judging by Catti-brie's smirk, unsuccessfully.

For the second time in a span of hours, Gromph had witnessed something beyond his understanding, something terrifying and alluring all at once.

He returned her grin.

What else could he do?

She was right. For all the danger, all the chance of complete disaster, to rebuild the Hosttower of the Arcane, she was right.

◆　◆　◆

"WE CANNOT LEAVE him," Artemis Entreri said out in the tunnels just beyond Menzoberranzan. He was with Jarlaxle and Dahlia, and with all their gear returned.

Jarlaxle laughed. "We surely cannot go and get him!"

"He would have died for us."

"He is probably already dead," the mercenary replied with a shrug. "Would you dishonor him and get all of us killed, as well? Or do you not understand the limits of a drow matron mother's mercy?"

Entreri spat on the ground and spun away, then stood up straight when he noted the approach of two dark elves.

Jarlaxle, too, noted them, and was not as surprised by the appearance of Yvonnel as he was by the other. "It cannot be," he said.

"Use your magic, then," Yvonnel answered. "You have the mask back in your possession. Is there another item that could so deceive the clever Jarlaxle?"

Braelin Janquay walked up in front of Jarlaxle and bowed. "Thank you for trying to end my misery," he said.

"You were a drider," Jarlaxle said. He looked past Braelin to Yvonnel. "You cannot undo a drider."

"Of course you can," she replied. "Or I can. I doubt others would have the courage to try."

"But Lolth . . ."

"She is celebrating the fall of Demogorgon," Yvonnel said. "She will forgive me."

"But why?" a suspicious Entreri demanded.

Yvonnel looked at him, and even tilted her pretty head to regard him more closely, then began to laugh and waved him aside. She motioned for Jarlaxle to follow, and walked back the way she had come.

"I do this for you," she said when Jarlaxle caught up to her. "A measure of good faith in expectation that you will serve my purpose."

"And that purpose is?"

"We will see, in time."

"Is he dead?" Jarlaxle asked, more seriously.

"Of course not."

Jarlaxle walked around to face the strange young drow squarely.

"You envy him," he dared to say.

Yvonnel snorted.

"You do!" Jarlaxle insisted. "You envy him. Because he is content in his heart that there is something more, some better angels and greater reason, and because he so easily finds his rewards, treasures as great as anything I or even you might know, in the contentment of moral clarity and personal honor."

"I envy him?" Yvonnel scoffed. "And what of Jarlaxle?"

The mercenary assumed a pensive pose, considering the words before finally nodding. "How many times might I have killed Drizzt for easy personal gain?" he asked rhetorically, with a helpless laugh. "And yet he lives, and I find that I would defend this Houseless rogue at the cost of my own life."

"Why?" Yvonnel asked, and sincerely. "Why you, and why that filth named Entreri?"

"Perhaps because secretly we all want to believe what Drizzt believes," said Jarlaxle. He waited for Yvonnel to look him in the eye. "You couldn't break him. You cannot break him."

She looks annoyed, he thought.

She waved him away. "Go," she said. "Remember that I gave your underling back to you. Remember that I let you walk away from this place."

"It will all be forgotten, I assure you, if you kill Drizzt Do'Urden," Jarlaxle warned.

Yvonnel scowled at him and waved him away.

◆ ◆ ◆

A TENDAY LATER, back in Luskan, Beniago stood with Gromph near the ruins of the old Hosttower.

"Jarlaxle will return on the morrow," he informed the archmage. "Catti-brie has entered the southern gate."

Gromph looked at the drow in human disguise.

"She will be here presently, I expect."

The archmage turned back to the ruins.

"You could be rid of her," Beniago offered, and Gromph arched his eyebrows at that surprising remark.

"Jarlaxle would not like it, but would he ever know?" Beniago asked when Gromph looked back at him again.

Gromph wasn't angry, of course. Beniago's words were perfectly consistent with everything about drow society and tradition—even within Bregan D'aerthe. But the archmage chuckled and shook his head. "Go back to your tower, High Captain," he said, mocking Beniago's silly station. "Let the artists work."

Even as Beniago started away, Gromph noted Catti-brie's approach, the woman riding upon her unicorn across the bridge from Closeguard Island.

In watching her, and now in appreciating the truth of this human woman, Gromph for the first time in his life was surprised to admit that he was jealous of a mere warrior.

She rode Andahar up to him, and slid from the saddle to stand in front of him.

"May I help you, Lady?" he asked, but didn't look at her.

"I forgive you," she said, surprising him.

"What?"

"I forgive you," she repeated. "For your telepathic intrusions. I understand now that you were not even there in my thoughts, and that it was only a suggestion placed for me to find."

"And to enjoy."

Catti-brie's expression went cold.

"Then I am no rapist," Gromph smugly replied to that look.

"You are a scoundrel and a fraud," the woman said. "But I expected as much from the outset. I forgive you because now I trust that you will not hold me in lust, in body, in mind, or in hatred."

"Interesting," Gromph admitted. "I did not think you cared."

"For you? No, I care for those you might harm. And I care most of all for those for whom you may do well. Can you do that, Archmage Gromph Baenre of Menzoberranzan? Can you just this once look beyond your own needs and desires and act for the benefit of others?"

"I am here, am I not?"

"Because you have to be, or because you want to be?"

Gromph gave a little laugh. "Good lady, let us finish this and make the new Hosttower of the Arcane more grand than the first."

"It will be," Catti-brie said with a nod, and then she offered a returned grin and added, "Just stay out of my thoughts."

It was merely an off-hand remark, a bit of levity among the continual tension, but to Catti-brie's obvious surprise, Gromph swung to face her, his expression very serious, and dipped a long, low bow. When he came back up in front of her, he said, in all seriousness, "Good lady. Catti-brie. I am Gromph Baenre of Menzoberranzan. Many times have I bowed to women—to do otherwise was to feel the bite of a snake-headed scourge. I say to you now, in all honesty, in all of my long life, that this is the first time I have offered a bow to a woman because I believe she deserved it."

Catti-brie fell back a step, for a moment seeming at a loss. "Am I to swoon now?" she asked with an unsettled laugh.

"If I thought you would, I never would have bowed."

And the great archmage turned back to the ruins and did not watch Catti-brie depart.

◆　◆　◆

DRIZZT SAT ON a comfortable divan. He wore fine, soft robes, and the meal in front of him would have satisfied Athrogate.

He had seen the dungeons of House Baenre, and now he witnessed the luxuries—though surely he felt this equally unnerving and exhausting.

"You could be a king," said Yvonnel, who sat across from him, her legs up and tucked, the slit in her comfortable gown revealing much of her shapely legs. "Do you even understand the possibilities before you?"

Drizzt looked across the room, where Matron Mother Quenthel, Sos'Umptu Baenre, and another priestess Yvonnel had introduced as her mother, sat staring at him. He could feel their hatred—almost as much for Yvonnel as for himself.

"Your companions are back on the surface now, nearing the city of Luskan," Yvonnel said. "That should make you happy."

Drizzt shrugged.

"Do you wish to join them?"

"Yes," he answered.

"You miss your friends and your home?"

He shrugged again.

Yvonnel laughed at him. "But did you not just come home? Are you not home now, among the drow, where you belong?"

"I came only to rescue Dahlia."

"Whom you do not even believe is Dahlia, correct? Because it is all a lie?"

Drizzt looked away, because he really did not have any answer to that. He still felt as if he were standing on quicksand, as if perception and reality were twined in terrible ways.

"Did you not come home?" Yvonnel pressed.

"This is not my home."

"I could make of you a king of Menzoberranzan!"

Drizzt shook his head.

"You could remake this city in your image. You are the champion of Lolth—all of the Houses witnessed your leap into the beast Demogorgon. You, Drizzt, destroyed that fiend and so we are saved."

"I was your arrow, nothing more."

"But they do not fully appreciate that, do they?"

"But I do. And this is not my home. Menzoberranzan can never be my home."

Yvonnel relaxed a little more in her chair, her expression one of amusement. "Do you have a home? One that matters? Isn't it all a lie?"

Drizzt shrugged.

"You are an insufferable one," Yvonnel said. "And so I have changed my mind." She motioned to the guards, who rushed out, returning with armloads of equipment, all of which Drizzt surely recognized. He looked on without even trying to hide his interest as Twinkle and Icingdeath fell upon the floor, and the belt Catti-brie had made for him, Taulmaril magically secured in the buckle.

And there, too, were Vidrinath and Orbbcress, along with Tiago's fabulously enchanted armor.

"To the victor," Yvonnel remarked.

Drizzt was looking past her, though, to see the profound scowls of Quenthel and Sos'Umptu, with the other, Minolin Fey, looking at the two with great concern. Yvonnel was playing her games as much for their benefit—or annoyance—as for his own.

"Take it, all of it," Yvonnel said. "And I will have Archmage Tsabrak send you to this place you call home. You are a fool to abandon so much. So much pleasure, and so much power."

Drizzt stared hard at her.

"If nothing matters, if it is all a wretched and twisted dream, then why not enjoy it?" she said.

When Drizzt didn't reply, she laughed and said, "Get out."

And so he did.

"How dare you?" Matron Mother Quenthel found the courage to argue when Drizzt was gone, his gear—and Tiago's—in hand.

"Should I have killed him, do you suppose?"

"Of course!" Sos'Umptu answered.

"Horribly!" Quenthel added.

"Would that destroy him, do you think?"

"He would be dead, or worse—a drider, as is fitting," Sos'Umptu replied.

"Better that!" Quenthel agreed. "You should have murdered him, yes, and painfully, over years."

"You cannot destroy Drizzt Do'Urden by destroying his body," Yvonnel explained. "He had long since moved beyond his corporeal form to become a creature of the heart and soul and not the flesh. His cries of pain would thrill you more than they would wound him, because he would hold his purpose and his truth. You cannot take that from him by torturing him."

"Then kill all who are dear to him, before his very eyes!" Matron Mother Baenre declared.

But Yvonnel simply shrugged. "To what end? Even then, we would only affirm the truth in Drizzt's heart. That heart would break at the sight of his beloved friends murdered, of course, but it would be a temporary victory. Breaking his heart is not the same as breaking his will."

"So you simply allow him to leave?" asked Sos'Umptu.

Yvonnel laughed, so wickedly, so knowingly, so sinisterly, that it sent a chill through the spines of the older women.

"Drizzt is not the Chosen of Mielikki," Yvonnel explained. "He is the Chosen only of what is in his heart, which he once accepted as the name of the goddess Mielikki. His faith lies in what he deigns truth, not a specific deity, and if there is a god for him, he believes he will find that god by following what he knows to be right and true. His apathy for the existence of a named truth, a god, will not chase him from his chosen course."

The two Baenre high priestesses glanced at each other uncertainly.

"His human wife's faith is less complicated. Catti-brie is a Chosen of Mielikki, willingly so," Yvonnel continued.

Sos'Umptu and Quenthel looked at each other again and shrugged, neither understanding.

"Trust the lingering curse of Faerzress madness," Yvonnel explained. "When Drizzt truly believes that he is deceived yet again, when he sees before him the ultimate ruse, he will reject it utterly and with explosive outrage."

"And?" the matron mother prompted.

Yvonnel turned a most awful grin over the women. "How destroyed do you suppose Drizzt Do'Urden will be when he comes to understand that in killing the lie, he has struck dead his beloved Catti-brie?"

The level of conniving evil had the Baenre sisters standing dumbstruck.

"I would find that more gratifying than merely torturing the fool," Yvonnel asserted, and she grimaced as she considered Jarlaxle's assertion that she could not break Drizzt, determined to prove him wrong. "Wouldn't you?"

◆